When
we
Fall

USA TODAY BESTSELLING AUTHOR
LENA HENDRIX

Developmental editing: Paula Dawn, Lilypad Lit

Copy editing: James Gallagher

Proofreading: Julia Griffis, The Romance Bibliophile

Model & Discreet cover design: TRC Designs by Cat

Model cover photography: Wander Aguiar

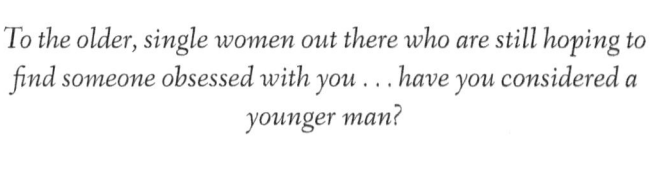

To the older, single women out there who are still hoping to find someone obsessed with you . . . have you considered a younger man?

LET'S CONNECT

When you sign up for my newsletter, you'll stay up to date with new releases, book news, giveaways, and new book recommendations! I promise not to spam you and only email when I have something fun & exciting to share!

Also, When you sign up, you'll also get a FREE copy of Choosing You (a very steamy Chikalu Falls novella)!

Sign up at my website at www.lenahendrix.com

AUTHOR'S NOTE

This book contains mentions of infidelity (of a parent, not any main character). There are references of a child feeling abandoned and unwanted. It also deals with self-concept after a divorce and the struggle to feel like yourself as a single parent.

There are several scenes containing yummy adult content between a single mother who's lost her groove and a very eager, younger man who is more than willing to help her find it. Enjoy!

WHEN WE FALL

STAR HARBOR
BOOK 2

LENA HENDRIX

LENA HENDRIX LLC

ABOUT THIS BOOK

I need a nanny. Not a distraction.

I certainly do not need a twentysomething man with a devastating smile, tattooed forearms, and an easy charm that could unravel a woman twice as composed as I pretend to be.

But when my daughter gets kicked out of after-school care (again) and my flaky nanny ghosts us (again), Austin Calloway moves into the duplex next door—and right into our lives.

Now he's helping with homework, cooking dinner shirtless, and showing up with coffee like he's always belonged here.

He's too young.

Too familiar.

Too good with my daughter.

Too close.

And the worst part? He sees through me—the cracks, the stress, the walls I've built to protect what's mine.

The more I try to keep him out, the more I ache to let him in.

But letting someone in means risking everything.

He's the wrong choice . . . unless we're finally ready to see what happens when we fall.

ONE

SELENE

My HAIR WAS a rat's nest, my tits were out, and I had exactly twelve minutes until I was late for my virtual meeting with the maritime museum.

I glanced at the clock again.

Where the hell is Amanda?

Amanda—my less-than-reliable babysitter—was supposed to be taking my daughter, Winnie, for the morning. I had hoped an outing like the park or even an ice cream cone would be enough to occupy and tire out my precocious five-year-old.

A deep ache settled between my ribs. I hated how much I missed her, even when she was right upstairs.

I would have loved for that person to be me, but post-divorce, I had bills to pay and a to-do list that seemed to grow with every passing moment.

"Mama!" Winnie's shriek flew down the stairs and slammed into my chest, right where my anxiety already lived.

I bristled and tamped down the urge to yell back up at her.

With a sigh I set down my coffee mug. I could always reheat it in the microwave later. I hastily buttoned my blouse as I walked upstairs.

"Win, how many times have I told you, we don't yell at each other in this house. If you need something from me, you can walk downstairs and—"

I stopped, staring at my five-year-old, who was standing on a step stool in the bathroom. Her hair was glistening wet and dripping with some kind of . . . goo.

Please be hair gel, don't be glue. Please be hair gel, don't be glue.

Her sticky hand smeared across the bathroom vanity as she leaned in closer to look at herself with a pout. "I want my curls bouncy like Auntie Elodie's."

Sadly, while Winnie's dark hair color did match my sister's, she had gotten my texture—a sad half-flat, half-frizzy mix that had always made me envious of my sister's effortless bounce.

I exhaled and offered my daughter a soft, understanding smile as I moved toward her. My hands cradled her face, squishing her cheeks and accentuating the pout across her lips. "I think your hair is perfect just the way it is."

I swallowed the echoes of the voices from my childhood. *You'd be so much prettier if you did something with that hair. Have you ever tried styling it like your sister?*

I looked down at her sweet, glum face. "I'll tell you what," I said. "If you really want to try to coax a curl, we'll bring in the professional." I tried to glide a few fingertips into her hair, but the sticky mess made it impossible. "We can cook dinner for Auntie Elodie and Cal, and I bet she would be more than happy to give you a few pointers."

Crisis averted, Winnie's big brown eyes lit up. "And Levi too?"

I chuckled. "Levi too." Levi was Cal's fourteen-year-old son and, in Winnie's eyes, the coolest kid to ever exist.

I stood behind my daughter, my hands on her shoulders. "What did you use so I know how to fix this?"

"Guh-ell," she said proudly.

Winnie had been adamant about wanting to learn to read before starting kindergarten, so I knew immediately she meant *gel*. Her phonics was strong, but she was still learning.

I heaved a sigh of relief. *Thank goodness.*

I mentally calculated the extreme lack of time before my meeting.

Our eyes met in the mirror—mine tired, hers impossibly hopeful. "How about this?" I got to work brushing her hair back into a ponytail. "Today we can try a slicked-back pony." I waggled my eyebrows at her. "Very chic."

Winnie eyed herself in the mirror as though she wasn't entirely convinced, then broke into a wide, gap-toothed grin that made my heart twist.

Crisis 1 of 876 averted. Check.

Once her hair was sufficiently slicked back, I gave her shoulders one more loving squeeze. "Time to go. Amanda should be here any minute, and I have a work call."

"What's that?" With a twisted face, Winnie pointed at my shirt in the mirror, and I looked down to find a mystery stain across the lapel of my cream-colored blouse.

With a huff I left the bathroom, then unceremoniously hauled the shirt over my head. "Please get dressed," I called over my shoulder as I tossed my top into my bedroom hamper.

As I was digging through my drawer for another suitable option, two knocks sounded at the front door before it pushed open.

"It's me," my little sister, Kit, called out.

My eyes lifted to the ceiling. *Thank god for tiny miracles.*

"Hey," I called down the stairs. "I'm just getting dressed. There's coffee in the pot."

Winnie, now dressed in a black-and-white-striped top and hot-pink tutu, danced down the stairs to greet her aunt.

I hadn't prepared a second outfit option when I had pulled out my clothes the night before, though with the way my life had been going lately, I probably should have. I selected a simple black knit top with a modest crew neck and short sleeves. At least if something got on that, the dark color could hide it.

I looked at the clock. *Four minutes.*

With no time for pants, let alone makeup, I bounded down the stairs in my sleep shorts.

Kit was perched atop the counter in cutoff shorts and a navy tank top, sipping her coffee and looking as unbothered as ever.

"Can I steal you for a half hour?" I pleaded. "It's an emergency. I don't know where the hell Amanda is and I have a call with the maritime museum starting . . ." I glanced down at my watch. "Literally now."

Kit raised her coffee mug in salute, talking around an enormous bite of blueberry muffin. "You got it, boss."

Relief and gratitude washed through me.

I picked up my cold cup of coffee before squeezing Kit's forearm. "Thanks. I'll be quick, I promise."

Kit nodded, then chuckled. "Is this a no-pants Wednesday?" she asked, noting my mismatched attire.

I shrugged. "Virtual meeting and I'm out of options." I pointed at each piece of my outfit. "Put together professional on the top." My hand dropped to my pajama shorts. "Struggling single mom on the bottom."

Without waiting for Kit's quippy response, I walked out the back door and hustled across the lawn to the carriage house in the back.

At first, living in a duplex on the edges of downtown Star Harbor had not been ideal, but I came to find it had its benefits. The European-style home came with a sizable carriage house in the backyard. I had known my property manager since I was little, and when I had asked Nancy if I could convert the unused space into an office and restoration space, she couldn't have cared less.

It was a sanctuary in the chaos of my life.

The carriage house sat nestled beneath a canopy of old sycamores, its weathered brick and white trim softened by climbing ivy and late-summer sunlight. Gulls wheeled high above, their cries distant beneath the rustle of dune grass pushing in along the fence line. On humid August mornings like this, the breeze carried a clean sweetness off Lake Michigan—fresh water and sand, edged with the sharp green of late-summer pines. I'd trimmed the hedges into something neat and intentional, but the wild bergamot near the porch steps refused to be tamed.

Inside my office, everything shifted. Cool, filtered light spilled through UV-protected windows. Flat files and worktables lined the walls in precise rows, tools arranged with quiet purpose—bone folders, pH pens, soft brushes placed just so. A blush-pink velvet chaise sat untouched in the corner, except when Winnie claimed it for an impromptu nap. It smelled like cotton gloves and history, and for a few blissful hours a day, it was mine—quiet, ordered, and entirely under control.

But as soon as I unlocked and opened the door, I knew everything was wrong.

The humidity in the air was off. I glanced at the dehumidifier, its light blinking an ominous red. That was a problem, but one that would have to wait until after the call.

A spider danced across the flat files, and I shrieked before swiping a hand and flinging it into the depths of god knows where. A full body shiver rattled my bones. I turned on my computer and tapped my foot as I waited for everything to boot up.

"Come on," I whispered, tapping the desk. "Come on, come on—"

I was already two minutes late.

After opening my digital calendar, I clicked the link to the meeting and smoothed a hand over my hair. My fingers snagged in a knot at the back of my head. I winced.

Shit.

I tucked my unruly strands behind my ears and straightened my shoulders. I did my best to paint my face with a polished, indifferent smile. "You've got this."

My flat smile wobbled at the edges, and I hoped the client didn't notice through the screen as we signed off. The thirty-minute meeting lasted nearly an hour.

I had been working with the local maritime museum on various projects—one project in particular was digitizing their registry. They wanted it uploaded *today*.

I flipped to a clean page on my yellow legal pad and added it to the top of a brand-new to-do list—the last one was now a graveyard of half-finished chaos.

I loved a good list, but it seemed like I was always

needing to start a new one before any of the tasks on the previous list were complete. My saving grace was the project I could start after the digitized registries.

I glanced at the shelf in the corner, my eyes settling on the thick, yellowed pages of my upcoming project.

A delighted giggle tickled my throat. Recently a client had dropped off a moldy, possibly cursed, wedding book from 1902.

She'd said it *smelled like secrets*, and I couldn't agree more.

I had earned a master's in museum studies with a focus on archival preservation. After working at a university library for years, I had returned home to Star Harbor after my divorce. Now I ran a small but prestigious private practice specializing in the preservation, restoration, and appraisal of rare paper-based materials—books, letters, maps, photographs, ledgers, that kind of thing.

It wasn't just restoring the photos or tracing my fingertips over the loopy handwriting that seemed to be lost in time that appealed to me. I was obsessed with what was hidden in plain sight.

Marginalia—the human traces left behind in books and letters. I liked knowing someone had been here before me. That their words mattered, even scribbled in the margins. Notes in margins, half-torn love letters, faded dedications . . . a wistful sigh escaped me.

For the time being, that project would have to wait.

I swiveled in my chair to face the windows that overlooked the backyard.

A loud cackle escaped my throat. Pressed to the glass, tongues out, cheeks puffed, were Kit and Winnie.

They slid down the glass and dissolved into a fit of giggles as I stepped outside. Clippings and sticks were clinging to their hair, and there was a suspicious, opened jar of peanut butter at Winnie's side.

I planted my hands on my hips and looked down at them. "What are you two up to?"

"Uh-oh. The fun police are here," Kit teased, earning her another playful laugh from Winnie.

Winnie kicked her feet. "I was trying to catch a squirrel for a pet, and Auntie Kit thought I might have better luck with peanut butter." To emphasize her point, Winnie stuck her dirty index finger into her mouth and sucked off the remaining peanut butter with a pop.

My nostrils flared as I inhaled and tried not to lose my shit on my little sister. "Is that so?"

Kit only laughed and shrugged before pulling herself up.

I helped Winnie to her feet, then crouched in front of her and dusted off her sparkly pink tutu. I held her hands as I looked up at her. "Remember, we talked about this. We can only make something our pet if we *truly* know they want to be a pet. Remember that raccoon?"

Winnie frowned and nodded. "He didn't want to be a pet."

"That's right." I rubbed her arms. "Do you think a squirrel would want to be a pet in a cage?" I looked up at the sycamore trees at the side of the yard. "Or do you think he would be happier, leaping and running and living outside?"

Winnie grumbled and stamped her tiny foot, but relented. "Living outside."

I stood and pulled her into an embrace, the smell of grass and peanut butter wafting off her. "I think so too."

I turned her shoulders toward the back of our duplex

and gently padded her forward. "Okay, go clean up. We've got to figure out where Amanda is."

"Man." Kit laughed, dusting off her hands.

"What?" I asked, walking after her.

"Selene Darling." She chuckled. "Professional good time assassin."

Carefree Kit shook her head and followed my daughter up the back steps of the duplex. My sister disappeared into the house, and I stayed behind in the yard, swallowing a sigh.

I stood with my hands on my hips, the scent of peanut butter and dirt clinging to the late-summer air. My shoulders were tight.

Through gritted teeth, I whispered my new mantra, "Don't die, don't cry, and don't kill your sister."

I turned toward the house.

The screen door creaked. I stepped back into the kitchen and let the storm door slap shut behind me. The quiet was immediate—and suspicious.

I glanced around. Silence, except for the slow drip of the faucet and the faint tick of the wall clock.

I closed my eyes. Inhaled.

It's fine. I'm fine. Everything is fine.

Ping.

My eyes flew open. I reached for my phone, already bracing for it.

AMANDA

I'm so sorry, but I can't do this anymore.
Good luck!

I stared at the screen.

A single, peanut butter–slicked feather floated past the window.

I had exactly four and a half days to figure out a new morning routine before the school year shifted into full gear. That meant juggling drop-off and pickup times, managing Winnie's five-year-old dramatics, and keeping my business from collapsing under the weight of historical ledgers and digital deadlines.

I picked up my mug and took a long sip of cold coffee, now lukewarm and slightly bitter.

Then I turned around and screamed silently into the pantry.

TWO

SELENE

THE MORNING AIR was thick with lake humidity, a soft heat that clung to my skin and made the porch boards sweat beneath my bare feet and turned every tiny task into an annoyance. I sat on the back step with my second cup of coffee, watching a chipmunk dart beneath the hedge. The neighborhood cat, unimpressed, watched with matching energy from across the lawn. For a moment it was peaceful, or as close to peaceful as life got lately.

I'd been operating under the illusion that Amanda would return from her spontaneous "mental health week" and reclaim her post as the world's most inconsistent nanny.

Spoiler alert: That illusion had popped like a balloon in a porcupine pit.

I took another sip. The coffee had already cooled, the bitterness curling across my tongue as I scrolled through my inbox on my phone. Restoration quotes. Overdue invoices. A polite-but-firm reminder that the maritime museum's registry was still missing twenty-seven scans.

I could do this.

I just needed a little grace. A little time. Maybe a miracle.

That was when I heard it—the low rumble of a truck engine, followed by the distinct clatter of something heavy being hauled up a porch.

I glanced over.

And then immediately wished I hadn't.

With his back to me, he was shirtless.

Of course he was shirtless.

Standing near the back alleyway of the empty duplex unit next to mine—now apparently not so empty—was a man who looked like he'd stepped out of a fitness influencer's thirst trap.

He had a box tucked under one arm; a backward cap holding in messy, sun-streaked hair; and the kind of tattooed forearms that made rational thought difficult.

Then he turned, and my stomach dropped. My mouth went dry. And yet my palms . . . those suddenly felt sweaty. His brown hair was a little too long as it started to curl at the ends. His jaw was sharp and precise. Even at a distance I could see his eyes were a haunting seafoam green.

Please no.

"Hey, you've finally got a new neighbor." My sister Elodie's voice floated behind me before she came into view, a coffee cup in one hand, sunglasses perched on top of her wild dark curls like she belonged in a vacation ad.

She was effortlessly pretty in a sun-warmed, farmgirl kind of way—green eyes bright, skin glowing from long afternoons spent prepping the land for the Star Harbor Family Farm project she'd come back to build.

I didn't answer, because I couldn't.

I was actively choking.

Elodie blinked at me. "Are you okay?"

I coughed, hard. Coffee sprayed down the front of my T-shirt, and I clutched my chest like the caffeine itself had betrayed me.

Elodie, ever helpful, handed me a paper towel from her tote bag.

"Selene," she said, low and amused. "Do you always wheeze like that when a hot guy lifts heavy things? Who *is* that?" She tried peering around the bushes and fence that separated the lawn, without luck.

I cleared my throat and shook my head. "No one."

"No one? Hmm . . ." She tilted her head, clearly not buying it. "Because 'no one' has the arms of a demigod and is currently lifting a box with one hand like it's a tray of hors d'oeuvres."

Oh god, yes, I remember those arms.

One time. One wildly out-of-character, toe-curling, tree-bark-in-my-hair mistake.

Elodie grinned, her eyes lighting with the kind of trouble I absolutely didn't have time for. "It might be hard living next to a walking fitness model with great biceps. Should I be worried about you?"

"Please," I deadpanned. "My libido is in a coma and plans to remain there."

But inside, panic stirred. My entire body was trying to decide between melting into the earth and launching into orbit. The last time I saw that man, I was half drunk on blueberry wine at a jazz bar that served Brie on toast points and advertised itself as funky and intimate.

Just over a month ago I had needed a night out. Just one night of feeling wanted, feeling like someone else. I'd known he was younger than me, but I hadn't cared. He had been leaning against the bar, all crooked grins and confidence, and I had convinced myself a little flirting would be harmless.

He'd offered to walk me to my car. I'd said yes. Then we'd ended up walking together down a path in the woods at twilight. Before I knew it, bark was digging into my spine, his wide palm pressed flat against my ribs, and we were panting in the humidity.

We never exchanged names. That had been the deal.

Until now.

Now he was moving in next door.

"Oh, shit!" Elodie raised a hand and gave him a friendly wave and huge grin. "Is that Austin?" she said, half to herself with a hearty laugh, and looked at me again. "It's Brody's brother. What are the *odds*?" The back of her hand slapped against my rigid shoulder.

He looked across the lawn and saw us. Austin grinned and *waved back*.

I took another sip of my tepid coffee and prayed the mug would hide the horror on my face.

By MIDAFTERNOON, the panic had settled into something closer to despair. The nanny agencies had nothing—too short notice, too few applicants, not enough incentive to lure someone into part-time, early-morning / early-evening care in a town where most college students had already moved on to fall internships.

I'd spent the last hour bribing Winnie with Goldfish crackers and an episode of her favorite ghost-hunting show while I tried to scan a fragile nineteenth-century ledger without crying on it.

Kit, of course, had breezed in and out like some kind of

helpful-but-sassy hurricane, offering to *manifest childcare solutions* and then promptly disappearing with a half-eaten muffin in her bag.

At six thirty, I pulled on clean clothes and slipped into a pair of sandals. Wednesday nights were technically Winnie's time with her dad, Brian. He taught evening classes at the university, so drop-offs were often last minute and tended to be inconsistent. Still, she'd gone with him tonight, which meant I had a rare window of quiet.

The Star Harbor Historical Society, informally known as the Keepers, met every week, and I hadn't missed a meeting yet—not since I'd moved back to Star Harbor. It was part civic duty, part tradition, and part much-needed distraction.

Tonight we gathered in my property manager Nancy Strickland's hydrangea-heavy backyard. It was a garden that looked like it came with a staff. The wine was cheap but cold, the air smelled like fresh-cut grass, and conversation buzzed around me like bees to sugar.

The topic, of course, was the Lady of the Dunes.

"I'm telling you," one of the older Keepers said, her glass waving dramatically, "Elodie may be onto something. Those letters are worth looking into."

Over the summer my sister Elodie had uncovered a long-forgotten trunk containing old letters while renovating the Stafford Farm. She was convinced that there was more to our local legend than we knew. I couldn't wait to get my hands on anything she'd found.

"You think the Lady left on purpose?" someone asked.

Star Harbor's entire identity was wrapped up in the story of the Lady of the Dunes. A ghostly woman in a flowing white dress, seen walking barefoot through the coastal dunes with a bouquet of wildflowers clutched in her hands. Some said she was searching for the lover she lost to a stormy shipwreck in the late eighteen hundreds. Others believed she was seeking revenge. The legend had been passed down for generations, warping with every telling until no one really knew who she was or what she wanted— only that she haunted this place like a memory refusing to fade. People swore they'd seen her at twilight, her dress glowing, her eyes hollow.

Whether they believed it or not, every single person in Star Harbor knew her story. Now some of us—against our better judgment—had started to wonder if it was entirely true.

"I think she had a reason to disappear." Elodie leaned forward, bouncing her eyebrows. "Doesn't every woman at some point or another?"

Laughter circled the group, and I offered a tight smile, my attention drifting toward the flicker of fairy lights strung along the fence line as my thoughts wandered.

Austin's arms. His smirk. That voice, low and amused, asking whether I'd ever been kissed under Michigan starlight.

I needed to focus.

My attention snapped back as the women discussed the upcoming fall events. I took notes, offered to follow up on a boardinghouse ledger someone had mentioned. When I slipped out an hour later, I felt no closer to peace than when I'd arrived.

～

MONDAY UNRAVELED FAST.

Over the weekend, Winnie had been confirmed for before- and after-school care, and I was clinging to that precious gift like a life raft. I dropped her off with a rushed hug and a banana she refused to eat, then raced home to prepare for a client call and catch up on the maritime registry files.

By 3:19 my phone rang.

"Ms. Darling?" The voice on the other end belonged to the aftercare program coordinator. My stomach dropped. "I wanted to inform you that we had a small incident with Winnie after school today."

My teeth clenched. "What kind of incident? Is she okay?"

A pause. "Yes, she's fine. But she told the other children that ghosts live in the attic of the school and that if they misbehave, the Lady of the Dunes will eat their toes."

I closed my eyes. "Oh no."

The woman tsked. "Two of the kindergartners cried so hard they had to be picked up early."

Of course they did.

"Our program may not be the best fit for a child with such . . ." The woman searched for words. "Spirit."

Nerves wobbled my voice. "No, your program is perfect for her. I promise this is just a blip. I'll talk to her."

"I'm sorry," the woman continued, "we can't have other children *afraid* while they're here. We're going to have to remove her from the program, at least temporarily. You understand."

My carefully color-coded to-do list spontaneously combusted. I offered a flurry of apologies, assured them I would speak with her, and ended the call with the brittle calm of a woman at the end of her fraying rope.

By evening I was sitting on the back steps of the carriage house with my laptop balanced on my knees and a legal pad limp in my lap. All the ice in my lemonade had melted, leaving behind a watery, disappointing refreshment. The only thing I'd managed to accomplish was burning a grilled cheese and snapping at the antique brush I'd dropped down a vent.

My shoulders ached. My head pulsed. Everything felt too loud. The cicadas. The deadlines. My own thoughts.

Across the fence line, I heard him.

Austin.

He was laughing and talking to someone as they unloaded a secondhand sofa from a trailer. His voice was low, steady, easy.

Of course it was.

The last thing I needed was a reminder of how easy things came to people like him.

Young. Untethered. Uncomplicated.

At thirty-six, I didn't need charm or tattoos or one more reckless mistake. I needed someone I could trust with the most important thing in my life.

I refreshed the nanny job board.

Still nothing.

THREE

AUSTIN

I HAD no plans to stay. Not in Star Harbor. Not in Michigan. Not anywhere, really.

But there I was—unloading the last box from the back of my pickup, the tailgate creaking like it held an opinion about my life choices. A summer's worth of sand still clung to the floorboards, and my baseball glove, worn smooth from years of rec-league games, rolled off the seat and landed at my feet.

I was just happy to no longer be couch surfing. I needed privacy. A place of my own.

That wasn't something I'd had much of. Mom had always been the fun one—spontaneous, beautiful, a little reckless. She was a parent who let you eat ice cream for dinner but forgot to pay the electric bill. I learned early how to take care of myself. How to pack fast and not get too comfortable.

Brody had had a much different life. Steady. Solid. He was the older half brother I'd watched from a distance—not close enough to reach, but just near enough to want more.

Somehow I'd deluded myself into thinking a man who

was told I shouldn't exist might want to get to know me. Brody hadn't pushed me away, and that was more than I'd let myself hope for. I just had to figure out how not to mess it up.

Half of a weathered duplex wasn't much, but it had a roof, decent plumbing, and the kind of quiet that suggested no one would be screaming through paper-thin walls. I'd take it. I hadn't stuck anywhere long enough to decorate since college, so it might be a fun change of pace.

Brody had helped me find it. Technically his friend Wes had called in the favor, and I owed them both more than I could articulate. Wes was finally home from the hospital, recovering from the car wreck that had cost him his leg. He'd pushed his friend Hayes out of the way of an oncoming vehicle, taken the hit full-on, and somehow come out shattered, but alive.

Lately I'd been filling in for him on his construction sites while he healed. Swinging hammers, hauling lumber, and trying to stay out of my own head.

Maybe that was the problem. The longer I stayed in Star Harbor, the more I found myself wanting to, and wanting anything too much had always meant trouble.

I dropped the last box on the porch and stretched, my shoulders cracking with the effort. The morning sun baked against the back of my neck, and for a moment everything felt still.

Then I heard it.

Laughter.

High, bright, and warm. The kind that didn't just fill the air but changed it. I turned my head toward the sound and—

Froze.

She was there. Standing in the backyard with a little

girl, both barefoot in the overgrown grass. Her hair—wild and mousy brown, though I'd argue it looked more like sun-warmed beach grass—was twisted into a loose knot, a few strands escaping to catch the light. She was holding a glass of what looked like pitifully weak lemonade, and she was smiling. Laughing.

She was glowing.

Not the polished, curated kind of beauty I was used to seeing in airports and bars and brief encounters. No, this was something else. She looked like sunlight caught in skin. Solid. Soft. Alive.

And then it hit me.

Holy shit, it's her.

I had absently waved to the neighbors when I'd moved in, but I hadn't taken the time to really look.

Of course it was her—the woman I still dreamed about lived twenty feet away.

I watched her say something to the kid, bending slightly as the girl shoved what looked like a dirt-covered earthworm into her hand. She didn't flinch, but grinned and accepted the gift, wiping it off with the hem of her shirt.

I couldn't stop the smile stretching across my face.

My mystery woman is a mother.

It hadn't been a night I'd expected to remember.

The bar was tucked off a narrow side street in a town I didn't know well—jazz humming through cracked windows, the kind of place that smelled like old wood, burned sugar, and red wine someone had spilled years ago but never really cleaned up. Everything glowed amber in the low light. Intimate. A little timeless.

I spotted her the second I walked in.

I'd seen the woman around town a few times over the summer. At the farmers' market once, dragging a wagon full of peaches. Walking out of the library with a tote bag full of hardbacks and a look that said she didn't have time for anyone's bullshit. I'd asked someone once—maybe Cal— what her name was.

Selene.

It suited her. Sharp and soft at the same time. I knew it was her but hadn't found the right moment to approach her.

She was sitting alone at the corner of the bar, perched on a high stool like she'd been carved there—back straight, legs crossed, fingers curled around a sweating glass of berry-colored wine. Her hair was loose, a wild mess of soft brown waves that caught the light every time she turned her head. She wasn't watching the band.

She was watching the exits.

There was something about the way she scanned the room—sharp, assessing, like she was waiting for someone and hoping they wouldn't show up.

I posted against the bar and ordered a drink. Whiskey, neat.

After making eyes at each other for a while, I tried to act casual as I slid onto the stool beside her. I made some ridiculous comment about the trumpet player's hat. She didn't laugh, but she looked at me—really looked at me—and gave me this half smile that cracked something low in my ribs.

"Aren't you too young for jazz?" she asked, her voice smooth as the rim of her glass.

I grinned. "I'm too old for cartoons."

She snorted, took another sip, and didn't move away.

We talked. Nothing deep. Teasing, mostly. We realized we both actually *hated* jazz, which allowed us to share a laugh over another drink. The woman was sharp—quick with her words but soft with her eyes, like she hadn't decided yet whether I was worth her time.

She asked how old I was. I told her—twenty-eight.

She hummed. "Still a baby."

I leaned in a little. "I'm no baby, ma'am. I can promise you that I'm old enough to buy you another drink, if you'll allow it."

That earned me a genuine smile and the prettiest flush of her cheeks. Sure, she may have been a few years older than me, but I didn't care. She was cool and mysterious, and we had enough in common that we laughed and the conversation was easy.

She didn't tell me her name, and she said knowing would ruin the magic. Though I'd known her name, I let her take the lead.

"You really want to know it?" she asked, tilting her head.

I shrugged, trying to play it cool. "Only if you want me to remember you."

She looked down at her glass with a soft laugh. "I don't."

Selene finished her wine and slid off the stool without a word. I watched her walk toward the front door, not sure whether I was supposed to follow or simply watch her slip into the darkness.

She glanced back once, and that was all it took.

Outside, the air was thick with summer heat, crickets singing in the trees. She said she needed air. I offered to walk with her.

We didn't say much, but she didn't pull away when my fingers tangled with hers.

The music from inside dulled behind us as we wandered past the parking lot and onto the path that led into the woods behind the bar. The trail was barely lit—just moonlight slipping through branches and the occasional shimmer of fairy lights someone had strung up long ago and forgotten. It smelled like pine sap and damp leaves, and her perfume—something clean and soft, like cotton sheets after a thunderstorm. Her scent wrapped around me with every breath.

She stopped walking just as the music disappeared completely and turned to me like she'd made a decision.

Then she kissed me.

No hesitation. No question. Just fingers in my shirt and mouth on mine like she'd waited years to do it.

I kissed her back.

God, I kissed her back like it was the only thing I'd ever been good at.

It wasn't frantic, but it was fierce. Her hands were everywhere—my neck, my chest, the waistband of my jeans—and I couldn't think past the sound of her breathing or the press of her body against mine. She backed me up against a tree, her thighs pressing between mine, and I let her take what she needed. I wanted to give her more.

We didn't talk.

We didn't need to.

The cicadas sang. The forest held its breath. Her mouth found the edge of my jaw, the hollow of my throat. Then I took control. We moved deeper into the forest, stripping clothes enough to feel everything—skin on skin, bark at my back, her fingers tangled in my hair as she moved against me, hot and hungry and gone.

It wasn't rough. It wasn't sweet. It was something between. Like we both knew it would end but didn't want to rush a second of it.

She came apart in my arms, shaking as her moan echoed through the trees.

When it was over, when we were both catching our breath beneath the heavy silence of the woods, she didn't kiss me again. She just looked at me—eyes wide, wild, like she wasn't sure what she'd just done.

I went to speak when her fingers pressed against my lips. "This doesn't leave the trees," she whispered.

I wanted more—for her to give me her phone number and let me take her out on a proper date.

Instead, she was already pulling her skirt back down, smoothing her hair, walking away toward the glow of the bar like she hadn't just undone me completely.

I stood there for a long time before I followed.

I'd been thinking about her ever since.

BRODY WAS MANNING the grill in his backyard like it was a crime scene—calm, focused, unbothered by the smoke curling into his face. He had changed out of his police uniform and flipped a burger with one hand while holding a beer in the other. He had his sleeves pushed up, posture loose.

"So," he said as I stepped through the gate, "you finally moved in. Nancy didn't warn you the place was haunted?"

I snorted and let the gate click shut behind me. "Haunted by what? Mosquitoes and drywall rot?" I reached into the cooler at his feet. "Nah, it's all right."

He grinned and clinked his bottle against mine. "I'm glad you came by."

This was how we operated lately—light, easy, like we didn't have years of missed birthdays and awkward history sitting between us. Brody was a man people looked at and immediately trusted. Solid. Sharp. Sheriff's deputy of Star Harbor with the kind of reputation small towns carved into stone.

He was also the half brother I didn't really grow up with.

We didn't share a roof or happy memories. Just blood. He got the badge and the father who showed up at football games. I got a rusted-out motorcycle and a mom who taught me to dance in the kitchen but forgot to pick me up from school half the time.

Still, after a few awkward phone calls, I showed up here. A few months ago I rolled into town and conveniently stepped up to help out while Wes recovered. At least that was what I told people.

The truth?

I wasn't exactly sure yet. I wanted to get to know my brother. Brody always seemed just out of reach—like a life I couldn't have, but something about this place had started to feel like it might let me stay.

We talked about Wes for a while and how Hayes Darling hadn't been the same since the accident either.

"He's doing okay," Brody said, flipping a burger. "Physically at least. Mentally? He's pacing trenches in his backyard. Sometimes the guy can't sit still. He thinks it's his fault that Wes lost his leg."

I nodded, not entirely understanding my brother's friends, but trying. "Wes was in the army, right? Guys like that always come back stronger. Hayes probably needs someone to keep him from blowing the place up in the meantime."

Brody nodded like he knew I meant it.

"Are you still playing ball?" I asked, knowing my

brother was on a softball team that regularly got their asses handed to them.

Brody smiled. "Damn right. Twelve-inch slow pitch. There's a game this week and we could use a player. You want in?"

I smirked. "Are you asking because you need another bat or because Cal's too slow to run bases?"

"Yes," he said, grinning.

"Yeah, I think I can make it." I suppressed the cheeky smile that made me feel twelve years old again.

Brody flipped another burger, the sizzle sharp in the quiet. Then, like he hadn't just dropped a grenade, he said, "You know you're next door to Selene Darling, right? That's Hayes's sister."

I took a sip of beer to buy myself half a second.

"I've seen her around," I said. "Maybe met her once or twice."

Brody nodded, like that was enough.

"She's had a rough go of it," he said. "She could probably use a hand. She's been on her own since her divorce. He still teaches at the university. Big brain, no backbone. Word is he's okay, but leaves her and the kid in the lurch sometimes. He shows up for PTA with espresso and excuses."

I let out a low laugh, but Brody's tone was anything but casual. "How do you know that?"

Brody shrugged. "People talk and I listen. Selene's been doing it all on her own. Juggling the kid, her business, everything. I've never heard her complain, and she doesn't ask for help. Which means—if she ever does?" He looked at me, something knowing in his eyes. "You say yes."

My grip tightened on the bottle.

Yeah, well—I'd already said yes. With my mouth, my hands, every reckless inch of me that should've known better.

That night with Selene was the hottest night of my life, but maybe the most ill-advised, because Selene Darling wasn't built for something temporary and I've never been anything but.

I gave Brody a tight nod and looked down at the label on my bottle.

∿

LATER THAT NIGHT I sat on the back stoop with a beer in one hand and my phone in the other, not really scrolling—just pretending to so I wouldn't look like a guy staring across the yard, thinking about a woman who didn't know she lived in my head.

I got up to pace the backyard and redirect some of the blood that had inadvertently gone straight to my dick at the thought of coming face-to-face with Selene again. She was *so close* it was bound to happen sooner rather than later.

The sun was melting down behind the trees, casting the whole yard in a thick, gold-laced light that made the world look warmer than it was. Crickets had started up in the hedges, and the scent of late-summer pine and cut grass drifted in with the lake breeze.

I looked up and saw her through the window.

She moved through her kitchen like a storm barely contained. A smudge of something smattered across one cheek. She was wrangling a backpack, a half-dressed child with wild hair and a plastic tiara, and what looked like a foil-covered monstrosity that might have once been a volcano.

I laughed under my breath, watching her try to shove

something into the trash with one hand while holding a juice box aloft with the other.

She looked exasperated. Exhausted. Real.

And like she could still bring me to my knees with a glance.

I took a long pull from the bottle. The glass was sweating against my palm, but it grounded me. It kept me from doing something stupid, like crossing the yard just to see if she'd smile at me the way she had that night.

She doesn't know I remember her, but I do.

Every minute. Every breath. If pressed, I could recall every damn leaf in that forest.

And now she was my neighbor.

Selene clearly needed help—even if she wouldn't ask for it. I probably shouldn't even offer any.

I wasn't there to get involved.

I reminded myself of that as I crossed the lawn back to my place, step by step, as if distance could fix what memory wouldn't let go.

FOUR

SELENE

The Star Harbor public softball field was attached to our local park, so the moment my sister Elodie opened her big fat mouth in front of Winnie, asking if we wanted to watch the softball game, I knew I was trapped.

Winnie's delighted shriek disappeared as she pounded up the stairs.

"Don't forget bike shorts!" I called up after her. I turned to my sister. "Winnie is in a dress phase."

Through the thin walls of the duplex, I could hear the muffled droning of a television. When it flicked off, my eyes shifted back to my sister.

"How's it going with the new neighbor?" she asked.

I tamped down the cartwheel of emotions that fluttered low in my belly with a shrug. "It's fine. I don't ever see him."

In fact, it was easy to not see someone you were actively avoiding.

Sometimes I could hear his deep, throaty laugh through the wall. It rattled through my spine like a threat.

Or a promise.

Austin's heavy footfalls thudded around his side of the

duplex, and Elodie made a face. "Sheesh." She grimaced. "I know you said the walls were thin when the Jeffersons were having wild sex, but I just assumed you were being a prude."

I shot my sister a playful snarl. The previous tenants had moved out a few months ago, and, to be honest, it had been a relief. I found it depressing that two geriatrics in their late seventies had a far more exciting and active sex life than I did.

I didn't mean to, but over the last few days I would catch myself going still, listening to hear any movement from Austin's side of the home.

Winnie's tiny feet thundered down the stairs, and I caught her at the bottom with a hug. "Walking feet, please." I set her on her toes. "Don't forget we have a neighbor again."

"Sorry, Mama," Winnie said.

"Meet you there?" I asked my sister, who nodded. I hoisted my purse over my shoulder. "All right, let's go, kid."

I let my annoyingly attractive new neighbor slip from my mind as Winnie filled the car with conversation now that my workday had been shortened by the lack of before- and after-school care.

My brain was filled to capacity juggling being a single mom and full-time business owner.

"Mom." She groaned my name like a full-blown teenager. "Did you hear me?"

My eyes flicked to hers in the rearview mirror. "What, sweetie?"

Winnie huffed and rolled her eyes. "Nothing."

I fought back tears. I didn't want her to remember me like this—stretched thin and half listening.

I hated that my stress seemed near constant at this

point, and poor Winnie was catching the brunt of my distraction. I swallowed back tears as my grip tightened on the wheel. "I'm sorry, bug. I've just got a lot on my mind lately." I hoped she could understand and hear the sincerity in my voice. "I'm trying my best, I promise."

Winnie kicked her feet and stared out the window without a response.

The Remington County Men's Softball League played every Wednesday night. Not all the games were in Star Harbor, but we tried to attend the ones that were.

As I put my car in park, Winnie didn't wait before she was unharnessing herself and flying out of the vehicle, running as fast as her little legs could carry her.

"Just be careful!" I called. Up ahead, my sister Kit shouted, "I got her! And if I have to, we'll trade her for a funnel cake." Kit tickled Winnie as they hugged.

I raised my hand in thanks. After grabbing a blanket from the back and a small cooler filled with snacks, I made my way toward the field.

The men's twelve-inch softball league games could be pretty fun. Sure, our guys were the second-oldest team in the league, but it was humorous, if nothing else.

A portable speaker was blaring a mix of early country and nineties R&B. The rusted stands were nearly full, and lawn chairs in uneven rows lined the foul lines. Off to the side, a group of small children were setting up a lemonade stand.

I scanned the crowd and smiled when I saw Winnie perched high above my brother Hayes's shoulders and Elodie waving me over to a spot she had saved. I squeezed in next to my sister Kit.

"Thanks for saving us a spot." With a sigh, I unloaded all our belongings.

I looked at my oldest brother, squinting in the late-afternoon sun. "Are you playing tonight?" I asked.

"Yeah," he grunted as he hoisted Winnie off his shoulders, settling her feet onto the ground.

I examined his too-tight T-shirt. "What are you wearing?"

Hayes's nostrils flared as if he was as thin on patience as I was. "Getting out of my truck, I snagged it. Tore a hole the size of my face. It was unbelievable. I had to borrow a spare shirt and all they had left was a small."

Hayes stretched his arms in front of his chest. The sleeves nearly tore, and it was so short, you could see a small strip of his abdomen. It was cut high enough to qualify as a crop top and tight enough to pass for a second skin. The shirt looked like it was almost small enough to fit Winnie.

I bit down a laugh. "Ah," I said with a knowing nod.

Poor Hayes seemed to have almost comically rotten luck. Ever since the end of his senior year of high school, he had been plagued by it. That meant, in our small town, rumors swirled about him being cursed by the Lady of the Dunes.

Of course, none of us believed it, but sometimes it was hard to ignore that our moody, forlorn older brother had absolute shit luck.

The team started to take the field and Kit clapped. "Well, get out there, big dog. *Woof, woof,*" she barked.

He groaned and rolled his eyes, but he also cracked a rare smile.

"There he is!" Winnie pointed, drawing our attention to the field. "There's Cal."

I swear, my little girl, side by side with her aunt, sighed wistfully as Elodie's boyfriend jogged onto the field. Ever since he'd put himself in the path of a rogue foul ball and saved Winnie, he was a hero in her eyes.

I looked at my younger sister, and a tightness twisted in my chest. She had come to life over the last few months—thriving and happy.

"Ooh, girls, looks like we got some fresh meat on the team in front of us." Three older women I recognized as fellow Keepers peered into their own sets of binoculars.

I followed their line of sight, my eyes landing across the broad shoulders of none other than Austin.

"Oh, that's so fun," Elodie said, turning to Kit. "Did Brody convince him to fill in for Wes?"

My youngest sister's face twisted. "How the hell should I know? Brody is Hayes's friend, not mine."

A disbelieving rattle formed in my throat before I could stop it, which earned me a slicing glare from Kit. Brody and Hayes had been best friends since elementary school, and Kit had been teased for many years about the summer she followed them around with stars in her eyes, mooning over him.

The crush lasted only a summer, and once Tommy Fitzsimmons moved to town, her crush on Brody had all but evaporated. But every once in a while I wondered whether there was still a tiny bit of that ten-year-old Kit lingering at the edges, hoping for her brother's best friend to notice her.

To me Brody would always be the protective older-brother type, but *his* brother was a different story entirely.

I knew Austin was twenty-eight. Old enough to be considered a man, but far too young for a delusional thirty-six-year-old single mom to fantasize about. Austin was in the shortstop position, and as they warmed up, a ground ball quickly rolled his way. He was impossibly fast, scooping up the ball and effortlessly throwing it to Cal at first base. The sharp whack of the ball hitting Cal's glove made me jump.

Cal pulled his hand from the glove, shaking it out. With a grin, Cal pointed at Austin. "Hell yeah, let's go."

"Maybe with Austin on the team, we'll actually win a game," Kit mumbled, hiding her giggle.

The team could use a win, especially after all the worrying about Wes.

I leaned forward to speak to Elodie. "Wes is home now, right? We haven't really seen him around or anything." My voice trailed off. Wes was healing, as was expected after such a traumatic injury.

Elodie nodded, sadness washing over her features. "He's home. Cal visits him a lot and says that physically he's healing really well. Mentally it's been"—she paused, chewing the inside of her lip—"kind of tough."

My heart ached for poor Wes. He had grown up in Star Harbor and had always been such a fun-loving guy. Winnie was dangling from the back of the bleachers, using them as a makeshift jungle gym. I reached into our cooler to grab a sparkling water and hopefully ease my parched throat.

Watching Austin bend in half to touch his toes and stretch certainly wasn't helping things.

"Has anyone heard from Clara?" I asked my sisters, desperate for a change of topic.

Clara, our middle sister, hadn't been back to Star Harbor in nearly a year. Her fiancé's thriving tech company did more than enough to keep her social calendar completely booked. Oftentimes I would reach out without hearing much back other than that things were fine.

Maybe it was my big-sister intuition, but something just felt *off*.

"She didn't come home once this summer," Kit accused. "It's like she thinks she's too good for this family."

I shrugged. "Maybe she just has a lot going on. I know Greg and his calendar keep them very busy."

"Greg and his calendar." Kit snorted a disgusted sound. "What a douche canoe."

Elodie and I glanced at one another and hid a laugh.

Winnie's head popped up from behind the bleachers. "What's a douche?"

Collectively we dissolved into a fit of giggles. "Come on, baby." I reached over and helped to haul Winnie back on top of the bleachers. "Let's focus on the game. It's about to start."

I tried not to stare, but *goddamn*. After effortlessly launching a ball over the outfield wall, Austin rounded home and jogged toward the dugout, grinning, sweat damp. He was completely unaware of how infuriatingly hot he looked.

His ball cap was turned backward, and as his eyes flicked up and locked on mine, my stomach took a nosedive.

Oh, he was *very* aware of how good he looked.

My thoughts jumbled. *He's just a man. A man with tattoos and forearms and a face like trouble wearing a backward cap. And a mouth I definitely don't think about. Ever.*

Kit's elbow bumped into my ribs. "So how's life with your hot neighbor?"

"Oh yes." Elodie leaned forward, resting her elbow on her knee and her chin in her hand. "What's he like?" she asked. "I've only met him a couple of times, and he just seemed so charming."

I schooled my face into a model of indifference. "I wouldn't know. We haven't spoken."

Kit lifted her nose in the air to tease me. "I wouldn't

know. We haven't spoken." She laughed. "You're telling me with those paper-thin walls, you haven't heard the shower running and thought of that man naked?"

Thankfully Winnie was out of earshot, working on twisting together a dandelion crown with a friend from school. I could feel the heat creeping up my collarbone and cheeks.

I'm certainly thinking of it now.

"You're hilarious," I deadpanned.

"I'm just saying," Kit chimed in, "that man looks like he could chop wood shirtless and ruin your life in the best way."

Elodie giggled. "I know on good authority there is almost nothing hotter than watching a man chop wood." Her gaze drifted to Cal as she smiled.

A part of me—one I usually kept locked up tight—wondered what it would feel like to be wanted like that again.

Recklessly. No questions asked.

I shook my head and tried not to imagine Austin as a shirtless lumberjack.

As the game wore on, I focused on the way the white puffy clouds floated across a clean blue sky, a bird digging for worms in the grass, Winnie's hair in tangles that she would surely fight me on as I brushed them out tonight at bath time.

Anything but sneaking glances at a particular shortstop whose ass looked like it was made from granite. When the game finally ended, we offered polite claps to hide the groans from another crushing loss. The other team and their fans celebrated while the majority of Star Harbor packed up their chairs and blankets and headed toward their cars.

As I packed the bits of discarded snack wrappers and

sucked down the remains of a half-finished juice box, my eyes flicked up and landed directly on Austin, but he was already looking at me.

My spine stiffened as he winked and started walking directly toward us.

Winnie also noticed and began waving wildly. "Hi! Hi!" She turned to me. "Mom, it's our neighbor." Then she turned back to Austin. "Hi."

It was the moment that my soul left my body.

My pulse hammered in my throat as Austin draped his forearms on the fence beside the dugout, his wrists crossing. "Hey, neighbor." His grin stretched across his face.

Think, think, think.

All I could do was blink at him until something sharp pinched my side—Kit.

"Hi," I choked out.

A throaty chuckle vibrated between us as his grin widened. "Are you ladies sticking around for a few rounds at the Lantern?"

It was common knowledge that the softball team celebrated wins and losses with beers at the local dive, the Lady's Lantern.

I had glanced at my sisters, hoping for any type of rescue, when Kit hopped off the bleachers. "Nope," the *P* popped effortlessly as she landed on her feet.

"Maybe." Elodie smiled as she moved away from the bleachers and wrapped herself in Cal's arms with a giggle.

"What about you?" Austin's eyes raked down my front, and I could feel every smoldering inch of his gaze.

"I have Winnie." I adjusted my attention to my daughter, occupying myself by fixing the hair behind her back. "No fun for me," I joked.

"I'm sure you get to have a *little* fun." His voice was thick and dripped with innuendo.

Oh god, he remembers.

He had to remember. He was smiling like he knew exactly what I tasted like and was dying to bring it up right in front of me.

"Of course we have fun, Mama," Winnie exclaimed. "We go to the beach and dance with the waves. We bake cookies and plant flowers."

I softened and smiled down at my daughter. "You're absolutely right, Win." I scrunched my nose at her. "We do have lots of fun, don't we?"

At that moment Brody jogged over to our little group, a towel around his neck, and handed Austin a Gatorade. "Hey, have you two officially met yet?"

"No."

"Oh yeah."

Our voices tangled over each other as my eyes flared in Austin's direction. He had the decency to wipe away his smile with a swipe of his hand.

Brody either didn't hear or chose to ignore our awkward interaction as he finished half of his Gatorade in one chug. "You should consider asking him for help with Winnie," Brody said. "He lives right next door, helps out with the construction stuff, and is good with kids. His schedule with Wes is flexible, so both mornings and evenings shouldn't be a problem."

My jaw and my stomach dropped. I nearly laughed, but instead the sound was more of a panicked, unhinged hack.

"Are you okay?" Brody asked.

"Fine. I just, um," I stammered.

"Just a thought." Brody shrugged. He slipped the towel

from around his shoulders and snapped it, whipping Austin in the butt hard enough to make him yelp.

I finished packing our things, doing whatever I could to steady my breathing as my heartbeat danced wildly out of control.

With Winnie tucked under my arm to keep her from running off, we headed back to our cars. I stared straight ahead, making a beeline for my escape.

The man I'd had completely anonymous, slightly illegal forest sex with was now playing softball with my family, waving at my daughter, and being recommended as my childcare solution.

This is not sustainable.

As I buckled Winnie into the car, I glanced across the lot to see Austin talking with my brother, Hayes. Somehow that man had gotten my impossible grump of a brother to actually laugh.

Winnie had noticed too. "I like Austin. He seems nice."

A half-hearted hum was all I could manage as my brain all but imploded.

FIVE

AUSTIN

The Lady's Lantern smelled like grease, floor wax, and defeat—though in a way that felt almost comforting. Postsoftball, the crowd had thinned into a familiar mix of barflies, off-duty mechanics, and men who probably had the same barstool every Wednesday, sipping domestics like it was tradition—and maybe it was.

I nursed a beer at the end of the booth while Hayes talked to the bartender, Cal leaned back in his chair with his boots crossed, and Brody flipped a coaster between his fingers. There was a postgame haze hanging over all of us, warm with adrenaline and muscle ache, a little sharper for me since my nerves were still chewing on the fact that I'd made eye contact with Selene Darling for more than two full seconds.

Not just eye contact. A spark. A jolt. Something I wasn't supposed to want but couldn't stop replaying.

"You keep looking like that and people are gonna think something is wrong with you," Brody muttered, his voice low as he slid another beer across to me. "Relax. You're allowed to have fun."

I flicked a brow. "This is my fun face."

"Then someone should tell your jaw." He leaned back, settling into the booth.

He followed it with a smirk, but I knew better. Brody had a casual way of watching people that made you forget he was doing it. He was all easy strength and dad jokes until he wasn't.

I learned quickly that when it came to Selene and her sisters, the guy went into full big-brother mode—whether anyone asked him to or not.

I couldn't help but wonder. "Do you think Selene really needs help?"

"She's just been through a lot," Brody said casually—but not really. His eyes stayed on the television in the corner, but the shift in his tone was impossible to miss.

"You mentioned that," I said, careful to keep my voice neutral.

He took a sip of his beer. "She doesn't exactly ask for help, but between her business and that little girl of hers, she's got more than any one person should have to juggle."

I nodded, slow. "The kid seems like a handful."

"Winnie's a firecracker," Brody said, and I didn't miss the way his mouth tipped up at the corner. "Smart as hell. Funny too. A lot like her mom."

I let the words hang between us for a second, unsure whether we were still talking about the kid—or if we'd drifted into something else.

My gut filled with lead, but I had to ask. "Is there like . . . a *thing* between Selene and you?"

"No." Brody chuckled. "Hell no. She could use a break is all," he added. "Honestly, you should offer. Mornings, afternoons—your schedule's flexible enough, right?"

"You really want me to babysit?" I blinked. When

Brody had first mentioned it, I thought he was joking, or maybe meant I could help her hang a picture frame or something.

"Not babysit. Just . . . show up. You're right next door. Kids aren't that hard. You're practically still one yourself. You can kick a soccer ball and tie a ponytail, right? That's the job description. It doesn't have to be complicated."

I wanted to laugh. He had no idea that it was *already* complicated.

I shrugged. "I can think about it."

Brody finally looked over at me then, and there was something behind his eyes—something more than just concern. He didn't know the truth, not really, but he wasn't blind either.

"She's one of the good ones," he said simply. "Just . . . don't give her a reason to dead bolt the door."

My grip tightened slightly around the bottle. "I won't."

He studied me a beat longer, then gave a single, satisfied nod and tipped his beer toward mine. "Good. Because Hayes wouldn't be the only one to beat your ass."

"Yeah." I smirked. "That tracks."

He raised a brow like that wasn't the answer he expected, then turned to join Cal in heckling the opposing team. I sat back and let the noise of the bar blur around me. I didn't need a warning.

Selene wasn't someone you messed with. She was the type of woman you moved through fire for.

And I was already burning.

THE NIGHT AIR smelled like grill smoke and cut grass, a scent that made it feel like maybe this town wasn't a city that tried too hard to impress you—it was content simply being what it was.

The duplex was quiet when I got home.

One of those split-down-the-middle jobs from the seventies—sloppy drywall surgery that took a perfectly good house and turned it into two crooked halves. You could still see the seams. A single front porch stretched across both units, the roofline sloping like it was tired of pretending it wasn't one place. I'd been told the kitchens and living rooms mirrored each other downstairs. Upstairs was where the lines blurred. Our bedrooms were back-to-back. Same narrow dimensions. Same creaking floorboards. Same cheap-ass, hollow wall in between.

Selene Darling was twenty feet away from me at all times. Ten, if we were upstairs, and most nights I pretended like I didn't know that.

But tonight? Tonight made it impossible.

I'd been in my place a week and already knew that Selene's bedroom was the one directly opposite mine. I also knew she liked to shower at night, because if you followed the lines of the original crown molding, hiding under layers of thick paint, you could see exactly where the primary bedroom had been cut in two. My guess was her half had the bathroom of an original en suite space.

I kicked off my shoes by the door, peeled off my hoodie, and climbed the stairs two at a time. The house smelled like fresh paint and laundry soap—new-tenant scent. My mattress was calling to me, a few unopened boxes stacked in the corner. I hadn't even bothered hanging anything on the walls. I told myself I didn't need to settle in if I didn't plan to stay long.

But I lingered anyway.

I slowed at the top of the stairs, fingers dragging across

the drywall as I passed the spot where her room pressed against mine.

Then I heard it. Singing.

I wasn't trying to listen, but when the house settled and was quiet, it was like the walls leaned in to whisper.

Soft, off-key singing floated through the walls. It was the kind of tenderness that made something in my chest seize up. A second voice joined in—smaller, higher, bubbling with laughter.

Winnie.

They were singing to each other. Warm and alive through the drywall.

My hand stilled on the doorframe. Not listening, not really. Just . . . existing in it. I let the sound of them fill the hollow space in my chest like insulation.

They didn't know I could hear them, and that was the part that got to me.

Selene's voice floated out again, reading some kind of story. There was a haunted tone in it—ghostly, spooky, maybe even a little ridiculous—and Winnie kept interrupting, asking questions with zero patience. Selene answered with laughter tucked into her words, with more patience than I'd ever seen in anyone. It was a far cry from the absent-minded tuck-ins of a working mother who was doing her best. Most nights I fell asleep wondering whether I would even see my mother in the morning before she left for work.

That sweet sound of a loving mother making sure her child was safe and warm—it hadn't been like that for me.

I sat on the edge of my bed, elbows on my knees, the lamp throwing amber light across the floor. I stayed there long after Selene's gentle storytelling faded. After a few moments, Winnie's voice quieted, followed by a soft hush.

It was hard to make out the rustling noises beyond the wall, and after a few minutes feeling like a total creep, I stopped trying. Instead, I took a shower in the bathroom down the hall and tried to scrub Selene Darling from my mind.

When I got back to the bedroom, I pulled on a pair of black boxer briefs and sat on the edge of my bed.

"No, I didn't mean to sleep with him," Selene hissed through the thin walls.

My attention was instantly piqued.

Her voice was low, but she must have been close to the wall, because even muffled, I could hear every word. "It was dark. There was alcohol . . . and possibly possession by a very hot demon."

I froze.

Her voice dropped to a whisper. "I'm serious, Kit. Don't laugh at me. I am *mortified*."

I leaned forward, pulse thumping hard in my throat.

"No, I am not totally sure that he remembers," she added, her frustration climbing. "I don't know if he knows it was me. God, this is a disaster." Selene paused. "I have to go. I'll talk to you tomorrow."

I bit down on a grin. My hand dragged across my mouth like that could stop the ache that bloomed behind my ribs. She didn't know I remembered. She thought I could forget.

She had no idea I hadn't stopped thinking about her since that night in the woods—how she kissed like she wanted to burn her past clean, how she eagerly took every inch like we were trying to outrun every mistake we'd ever made.

I lay back on the bed, one arm flung over my eyes.

"Yeah, sweetheart," I whispered to the ceiling, exhaling my frustrations. "I fucking remember."

Minutes ticked by, and I hated that I couldn't scrub her from my mind. I stared in silence, wondering what she was up to. I didn't need to be caught up with a hot-as-fuck single mom who could level me with one glance. My brother would be pissed if I fucked it up, and, let's be real, that was typically what ended up happening.

Then I heard a faint sound. A sharp inhale. Something too soft to be words and too heavy to ignore.

Something breathless. Then again, followed by a stifled moan.

My hand dropped from my face. I stared up at the ceiling like it could help.

Selene was touching herself.

I didn't know for sure. It could have been anything, but something inside me *knew*.

She didn't know I could hear. Just like she hadn't known I was the man in that dark forest.

The heat hit me hard—fast and furious and fucked. My hips shifted, the ache turning sharp as I dragged a palm down the front of my boxers. I didn't mean to. I probably shouldn't have, but I did it anyway.

I shut my eyes, letting the image flood in—her body against mine, the hitch of her breath, the way her fingers had gripped my shoulders like she needed something to hold on to or she'd fall apart.

My cock was already hard, straining against fabric, and I fumbled with the waistband like a goddamn rookie. I pushed my underwear down just far enough to wrap my hand around myself and squeeze.

"Fuck," I muttered.

Every gasp I remembered from that night came rushing back—hers, mine. How quickly and intensely we'd found a rhythm. The way we moved like we knew each other already, like it was the last time we'd ever be touched.

My hand stroked slow, firm, and greedy. I bit my lip to keep quiet, to keep it buried deep. The sounds through the wall kept coming—soft, uneven. Maybe she didn't know I was this close. Maybe she did.

I wanted to believe she was thinking about me.

I imagined her fingers between her thighs. Her breath catching. Her head tipped back.

I fucked into my hand with that image lodged so deep it ached. No teasing. No pretense. Just need, raw and ragged and sharp.

My back arched. My jaw clenched.

"Fuck, Selene," I whispered.

When her intake of breath was sharp, followed by a shudder of her orgasm, my release hit hard—violent, like it had been waiting since the forest.

I spilled over my stomach, panting hard, hand trembling where it still held my cock.

For a second everything was too quiet.

Then I laughed—quiet and bitter.

I reached for a tissue and wiped myself off, the heat of shame creeping up the back of my neck. It didn't belong to her. This secret. This wanting.

It was mine to carry. Mine to bury.

I rolled onto my side, staring at the wall between us.

"I just needed to get you out of my system," I murmured to the void, but even I knew that was a fucking lie.

I should've felt better, or emptier, but the ache wasn't in my dick—it was in my fucking chest.

~

I woke up early the next morning and did what any rational, emotionally balanced man with a guilty conscience would do in my situation.

I brought gifts.

I ordered two drinks from the café downtown—one hot chocolate with whipped cream and sprinkles for Winnie and one oat milk vanilla latte for Selene. It was a guess, but it felt right. Then I wrote a note on a bright-yellow Post-it and stuck it to the side of the cup.

If it helps, I was possessed too.
—The Demon

It was risky—letting her know not only that I could hear her conversations through the wall, but that I also *remembered*.

I left the drinks on her porch after knocking twice, then retreated back to my door and slipped inside like a man who absolutely hadn't been eavesdropping like a creep the night before.

But I waited.

Not long after, I heard the front door creak open, followed by a moment of silence. Then Winnie's giggle. "Mama! Did a demon bring us coffee?"

"He left a note," Selene murmured, and I could picture her squinting at it like she wanted to roll her eyes—but smiled instead.

I grinned into my mug and let the heat warm my palms. I couldn't pinpoint why Selene had such a hold on me.

But possessed or not—I could make one hell of a neighbor.

✥

THE SUN WAS STARTING to dip by the time I stepped into the backyard. The light hit everything sideways, slanting through the trees with that late-summer gold that made even overgrown grass look romantic.

I'd intentionally left the gate between our halves of the yard open. It seemed to stick a little, so I'd wedged it with a rock to keep it from swinging shut.

An opening.

I wasn't expecting to see Selene outside, but there she was—bent over slightly, gently teasing a dandelion crown from Winnie's hair while trying to keep her from dumping an entire bottle of bubble solution on the lawn.

"One more puddle and we're officially hosting a fairy water party." Selene laughed, but I could tell she was half exhausted.

Winnie skipped across the lawn, twirling into my yard, leaving Selene to stand alone in the light. Her slim shoulders were drawn tight to her ears like they didn't know how to relax. Selene tipped her face toward the sagging sun and exhaled.

When she turned, she spotted me before I could pretend I wasn't staring.

"Oh," she said, brushing her hair from her face. "Hello."

I tucked a hand into the pocket of my jeans. "Hi."

The muscles in Selene's neck worked as she swallowed. She pointed toward the open gate. "You might want to keep that closed. Winnie's known to wander over to your side. I keep telling her to stay out of your space."

I took a few steps closer, slow and deliberate. "Winnie's fine. I opened it so she could have more space. You too."

She narrowed her eyes. "Me?"

"Yeah," I said, leaning one hand on the fence post. "You can wander in anytime you feel like it."

She blinked. Then she rolled her eyes so hard I half expected her pupils to file a complaint, but she smiled.

It was small, but the smile was enough.

Selene's frustrated exhale was quiet. "You're impossible."

I nodded. "I can be."

She crossed her arms, but her voice was lighter than it had been all week. "About the coffee . . ."

My eyes narrowed, genuine curiosity getting the best of me. "Did I get your order right?"

"No." Her voice was all business, and a hearty laugh escaped me. I liked the challenge.

Selene bit her bottom lip, then let it go. "It was funny. The note."

I relaxed into my stance. "I meant what I said too. I was . . . enchanted."

Her eyes flicked up to meet mine, and for a split second everything got quiet.

Really quiet.

"Well . . . don't read into it," she said, her tone flat but her voice softer. "That night. It was nothing."

I chuckled and grinned. "Okay."

Her brows furrowed. "I mean it."

"I believe you." I leaned in slightly, just enough for my voice to drop. "But I still remember every second of it, and that was not *nothing*."

She inhaled, sharp and shallow.

"Okay, well, I should go." Her words ran fast, like they were chasing her heartbeat. "Winnie needs a bath."

Selene turned toward her yard when insanity took hold of me. "Oh, hey," I called out, and she turned, shading her eyes from the sun. "Brody was right. I could help you out before and after school. It wouldn't be a problem. So if you ever change your mind about needing help . . ."

"I won't." Her chin lifted, muscles tense.

My grin spread wide. "I know."

She turned, calling out for Winnie, who was now chasing a butterfly into my side of the yard. The little girl bounded over and took her mother's hand, dandelions still tangled in her curls.

Selene led her back inside, and I watched the door shut behind them.

The chain-link creaked, the sun dipped low, and I leaned back against the fence like it could steady me.

This pull between us?

I had a feeling it was just getting started.

SIX

SELENE

THERE WERE EXACTLY three sips of coffee left in my mug when Winnie's pink plastic unicorn cup went flying.

I tried to catch it and a splash of lukewarm caffeine hit my neck. My shirt. The counter. The floor. Winnie—oblivious as ever—giggled, her curls bouncing as she chased the runaway cup like we were starring in some deranged slapstick comedy.

I steadied my voice. "Winnie, I asked you not to bring your cup over here."

"But I was thirsty!" she insisted, indignant.

I pressed my fingers into my eye sockets and tried not to cry. The coffee was the only thing tethering me to the realm of the living this morning. Now it was soaking into the hem of my shirt and pooling beneath the toaster like some dark omen.

Somewhere in the distance—possibly on Mars—my phone buzzed for the fifth time in two minutes. Work texts, no doubt. I ignored them.

I didn't need help. I needed cloned versions of myself with better attitudes and lower cortisol levels.

"Mama, I can't find my purple sock!" Winnie yelled.

I gritted my teeth. "Then wear the yellow ones!"

She groaned. "They're itchy!"

I closed my eyes. Counted to five and breathed in. The air smelled like spilled coffee and syrup-sticky fingers. I cracked one eye open again and surveyed the kitchen—cereal scattered like confetti, shoes in the sink, Winnie in her pajamas, and me in a shirt that now looked like I'd gone twelve rounds with a latte.

From beyond the kitchen wall, I could hear Austin moving. His side of the duplex had its own rhythm—less chaos, more quiet thumps and purposeful steps. A door clicked shut. His footsteps trailed toward the back. Then silence.

I braced myself against the sink, letting my head hang. Austin's playful note from the day before had put a little pep in my step, but it looked like I was on my own this morning. At first I'd been mortified to learn that he had overheard me talking with Kit. The flush in my cheeks deepened when I thought about what *else* he may have heard through those thin walls.

The respectable, modest part of me wanted the earth to open up and swallow me whole, but the poised, assertive parts didn't care he might have overheard me pleasuring myself. In fact, I wondered what he might have said had he known I'd gotten off imagining him stroking himself on the other side of the wall.

Warmth bloomed low in my belly. It was safest to keep a lid on dangerous, yearning parts.

I shook out my shoulders. I had shit to do and *very* little time to do it.

Austin was gone for the day—or so I thought. The house was quiet long enough for the silence to settle and for me to start scrubbing the counter while I considered reheating yesterday's coffee—when the knock startled me.

Two short raps. Confident and familiar.

I blinked at the door like it had grown arms.

Another knock, followed by a muffled voice. "Everything okay in there? It sounded like someone was trying to wrestle a raccoon into a turtleneck."

Winnie shrieked with laughter.

I padded to the front door and cracked it open just wide enough to see him standing on the porch with two to-go cups in a cardboard tray. Austin looked irritatingly awake. Hair tousled but somehow still perfect. Black T-shirt and jeans with that cocky little half smile like he already knew how my morning had gone.

I opened the door a little more, just enough to reveal that I was wearing only one sock. His gaze dragged down my legs and back up, humor dancing in his eyes.

"Not a word," I warned.

He raised his free hand. "I didn't say a thing, but I did bring a peace offering."

And, damn it, I almost smiled.

He held out the tray. One cup was topped with a clear domed lid and whipped cream piled high with sprinkles. The other was marked with my name in Sharpie.

"Let me guess," I said, eyeing him suspiciously. "You heard the chaos and decided to rescue the damsels in distress?"

"Nope," he said. "I heard the chaos and thought, 'Wow, I bet she's already out of coffee.'"

I reached for the cup despite myself. "You're a menace."

The corner of his mouth lifted. "Only sometimes."

Winnie darted between us, flinging herself around his

waist like she did this every day. "Austin! You brought sprinkles!"

He crouched to her level, ruffling her curls. "Only the best for my new favorite tornado."

Winnie darted back into the house, probably to find something cool to show her new friend, no doubt.

I propped a hip against the doorjamb. "You seem like a man who has a lot of tornadoes in his life," I said before I could stop myself.

He looked up at me, slow and amused. "Nah. I've got a type. One-socked women with coffee stains and a death glare."

My mouth opened—then shut again.

From inside my house, something crashed and I closed my eyes.

"I'm on it," he said, already stepping inside like he belonged.

He set the drinks on the counter, scooped up the cereal box from the floor, and caught Winnie mid-spin before she collided with the table. "All right, small but mighty," he said to her, "let's find those socks before your mom self-destructs."

I just stood there, stunned, while he moved through the kitchen like he'd been doing it for years.

"Selene?" he said, glancing at me over his shoulder. "Why don't you go take five? Put on something without coffee in the fabric. I've got this."

I didn't move.

"Seriously," he said, softening. "Go. I've got this."

And, apparently, he did.

I hesitated at the bottom of the stairs, waiting for him to second-guess himself, to need direction, to prove I couldn't let go even for five minutes.

But he didn't. He just moved around like the kitchen belonged to him, Winnie trailing behind like he was the sun and she was some wild little planet in his orbit.

I turned and climbed the stairs—quietly, reluctantly—listening as his voice drifted up through the old floors, low and calm and steady.

And somehow that was the part that undid me most.

When I came back down, the kitchen was still a mess, but somehow the noise had settled. Winnie munched on a granola bar at the table, swinging her legs under the chair and humming to herself like this was any other day. Austin leaned against the counter, one ankle crossed over the other, sipping coffee like he belonged there—like this wasn't the weirdest morning of my week.

I stayed in the doorway, arms folded, trying not to over-analyze the fact that he'd poured Winnie's milk into a mason jar because he couldn't find her cup, or that she'd happily accepted it without a second thought. Or that he had somehow managed to talk her into putting socks on without either of them ending up in tears.

"She's a negotiator," he said, eyes flicking toward me as he handed her a paper towel. "I think she could run a boardroom if the snacks were right."

"She's five," I muttered, but the corner of my mouth tugged up anyway. "And she's not supposed to eat in here without a plate."

He held up both hands like I'd caught him mid-crime. "Noted. Next time, full table settings and linen napkins."

I stared at him. "There's not going to be a next time."

Austin just shrugged and took another sip of coffee. "Okay."

I crossed the room and grabbed a banana, peeling it with a little more force than necessary. "I mean it."

He nodded. "I know."

"I'm serious." My hand propped on my hip.

Austin smiled. "I can tell. You've got your serious banana-eating stance going."

I looked down at the banana like it had betrayed me, then exhaled hard. "I don't like needing help."

Austin's voice was laced with understanding. "Most people don't."

I gritted my teeth. "I'm not most people."

He chuckled, but somehow I didn't feel like he was making fun of me. "I'd gathered that."

We stood there for a second—me with my half-peeled banana, him looking aggravatingly calm—and something in my chest twisted. I hadn't invited this. I hadn't asked for anyone to step in, but he had. Winnie had accepted him with open arms, and now there we were.

My eyes narrowed at him. "Don't you have a job?" I looked around the duplex. "Somewhere *else* to be?"

Austin's cheek twitched. "I'm employed."

I shot him a blank stare.

He chuckled and added, "I was working at the marina, but stepped away from that. Right now I am helping Wes's construction company while he's recovering. In fact, I'm working on a jobsite at Star Harbor Farms for your sister." His shoulders lifted. "It's physically demanding work, but I'm finding I actually enjoy it. The hours are flexible and the pay is more than fair."

I eyed him again. If anyone knew I was actually considering accepting childcare help from a one-night stand, I'd be the mockery of the school pickup line. As if their pity glances weren't enough, if they knew my only option was big-dick energy with a winning smile, my status as *tragic mess* would be officially cemented.

Still, it was hard to deny the convenience of a caretaker right next door who could accommodate before- *and* after-school care.

Shit.

"Just for this week." I rubbed my temple. "Until I can figure something else out."

Austin's smile was subtle, but it was there. "Sure. Temporary works for me. You're the boss."

Winnie popped out of her chair like a jack-in-the-box. "Does that mean you're my nanny?"

Austin choked on his coffee. "I think 'awesome neighbor helper guy' is a cooler title."

She tilted her head. "Do I get to make you a name tag sticker?"

He gave a solemn nod. "Only if it has glitter."

The timer on the stove buzzed—a reminder I'd set ages ago to switch the laundry that I never actually put in. I groaned, rubbing my eyes. "I need ten minutes. Can you keep an eye on her?"

He didn't hesitate. "Go."

I hesitated anyway.

"Selene," he said, voice low and even. "We can survive ten minutes. I've got her."

Something in his tone—something steady and unflinching—made it hard to argue. So I nodded and backed out of the room, only half listening to Winnie tell him her favorite knock-knock joke for the third time this week.

Halfway up the stairs, I realized I was breathing easier.

And that scared the hell out of me.

SEVEN

SELENE

Winnie didn't seem to care that we were already late for school. She skipped half the way there, swinging her lunchbox and singing a made-up song about unicorn crackers. Austin strolled beside her like we were just out for a walk in the sunshine and not barreling toward an unexcused tardy slip.

I checked my watch for the third time in as many minutes. "We should've left fifteen minutes ago."

Austin gave me a side glance. "We're already on the way. Unless you've got a teleportation device stashed in that purse, I don't think we can do much else."

His tone was easy, teasing, which only made my anxiety spike harder.

I gritted my teeth. "I don't like being late."

Winnie slowed to a bounce in place while waiting at the crossing. Her curls frizzed into little wings on either side of her head, and one of her socks had betrayed her ankle completely.

"She looks like she was raised by wolves," I muttered.

Austin grinned. "Nah. She's free-spirited. There's a difference."

We made it just as the bell rang—one long, shrill note that felt like a judgment.

The teacher at the door smiled as we approached. "Oh, Winnie! Good morning, sweetheart. Cutting it close today, huh?"

Before I could respond, Winnie pointed. "This is Austin. He's taking me to school now."

The teacher—Ms. Evelyn, young, pretty, and exactly the kind of woman who probably drank water regularly and had time to exfoliate—turned her attention to Austin like a sunflower following the sun. Her smile widened. "Nice to meet you. Are you new to Star Harbor?"

I cleared my throat. "Austin's our neighbor. He'll be helping with school drop-offs this week—" I threw a glance at him.

"And pickups," he added smoothly, offering a handshake that somehow looked casual and confident at the same time.

Ms. Evelyn took it, a bit too eagerly if you asked me. "That's wonderful. Winnie's such a delight."

Winnie beamed. "I had sprinkles for breakfast!"

I set my shoulders. "She had real breakfast too," I added quickly.

Austin gave her a wink. "Only the best for our girl."

I didn't miss the look Ms. Evelyn gave me after that—curious, maybe a little surprised. And why wouldn't she be? I looked like a woman hanging on by a thread, and he looked like a walking Pinterest board of hot husband material.

She probably thought we were together. And worse—she probably thought I wasn't good enough for him.

Which, objectively speaking, wasn't completely inaccurate.

We said goodbye to Winnie, who launched herself through the classroom door without a backward glance.

We walked in silence for a few steps, the air already warming with early sun. My shoulder brushed his once. Not on purpose, but I didn't move away.

He didn't either.

After a while, he said, "So. Just to clarify. I'm not your employee, right?"

I huffed a laugh. "Please. I'm not even sure I can afford you."

He looked over at me, a lazy smile tugging at his mouth. "Then I guess we'll have to negotiate my rate."

Those playful words did something to me I didn't want to examine. I swallowed hard and looked away. "You're really good with her."

His tone was quiet. "She's a good kid. Fun."

I fought a smile. "She likes you."

"Yeah," he said. "She makes it easy."

We stepped up onto the porch. I hesitated at the door. "Do you want to come in? For coffee?"

He nodded once. "Sure."

The kitchen was still a mess, but I didn't bother apologizing. He didn't seem to notice.

I poured the coffee this time and handed him a mug. He leaned against the counter, eyes scanning the space like he was already memorizing it.

I sank into a chair and rubbed at my temple. "I keep thinking I'll catch up. That there'll be a break, but the break never comes."

Austin didn't say anything at first. He just sipped his

coffee and studied me like I was a riddle he didn't want to solve too fast.

"Then I guess we hold the line until it does," he said.

It wasn't advice. It wasn't a fix. Just a simple, solid thing to say. Like anchoring a tent in a windstorm.

His words lodged somewhere in my chest.

We sat there for another minute or two, silence stretching between us. It wasn't uncomfortable. It just . . . was.

Eventually he stood. "All right. I should let you work. I'm heading to the job at Elodie's place, but I'll be back in time for after-school pickup."

I walked him to the door. He paused on the threshold, like he was going to say something else, but he didn't.

Austin tipped his chin and stepped out into the sunlight, and I watched the door shut behind him before sinking to the floor in a puddle.

THE LIBRARY'S community room smelled like old paperbacks and lemon-scented floor cleaner—the sterile freshness that never quite masked the scent of time. The Keepers were already mid-chaos when I arrived, embroidery hoops and tea canisters spread across two folding tables like we were planning a very polite coup on a Friday night.

Elodie was perched at the head of the table, arranging mismatched china into neat little rows while the head Keeper, Helen, fussed with a lace tablecloth that refused to sit straight. I moved toward a seat by the window and pulled out my needlework, though calling it that felt generous. My sunflower looked like it had survived a small but devastating fire.

"You're late," Helen said without looking up. I had known Helen since I was a kid. She was in her sixties now but just as youthful as I always remembered. She was always smiling, her freckles dancing across the bridge of her nose as it crinkled. Her dark-brown eyes seemed to twinkle with some secret knowledge. Her salt-and-pepper hair had changed styles throughout the years, but lately she was keeping it in short twists that brushed her temples.

"I'm here," I said, dropping my purse into a chair. "That's the best I could do."

"I saw your . . . helper today," my mom, Angela, said with a grin, looping the word like a lasso and tossing it straight at me.

I kept my eyes on the teacup in front of me. "Helper?"

"You know," she said, nudging my sister Elodie with an elbow. "Austin. The tall, handsome one who looks like he was carved out of someone's daydreams. The man who picked up Winnie at school this afternoon and had every mom at the pickup line sucking in their stomachs."

Elodie's face twisted. "Why were you at the school?"

Mom blinked innocently. "I was just passing by on my walk. It's important to stay limber and fit as you age."

I harrumphed.

Mom was a busybody. Her walks were almost certainly a part of her mission to know everything about every*one* in town, her daughters included.

"Austin is our new neighbor and is just filling in. Temporarily." I clattered the teaspoons into the saucers a little louder than necessary. I gestured at the delicate porcelain in front of me. "What are we even doing here?"

Kit shrugged. "Tea party, obviously."

"Oh, so he's the *manny*," Helen said brightly, not letting me change the subject so easily. "Lucky you." She waggled her eyebrows.

"He's not the manny," I muttered, though admittedly the title was kind of hilarious.

Mom tilted her head. "No? Because from what I could see it kind of looked like he was walking Winnie out like he owned the place."

"Is there *any* privacy in this town?" I inhaled slowly through my nose. "Austin is just helping out for a few days. It was Brody's idea."

"Mmm. Helping," Mom echoed, not bothering to hide her smirk. "How chivalrous."

I pinched the bridge of my nose. "Can we please talk about something else?"

That only made them smile wider. It was a blood sport, really. One flicker of discomfort and they circled like sharks.

"Fine, fine." Elodie poured the first cup of tea. "I vote we talk about the Lady instead."

Thank god for small miracles.

A low buzz of *oooh* rose around the table like schoolgirls sharing secrets behind the bleachers.

Elodie grinned and pulled out her notebook. "So here's what we know: In 1903, a young woman's body was found on the dunes with a locket with the initials A.L. engraved on it, but there was no mention of the woman's true identity. Alma was engaged to William Lovell and wore a locket with the initials A.L., so it's safe to assume the lady haunting Star Harbor is Alma."

Gentle hums filled the space. We were familiar with the lore of the Lady, but something about how Elodie was suggesting a new twist on a familiar ghost story was enchanting.

"But if they were only engaged, her name wouldn't be Lovell. At least, not yet, right?" Kit asked.

"That's true." I nodded.

"Unless . . ." Elodie's eyes sparked with delight. "The locket was a gift for his bride-to-be. A claim on her or promise of some kind with her soon-to-be married initials?"

"That's sweet." Kit sighed wistfully.

"Or controlling," I grumbled, which earned me a few slanted looks. Kit bumped my shoulder and I playfully scowled at her.

"I have thoughts," Elodie continued. "Helen confirmed that there are no records of William Lovell after that engagement announcement. It became assumed that he disappeared right alongside his lovesick bride-to-be."

Kit shrugged. "So maybe he was the long-lost lover who died at sea—just like the legend goes."

Elodie frowned. "Maybe. *But*"—her eyes flicked to Helen, who gave her a reassuring nod—"I have a different theory."

The air in the library grew thick with tension. No one dared to move as we all clung to my sister's words. "The engagement announcement never mentioned the woman's last name. I'm still wondering about Alma's true last name. I think there's a very real possibility that Alma Lovell was really Alma Barker."

"The Barkers who owned the Drifted Spirit Inn?" Tara Smithton, another Keeper, asked.

Elodie nodded with wide eyes. "I think Alma Barker was engaged to William Lovell and the locket was a gift for his bride-to-be. But"—she held up a finger—"Alma had a secret."

Elodie carefully spread faded paper across the table. I cringed, knowing how delicate the paper was.

"After the barn burned down, I found an old trunk in the root cellar. This letter, and others, were tucked inside—dated sometime around 1903, signed only with the initials A.B."

Curious eyes roamed over the letters. The legend of the Lady of the Dunes was so well known in our town that new information was rare. A little thrill danced through our group, and we collectively leaned in.

"Her letter is odd," Elodie added. "I think the legend is wrong—at least, parts of it. I don't believe Alma was waiting for her lost love." My sister set her shoulders. "She was hiding."

That quieted the table.

Mom spoke up. "If she was hiding, from who? Or what?"

"That," Elodie said, barely containing her excitement, "is what we need to find out."

The group murmured, speculation already buzzing—jealous lovers, false names, disappearances. I leaned back and glanced toward the doorway, as if someone might walk in and confirm it all.

My fingers tingled. Seeing the faded, loopy cursive on time-worn paper was intoxicating. I couldn't wait to examine it up close. "Maybe I could look into it a little. Nothing deep, just—see if I can dig anything up. Old property records, boardinghouse logs. That kind of thing."

Helen raised an eyebrow. "Maybe you can see if there's anything on William or even more about the Barker children."

I shrugged, pretending not to notice the way Elodie tried—and failed—to smother her smile. "Winnie's been asking about the ghost again. This might scratch the curiosity itch and keep it from turning into a full-blown obsession."

"She can be in charge of dioramas," Elodie teased.

"Exactly." I smiled. "She's five—that's her version of a dissertation."

"Still," Helen said, focusing the conversation. "Do you really think there's something there?"

I didn't answer right away. The warm light caught on Elodie's notebook, the pages filled with scribbled theories and sketches of old signatures. I thought about the mysterious letter—how something so small could unravel so much history.

"I think it's probably nothing," I said at last. "But I've got some research tools. We might as well put them to use."

With a delighted squeal, Elodie raised her teacup. "To ghosts, gossip, and good intentions."

The others echoed the toast with laughter, but I just sat there, smooth porcelain beneath my fingers, feeling the strange weight of the mystery settle into my chest.

I didn't believe in ghosts.

Not really.

But I was starting to believe in unfinished stories—and the way they had a habit of pulling you back in, even when you swore you were done stitching them together.

EIGHT

AUSTIN

It was Monday morning and I rolled over to check the clock for the third time. With Selene's reluctance to accept help, we hadn't really discussed a start time, so I had spent the last hour lying in bed and listening for sounds of chaos through the wall.

It only took a simple internet search to learn that Winnie's school day started at eight thirty. If all went well, I could drop Winnie off at school and still be at Star Harbor Farms and on the jobsite before nine.

Piece of cake.

By seven, Winnie's footsteps were thundering across the floorboards, and I hauled myself out of bed for a quick shower. Afterward, I walked out my front door and across the porch to theirs.

Before my knock even had time to land, the front door was flying open. "Good morning!" Winnie shouted with excitement.

Selene stood in the doorway, breathless and rearranging her robe like she hadn't meant for the door to open at all. Her hair was wild, her cheeks flushed, and it took every shred of decency I had not to stare.

"Winnie, I told you not to—" She looked at me. "Sorry."

I raised my palms. "We hadn't talked about a start time. I made my best guess, but I can come back if you don't need me right now."

My mind flickered across the rogue thought that Selene might be naked beneath that robe, and my brain short-circuited for a full three seconds.

She flicked a hair from her face, drawing my attention back to the present. "No, it's okay." Selene let a soft smile grace her shapely lips. "You have impeccable timing, actu-ally. Winnie was just getting dressed." Selene grinned at her daughter and redirected her shoulders to point toward the stairs, to which the little girl grumbled, but complied.

She turned to me. "I was just finishing her lunchbox and wanted to go over a few ground rules with you."

When Selene stepped aside, I entered her house and turned to her with my hands on my hips. "Rules?"

She shrugged and it took every part of me to keep my gaze respectable and not linger on the way the thin fabric of her robe sagged on one shoulder.

"Expectations," she said. "I figured I would give you the same rundown as Amanda, and we can go from there."

"You're the boss," I simply said, which earned me a playful eye roll.

Selene walked deeper into her home, and I obediently followed. "Around seven thirty or seven forty-five would be the most helpful," she said. "That way you can help get her ready for school, and I can get myself ready if I have an eight o'clock meeting. School lets out at three-oh-five, and I would love to be able to work until about five." Her hazel eyes sliced to mine. "If that works for you, of course."

I smiled. "That works."

"Some days my schedule is flexible, and if I can, I would like to walk her to school myself or pick her up. So . . ." Selene's teeth captured her lower lip as she glanced up at me through heavy-lidded lashes. "We should exchange numbers so I can give you a heads-up if the schedule changes, or you can let me know if you have any issues and can't help out."

I smirked. "First names *and* phone numbers. Wow."

Her eyes flared. "We do not speak of that night ever. That's the first rule."

My nose scrunched. "These rules aren't very fun."

"I'm serious," she said. "If there's any chance in hell this is going to work, for my own sanity, I need us to both pretend that that night never existed."

I blew a steady stream of air through my lips and shook my head. "I don't know if that's possible"—I stuffed my hands in my pockets—"but I'll do my best."

She looked exasperated, so I thought I'd cut her some slack.

"All right, hit me with the rest," I said. "What are the other rules?"

Selene's chin dipped as each rule was checked off her mental to-do list. "We don't do any screen time before school, or until at least after dinner. I would prefer never, but I'm not a total monster. Processed sugar is dicey. If you give it to her, you may have a maniac on your hands. So if you want to preserve any of your sanity, save anything like that for an after-school treat. She needs closed-toe shoes for school. And no matter what she says, under no circumstances, are we adopting a pet. I don't care what she says or how cute she looks when she asks."

I couldn't help but laugh at the last one. "No adoptees."

I chuckled. "Got it. I think I can handle that. Anything else, boss?"

Selene groaned. "God, why are you being so nice?"

I leaned against her kitchen counter. "Why are you so surprised that people don't mind helping you?"

Selene eyed me suspiciously, but it was clear she was more than a little tired and grateful for me to lend a hand.

With her finger in the air, Selene stepped forward, eyes narrowed. "Just because you're charming doesn't mean I trust you."

God, she was cute when she was trying to be tough.

I dipped my chin. "That's fair, but I'm sure I'll win you over with sheer tenacity and my superior granola bar management skills."

A half laugh rattled in the back of Selene's throat, and I was rewarded with a sly smile at the corner of her mouth.

Selene eased past me with graceful movements. "We'll be down in a few minutes." She tipped her head toward the coffeepot in the corner. "The coffee is hot. Sugar's in the jar next to it, and cream is in the fridge."

I nodded without responding, and as she slinked upstairs, I took in the space around me.

It was uncanny how you could clearly see a beautiful home had been divided and made into this monstrosity of a rental property. Modern walls had been shoehorned into a once-historic building. You could see it in the way the original crown molding disappeared on her side but continued on mine.

Out in the joint backyard a smattering of rain made music on the back steps. Listening for any signs of trouble upstairs, but not hearing any, I hurried over to my apartment side to grab an umbrella.

When I stepped back into their side, Winnie was just

coming down the stairs. Her little grin with one front tooth missing was too damn cute.

"Almost ready, kid?" I asked.

Winnie was dressed in a pair of knee-length denim shorts and a red-and-blue-striped shirt.

"Almost," she chirped. "I want a French braid and a big bow." She turned back up the stairs. "Mama!"

I stepped forward. "Oh, whoa, hey—maybe there's something I can help with." I shrugged.

Winnie eyed me skeptically, her hands propped on her little hips. "You know how to French braid?"

"Absolutely not." I shook my head with a chuckle. I spun my finger in a circle. "Give me a quick twirl."

Happy to be the center of attention, Winnie obliged, twirling in a big circle and ending on a curtsy.

"How would you feel about a mediocre ponytail with that big bow? That I think I can handle."

Her lips pursed, but almost immediately she shrugged. "Sure, why not," she relented, and I breathed a sigh of relief.

I opened my arms. "Well, step on up to Austin's beauty parlor."

Winnie chuckled and turned so I could gather her wild hair into a ponytail. Her brown strands were past her shoulders, half of it curly and the other half poking out in different directions. I did my best to gather it behind her, smoothing the front and sides without tugging too hard on her scalp.

"High or low?" I asked.

Winnie shot a skeptical look over her shoulder. "High," she decided. "And how do you know how to do a ponytail?"

I laughed, piling her hair higher on her head. "Well," I explained, "right after college, I moved from Michigan to

California. I thought being a surfer sounded really cool. I even grew my hair out long so I would look the part."

"What happened?" she asked.

My mind drifted briefly to the wild, reckless time when I was an aimless kid simply looking for acceptance and purpose in my life.

"Scrunchie," I called, and Winnie lifted her wrist so I could pluck the elastic band and begin twisting it in her hair. "Turns out it's a lot harder for a guy who grew up in the Midwest to learn how to surf." I tightened her ponytail and accepted the large red ribbon she held out, looping it into an exaggerated bow. "I was a *terrible* surfer," I continued. "But I learned how to tie a pretty good ponytail." I patted her shoulder. "What do you think?"

Winnie moved to the mirror in the hallway to examine my work. She turned her head left, then right. She tilted her head and raised her eyebrows. "It's pretty good."

Who knew a simple compliment from a precocious five-year-old could hit you right in the damn chest?

"Thanks," I said with a proud smirk, just as Selene came down the stairs.

"Austin did my hair, Mama," Winnie announced. "We're ready to go, and you're making us late."

Selene stopped before she hit the last step and blinked in my direction. "Oh. Thanks."

"Piece of cake . . . and you're not making anyone late." My eyes flicked down her outfit. She had chosen a pair of denim cutoffs and a black-and-white-striped T-shirt. Over the top she wore an unbuttoned denim shirt.

"You look beautiful," I said.

Her eyes widened. "You can't say stuff like that."

My eyebrows pinched down. "Another rule?"

"Yes." She breezed past me with a huff, and her shoulders sagged as she looked out the front window. "Shoot. It's raining, so the walk will be pretty miserable."

Selene glanced at the small slim gold watch on her wrist. "I can probably drive her and be back in time for my meeting."

"I can drive Winnie to school, that's no problem. That's what I'm here for." I eased back on my heels.

"She's not riding on a motorcycle." Selene's eyes narrowed at me. "Is the truck safe?"

When we had met, I was riding an old motorcycle. After my father died, the motorcycle was the only thing I had from my dad. Brody had given it to me, more than likely because he felt guilty that our father left nothing that even acknowledged my existence. Now the bike was sitting unused, and Selene had seen the piece-of-shit pickup I'd moved in with.

Once I'd really considered the idea of helping Selene with her kid, I figured a better car would be necessary. I hadn't specifically bought that vehicle for Winnie or Selene, but there was something I liked about being the kind of guy who'd think to buy it for someone like them.

"That SUV in the drive is mine." I smiled, hoping she'd just give in already. "It's new. Safest one they had."

"I'm not sure . . ." Selene chewed on her bottom lip as she considered my offer.

"Selene, it's literally what I'm here to do—help you in the mornings with Winnie so you can get to work on time and not be so stressed in the process. Come check out the booster seat I have for her and make sure it will work for her size. I had some help at the store, but I sort of had to guess at her height and weight."

For a second Selene just stared at me. "You got a booster seat for her?"

I shrugged. "I figured Star Harbor is pretty walkable, but there might be times we have bad weather or we don't feel like it, so at least we have the option to drive."

Her pert mouth popped open like a fish, but she quickly snapped it shut at my simple logic. Leading the way, I walked outside toward my brand-new crossover SUV.

Looking down her nose, Selene examined the car seat and how it was attached to the anchoring system.

She tugged on the seat and straps once for good measure before lifting her eyes to mine. "It's perfect."

Her approval was like a shot of adrenaline, and my face lit up. "Yeah? I did good?"

Selene rolled her eyes and chuckled. "It's even nicer than the one I have." She shook her head. "It's more than okay. Thank you."

"All right." I grinned at her. Over her shoulder I called Winnie down from the porch. "Well, kid, let's do this. Load up."

Winnie bounded down the stairs, plowing into Selene with a great big hug. "Bye, Mom, see you later."

Selene hugged her daughter and clung to her for a fraction of a second longer. When she looked up, I could see she was fighting tears of exhaustion.

"Thank you," she whispered.

I drove to school, floating six inches off the ground.

NINE

AUSTIN

THE CAR LINE was at a dead stop, parents waiting outside their vehicles for the kids like they always did at pickup. Over the past few days, I had learned that the line was long enough to make a man start contemplating whether kindergartners truly needed an education. I leaned against the side of the SUV, letting the warm breath of late afternoon drift through. Sunlight hit the paint in sharp, slanted beams and lit up the dust on the dash like golden mist. It was light that made everything feel softer, even the tightness in my chest that always showed up when I was waiting.

Then—there she was.

Winnie Darling came flying down the steps of the elementary school, her backpack thumping against her small frame, arms flung out like she might take off if she caught enough speed. A teacher's aide tried to wave her into a more dignified walk, but she ignored it completely, focused and grinning like she had a secret she couldn't wait to spill.

I yanked open the passenger door, and she scrambled

into the seat, already talking before the buckle clicked. "You're not late."

I raised a brow as I adjusted the straps on her booster seat. "Have I ever been late?"

She shrugged and popped the cap on her pink water bottle, like that was irrelevant. "Not yet."

The words weren't bitter, they were casual. A simple fact, but they landed hard in the small, quiet place in my chest that was growing more and more aware of the unspoken gaps she'd already learned to sidestep. I shook my head as I climbed back behind the driver's seat.

Before I could respond, she narrowed her eyes, examining me like a biologist discovering something half interesting in a puddle. "You're dirty."

I looked down at my shirt—smudged with drywall dust and a thin streak of joint compound across the hem from the job I'd barely finished in time to make it here.

"Rude," I said, feigning offense. "This is called looking rugged."

Winnie grinned like she didn't believe a word of it. Then she reached into her glitter-covered backpack and pulled out something small clutched in her palm.

"For you," she said, holding it out on her open hand like it was something sacred.

I took it slowly—a small, shimmery stone, flecked with bits of mica that caught the sun like stars—red and purple with a faint swirl of silver.

"It's a protection stone," she said seriously. "Just in case. For the coming week. I had to do a blessing with it last night, but the magic should hold."

I stared at the stone for a long second, caught off guard by the earnestness in her voice. No teasing. No performance. Just childlike truth—the kind only kids knew how to hand out without apology.

"Thanks," I said, quieter now. I slipped it into my pocket without a joke. It didn't need one.

"I got Mama one too." She grinned.

"She needs protection too?" I asked.

Winnie shook her head. "Hers is for relaxing. Mom has the best laugh when she's not stressed out."

A puff of air shot out of my nose. *This kid.* "She does, doesn't she?"

Winnie settled back in her seat, humming a song I didn't recognize as she pulled her legs up cross-legged like the car was her living room.

As we drove around the parking lot and out into the street, I asked, "So what's new in the castle?" Winnie and her friends had been spending their recess time playing make-believe. It was hard to keep up sometimes, but the drama was better than any TV show.

Without looking at me, Winnie said, "There's been a coup in the Lavender Wing. Queen Esmerelda tried to take over the North Hollow during second recess, but Felicity—she's head of the Moon Court—said that was against treaty rules. So now there's going to be a magical trial by winged combat."

I blinked. "Dang. That's intense."

"Ms. Evelyn says I have too much imagination." She wrinkled her nose at the accusation. "But she just doesn't understand Fae law."

I shook my head. "Well, I think that's a pretty serious oversight on her part."

Winnie grinned. "Right? I mean, the Hollow's territory only goes up to the hopscotch line. Everybody knows that."

I nodded solemnly. "Obviously. Boundaries are important."

She beamed. "Exactly."

The street finally cleared ahead, and I eased into the late-day traffic with one hand still resting near my pocket where the little stone sat, warm from the sun and her palm. It was nothing. A simple rock, but I couldn't stop thinking about it.

I wasn't her dad or her stepdad. I wasn't anything, really.

Except maybe something she counted on.

That thought settled somewhere deep inside me, quiet and unfamiliar. The kind of weight that didn't feel heavy, just permanent, like a key left in a lock.

She pointed up ahead. "Can we drive past the pink house again?"

I smiled. "The one with the cat in the window and the mailbox shaped like a mushroom?"

She nodded. "That's where I think Queen Esmerelda's hiding until the trial."

"Then absolutely," I said, flipping on my turn signal. "We can't let her get away with a hostile takeover."

Winnie raised her water bottle like a toast. "To the Resistance."

I reached back to tap my knuckles against hers. "To the Resistance."

And we drove on.

By the time we pulled into the driveway, the sun had dipped low behind the tree line, turning the sky a dusky watercolor of plum and gold. Winnie kicked off her sparkly sneakers at the bottom step and darted up the stairs with an energy only children seemed to store in endless supply. I followed at a slower pace, the weight of the day settling into my shoulders, the slight ache in my knees reminding me I was pushing my limits.

I looked out at the carriage house. I couldn't hear the muted click of Selene's keyboard, but I could see her. Her back window glowed with warm light, casting her silhouette in motion—shoulders hunched slightly, one hand braced against the desk, the other moving fast as she typed. She worked like she lived—quietly focused, with no room for distraction unless someone needed her. When she realized we were home, she dropped everything without hesitation.

Winnie flung open the back door. "Mom! We're home! And guess what—Austin says Queen Esmerelda is totally overstepping her boundaries!"

I watched as Winnie flopped onto the couch, already unzipping her backpack and pulling out a tangle of worksheets and a crumpled granola bar wrapper.

A minute later, Selene padded in barefoot, glasses sliding down her nose and a pencil tucked behind one ear. Her hair was up in a twist, and she wore a soft oversize T-shirt that hit just below her hips, paired with leggings that clung to the curves I still hadn't gotten used to seeing this close.

"Thank you for picking her up," she said, leaning down to press a kiss to the top of Winnie's head before looking at me.

"Anytime," I said, rubbing the back of my neck. "She's excellent company. Gave me the full rundown on the fairy kingdom's legal system."

Winnie pointed a crayon at me. "He agrees with my interpretation of the treaties."

Selene gave me a mock-stern look. "So now you're a diplomat?"

I shrugged. "Apparently."

She shook her head and smiled, a small, tired thing that tugged at my chest in a way I wasn't prepared for. Her glasses slipped lower, and she pushed them back with the heel of her hand.

When her phone buzzed again, she sighed and pinched the bridge of her nose. "This is a call I should take. You mind hanging out for five more minutes?"

"I've got her," I said. "Take your time."

Selene's hand brushed my forearm briefly—barely there, but enough to spark heat under my skin. "Thanks," she murmured, already backing toward the hallway.

I moved to the kitchen, unboxing the emergency mac-and-cheese stash I'd picked up last week after discovering Winnie's aversion to anything green that wasn't a sprinkle or candy. Then I moved toward the fridge and pulled out a bag of broccoli florets.

Winnie groaned as she walked in. "No. No green trees. I already had fruit today."

"You had half a strawberry yogurt for breakfast," Selene said as her head popped back into the kitchen.

"And I sniffed a grape," Winnie added.

"Not the same thing," her mom muttered under her breath as she listened to the voicemail.

I cleared my throat. "What if we made a deal?"

Both turned to look at me. Selene's eyebrow crept toward her hairline. Winnie narrowed her eyes like a seasoned negotiator.

I pointed a spoon at the pot. "If you try one bite of broccoli tonight—just one—I'll build a vegetable garden out back. You get to pick what we grow. I'm talking candy-striped carrots, purple beans, weird tomato hybrids . . . whatever you want. Then, if it's okay with your mom, the only veggies you have to eat are the ones you grew."

Winnie considered this, tapping her chin dramatically. "I want a fairy pumpkin."

Selene's eyebrow creased. "What is a fairy pumpkin?"

"It's very small and glows in the moonlight," Winnie explained with a gap-toothed grin. "Obviously."

I leaned toward Selene. "Is that a real thing?"

She lifted her shoulders and I laughed. I nodded solemnly at Winnie. "We can start planning tomorrow."

Winnie gave me a regal nod and disappeared back into the living room.

Selene mouthed *thank you* at me over the stove, and I just shrugged, but something about it stayed with me—how she looked when she said it. Grateful. A little surprised. Like maybe she wasn't used to backup.

Selene held her hand over the mouthpiece of her phone. "I'll be back soon."

I waved her off and then found Winnie sitting cross-legged on the couch, absorbed in a book about underwater fairies and their pet dolphins. We made up a game—trading turns reading in the voice of the sea witch, trying to one-up each other in dramatics until we were both doubled over with laughter.

Selene returned twenty minutes later to find Winnie curled up beside me, her cheek resting on my arm.

I started to pull away, unsure—but Selene shook her head and whispered, "She's fine."

"I'm heading out," I said quietly, carefully slipping out from beneath Winnie's cheek.

Selene walked me to the door. "Thanks again," she said. Her voice was warmer this time. Closer.

I hesitated on the porch, one hand still on the knob. "You work too hard," I said, nodding toward the carriage house. "Did you even eat lunch today?"

"I'll devour that broccoli mac and cheese." She waved me off. "It's fine. I'm used to it."

I didn't say anything then, but I gave her a faint smile and walked back to my side of the duplex.

TEN

SELENE

THE STORM HAD PASSED JUST before bedtime, leaving the windows streaked and the air heavy with the scent of wet pine and pavement. Thunder had rolled through earlier like a giant dragging furniture across the sky, but now only the occasional drip from the gutters broke the quiet.

Winnie padded down the hallway ahead of me, her blanket trailing behind like a cape, one fuzzy sock half off her foot. She clutched the book we'd checked out earlier from the library—*The Legends of Star Harbor*—her fingers smudging the worn cover. The library tag was worn at the corners, and the binding had nearly come undone. I'd found it tucked between old maritime histories and out-of-date census ledgers in the reference section that no one but retirees and weirdos like me ever touched.

Winnie had spotted me looking through it and begged to take it home. I almost said no—ghost stories weren't exactly on my list of calming bedtime reads—but she'd been so insistent, so sparkly-eyed and earnest, that I gave in. We could read it at bedtime and I'd leave out any part that might seem too scary. I figured it was better than letting her spiral down another YouTube hole of haunted dolls and cursed playgrounds.

On the way to bed, her stuffed unicorn dangled from the crook of her arm, well loved and trailing ribbons from its tail.

"You brushed your teeth, right?" I asked, already knowing the answer.

She turned and flashed me a toothpaste-smeared grin, which was answer enough.

"All right, hop in," I said, flipping on her night-light shaped like a little lighthouse. Its glow washed the walls in pale yellow, the beam slowly rotating across the ceiling like we were inside a tiny ship cabin.

Winnie scrambled into bed with a dramatic sigh and flopped backward, her arms wide, the book landing on her chest with a soft thud. "You said we could read the ghost parts."

"I said *one* ghost part," I reminded her, sitting beside her and tugging the blanket up over her legs. "And only if you promise not to wake me up in the middle of the night scared of haunted beach brides."

She giggled and tucked the unicorn under her chin. "I won't. Promise. I'm not scared of the Lady. She's just sad."

I hesitated, surprised and charmed by her earnestness. "You think the Lady is sad?"

Winnie nodded solemnly, her eyes wide. "She's all by herself. That's the worst part."

I opened the book to the page she'd bookmarked with a Post-it and a heart sticker from her backpack. The musty paper crackled as I smoothed it flat, and I began to read in a low, steady voice.

"It's said the Lady can be seen walking the dunes in her

white wedding gown, holding wildflowers. She is waiting for her love to return from the sea—but he never comes."

Winnie's hand found mine beneath the quilt. Her palm was sticky with residual jelly from dessert.

"She waited forever, right?" she whispered.

"So the story goes," I said, brushing her hair gently back from her face. "But no one really knows what's true. It's an old legend. Sometimes things get mixed up."

She was quiet for a moment, her little brow furrowed in thought. "Do you think Daddy will still come next weekend?"

My heart pinched. "He said he would," I said carefully, smoothing the blanket higher on her chest. "But sometimes . . . schedules change."

Winnie didn't say anything. She just turned her head to the side, staring at the wall. Her thumb crept toward her mouth but paused halfway, like she was trying to act older than she felt.

"He was supposed to take me to the zoo last time," she whispered.

"I know." I reached out and tucked her unicorn tighter against her side. "If he has work, we'll do something fun here instead. Just you and me."

Brian and I shared the same workaholic tendencies, but more and more it was affecting our daughter. His work at the university had always been important, but he didn't seem to notice the way her sweet little face fell any time he had to change plans.

There was a long beat of silence, and then Winnie murmured, "Maybe Austin would take me."

I blinked. "What?"

She rolled to face me, her eyes round and sleepy but

insistent. "Austin would take me to the zoo. He listens to me and he laughs at my jokes, even the really bad ones."

I laughed softly, my throat suddenly tight. "You do tell a lot of bad jokes."

"He helps me with stuff even when I don't ask," she continued. "He didn't get mad when I spilled juice in his new car, and he gave me his last gummy bear. He didn't even pick out the red one to keep for himself."

"Wow," I whispered, teasing. "That's pretty serious."

"It's fun when he picks me up from school," she added, already drifting. "He makes me feel happy in my tummy. Not twisty or sad."

There it was. Gentle and childlike—but clear. She didn't say *anxiety* or *disappointment*. She didn't have the words for those yet, but I did. I was all too familiar with what a twisty tummy meant.

I swallowed hard, smoothing her hair again as her eyes fluttered closed. "I'm glad he makes you feel that way, baby."

She yawned, the unicorn's mane clutched in one hand. "He's handsome like a movie person, but in real life."

I chuckled and pressed a kiss to her forehead, breathing in the scent of watermelon shampoo and a faint trace of peanut butter.

"I think you're the movie star," I whispered. "Sleep tight, my love."

She was out before I stood up and flicked on the video monitor. I hoped to get caught up on work and always felt better knowing I could use the monitor to check in on Winnie from the carriage house.

Her lighthouse night-light swept another slow arc across the ceiling as I pulled the door almost shut behind me, the legend book still in hand. I held it against my chest, suddenly unsure whether I was more haunted by the ghost story or the man living in the space next door.

I looked at the wall as if I could sense him, just on the other side.

Austin.

Too young and too charming. He was far too good with my kid. I could never have guessed that one night of letting loose and having fun would haunt me so thoroughly. On many nights, I caught myself lying awake, staring at the paint on the ceiling and recalling every detail of our night in the forest. The cool breeze on my thighs as he lifted my skirt, his warm breath against my skin, the shiver of antici-pation rippling down my spine. There was a part of me that desperately wanted to feel that alive—that *free*—again . . . and temptation was residing literal feet away.

I exhaled and shook my head as I padded into the hall-way. In the quiet of the house, I could hear the slow tick of the kitchen clock and the sound of rainwater still dripping off the eaves. I needed something to keep my mind off my incredibly inappropriate, yet altogether irresistible, neigh-bor. I slipped on a pair of rubber garden boots to make the trek across the wet lawn.

Once inside the carriage house, I moved to the small desk where I'd stacked the materials Elodie had handed off —fragile, water-warped letters and a few odds and ends from the trunk she had found. She had dropped off the letters after the Keepers' meeting, each carefully wrapped in acid-free sleeves and tied with string like some forgotten treasure trove.

I placed them next to ledgers from the boardinghouse and old pages I hadn't sorted through yet. I added the library book to the pile and started looking through some old folders to try to make room for everything.

I sifted through my own stack of historical documents. Most were brittle ledgers or handwritten menus and maps. Cal had let me borrow a stack of water-damaged guest registries from the Drifted Spirit Inn's earliest days. A few were nearly illegible, the ink dissolved into foggy blue-gray swirls, but others still held faint outlines of names, dates, and room numbers.

Between two brittle pages of a late-1890s boarding ledger, something stiffer caught my fingers. I slid it free, careful not to tear the fragile binding. It was a photograph—faded and curling at the corners. The kind printed on albumen paper, its edges scalloped like lace. A woman stood at the center, long dark hair coiled beneath a simple hat, her figure posed in front of a familiar porch railing I couldn't quite place. Her eyes had been scratched out in tiny, deliberate X's.

I turned it over.

A name had been scribbled on the back in pencil, so faint it nearly vanished beneath the smudges of time.

Barnes? Barlow?

The handwriting was uneven, hesitant and faded. It was hard to tell. The name wasn't clear, but my pulse quickened anyway.

Barker.

A shiver danced up my spine. There had been Barkers in Star Harbor's early history, I was sure of it. Not just passing names in a ledger—but landowners. The Drifted Spirit Inn had once been the Barker family's homestead, long before it was converted into an inn. If I remembered correctly, they'd also owned the land just west of the property—land that eventually became what is now Elodie's Star Harbor Farms.

The Barkers had two children, a boy and a girl. That much was recorded, but little else.

No marriage records. No graves. Just a surname that faded from town documents like fog lifting from the dunes.

My pulse skipped. *Could this be her? The woman from the photo—scratched eyes, secretive smile—could she be the Lady? Not just some nameless ghost, but someone real? A person with a past, a family, and a real name?*

The image would need to be stabilized, scanned, and carefully cleaned. But more than that—I'd need to dig deeper. I wanted to cross-reference land deeds. Track ownership transitions. Compare dates. There might be something here. Something *true*.

I didn't know what it meant yet, but I knew better than to ignore it.

I rolled my aching shoulders. I slipped the photo into an archival sleeve and tucked it among the rest of the documents before sucking in a deep breath.

I stretched my neck, reaching back to massage my tight shoulder with a groan. I knew that when I got wrapped up in a project as intriguing as that, it was like my mind raced down a single track. I glanced at my watch. If I wasn't careful, I could easily stay up into the wee hours of the morning, poring over documents. That would inevitably create a long and tiring following day, so I exhaled and pushed myself away from the desk.

When I locked the carriage house, I heard the low hum of music drifting from the other side of the duplex. My stomach tightened. When I looked up, my belly swooped low and I fought a smile.

Austin sat on the steps, legs long and sprawled in front of him, a bottle of something resting between them. His shirt was rumpled, his muscular arms testing the limits of the short sleeves. I noticed the faint scrape of a bruise coloring the inside of his forearm. Probably from hauling lumber earlier.

He lifted his head as I padded across the wet lawn. "Late night working?"

A smile dusted my lips. "Just organizing some things." I sucked in a lungful of night air. "Getting some fresh air."

"Looks like you found it." He smiled as I walked through the gate he left open. Austin scooted to the far end of the steps, making room for me.

I sank onto the top step beside him, careful to leave a few inches of space between us. He didn't say anything right away, but he handed me a bottle of bourbon.

Feeling brave, I took a sip, winced at the heat that scorched my throat, and handed it back with a cough.

We sat side by side for a beat, soaking in the quiet hum of small-town living. The stars were faint tonight, blurred by leftover clouds, but the crickets had returned, and the world smelled like earth and something wild.

"She said you make her tummy feel good," I said, studying my black rubber boots.

Austin didn't look at me. "She's a cool kid."

I laughed. "She's impossible. Moody. Dramatic. Smart in a way that actually terrifies me." I exhaled dramatically. "But she really is the best."

He let out a soft laugh. "I think I understand her."

My body tilted slightly in his direction, and I hated that I didn't correct it. I wanted to lean in, to press closer. I could smell him—woodsmoke, rain, something a little spicy clinging to his skin.

"You're really good with her," I finally admitted.

His chin tilted toward me as an eyebrow crept up his forehead. "You sound surprised."

A laugh huffed from my chest. "I am."

Austin finally turned his frame toward me, and the way he did—like he was peeling back layers I didn't know I was still wearing—left my mouth dry.

"I don't want to be surprised," I added quickly. "I just . . . I didn't expect all this."

His voice dropped. "What did you expect?"

I swallowed hard. "Someone less invested. More temporary. More . . . typical."

He leaned in slightly. "Do I seem temporary to you?"

God help me.

His face was inches from mine now, and I could feel the heat between us, like it had its own gravitational pull. My breath caught, and he saw it—he had to. His eyes dropped to my mouth.

Then I blinked and straightened, and the moment shattered.

I turned slightly, creating distance that didn't feel natural. "I should go in."

Austin exhaled slowly but didn't move.

I stood, brushed imaginary dust from my shorts. "Thanks for the drink."

He stood, too, closing the gap. "Selene."

I looked up, already regretting the space I'd created.

"It's okay," he murmured, his fingertip burning a path down my arm before catching my wrist. "You can think about me later. When you touch yourself." His voice was low, deliberate. "I might even hear it through the walls. And if you ask nicely . . . I might even join you."

The words hit like a lightning strike—hot and delicious

and completely inappropriate. I turned without answering, walked back through the door on legs that didn't feel steady.

I closed it behind me, locked it with trembling fingers, and leaned against it, cheeks flaming and heart hammering.

I was in so much trouble.

ELEVEN

AUSTIN

THE SUN WAS warm enough to peel off the layers by midafternoon. I'd spent most of the evening hauling wood chips into the back half of the duplex lawn, where grass had given up and weeds had taken over. Winnie had drawn a map for me, complete with a garden marked by sparkly ink and ominous warnings in red crayon about fairy territory and cursed rocks that must never be moved.

I followed it like gospel.

I was laying out the first row of raised beds—just rough-cut frames for now, lined with cardboard and filled with compost—when I heard the door creak open behind me.

Music filtered out first. Something bright and bouncy with a retro beat. Then feet—two sets—tapping along to the rhythm on the back porch.

I turned, wiping my forearm across my brow.

Selene stood in the doorway of her place, holding her phone in one hand, the other extended toward her daughter. She was barefoot, laughing as Winnie tried to copy her movements, elbows flapping like a baby bird, braid swinging behind her.

"You're cheating," Selene said, twirling in place.

"I'm improvising," Winnie declared, nearly colliding with the railing.

Selene caught her just in time, steadying her with both hands, and then they were laughing again, spinning together. The sun caught in their hair. It painted Selene's face in warm gold, catching on her cheekbones, glinting off her collarbone where the neckline of her dress dipped just slightly.

She hadn't seen me staring yet.

I leaned on the handle of the shovel, pretending to inspect the garden bed, though my eyes kept drifting back to her. Her hips swayed as she danced, loose and easy, like no one was watching. Like she didn't even care if they were.

Maybe she didn't.

"Hey!" Winnie called suddenly, catching sight of me. "You too!"

I shook my head and straightened. "Nope. Busy. Very official garden duties underway."

Selene arched a brow, playful. "Scared you'll get shown up?"

I grinned. "Terrified."

Winnie ran through the gate toward me and grabbed my hand. "Just one spin. I don't care if you're dirty."

"Peer pressure is a powerful thing." I laughed, dusting off my hands and setting down the shovel before twirling Winnie's arm in a wide circle.

Selene clapped as she stepped onto my side of the lawn. Winnie beamed and gave a dramatic count-in like she was cueing a Broadway number. I took her hand, spun her once, then dipped her into a ridiculous bow.

She shrieked with laughter.

Selene shook her head, arms crossed but smiling. I caught her eye and gave her a wink.

She looked away too quickly, but when I handed Winnie back and spun to return to my side, I heard her murmur something under her breath.

"What's that?" I asked, pausing to look back at Selene.

She looked at me then. "You're really good with her."

It wasn't the first time she'd said that, and the compliment shouldn't have hit as hard as it did. I scratched the back of my neck. "She's easy to like."

Selene smiled again, but this one was quieter. Thoughtful. It lingered in my chest as I went back to my garden plot.

The buzz was still there hours later, even after the sun dipped below the horizon.

On Saturday, I was driving through downtown, and I hadn't expected to see them.

I'd just wrapped a grocery run—milk, eggs, a six-pack of whatever beer was on sale—and was heading down the main street in town when I spotted my favorite duo. Selene in jeans and a striped tee, Winnie bouncing beside her in light-up sneakers and a unicorn backpack, both holding ice cream cones that were melting faster than they could keep up.

They were laughing. Heads tipped toward each other, matching strides even though one had to slow down and the other had to half skip to keep pace.

I pulled over without thinking.

The window rolled down, and I leaned across the passenger seat. "You two planning to walk all the way back?"

Selene turned, startled. Then her mouth curved into something that made my mouth go dry.

"We're not that far," she said. "Just needed to get out for a bit."

Winnie ran to the window. "We saw fairies by the library!"

I blinked. "You don't say. Are they wandering into enemy territory?"

She shook her head. "They left glitter trails, and it's bad luck if you don't say thank you." She narrowed her eyes at me as ice cream dripped down her wrist. "Did you say thank you last time?"

My lips twisted. "I'm gonna be honest—I don't remember."

She sighed like this was exactly the kind of oversight that explained the general state of the world. "You're lucky you didn't get cursed."

Selene looked up at the sky. "It's getting late."

Winnie pointed dramatically. "That's when the Lady comes out. She walks the roads and looks for people who forgot to be kind. I hope we see her."

I tried not to laugh as Selene groaned. Winnie was into lore of all kinds, but you couldn't escape chatter about the Lady, and Winnie's young mind took the stories as fact.

I popped the door open. "In that case, you'd better hop in. I'd hate to be responsible for a ghost-related incident."

Selene hesitated, like she might insist they were fine, but then she glanced at Winnie, who had already climbed into the back seat, cone carefully balanced in both sticky hands.

"Thanks," she said quietly as she got in beside me. I nodded and reached across to the glove box and handed her a wad of extra napkins.

Winnie kept up a running commentary about magical portals and fairy physics, then trailed off halfway through a sentence. I glanced in the rearview mirror to find her slumped against the window, cone licked clean, fingers sticky, and eyes closed.

"I think she's out," I said.

Selene twisted to look, her expression soft. "She never makes it past eight these days."

I pulled into the driveway and killed the engine. The shared porch lights were on, casting everything in a warm, amber glow.

"I can carry her," I offered, already climbing out.

Selene opened her mouth, maybe to protest, but then she just nodded and got the door.

Winnie didn't even stir as I lifted her. She tucked into my shoulder, completely trusting, small and warm and smelling like watermelon candy, dirt, and sugar.

Selene led the way, holding the door, then stepping back so I could navigate the hall.

Her room was dim, the curtains drawn. I laid her on the bed and pulled the blanket up over her shoulders. She mumbled something incoherent and curled onto her side.

I stood there for a second longer than necessary.

Then turned to find Selene watching from the doorway, arms folded across her chest, something unreadable in her eyes.

"She's lucky," she said. "Having a friend like you around."

I didn't know what to do with that.

"I'm the lucky one," I said, before I could stop myself.

It felt too honest. Too close to something I hadn't admitted yet—not even to myself.

Selene looked away. I followed her out to the living

room. The night was quiet, the whole house still. A breath between things.

At the front door, I hesitated. "Okay, I'm going to head out."

She nodded. "Thanks for the ride. Sorry if she got ice cream all over your new car."

I turned the knob, but stopped.

Selene hadn't moved. She was still standing there in the glow of the hall light, arms folded like she was holding herself together.

I didn't know what the hell I was doing, but I knew one thing for sure:

This—her, Winnie, the routine of this life—it was starting to feel like something I didn't want to give up. Even if I wasn't supposed to want it.

"Night," I said.

"Good night," she echoed.

I stepped onto the porch, into the hush of early autumn air and crickets, and didn't look back.

TWELVE

AUSTIN

AT THE CONSTRUCTION SITE, the midday sun was already hot as fuck, but I didn't mind the heat. It soaked into my skin, loosening the knots in my back and slicking sweat down my spine. It was the kind of heat that made the air shimmer off a tin roof and left the wood smelling like sap and sunburn. The Midwest always did that—made you think summer was over, then blasted you with an unexpected heat wave. It was one of the things I missed most when I had moved away—familiar Michigan mornings that started breezy and cool, then transitioned to a warmth that left your muscles languid.

The construction crew was busy framing the inside of what once was a barn at Star Harbor Farms. Elodie Darling had somehow befriended the local Amish community and wrangled a deal that resulted in an incredible barn raising. Wes's construction company was now tasked with framing the inside to be transformed into a farm-to-table restaurant that Cal would run.

I looked around at the stacks of wood and the beams already going up, and I could see it. As a kid, I had always wanted to go to Star Harbor Farms to pick a pumpkin or go on a hayride, but my mother wouldn't have been caught dead in Dad's town. As was typical, I had been relegated to the outskirts, an outsider always looking in, and I'd never gotten to experience the charm of a family pumpkin patch. I remembered driving through Star Harbor, sitting in the car with the windows cracked, watching other kids carry pumpkins too big for their arms. Once, I'd begged. My mom had only lit a cigarette and told me to stop acting poor.

Elodie Darling had taken over the farm with the goal of bringing it back to its former glory, and I couldn't help but smile. I could already see how Winnie would tear through the corn maze or consume countless cider doughnuts without a second thought. I chuckled to myself.

"What's got you grinning like a fool? Hot date last night or just thinking about your babysitting duties?" Scott, a guy in his forties and known to stir the pot, grinned.

I looked at him but didn't engage.

"Leave Mary Poppins alone." Jackson snorted. "He's the hottest manny in Michigan. We should all be so lucky."

Scott whistled. "Hell, I'd be a manny, too, if it meant spending all my free time with Selene Darling. That woman's a whole meal."

That did it.

My jaw flexed. I wasn't blind—Selene was beautiful, but there was something about hearing it from Scott's mouth that made it sound wrong.

Like they didn't see the woman she was.

But was I really any better? My words still echoed, cocky and low: *You can think about me later. When you touch yourself.*

Where the hell did I get the balls to say that? The

audacity to think that a woman like Selene should be spoken to that way.

As I berated myself, the image of her smile and flushed cheeks flashed in my mind. A part of me hoped she not only didn't hate it, but also liked it a little bit. At least it didn't seem like she was holding it against me.

"Will you buffoons get to work? Otherwise I'm calling Wes, and trust me, he is in no mood to put up with any of your bullshit." Cal's stern voice echoed through the empty barn. "He also said if one more board goes up crooked, he's lighting this place on fire . . . again."

The crew chuckled at the crass joke—the barn *had* been on fire only a few months ago—but we softened at the mention of our absent boss's name.

The joke landed, but no one laughed long. Not when the weight of Wes's absence still hung over the jobsite like dust in the rafters.

Scott looked up. "Hey, I'll take the heat if that gets him out of that fucking house."

Murmurs and agreements and head nods rippled through the crew. Wes's accident had taken more than just his leg. It had taken its toll on his mental health, too, and we all could sense it. He'd been holed up in his house for weeks, only opening the door for a select few.

Cal was one of them. "Yeah, I know," he murmured but changed the subject. "Hey, it's hot today. I brought waters and Gatorades—don't work yourselves to death in here."

I caught his eye, and he tipped his chin toward the barn door. I pulled a rag from my rear pocket and used it to wipe the sweat from the back of my neck as I followed him outside. I stepped into the sunlight, squinting against the harsh rays.

"You still in for another game?" Cal asked.

I nodded before swiping a light-blue Gatorade from the cooler at my feet. I uncapped it and took a long, deep swallow. "I told you I could cover—for as long as you needed me."

Cal's lips pressed together and he nodded. "All right," he said, "just making sure you were going to follow through."

I swallowed down a heavy sigh. Cal barely knew me, but people in my past always seemed to think I didn't measure up. I had no reason to believe Cal was any different. I may be young, but I was getting really fucking tired of the expectation that I was a fuckup.

I was showing up every morning and evening for Selene *and* Winnie, then hauling ass in between to bust my balls on the jobsite. Most nights I was too dog-tired to do anything like go out or chase some tail, so I spent my evenings lying in my bed, staring at the ceiling, and trying to ignore the muffled sounds I heard coming from the duplex next door.

Sometimes I'd catch her laugh through the open window, soft and low, and I'd have to roll over and bury my face in the pillow just to get her out of my head.

"Yeah." It was all I could muster through my frustration.

I was used to being underestimated, but lately it was starting to bug me more than I cared to admit.

"So things are working out with your neighbor, I take it?" he asked.

I paused mid-drink to look at Cal. His stance was wide with his arms crossed over his chest and the familiar line creasing between his eyebrows. It was no wonder he and my brother were friends. They had the same grumpy-older-brother routine down pat. It was like they were passing me around like a project they could fix up with enough elbow grease and a few stern lectures.

I stuffed my free hand into my pocket. "The kid's a lot of fun. I don't mind helping out."

He nodded in a way that told me my answer was almost good enough, but not quite up to his standards.

Older-brother speech incoming in three, two, one . . .

"You know . . ." He cleared his throat. "You seem good with her. Don't screw it up by pretending it's all just for laughs."

My defensiveness reared its ugly head. "What is it about waking up at five a.m. or hanging out after my full-time job that says I'm not willing to go the extra mile? I'm taking it fucking seriously, okay?"

Cal's wide-eyed shocked expression mirrored my own internal surprise. I hadn't meant to bite his head off, but his comment had hit something tender beneath my skin.

His palms raised up. "We're all just looking out for Selene and Winnie. I didn't mean anything by it. We care about them. That's all."

I finished my Gatorade in a single drink and tossed the empty bottle into the trash. "Yeah, well, I care about them too."

"All right." Cal nodded. "Noted. I'll give it a rest then." His attention flicked over my shoulder before drawing back to me. "Better look alive, kid. Looks like both our bosses are headed this way."

I turned to find Selene walking next to her sister. The breeze kicked up just enough to rustle the trees along the back field, and then there she was—like some goddamn daydream—walking beside Elodie with her sunglasses pushed into her hair and her sundress catching in the wind. Elodie was practically vibrating with excitement and skipped the last few feet to launch herself into Cal's arms. He pulled her body against his, kissing her long and deep.

Long enough for Selene and me to exchange an awkward glance. We both suddenly found the sky fascinating. Anything to avoid watching Cal suck face with Elodie in broad daylight.

I cleared my throat and Cal put her down.

"Hi," she said, breathless.

"Good morning," I greeted Elodie, then shifted to Selene. "Ma'am," I drawled with a slow grin, tipping my chin toward her. "Well, I better get back to it." I held out my hand for Cal, and he took it. "Especially now that the bosses are here." I glanced at Selene and shot her a playful wink. Her lips parted, maybe in surprise, but her chest and neck flushed the prettiest shade of pink before she dragged her gaze away.

The trio stayed outside the barn, chatting about something as Elodie waved her arms around wildly. Cal nodded and Selene stood next to her vibrant sister, looking like the pinnacle of patient grace and sophistication. She was wearing some kind of breezy linen dress that billowed with each small gust of lake wind. On top was a formfitting tank that hugged her curves in a way that made me want to groan out loud.

I already knew exactly how Selene felt under my hands, and I tamped down that memory, stuffing it into a box and trying to forget about it altogether. When I caught her eyes slicing in my direction, I grinned. Her gaze snagged on mine like a hook beneath my skin—sharp, swift, and impossible to ignore. I felt it land, linger, and burn.

Hell if that didn't make me want to push it just a little bit further.

I grabbed the back of my T-shirt and peeled it up slowly, just to be a dick. Sweat clung to my skin, catching the sunlight as I dragged the fabric over my head and tossed it aside. Out of the corner of my eye, Selene's jaw went slack. I raked my hand across my chest, pretending not to notice. It was a slightly unfair, yet coordinated, tactic, but I didn't care. If she was going to keep sneaking glances, the least I could do was give her a good show. If she wanted a peek, I'd give her a memory she could blush over later.

"Showing off again, pretty boy?" Jackson muttered, giving me a backhand to the stomach and dragging my attention again to the crew.

"Fuck you. It's hot," I ribbed back.

"Oh, you know what? I think you're right." Ben, a grizzled man who'd worked construction all his life, started pulling at the collar of his T-shirt, exaggerating how hot he was before he started gyrating his hips. "It is hot." He grabbed the bottom hem of his T-shirt and started rolling it up over his protruding beer belly.

"Oh man, I'm overheating." He pulled his shirt completely off and started swinging it around. His belly jiggled as he twirled his shirt over his head like he was headlining the worst Chippendales act in history.

Another guy from our crew took the opportunity to empty a bottle of water over Ben's head. Collectively, we laughed. Ribbing and a little ball busting was all a part of the job.

"Are you idiots done getting naked?" Cal's irritated voice thundered through the open doorway as he leaned in.

"I don't know, boss," Jackson mocked as he slowly started to unbuckle his belt. "I'm feeling so . . ." He opened the buckle. "So steamy."

When Cal threw his hands in the air and walked away, we all dissolved into a fit of giggles like a gaggle of hens. I watched as he trailed after Elodie and Selene, who were heading toward the small cottage at the edge of the property. I caught Selene turning, just a flick of her head over her shoulder—but it was enough. Our eyes met for half a heartbeat, and I swore the world narrowed to that look. I held it. Grinned like a bastard. Then dragged my shirt on— slow as hell—just to let her watch.

I didn't know whether she could still see it clearly, but I shot a wide grin just for her.

LATER THAT AFTERNOON, my back ached and my muscles screamed at me from lifting lumber overhead for the better part of the day. I glanced at my watch and used the impact driver to place one last screw into a support beam.

"Gotta go, boys." I hung the tool on my belt and turned toward the crew. My shirt clung to my back, damp with sweat, and the sun had baked my neck a shade darker than I meant to. I rolled my shoulders, trying to shake the ache from a long-ass day of lifting lumber like I didn't still have to wrangle a five-year-old.

"Everyone say goodbye to the hottest manny in Michigan," Jackson teased.

A chorus of goodbyes and chuckles floated over me. I shot them a middle finger over my shoulder and didn't bother hiding my grin. They were assholes, but they weren't wrong. Without bothering to respond, I packed up my gear and walked along the edge of the pumpkin patch toward the Drifted Spirit Inn.

The pumpkin patch stretched out in crooked rows, green vines curling across the dry earth, dotted with young orange orbs just beginning to swell. In October, it'd be chaos with kids and cider and hayrides, but now it was quiet— blooming with potential. I liked it better like this—when the world was quiet and full of possibility. It was easier to believe in things when you saw them the way Winnie did.

I bet Winnie would pick out a weird-looking one— something misshapen or full of those wartlike bumps just because it was funky and different. It was one of my favorite things about that kid. She liked things simply because she liked them, not because they were perfect.

In fact, I was pretty certain that perfect in the eyes of that particular five-year-old was entirely too boring. Maybe that was why she liked me at all. I wasn't shiny. I was just . . . there.

The Drifted Spirit stood like it had been pulled out of a postcard—three stories of clapboard and freshly painted trim, with flower boxes spilling over in red and yellow blooms. A wide wraparound porch circled the front, like the building had always been waiting for someone to sit a while and stay.

When I had agreed to help out Selene, Cal had suggested I save time on going home to shower before picking Winnie up on days when I couldn't get away from the job early. Today was definitely one of those days.

As I entered the inn, I wiped my boots on the mat and tried not to look like a man who'd spent the last several hours sweating his ass off in sawdust. I stepped up to the concierge desk and drummed my fingertips on the solid oak surface. "Afternoon, Miss Helen. Any chance I could sneak in a shower?"

Her long bony fingers clacked on the keyboard of the computer behind the desk. "The Mariner's Room is all yours," she said. "Fresh towels, peppermint soap, the works."

Since Star Harbor was such an active tourist destination, the Drifted Spirit Inn was unique in that, even after guests checked out in the morning, if they planned to explore or sightsee, they could come back to the inn to rest or shower or freshen up before their drive or flight out of town.

I often used it as an opportunity to not be so rank when picking up Winnie after school.

"Thanks, Helen. You spoil me," I teased, flashing her a grin. "Pretty soon I'll be impossible to live with."

"No problem," she answered with a smile. "Though it sounds like you might be off the hook before too long."

I stopped, craning my neck in her direction. My hand froze mid-reach for the key. "What?"

"The way I heard it, Selene had a pretty amazing childcare candidate come through today. She's new in town. Sweet girl. Polished and smart. Did her degree in early childhood development. Selene said she was perfect. Dale the mailman's niece came up from Ann Arbor to 'find herself,' and she found Selene instead. After college she's spending the summer in Star Harbor. She was looking for work and was pointed in Selene's direction." Helen shrugged as though she hadn't just delivered a swift punch to my gut. "If it works out, she can start shadowing next week. Seems like it works out for the both of you."

An experienced childcare worker with a degree. Polished.

I looked down at calloused hands streaked with grime and rubbed them together. I was all rough edges and second choices. A guy you picked when your first plan fell through.

"Yeah," I said, "that's great news." My voice sounded like a stranger's. "That's . . . just great." The words burned like a scraped knuckle. I turned away before she could see how much it had hit me. I walked back to the Mariner's

Room with the painful reminder that I was never supposed to be permanent stinging in my veins.

From my perspective, we had settled into a comfortable routine. I had hoped I was making progress with Winnie and Selene, but of course she would pick the one who makes sense.

Hell, I wouldn't pick me either.

My AFTERNOON with Winnie was a sad case of me going through the motions. I tried to act completely unbothered by the fact Selene was still interviewing other caretakers, but I couldn't shake the clawing sense of dread.

Winnie had been her usual hurricane of weirdness and wonder, but I was off my game. My jokes landed flat. My heart wasn't in it. I was stuck in my own damn head, and the view from there wasn't great. The minute Selene walked out of the carriage house to relieve me of my duties, I practically ran to my side of the duplex without a backward glance.

Selene barely looked at me when she came out the door. I got a smile and a quick "Thanks."

I didn't know what I expected. A thank-you parade? A promise she wasn't replacing me? I needed to get a grip.

I was sullen and pouty, and I sure as hell didn't like it.

I considered calling Brody to see whether he wanted to hang out or maybe even go to the Lantern for a few beers or to find some tourists to spin around the dance floor, but I couldn't muster the energy. Usually the thought of a cold beer and a warm body was enough to shake off a shitty mood. Tonight it all sounded hollow.

Plus, I didn't want to have my mood shitting all over

Brody's evening either. So instead I sulked in silence perfectly in line with the gigantic baby I was acting like.

A knock at the front door caught my attention, and I glanced at the clock. I hadn't made that many new friends since moving to Star Harbor, and anyone I did know had my cell phone number.

So who the hell would be knocking at this time of night?

I yanked open the front door with an irritated scowl. I almost barked out "What?" before I even opened it. But then I saw her—standing there in cutoffs and confidence—and every ounce of irritation drained out through my boots.

My gaze dropped before I could stop it—those shorts should've been illegal. My hands twitched at my sides. Selene blinked and took a tiny step backward from the force with which I'd opened the front door.

I stopped short. "Oh, hey." I glanced toward her place. "Everything okay with Winnie?"

Selene's slim shoulders were set straight. She swallowed and gently cleared her throat. "Yes, perfect." Selene's palms swiped down the front of her denim cutoff jeans. "Things felt just a little awkward this afternoon, I guess." She chuckled a little at herself. "I just wanted to make sure that you were okay."

I set my jaw. I had no intention of trauma-dumping my insecurities on Selene. "I'm fine."

Her lips twisted and she hesitated. "Okay, so the rumor mill in Star Harbor is a strange and horrendous thing. I got wind that Helen may have told you about an interview I did today. I thought maybe because you heard about that through the grapevine and not from me, that maybe you were mad. I don't know, it's silly." She bit her lip, laughed a little too loud, then winced like she wished she could take the whole speech back.

My stance widened as I strengthened my defenses and lifted my chin. "I heard about it, but figured you're just doing what you think is best for your kid. I told you I would help out as long as you needed me."

Selene pulled her bottom lip between her teeth, and I hated myself for imagining what those lips tasted like.

"So here's the thing," she continued. "I did agree to the interview, but only because Dale is an old family friend of my parents and I wanted to give his niece a fair shake. But I've made my decision. Winnie needs somebody who can be there for her when I can't be. I need someone that wrangles in the chaos of our lives and is a partner, someone I can count on." As Selene rambled, she shook her head in disbelief. Her eyes shifted to mine. "I need to have faith in the person that I let into our lives. Do you understand that?"

I nodded, and my molars ground together. I wanted to be cool. Chill. Shrug it off like it didn't matter, but her words felt like rubbing salt in a wound I didn't realize was still bleeding. "I understand."

"And the thing is . . ." She blew out a huff. "That person is . . ."

Here it is. Prepare for the blow.

"You."

The word landed like a fist to my sternum. One syllable. One second. And everything shifted. My throat tightened, and I prayed she couldn't see it. Her voice sounded just as surprised as I felt. It took a few seconds for her words to register as I stared at her.

Selene exhaled sharply. "So now that's cleared up, I don't have to walk around feeling guilty all night. As long as you're in—"

"I'm in." I didn't even hesitate.

"Great." Selene's smile bloomed and my chest ached.

She turned toward her side of the duplex before pausing and looking over her shoulder, one hand cocked on her hip. "Oh, and Austin." Her voice was like honey poured over a blade. Her long lashes swept down, then up again. "When I decide I need help touching myself, I'll let you know."

Stunned, I simply stared after her.

I didn't even get to respond. Instead, I just watched her walk away and tried not to follow her, like a dog on a leash. The door clicked shut behind her and I just stood there, shell-shocked, shirtless, and hard as hell.

Jesus Christ. I am so screwed.

THIRTEEN

SELENE

It had been only three weeks, but already it felt like Austin had always been here—this shadow moving through my mornings, a steady presence in the house beside mine. Winnie was humming to herself as she picked at the moss in her fairy garden, rearranging tiny ceramic mushrooms around a pale-pink bench that Austin had added one morning last week. He hadn't said a word about it—just left it there like a secret offering. She'd discovered it on her way out to water the dandelions, and the sight of it had clutched at her chest harder than I'd expected. Now it sat beneath the hydrangea bush, a part of the ever-growing world my daughter was building.

One she believed in.

One Austin kept adding to when no one was watching.

I stood on the back step, coffee warming my palms, pretending not to stare at him as he watered the row of planters along the shared porch. The tank top he wore was threadbare and loose around the neck, but it clung to his back where sweat darkened the fabric in a familiar triangle between his shoulder blades.

He didn't glance my way, but I saw the faint twitch of his mouth.

He knew.

Of course he did.

This was our new rhythm.

By early September, it had settled into something that felt suspiciously like routine. Winnie's school year had begun, and Austin—whom I'd officially hired without any real end date in mind—slid into our days as if he'd always belonged here.

In the mornings he slipped in just after I finished brushing my teeth. I'd leave the door unlocked. Sometimes he brought over muffins. Sometimes he just made my coffee. But he always left something—small, quiet things I wasn't meant to find right away.

A note on the fridge:

DECAF AGAIN? WHAT DID CAFFEINE EVER DO TO YOU?

A sticky note on the mirror, after fixing the drawer that had stuck for weeks:

YOUR BATHROOM'S NICER THAN MINE. I'M FILING A FORMAL COMPLAINT.

They were silly. Teasing. Just ink on paper, but I couldn't bring myself to throw them away. I kept them tucked in the back of my top drawer, underneath my bras, as if they were too private to be seen—even by me.

We'd also managed to keep any interactions strictly PG —no more mentions of touching ourselves, or each other.

Though I couldn't say the same about what I *actually* did in the privacy of my own bed.

He was everywhere. In my home. In my daughter's orbit. In my routines and rituals and quiet moments when I used to have space.

I took a long sip of coffee, letting it coat my tongue before swallowing.

"Fairy Queen," Austin called to Winnie. "Are you good out here while I run in for breakfast cleanup?"

I straightened. "I can do it."

Austin flashed me a smile. "Nah, it's no big deal. Enjoy a few more minutes with her." My heart thunked against my ribs.

Winnie gave him a thumbs-up with both hands, face scrunched in concentration as she fixed something in the fairy garden. "Next time please don't touch the moss. It's *curated*."

He laughed, a deep, full sound that felt too large for the porch. "I wouldn't dream of it."

As he passed me on the step, his hand ghosted the top of my shoulder for a fraction of a second.

It wasn't long enough to be real.

Just long enough that I still felt it minutes later.

WE WALKED. Not because we had to, but because the morning air was still laced with summer softness, and Winnie liked to skip over the sidewalk cracks in her pink sneakers. When she'd asked me to join them, I couldn't resist.

Winnie clutched Austin's hand, launching into a detailed

retelling of how Waffles—the class frog—had escaped his tank during story time yesterday. Her ponytail swished behind her with each hop, a glittery scrunchie keeping it wrangled. Austin listened with his whole body, nodding and murmuring at all the right places, his laugh low and unhurried, like the story really was the best part of his morning.

I trailed beside them, a few paces slower, letting the two of them take the lead. From the outside, we probably looked like a family. The thought knotted something deep in my gut. It wasn't unpleasant, just . . . dangerous.

I saw the way a woman slowed her car just slightly as she passed. The way a man nodded politely and then glanced back a second time. People in town were noticing.

Austin, of course, was oblivious.

He didn't see the glances. Didn't clock the subtle curiosity in the expressions of the other parents lingering at drop-off. Why would he? He wasn't the one doing calculus in his head over how it might look—him, younger, tattooed, handsome in that distractingly rough-cut way. Me, older, composed, trying not to fidget with my sleeve or wonder whether they thought I was babysitting *him*.

When we reached the school steps, Winnie dropped Austin's hand to hug my waist. "Are you coming with me today?"

"Just to the door, kiddo," I said, brushing a crumb from her cheek. "You'll have a fun day—you've got music."

She lit up like a sunrise. "We're learning to play 'The Ants Go Marching.' Austin, you'll love it."

"I can't wait," he said, pressing a hand over his heart.

At the doors, she kissed me and ran inside, her little backpack bouncing behind her.

The walk back was quiet at first. Our steps fell in rhythm. Austin didn't fill the silence and didn't reach for banter. That was something I'd come to notice about him—he had this way of not needing to talk just to fill space. Sometimes he simply let silence breathe.

Still, I felt the weight of curious eyes. Other parents milled about the schoolyard, saying goodbyes, sipping coffee from travel mugs as they chatted. A couple of moms glanced our way, the polite kind of curious that wasn't quite gossip. I didn't blame them. I was aware of us too. Me, walking beside a man who was younger and indecently handsome. Tattooed forearms, work boots, and a worn ball cap pulled low. He had a look—the kind that made people glance twice.

Austin, of course, was still completely unaware.

He turned to me as we rounded the corner. "Do you always wear heels on Tuesday mornings?"

I glanced down at my boots—block-heeled, leather, more fashion than function. "I have a meeting in town."

He nodded. "You clean up nice for a school drop-off."

I lifted an eyebrow. "I wish I was in sweatpants right now."

His mouth curved.

We stopped at the crosswalk, waiting for the light. I folded my arms, trying to ignore the warmth blooming at the base of my neck. "Are you always this charming before nine a.m.?"

Austin crossed behind me, making sure I was on the inside of the sidewalk. "Only when I'm walking back with you."

There it was again—that unstudied, easy confidence that never tipped into arrogance—and it was doing something to me. Something traitorous.

The duplex came into view—two connected units with matching cedar siding and flower beds that Austin had sneakily weeded last week while I was working late. He hadn't even mentioned it. I just came home to tidy mulch and a clipped hydrangea bush, like it had magically fixed itself.

I unlocked the door and stepped inside first, toeing off my boots. Austin followed and headed toward the kitchen like it was second nature now.

The door clicked shut behind him, quiet and certain.

In the stillness that followed, the house exhaled—just a soft settling of silence—but I felt it in my chest like a shift, like something was changing.

Austin moved through the kitchen with an ease that made my stomach twist. He didn't ask where things were anymore. He didn't hesitate when he opened drawers or reached for the bag of coffee. He knew where I kept the mugs. Which one was mine. The stupid pink one with the cracked handle and faint lipstick ghost that wouldn't scrub off.

He set his own tumbler under the machine, waiting for the slow, steady drip to finish. Then he rinsed my cup from the morning and turned it upside down beside the sink.

He didn't say anything, because he didn't need to.

It had become a ritual of sorts—small, unspoken, and somehow intimate. The cup was always there when I wandered out mid-morning between meetings, warm from the rinse, placed precisely where I would reach without thinking. The first time it happened, I nearly dropped it, heart lurching with the simple suggestion of *thoughtfulness*. Now I just stared at it, quiet, like it had said something too loud in the hush of the kitchen.

"I'll get that later," Austin said, tapping a finger on the loose drawer handle. His voice was casual, easy—already halfway out of the moment. "It's coming off the track."

He pulled his travel mug free, screwed the lid on tight, and ran his hand over the back of his neck. I watched the movement, the long line of muscle shifting beneath the sleeve of his shirt. His biceps stretched the cotton just enough to draw the eye—and mine went there, traitorously.

I folded my arms tighter, trying to ignore the way the house smelled like him now—like pine soap and clean cotton or like the faint, sun-warmed scent of whatever detergent he used. It clung to the air and to the couch cushions.

My home—the one I had fought to rebuild—was no longer entirely mine.

Winnie had started drawing pictures of him.

Crayon stick figures with big smiles labeled in wobbly block letters: AUSTIN. Her latest drawing had been slipped under a magnet on the fridge, and I hadn't moved it.

He was in her art. Her morning routines. Her vocabulary. He was in my walls.

And worst of all—I didn't want to chase him out.

"You sure you don't need anything before I go?" he asked, thumb hooked in the belt loop of his jeans.

I shook my head, maybe a little too quickly. "No, I'm good."

He lingered, just long enough to stretch the moment taut.

My voice caught somewhere between my throat and my ribs. "So I'm . . . thinking about pizza tonight."

Austin's brows rose, his hand pausing at the strap of his backpack. "Yeah?"

I knew he must be tired. Austin was essentially working two jobs—one without pay since he wouldn't take my money, I might add. After surviving our morning chaos, he worked a hard labor job. Feeding him was the least I could do.

"Yeah." I cleared my throat. "I thought I'd order something easy for dinner. Winnie's been asking for pizza."

Something flickered in his eyes—something warm, unguarded. "You want me to stay?"

It wasn't a loaded question. At least, not on the surface, but it pressed against the line we hadn't talked about since I hired him.

He helped. I worked. He left. That was the rhythm. Our safety net.

Inviting him to stay wasn't nothing.

I tried to sound casual, breezy. "Only if you're free."

Austin nodded slowly as a smile ghosted on his lips. "I'm free."

Of course he was.

He gave a soft knock to the counter with his knuckles and stepped back. "I'll see you after work, then."

I nodded. "Thanks again."

His brows pitched down. "For what?"

I opened my mouth, then closed it.

For knowing how I take my coffee.

For slipping into our lives without forcing his way in.

For fixing things I hadn't even noticed were broken.

"For the mug," I said instead.

He smiled, the slow kind that curved just one side of his mouth and stayed there as he turned and left, the front door whispering shut behind him.

The silence that followed felt less like stillness and more like absence.

I stared at the upturned mug by the sink for a long moment before finally moving to grab my laptop.

～

THE SCENT OF PEPPERONI, fresh basil, and melted cheese drifted through the kitchen, warm and savory and comforting in a way that made the place feel like a real home —like something we'd built together without meaning to.

Winnie sat cross-legged on a barstool at the counter, her little fingers greasy from tugging cheese off her second slice. She'd insisted on the "special pizza," the kind with stuffed crust and pineapple, and had declared it the "best idea ever" at least three times already.

Austin leaned against the opposite counter, one ankle crossed over the other, sipping from a glass of soda like he wasn't aware of how domestic the entire scene looked. His sleeves were pushed up, forearms streaked with flour where he'd helped cut up Winnie's pizza into small squares. She'd pressed a sticker from her pizza box to his shirt and dubbed him the "Cheese Boss." He had obliged without complaint.

My heart ached in that hollow, unfamiliar way it did when something felt both perfect and unsustainable.

He caught my gaze and smiled—lazy, lopsided, the kind that felt like being let in on a private joke.

"You know," he said, glancing at Winnie, who had now moved on to arranging pepperoni slices into a face on her plate, "I think she's finally accepting me as a full-time member of the club."

"Don't get cocky," I warned, reaching for another slice. "You still haven't passed the bedtime-story trial."

"Oh, I'm saving my best material for that." His voice was low, teasing.

Winnie let out a dramatic yawn, arms stretched high, and declared, "My tummy is sleepy."

"Is that so?" I raised a brow. "This is the first I'm hearing of this expression." I moved toward her to tickle her *tired tummy*.

"It means," she said between giggles, "it's time for Austin to read me a story."

She slid off the stool, fingers reaching for his, and she dragged him toward the stairs, her trust tethered between them like a string.

I'd managed to wrangle her to the bathroom sink first, washing her hands and face before brushing her teeth. Her lids were heavy, and I would have bet good money she'd be sound asleep in a matter of minutes.

When we finished, I followed them into Winnie's room and leaned against the doorframe as Austin settled into the little armchair in the corner of her room. She climbed into bed with her stuffed giraffe and handed him a pink hardcover book with sparkles on the spine.

He didn't hesitate. Instead he opened the book and began reading in a ridiculous accent that made Winnie dissolve into peals of laughter. He even did voices.

I stood there and stared. I watched the way his voice softened in the quiet parts and the way his fingers turned the pages with care. Her breathing slowed and she reached out to touch his arm as she finally drifted off.

Eventually he closed the book. Winnie's lashes fluttered against her cheeks, her hand still resting against his forearm.

I stepped in and gently lifted her wrist to tuck her in. "Night, bug," I whispered before dropping a kiss into her hair.

She barely stirred.

Austin rose, and for a moment we just stood there—together, alone, surrounded by glow-in-the-dark stars and the faint hum of the white noise machine.

I turned off the bedside lamp and nodded toward the hallway. We moved in silence until we reached the kitchen again, now dim and quiet and smelling faintly of garlic and pepperoni.

Heavy moments passed as I stared up at him.

His throat cleared. "I should head out," he said, glancing toward the back door.

I hesitated, thumb circling the lip of my wineglass on the counter. "Thanks. For . . . everything."

His eyes met mine. "Anytime."

He meant it. That was the dangerous part. My eyes dipped to his lips for a fraction of a second.

What would happen if I let it all go and kissed him?

A yearning ache bloomed low in my belly. Too scared, I nodded and turned to start rinsing the plates. He gathered his hoodie from the peg by the door and slipped out without another word.

Only after the door closed did I finally exhale.

I tried to clean the kitchen like it mattered, scrubbing plates and forks longer than necessary, aligning the silverware like that small order would help restore the larger one slipping out of my grasp. Once everything was spotless, I poured myself a glass of wine and retreated to my bedroom. I took a sip and stared at the tub in my en suite bathroom.

I needed something—steam, solitude, something simpler than all the feelings pressing against my chest.

The tub filled slowly, the sound of water lapping against porcelain dulling the edges of my thoughts. I lit a candle— fig and sandalwood—and sank into the heat. The wine was dark and dry and bitter in a way that felt luxurious.

I opened the book resting on the windowsill. Not a new one—an old favorite from college. Dog-eared. Annotated. The kind of book where someone else's thoughts lived in the margins beside my own. I traced the ink with damp fingers, barely reading. The words blurred and scattered, like my focus had lost its footing.

There it was again—that sense of being watched from the inside. Not in a haunted way, but in a known way.

Outside the bathroom window, the breeze whispered through the trees. I could make out muffled crickets and a far-off car. Inside, only the faint flicker of the candle and the clink of my nail against the glass as I reached for another sip.

Then the record player started.

The sound was soft at first, the telltale crackle of needle to vinyl. A low hum that seemed to travel straight through the wall vibrated faintly in the pipes.

Then came the voice.

Dean Martin. Warm. Winking. Romantic in a way that made everything float away. I closed my eyes and let the music wrap around me, seeping into the corners of the bathroom like river water over stone.

I chuckled to myself. Of course he liked Dean Martin and not Sinatra. Somehow Austin always seemed to like the less obvious choice. I listened as one track faded into the next.

When the bath water finally cooled, I drained the tub and blew out the candle.

I wandered naked across the floor to my dresser. The music still played. Faint. Steady. I dressed, then pressed my forehead to the wall between us. The walls were just thin enough to hear him.

To *feel* him.

I curled into bed, pulled the blanket to my chin, closed my eyes, and waited for silence. It came slowly, like the record reaching its end, and the static settled. Then, just as sleep began to take me, I heard it.

Low. Quiet. A thread pulled straight through the drywall. "Good night, Selene."

My eyes snapped open. I didn't move. He didn't say anything else.

I pressed my hand to my chest, heartbeat tangled somewhere near my throat.

FOURTEEN

WINNIE STOOD on the back step with her hands on her hips and glitter on her forehead like war paint.

"Three rounds," she declared. "I'm the seeker. No take-backsies."

Selene blinked at her. "Lovebug, what's a 'take-backsie'?"

Winnie narrowed her eyes, deeply offended that neither of us knew the rules to a game she had just made up. "It means no changing the rules once we start."

Selene and I shared a look—equal parts amusement and exhaustion. It had been a long day. Our morning routine, school drop-off, work, and a post-school spilled bottle of blue glitter that had turned the kitchen into something out of a disco ball crime scene.

Thankfully Winnie and I had cleaned it up before Selene could stress about the blue streaks across the wood floor. When she'd emerged from the carriage house, blinking at the afternoon sun, I'd bent down to whisper into Winnie's ear, suggesting she ask her mom to take a break for a quick round of hide-and-seek.

"I'm going to count," Winnie announced, already turning toward the porch post like she'd done this before. "You better run and hide somewhere good."

"I didn't stretch for this." Selene groaned as she arched her back. My mouth went dry at the sight of her perfectly round tits straining the fabric of her shirt.

"You'll be fine," I said, tugging the hem of my shirt lower and readying myself. "Just don't pull anything."

"I'm wearing ballet flats, Austin. This is not a regulation sport outfit." She smiled, but once Winnie started counting, Selene bolted across the yard with surprising speed.

I took the opposite route, circling toward the back of the property, behind Selene's office in the carriage house. The afternoon air was thick with lake humidity, the earth still soft from yesterday's rain. My boots made almost no sound against the moss and mulch as I slipped into the narrow gap between the brick wall and the wooden fence. It was tighter than I would have guessed, overgrown with ivy, and shadowed in a way that made it feel like stepping into a pocket of time.

I crouched, breath steady. My heart wasn't pounding from running. It was thumping hard from what this felt like —how easily the three of us played house. How quickly this place, these routines, had become mine too.

Somewhere behind me, I heard Winnie call, "Thirty! Ready or not!"

Then the thump of her feet pounded across the yard. I smiled, ducking lower into the darkness.

And then—a soft sound. A whisper, not much more than the hush of fabric against skin, "Is she close?"

That voice. *Selene*.

I turned just as she ducked in beside me, nearly brushing her forehead against mine.

"Jesus," I muttered, shifting back a hair. "You scared the hell out of me."

She grinned, unbothered. "You're hiding like a criminal."

I smirked. "I'm hiding like a man who doesn't want to get caught by a five-year-old with no mercy."

"Scooch over," she whispered again, shifting her body as we crouched against one another in the too-small space.

I didn't move. "I am scooched. I'm six foot three."

Selene smiled but stayed quiet as her eyes darted, searching for Winnie. I studied her profile.

"She's ruthless," Selene whispered. "I swear I don't know where she gets it from."

"She's strong . . . just like her mother," I murmured, my eyes landing on Selene's lips.

We stayed there, still and pressed close in the space that barely held us both. I could feel the heat coming off her body, her figure just brushing mine again, like a live wire.

It would've been easy enough to shift or step away, but neither of us did.

Her arm was bare, pressed lightly against mine. The afternoon sunlight filtered through the slats in the fence, casting her face in warm shadows. I could smell her—something green and sharp from her perfume, humidity in her hair from the lake breeze, and the warm, almost sweet scent of her skin. My body tightened in response, involuntary and insistent. My cock thickened against the zipper of my jeans, and I shifted to ease the ache.

I could've sworn the air got thicker between us, like time was holding its breath.

I couldn't look away from her mouth. The words were soft, but her lips were so close I could almost taste them. My entire body responded before my brain could catch up, lighting up like she was the sun and I was pulled into her orbit.

The brush of her thigh near mine, the way her chest lifted when she took a breath—I registered all of it with painful precision. It was too much, too close, too easy to imagine what would happen if I just leaned in and pressed my mouth to hers.

Not until she exhaled a shaky laugh and shook her head. "This is insane."

I cleared my throat. "Yeah. Probably."

Winnie was circling the lawn, jumping behind bushes and peeking under the porch. She was dangerously close to finding us, but I didn't move, and neither did Selene.

Her gaze slid to me and her expression shifted—barely, but I caught it. Something flickered behind her eyes, a mix of uncertainty and something else she wasn't ready to name. Her gaze dropped to my mouth and lingered.

The silence between us stretched, pulling tighter.

Somewhere across the yard, Winnie shouted something about bunnies in the hydrangeas.

But there, in this sliver of shadowed space, the world narrowed to the sound of Selene breathing beside me and the roar of my own pulse.

She turned to look at me again, slower this time. Her face tipped up toward mine, her breath brushing my jaw. My hands twitched at my sides. I wanted to touch her.

God, how I want to touch her.

I shifted, barely. The toe of her shoe grazed mine. She didn't pull back.

For one full second I thought we'd do it. I thought I'd finally say screw it and close the space between us. I wanted to let my hands memorize her face, her waist, the slope of her hips. I thought I'd feel her sink into me like she did in every version of my dreams.

A cackle rang out. "Found you!"

Winnie burst into the space with triumph smeared all over her cheeks, her braid unraveling like a flag of war. Selene jumped, startled, and I blinked hard, the moment evaporating like steam off pavement.

"You shouldn't hide *together*." She laughed. "It makes it too easy to find you."

"Win," Selene said, breathless, pressing a hand to her chest. "You are terrifying."

Winnie beamed like it was a compliment. "I told you I was good."

"You were born for this," I said, unfolding myself and stepping into the sunlight. "I'll have to find somewhere even trickier next time. But right now I've got to run. I have a rescheduled game tonight." I ruffled Winnie's hair, and just like that the spell dissolved, but it didn't really fade. It stayed under my skin, crackling and hot.

I caught Selene's eye one last time as we walked back toward the porch, her hand brushing lightly against her hip like she could still feel the space where I'd almost touched her.

She moved toward her daughter with that careful ease she used when she didn't want me to see she was flustered.

I just watched her, my hands still balled at my sides, realizing that pretending got harder by the day.

THE SUN HAD DIPPED LOW by the time we wrapped up the game, the whole field awash in a burnt-amber glow that stuck to our skin like sap. Hayes had sweat slicked down the back of his neck and Brody was nursing a beer like he'd just run a marathon instead of half jogged through six innings. Cal was the only one still energized—too competitive to pretend it was just a small-town league game.

Collectively the team voted for tailgating in the parking lot instead of making the trek to the Lantern. We dragged lawn chairs out of the back of Hayes's truck and let them scrape across the gravel like we were staking claim. Music played low from Hayes's phone, all scratchy classic rock, and someone had cracked open a cooler that smelled like hops and melted ice.

I grabbed a beer, still cold enough to sting my palm, and sank into the folding chair across from Brody. The plastic sagged under my weight. It was the first time all day I felt still.

"Domestic bliss looks good on you, kid," Hayes said with a smirk, peeling off his batting gloves with too much flair. "You're showing up early, remembering the snacks. Was that a wet wipe I saw you use earlier?"

"The man's folding laundry too." Brody lifted his chin, happy to join in the teasing. "You can see it in the shoulders."

I laughed, slow and easy, because it was better than saying what was true—that they weren't wrong. The towels in Selene's bathroom had creases in them from my careful folding. My boots had found a home just inside her front door.

I shrugged like I hadn't memorized the way her mouth looked when she was half asleep and curled on the couch, pretending she wasn't exhausted from a long day hunched over her desk. "She's my boss," I said.

That earned me a round of side-eyes.

"Sure, man," Brody said, dragging the words out slowly. "Keep telling yourself that."

"No, really," I added, and the words felt like chewing on gravel. "I'm there for Winnie when Selene needs to work. That's the job."

Nobody said anything for a beat. Just the low clink of a bottle against teeth.

Then Cal said, "She definitely seems less stressed out."

I didn't answer, only swallowed past the gravel in my throat.

"And that," Hayes said with a laugh as he clinked his bottle against Cal's, "is a damn miracle. My sister has been all go and no whoa since the minute Winnie was born." His eyes narrowed on me and I tried—and failed spectacularly—not to squirm in my seat. "What's she paying you anyway? I'll double it as a thank-you."

"Uh—" I cleared a scratch in my throat. "Nothing, actually. I'm just helping out."

"You see that?" Brody leaned in to punch my leg. "A Good Samaritan."

Hayes's noncommittal hum wedged in my chest. That man may have the shittiest luck alive, but it didn't take luck to see what I was barely hiding.

I was a fucking wreck over his sister. Ever since hide-and-seek in the yard, I couldn't stop thinking about her—us hiding behind the carriage house together. Her breath shallow. Her mouth so fucking close.

I took a pull from the bottle, swallowing around the ache that had lodged deep in my throat and hadn't budged in weeks.

Hayes kicked at a pebble with the toe of his cleat.

"What ever happened to that girl you were seeing—the one from Muskegon?"

A laugh cracked out of my chest, a bit too loud and way too fast. "That really wasn't anything. It fizzled fast."

It was months ago and had fizzled because she wasn't Selene. All because I'd met a stranger in a shitty jazz bar and had the best sex of my life. No woman measured up, and, frankly, I wasn't all that bothered by that.

No. Selene was the only woman to leave me pacing the other side of a wall while she soaked in the tub with a book, and the sound of her sighing behind the door drove me half insane.

"Man," Brody muttered, smirking, "you are fucking done for, kid."

My scowl sliced in his direction. "Shut up."

But they all knew.

A chorus of laughter rumbled through the group. I leaned back and closed my eyes, letting the breeze cut through the heat still clinging to my skin. The sun was behind the trees now, but the sky held on to that early autumn bruise-blue tint.

I had played a lot of games in my life and taken a lot of hits, but this felt like standing still and getting wrecked anyway.

When I opened my eyes, Hayes was watching me. Not judging, just . . . assessing.

"She looks at you differently, you know," he said simply. "They both do." Hayes stood, stretching his back before clamping a hand on my shoulder. "Just don't fuck it up."

My jaw clenched. I didn't answer, because I knew the truth. She did look at me differently, and I looked at her like I couldn't stop.

I TOLD myself I was just swinging by to grab my hoodie—the one Winnie had claimed and Selene had threatened to donate if I didn't take it home.

It was an excuse. One even I barely believed.

The house was quiet when I pulled up. The porch light was on, just like always, but there was no TV glow through the window. It was surprising how quiet it was without Winnie's voice tumbling through the screen door in a swirl of questions and glitter.

It was late. Her bedtime had come and gone, and because of that, I didn't want to knock too loud. I wasn't here to cause a scene or to wake up a sleeping kid who thought I hung the damn moon.

I knocked softly and waited. When there was no answer, my ears strained to hear anything coming from inside the duplex, but it was quiet.

I slowly cracked the door open and peeked inside, voice low. "Selene?"

No reply.

Then I could hear her. Faint movement toward the rear of the house. I knew the layout like the back of my hand—how the floor creaked just before the hallway turned, where the overhead light hummed near the laundry nook, the way the kitchen curtains fluttered with the slightest breeze.

I stepped inside quietly, closing the door behind me. My shoes thudded softly against the rug. The kitchen was dim with just the stove light on. A pan from dinner still rested beside the sink. It smelled faintly of tomato and basil. Something sweeter clung to the air—her shampoo, maybe, or the dryer sheets she liked.

The tumble of the dryer led me to her.

Selene was barefoot, wearing soft shorts and an old college tee that clung to her back in places and stretched loose in the neckline. Her hair was up, but barely—half undone in that way that made me ache. She had earbuds in, swaying slightly to music I couldn't hear. Her hands moved with practiced rhythm as she folded a towel and dropped it into the basket.

I froze and stared for a heartbeat. Maybe longer.

The sight of her like that—unaware, relaxed, truly at home in her skin—hit me square in the chest. There was nothing performative there, just Selene, warm and wild and so fucking beautiful it almost hurt.

She turned and startled when she saw me.

A hand flew to her chest. "Jesus, Austin—"

I laughed and held up my hands. "I'm sorry, I didn't mean to scare you."

She pulled the earbuds out. One side of her shirt slid lower as she moved, baring the soft curve of her shoulder.

"You scared the hell out of me," she said, but there was laughter in her voice.

I smiled, stepping closer. "I didn't want to wake Winnie, but I came for my hoodie."

"She's out. Long day of fairy hunting." Her eyes flicked over me. "Did you guys win?"

I shook my head. "Nah. We got our asses handed to us. Brody gave me shit, saying they'd only asked me to play to secure a win." I shrugged playfully. "Turns out even I can't help us."

She chuckled and turned back to the dryer. "How's Hayes?"

I lifted a shoulder. "He showed up late again. He swore a seagull shit on his windshield and stole his sandwich while he was parked at the marina for dinner. Brody accused him of lying, but I saw the mustard on his windshield."

Selene sighed and shook her head. "He has the *worst* luck."

My brows furrowed. "Is what I've heard true? Do you think he's cursed by the Lady?"

"No." She gave me a sad smile. "Maybe?" Selene exhaled and looked at the shirt in her hand. "He has the worst luck imaginable, but I don't really believe in curses . . . I don't think. Hayes doesn't like to talk about it." Her head tipped sideways. "Your hoodie's over there. Freshly washed."

"I see that," I said, but I didn't reach for it.

I stepped up behind her, close enough to feel the warmth rolling off her skin. Close enough to smell the faintest trace of coconut and clean laundry. Her breath hitched.

"You fold like a fucking goddess," I murmured, my voice low and rough.

She snorted. "That's a new one."

I reached past her for the hoodie, intentionally brushing her hand in the process.

Her body went still, and so did mine. Her skin was warm. The air shifted. Every inch of space between us vanished. Her breath caught. My pulse spiked.

She didn't look at me, but I could feel the awareness snap tight between us. The buzz of the dryer. The creak of the floor. The throb of need so thick it made my head spin.

I leaned in, voice barely audible. "Do you always smell this good, or is it just when you're trying to kill me?"

Selene's shoulders rolled back, her breath sharp and shaky as her back pressed against my front. "You're—*God*, you're impossible."

I pressed my mouth to the curve of her neck, just once, just a whisper of skin.

"Tell me to leave," I murmured, praying she wouldn't. "I will. Just say the word."

She didn't speak, so I let my mouth roam. My tongue laved over the delicate curve of her neck. She arched into me as I sucked and moaned into her skin. My hands dug into her hip bones as I struggled to remain in control.

My cock twitched as every nerve ending in my body lit up. Gripping her hard, I spun her around. For a beat I stared down at her. Selene's cheeks were flushed, her pert mouth slack as if she couldn't believe what we were doing. My eyes searched hers, begging for her to tell me to stop before it was too late.

A rumble gathered in my throat. "Fuck it."

My mouth crashed to hers. The kiss wasn't delicate; it was filthy.

Her mouth opened to mine like she'd been waiting for it —hungry and wild, like she needed it just as badly as I did. I crowded her against the dryer, hands kneading her hips, pulling her against my aching cock.

She whimpered when I rutted forward, and that fucking sound . . . it ripped the breath from my lungs.

"You don't know what you do to me," I growled, dragging my mouth along her jaw.

Her hands clawed at my shirt, tugging me closer. "Then show me."

I leaned in, arching her back against the warm dryer. My thigh shoved between hers and her hips ground against me like it was instinct.

"Christ, Selene," I breathed. "You feel that? That's what you've been doing to me."

Her fingers dug into my shoulders, her head falling back with a gasp.

"I think about this every damn night," I said, dragging her top down farther to expose her shoulder. "I think about your cunt on my tongue. About you begging me for more. I've been thinking about it ever since that night in the forest."

She let out a desperate sound, and I swallowed it with another kiss—hot and deep and filthy enough to burn.

"Do you want that?" I asked. "You want my mouth on you?"

She nodded, wild-eyed. "Yes. Please. *Fuck*—Austin . . ."

I dropped to my knees without hesitation. We'd been too hurried to go slowly the first time, and I wasn't about to make the same mistake twice. I'd been dreaming about the taste of her for *months*.

Selene tried to say something, but I grabbed her thighs and pulled her forward.

"Shh," I said, mouth already pressing hot kisses up the inside of her leg. "I've got you."

And then—

Footsteps above.

A creak of the upstairs floor.

Selene went rigid as her hand clamped on my shoulder. I blinked up at her, both of us panting like we'd just run a mile.

She shook her head, eyes blown wide. "I can't. Not here."

I nodded once, jaw clenched, swallowing down every last ounce of want like it might kill me.

She straightened her top, flushed and trembling. "I'm sorry."

"Don't be." I stood slowly, brushing my thumb across her cheek. "But just so we're clear . . ."

She looked up, blinking.

"I'm not done with you." I grabbed my hoodie and walked out the door without looking back.

I knew then—and so did she—that the pretending was over.

FIFTEEN

SELENE

I STARED AT THE CEILING, still and silent, as the fan rotated in slow, hypnotic circles above me. The early-morning light cut in through the blinds—angled and soft, warm against the sheets that had twisted around my legs sometime in the night. I hadn't really slept. At least, not in any way that counted.

My body hadn't forgotten.

It still buzzed with the memory of *him*—his mouth against mine, the press of his body pinning me against the dryer, the way he'd groaned my name like he wanted to take whatever I was willing to give. I rolled to bury my face in the pillow.

What was I thinking?

I'd nearly let him fuck me in the laundry room. I would have if he hadn't stopped. If he hadn't stepped back with that wrecked expression like he wanted to stay but knew better.

And what does it say about me that I was disappointed he had?

I turned my head on the pillow, already hating myself

for the way my heart squeezed, for the heat that stirred low and shamefully between my legs. I shouldn't be thinking about this—about him. About how it felt to be touched and wanted like that. It had been too easy to lose myself in him, to forget that there was a child upstairs and a life I was barely holding together most days.

I pressed my thighs together under the sheet, searching for relief I hadn't earned. My nipples ached beneath the thin cotton of my top, overly sensitive, the fabric rasping against them just enough to make me squirm. I could still feel the ghost of his hands—broad, calloused, and confident. I recalled the way they'd slid down my sides, not possessive or hurried, but like he'd known what he was doing. Austin was patient, like he'd been waiting for me to catch up to the truth we'd both been circling for weeks.

I let my eyes fall closed and gave myself one single second to remember it. His voice—low, frayed, filthy.

You feel that? That's what you've been doing to me.

I swallowed hard, my body responding with a throb that felt delicious and dirty all at once. I was too old for him. He was helping me take care of my daughter.

And yet I couldn't stop remembering how his thick thigh had slotted between mine, how my hips had tilted up for more without thinking. I'd been soaked for him. Aching, open, and desperate. My pussy clenched at the thought, traitorous and slick just from the memory.

I'd been one look away from losing every boundary I'd spent years reinforcing.

And he—he had been the mature one.

He'd left when we heard Winnie upstairs.

That was the part that wrecked me the most.

It wasn't just that he hadn't pushed, but that he'd read the fear on my face and stepped back with enough restraint for both of us. He was level-headed while I had stood there, mouth swollen, pulse racing, knees weak, and ready to undo every rule I'd ever made.

I rubbed a hand over my face, willing the heat in my cheeks to fade. I wasn't this woman. I wasn't careless. I didn't do reckless anymore.

Not since Winnie.

Not since everything fell apart and I was left to put it back together by myself.

It was just an attraction. Physical. Hormones and proximity and the fact that he looked like a goddamn thunderstorm made of muscle and slow smiles.

Surely that was all it was.

But even as I tried to rationalize it, I knew I was lying, because it wasn't just lust that had tangled me up.

It was the way he'd tucked Winnie's stuffed unicorn under her blanket when he thought no one was watching. The way he'd listened when she talked about her imaginary fairy kingdom like it was as important as any adult problem. It was how he noticed things without making a show of it— how he saw me.

Not just the mother. Not just the provider. *Me.*

That was what terrified me the most, because deep down I wanted that. I wanted to be seen like that. Touched like that. I wanted the press of his mouth against mine again, the rough scrape of his stubble across my throat, his cock inside me, filling me until I forgot every name that wasn't his. I wanted to arch for him. To come on his fingers, his tongue, his—

I groaned and turned over, burying my face into the pillow, this time allowing a scream to burn in my throat. My thighs were still pressed together, tightly enough to feel the wet heat that had gathered there.

I couldn't. I wouldn't.

Because the second I stopped thinking with my head and started thinking with my body, I risked losing everything I had worked for—our routine, our safety, the quiet, stable life I had built one brick at a time.

I didn't get to have a flirty fling—at least not the way other women did.

Not the sex, not the heat, not the magnetic pull of a man who made me feel like a woman instead of a checklist.

Not the way he made me ache to be ruined.

So I swallowed it down, again, like I had a thousand other times since I became a mother. I pushed away the burn in my chest and the wetness between my thighs and reminded myself of all the reasons I couldn't afford to want him.

And still, somewhere deep in the marrow of me, a voice whispered:

Maybe just this once you could want him . . . maybe you already do.

Saturday mornings used to be my favorite. No alarms. No school lunches to pack. Just me and Winnie and the loose, cozy rhythm of a day that didn't demand too much, but this morning felt off-kilter.

The sun filtered in through the kitchen blinds, casting long golden bars across the counter like a watercolor painting that had lost its vibrancy. I moved through the motions like I was underwater—filling the coffeepot, setting out two bowls, pouring cereal into one of them without even asking which kind she wanted.

Behind me, Winnie hummed under her breath, still in

her pajama set with the faded mermaid print, perched cross-legged at the kitchen table, a spoon clutched in one hand and her unicorn stuffie in the other.

"Mama?" she asked, her mouth full of cereal. "How come Austin's not here today?"

At the mention of his name, my hand froze on the coffee canister.

"He doesn't usually come on Saturdays," I said, careful not to sound as strange as I felt. "He has his own things to do. It's his day off."

Winnie made a small noise in the back of her throat, like she didn't agree with that logic. "He's still allowed to come over, though. Right?"

I turned slowly, clutching my mug like it could anchor me, and smiled. "I mean . . . I guess. But sometimes people need breaks."

She blinked, spoon halfway to her mouth. "I don't."

That got a small laugh out of me. I came around the table and smoothed a hand over her head, my fingers catching in a tangle near the crown. Her hair smelled like kid shampoo and the faint scent of lavender body spray she liked to overuse.

"You definitely don't," I murmured. "But grown-ups get tired sometimes."

She squinted at me, her spoon paused midair. "You look funny today."

I blinked. "Funny how?"

She tilted her head, studying me with that tiny furrow between her brows like she was solving a puzzle. "Like . . . your face is doing a secret."

That startled a laugh out of me. "My face is doing a secret?"

Winnie nodded seriously. "Uh-huh. Like when you smile, but you're not saying why you're smiling."

I pressed my fingers to the corners of my mouth, trying —and failing—to smooth it away. "I don't know what you mean."

Her eyes lit up. "Do you have a present for me?"

I laughed and shook my head. "Sorry, kid. No surprises today."

Winnie pouted but went back to her cereal, completely unbothered. "Maybe you're thinking about something that makes you happy. Your face did that when we saw Mr. O'Brien and you said his cat was cute."

I snorted into my coffee. Mr. O'Brien was a sweet old man who walked his cat downtown on a leash. "His cat is really cute."

She gave me a knowing look, five going on forty. "Your voice got soft like a marshmallow. I think it means we should get a cat."

Winnie's logic was impressive. Avoiding the topic of getting a pet cat, I retreated back to the counter, heart thudding like I'd been caught doing something criminal. I tried to examine my reflection in the toaster, but it was no use.

Winnie had always been perceptive—more than most kids her age. She saw things, felt them, and the truth was, I probably did look different.

Because I *felt* different.

Austin had gotten under my skin, and I didn't know how to dig him out.

As I reached for the coffee again, Winnie rambled on about cats and I found myself thinking about marginalia.

Those quiet notes readers left in the margins of books— half thoughts, underlines, delicate nothings that felt like secrets. I loved to collect those moments, both in a literal sense, but also in the way I'd press my thumb to the page and wonder who else had felt that line deeply enough to mark it. I'd always loved that—evidence of someone who'd come before me. A life brushing up against mine in the smallest, most intimate way.

And now I couldn't stop wondering: What was I leaving behind? What kind of marginalia was I writing into my daughter's life? Was it all tired routines and microwaved dinners and reminders to wear socks with her boots? Did she see me as a whole person? Or just the scaffolding that held everything up?

I glanced over at her—pink cheeks, wild brown hair, a cereal drip making its way down the front of her pajama shirt—and I felt the ache of it in my bones. I loved her more than I had ever loved anything in my life, but I was starting to wonder what else I was supposed to be.

If I was supposed to be just this.

If I was teaching her that mothers didn't get to want anything outside of their children. That being responsible meant locking your desires in a drawer and throwing away the key.

I wanted more.

Not *instead* of being her mother, but because I was. I wanted to teach her to live fearlessly.

I wanted to show her that women could be complicated. That they could want stability and still burn with hunger. That they could make mistakes and survive them. That they could crave comfort and risk, sometimes in the same breath.

And Austin? Something about him made me feel like I could be that kind of woman again.

Capable of ruin. Capable of joy.

I finished my coffee in silence and rinsed the mug in the sink, placing it upside down just like Austin did. Winnie had wandered over to the back door by then, dragging a blanket behind her and talking to her unicorn about whether they should plant flowers or a vegetable patch in the garden Austin was building.

The house was quiet. Too quiet.

I miss him.

It scared me how much I missed him, but more than anything I was terrified of the voice in my head whispering that my moment for happiness had passed me by a long time ago.

SIXTEEN

SELENE

Our local café and bookstore was called the Crooked Spine. It was tucked between the bookstore's ivy-covered side wall and an antique map shop that rarely opened before noon. Inside, it smelled like espresso and old paper, with mismatched chairs and creaky wood floors that whispered with every step. Fat, sleepy cats draped themselves across armchairs and windowsills, basking in squares of sunlight like royalty. Winnie had named them all—Marmalade, Sir Pounce, and Biscuit Head among them—and greeted each one like a longtime friend. She'd begged me to sit at the table by the window "because that's where Biscuit Head curls up," and sure enough, he was already there, loafing beside the glass like a furry paperweight.

The bell above the café door chimed with its usual delicate jingle, but I barely noticed it. My eyes were on the book in my lap, a paperback with dog-eared pages I'd already read twice but had pulled off the shelf for comfort more than plot. Winnie sat across from me, legs swinging under the table; marshmallow foam clinging to her upper lip as she sipped hot cocoa from a yellow ceramic mug that looked far too big for her hands.

She was humming something—some tune she'd learned in school or made up on the spot, impossible to tell the difference—and I tried to lose myself in the words on the page, but they blurred.

Everything blurred lately.

My body was still betraying me. Every time I closed my eyes, I could still feel the hot press of Austin's mouth at my jaw, the way his voice had rasped my name like a secret in the dark. My insides went molten just remembering. Even now, sitting in the middle of a public place, my thighs squeezed together under the table like they had a mind of their own.

And then—

"Didn't expect to find my two favorite girls here. Are you stalking me, or is this fate?"

My head snapped up, pulse stuttering.

Austin stood just inside the threshold, sunlight hitting his shoulders like a spotlight. He wore a worn gray Henley with the slutty little buttons undone, jeans low on his hips, and that stupidly easy grin that made breathing feel optional.

He was already walking toward us, unhurried, and completely at home in his own skin.

He stopped at the edge of our table like it was the most natural thing in the world. Like he belonged there.

Winnie lit up like a sunrise. "Austin!"

He crouched next to her chair, his attention fully hers. "What's the cocoa verdict today, kiddo? Is it any good?"

"Mom thought the cocoa was a little too hot to drink," she said seriously. "She was right, but the whipped cream helps."

Austin's flirty gaze flickered my way. "I bet there isn't much your mom is wrong about, but can I trust your taste buds?"

She offered him the mug with no hesitation. He fake-sipped, smacked his lips, and nodded solemnly. "Yep. That's solid cocoa. You've got a good thing going here."

She beamed, already back to sipping like she hadn't just handed over her drink to a grown man with zero suspicion. That was the thing about Austin—he made people feel safe. Instantly. Easily.

And me?

I was watching him like he was made of fire.

He looked at me then. Really looked. Not just with his eyes—but with something heavier and deeper, like he remembered every inch of last night's heat and wasn't sorry for any of it.

I tucked my hair behind my ear, trying to stay steady. "I didn't peg you as a café bookstore guy."

"I saw you two in the window." He stood to his full, impressive height, smile still teasing. "I'm still trying to crack the code on your coffee order."

I raised an eyebrow. "What?"

His arms crossed. "I've been guessing for weeks. You keep switching it on me. First it was vanilla something, then the cinnamon one." He frowned down at the foamy cold brew in front of me. "Today there's ice and it's got a dusting of something. Is that nutmeg?"

I blinked, then looked down at my cup. "You've been paying that much attention?"

"Maybe." His grin went crooked. "It would be a hell of a lot easier if you'd stop changing it up every day."

My chest went tight. I hated how much I liked his answer.

Winnie slid out of her chair to dig in the little basket of books at the end of the table, humming again. Austin's gaze followed her for a beat, soft and warm, before coming back to me.

"It's weird, right? Not seeing each other in the mornings?" he said, voice lower now. "I almost stopped by before I realized it was Saturday."

I nodded, because I didn't trust my voice. Because yes. It did feel odd. Having Austin around had quickly felt comforting. It was almost like he had always been here, like his laugh belonged in our kitchen and his shoes belonged by the front door and his goddamn voice belonged in my ear at night.

He held my gaze, but I looked away first.

"Well, I'm headed to the nursery," he said casually. "Thought I might grab a few plants for the garden. You're welcome to pick some out . . . unless you two had plans?"

Winnie whipped her head around. "I wanna go!"

I opened my mouth to say no, to offer an out. "I mean, we could go, but it's your day off. You probably need a break from us," I said gently.

He tilted his head, brows lifting just slightly. "Selene," he said, voice like velvet dragged across skin, "if I wanted to be anywhere else, I would be. Spending time with you two isn't a job. It's just . . . where I want to be."

And just like that, I was melting all over again.

I gave him a slow nod as he extended a hand toward Winnie. "Let's go find some veggies, kid."

She squealed and darted ahead of us. I grabbed my bag, still rattled, still aching.

As I passed him on the way out, Austin's hand grazed the small of my back—it was definitely *not* by accident.

"Are you going to keep looking at me like that," he

murmured so only I could hear, "or are you finally going to admit you like having me around?"

I didn't answer, but I knew he saw my smile.

THE NURSERY SAT at the edge of town where the gravel turned to dirt and the fields stretched wide and sun-bleached, preparing to sleep. Autumn had settled in with its crisp quiet that made the air smell like dried leaves and earth still clinging to the last of the harvest.

We pulled into the lot just as a gust of wind kicked up a swirl of golden birch leaves, sending them skittering across the hood of my car. The greenhouse glowed in the slant of early-afternoon sun, its arched panes fogged slightly with warmth and life.

Austin's SUV parked beside ours, and he pulled open my driver's-side door and grinned as Winnie frantically tried to unharness herself. He turned to me. "You think she's excited?"

"She's vibrating," I murmured, shaking my head.

Austin waggled his eyebrows. "I've got that effect on women," he said under his breath, then winked before giving me room to get out and open Winnie's door for her.

My laugh caught in my throat, and a low roll of heat curled through me.

Winnie was squirming in the back seat. "Do you think they'll have sugar snap peas? You said fall is for planting peas."

"I said that one time." Austin shook his head and smiled as he helped her unbuckle. "You've got a memory like a steel trap, kid."

She beamed. "I'm very smart."

His smile bloomed, blinding and bright. "That you are, Win."

I stepped out of the car, grounding myself in the crunch of gravel underfoot, and in the sound of the wind chimes tinkling just above the entrance. A part of me still couldn't believe we were here. Together. I glanced around, wondering whether this was something people noticed or if I was too caught up in my own thoughts.

Austin opened the greenhouse door and held it for us like being a gentleman came naturally for him. It wasn't a date . . . but somehow felt like one anyway.

Inside the nursery, the scent of damp mulch and cedar pots wrapped around me like a sweater. Tables were lined with hardy greens, cool-season lettuces, and little fruiting plants in ceramic pots—kale with deep-purple veining, stubby cabbages, and even a few late-bearing tomato varieties already straining against their cages. It was quieter than in spring, the planting rush long past, but there was something peaceful about the stillness. Humidity and the trapped sunlight warmed me, so I slipped out of my jacket, draping it over my arm.

Austin nudged Winnie toward a flat of broccoli seedlings and whispered like it was a secret mission. "Do you think your mom would eat these if you grew them?"

She squinted at him like she wasn't sure whether that was a trick. "Only if they turn into cheese."

They laughed at my expense, but it filled me with happiness. My cheeks pinched and my heart was full.

The greenhouse curved overhead in a long glass arch, soft light diffusing over rows of herbs and starter plants, little signs stuck into pots in loopy handwriting—basil, zucchini, beefsteak tomato, and something called 1,500-year-old cave beans.

Austin crouched beside her as she ran her fingers over fuzzy leaves. "You remember what we talked about, bug? You have to pick at least one thing you're willing to try eating."

She scrunched her nose and looked up at him with a wrinkle of suspicion. "Even if it's weird?"

"*Especially* if it's weird," he said solemnly. "That's what makes it fun."

She pointed to a tray of rainbow carrot sprouts, still tiny and wild-haired. "These look funny."

He grinned. "Perfect."

I stood a few steps behind them, arms folded, trying to seem casual, but my chest was tight and my skin too warm, even without my jacket. Austin scooped her up effortlessly to let her see the hanging baskets overhead—long tendrils of sweet potato vines and bursts of red geraniums.

His hand cradled her back. His laugh was soft.

I felt it again—that ache that wasn't just physical. It was the one that whispered *what if.* The one that threatened to swallow me whole if I let it.

Winnie pointed to a ceramic frog statue with a cracked eye. "I love him. Do you think he has a name?"

Austin glanced over his shoulder, catching my eye. "What do you think, Selene?"

I blinked. "Me?"

"Yeah," he said, voice low and just this side of intimate. "You look like someone who'd name a frog."

I gave a wry smile. "Charming."

He smirked. "Come on. Don't let the frog down."

"Willie." I shrugged and immediately regretted it.

"Old One-Eyed Willie." Austin's grin widened. "It's perfect." He grabbed Willie by the neck and tucked the figurine into his armpit.

I turned away, pretending to examine a tray of lavender plants, but I could feel the smile tugging at my mouth anyway.

We bought far too many plants. More than would ever fit in the tiny raised bed he'd built behind the duplex, but Winnie was too thrilled to stop, and I didn't have it in me to break the spell. The woman at the register gave a steep discount for Willie since he was cracked, and Winnie's smile beamed the entire time.

As he paid, Austin's hand grazed the small of my back, light and intentional.

My breath stuttered and I didn't move.

"Are you okay?" he murmured, voice pitched just for me. "You're looking a little . . . flustered."

I swallowed, pulse thudding. "I don't know what you're talking about."

His hand didn't move. "Sure you don't."

He turned toward Winnie before I could respond, but the heat of his palm lingered long after it left me.

As we stepped back into the sunlight, arms full of starter plants and a ceramic animal we didn't need, he adjusted the flat of marigolds under one arm and glanced at me. With my jacket off, I should have felt the chill in the air, but the warmth of Austin's touch lingered like it had been burned into my skin.

"See you at home," he said easily.

Home.

It shouldn't have made my heart clench like that, but it did.

SEVENTEEN

AUSTIN

Another week had gone by since our trip to the nursery. I was sitting on the front porch when their door opened.

The rusted screen let out a familiar creak as Selene stepped outside with Winnie, both wrapped in the golden spill of late-afternoon light. Winnie was mid-story about something that had happened in art class—there'd been glitter, maybe glue, and a very dramatic betrayal involving someone named Harper.

Selene's eyes met mine as she closed the door behind them. She looked tired, but that warm, distant kind of tired —the kind that had less to do with sleep and more to do with holding too many pieces of yourself together at once.

I stood slowly, one hand braced on the porch rail, and offered a half smile. "Big Friday-night plans?"

"We're waiting for her dad," she said, tugging Winnie's hoodie sleeve down over her wrist. "He's supposed to pick her up for the weekend."

The words felt neutral on her tongue, but the way her shoulders tensed betrayed the truth.

Winnie twirled on the sidewalk, her backpack bouncing against her small frame. "We made cinnamon muffins for the drive."

"I supervised," Selene clarified with a smile. "Which mostly meant saying 'Please stop eating the batter' at thirty-second intervals."

I chuckled and slipped my hands into the pockets of my jeans. "I should probably head out. Give you some space."

She looked at me, something unreadable passing through her eyes. Then she shook her head. "No. You're fine."

Sick curiosity was eating at me, so I stayed.

At least ten minutes passed, long enough for the sun to fall behind the rooftops. Shadows stretched across the lawn. Winnie sat cross-legged near the steps, chattering to herself as she arranged leaves by color.

When the black sedan finally pulled up to the curb, I watched Selene brace herself like a wave was coming.

The car door opened and a man stepped out, dressed in a crisp button-down and dark jeans. His phone was in hand, sunglasses still on even though the light was beginning to fade.

He looked like a man who used words like "pedagogy" in casual conversation and expected everyone around him to nod thoughtfully.

Winnie stood tall as he walked, unhurried, toward his little girl.

His eyes swept over the porch, pausing when they landed on me.

His gaze flicked from me to the front of the house, then back to me before asking Selene, "New neighbor?" He held a hand out to me. "Hi, I'm Brian."

I didn't answer right away, because the prick hadn't even greeted Winnie.

"Brian, I—" Emotion flickered across Selene's face, though I couldn't quite place it—exhaustion or frustration maybe.

I stood and placed my hand in his. Before I could open my mouth, Winnie darted up the porch steps to stand beside me and said with all the confidence in the world, "He's not a neighbor—he's my nanny!"

I bit down on a laugh. Not because it wasn't funny—though it was—but because of the way Brian's jaw ticced. He looked at Selene, who had just stepped off the last porch step, arms crossed over her chest, eyes unreadable.

Brian didn't look pleased. "Didn't know you were hiring live-ins, Sel," he said, voice light but not casual.

There was a moment—just a sliver of it—where I wondered whether I should say something, whether I should just let his dig slide, but I couldn't.

"Nice to meet you, Brian. I'm Austin." I stepped forward, calm and steady, my voice even. "She's in good hands. That's what matters, right?"

I hadn't mentioned which *she* I was referring to, but I'd let that be open for his interpretation. Brian's head tilted like he might say something else, but he must have had an ounce of self-preservation, because he held back.

Selene didn't flinch. "Winnie's backpack has everything she needs. I expect her home by six thirty Sunday night. Please do not be late again."

Brian looked at Winnie and smiled. "Let's go. Clock's ticking."

She glanced up at Selene. "Can we do movie night on Sunday when I'm back?"

Selene knelt, her arms around her daughter before she'd even finished asking. "Of course, my love. I will miss you every minute."

They hugged again, and there was something about the way her hand lingered on her daughter's shoulder that got to me, like if she let go too fast, something might unravel.

The car door slammed, the engine turned, and they disappeared down the street.

Selene stayed on the sidewalk, staring down the roadway, as they drove away. Her arms were wrapped around herself, like she was trying to stay inside her skin. Her eyes tracked the red taillights until they vanished behind the bend in the road.

I stepped up beside her, not touching. Just there.

"You okay?" I asked.

She let out a breath like she'd been holding it all day. "I hate it," she said. "Watching her go. It sucks every time."

I didn't say anything, but just waited. The truth was still building behind her eyes.

"But"—she exhaled slowly—"it's also a bit of a relief to just breathe for a second. Isn't that awful of me?"

"No," I said with a shake of my head. "That's real. You work hard and it's not wrong to take a break sometimes."

Selene turned and looked at me. Really looked. Her eyes were tired, but there was something behind them—like the part of her that had been locked up for a long time was stirring and shifting beneath the surface. It wasn't quite ready to come out, but a part of her was close to breaking free from the walls she'd built.

I took a step back, wanting to give her space to feel whatever she needed to feel. I cleared my throat. "How do you feel about someone else making dinner for a change?"

Her brow arched, suspicious. "Are you offering?"

"I'm not just pretty," I said with a grin. "I can cook too."

A smile bloomed on her face as her arms crossed. "Is that so?"

My chest tightened. "Yep. You can sit and I'll feed you. There might even be wine involved."

"Hmm . . ." Selene nodded and walked up the porch steps. She didn't say yes, but she didn't say no either.

She just turned and opened the door to her side of the duplex, and I followed her inside.

Selene moved through the house like she was still half waiting for the other shoe to drop.

She hadn't taken off her shoes. Her arms stayed crossed, like some part of her was holding herself together with invisible thread. The thunk of the door closing behind us echoed louder than it should have, like it marked some line neither of us wanted to acknowledge just yet.

I didn't say anything. Just toed off my boots, washed my hands at the sink, and started pulling open cabinets like I'd done it a hundred times. Because, in reality, I had. I had navigated her kitchen enough times that I knew where the olive oil was, where she kept her sharpest knife, and how she labeled her spice jars in neat, looping script.

Behind me, she hovered. I could feel the weight of her gaze—low, lingering, and curious in a way that made the skin at the back of my neck tighten.

"I don't have much," she said after a beat. "A few vegetables. Maybe some pasta."

"I'm a bachelor. I've worked with less," I said, turning to flash her a grin. "You've never seen what I can do with a sad zucchini and half a box of spaghetti."

A breath of laughter escaped her. She leaned against the kitchen doorway, finally uncrossing her arms. "Is this your seduction technique? Feeding exhausted single mothers until they forget their morals?"

I smirked as I sliced into an onion. "Only the ones who smell like cinnamon muffins and temptation."

That earned me a full smile. I filed it away like a win.

The radio was still tuned to some local station, playing a soft indie track with scratchy vocals and melancholy guitar that made the room feel smaller in the best way. I turned the volume up just a little. The music was enough to fill the silence without trying to erase it.

I moved around her kitchen with practiced ease— boiling water, tossing vegetables in a hot pan, coaxing flavor out of garlic and butter.

Selene watched from the stool by the island, a glass of red wine cradled in her hands. I hadn't asked. I'd just poured it and handed it to her, fingers brushing hers in the exchange, reveling in the fact that she didn't pull away.

I swallowed hard as something tugged in my brain. "Can I ask you something . . . about Winnie?"

Selene blinked at me, but nodded.

"You and Brian were married, right? But Winnie has your last name. How did that come about?"

A smile twitched on her lips. "About a year ago I decided I wanted to go back to my maiden name, Darling. Winnie liked it too. Brian didn't fight me on it . . . and that was part of the problem. He never fought for anything, including me."

My throat was thick even though Selene scoffed like what she'd shared wasn't a huge fucking deal. I couldn't imagine a world where a man wouldn't claw his way to the ends of the earth for those two.

"So," Selene continued, "when we changed our last

names, she talked me into a new middle name too. Winifred Elizabeth *Amaryllis* Darling because—"

"Amaryllis means sparkle," I finished with a laugh. "I know, she told me." I shook my head as I continued to pull ingredients for dinner. "That kid is something else."

"That she is." Selene's laugh was soft and melodic. Then she hummed along to the radio and watched me work. "Do you do this often?" she finally asked, voice low, a little rough around the edges.

"Cook for beautiful women in their kitchens?" I glanced over my shoulder, just in time to catch the flush rising in her cheeks. "Not nearly as often as I'd like."

She rolled her eyes, but her lips curved. "You're impossible."

"I'm a delight," I corrected, grabbing two plates from the cupboard. "Please, tell your friends."

She scoffed. "I don't have time for friends. My friends are my sisters—and they have to love me."

"You've got time for dinner," I said. "That's a start."

Dinner was simple—pasta tossed with garlic, blistered tomatoes, and hunks of salty Parmesan that melted into the heat of the noodles. We ate at the table, knees brushing, shoulders leaning closer than necessary. Selene twirled her fork slowly, the bite held midair as we talked about nothing in particular—old teachers, worst meals ever cooked, the way her daughter insisted every weed was a flower that needed some love.

Selene's laughter came easier with each sip of wine, and I savored the sound like it was something I could pocket for later. She moaned around one bite—an honest, delighted sound that made my cock twitch—and I nearly dropped my fork. She didn't even notice, just grinned and went back for more.

When we finished, Selene looked down into her wine like it might have answers for her as I walked our dishes to the sink. The glass caught the light as she tilted it, just enough to let a drop roll off the edge and catch on her bottom lip.

My brain short-circuited.

Her tongue flicked out to catch it, and I swear I forgot what I was doing. My hand tightened around the spatula.

Every muscle in my body went tight with restraint. "Selene."

Her eyes lifted, slow and curious. "Hmm?"

"Come here." My voice was low and demanding.

She blinked, still holding the glass, then slid off the chair and crossed the kitchen floor. She stopped a foot in front of me, close enough to feel her body heat. Close enough to feel her breath when it caught in her throat.

I reached out and brushed my thumb beneath her bottom lip. Her skin was warm and soft.

"That drop of wine," I murmured. "I can't stop thinking about it."

She didn't move. Didn't pull back.

I leaned in and kissed her—slow and deliberate, just a brush of my tongue over the place that wine had touched.

She tasted like tangy fruit and sin and something I hadn't let myself want.

Her breath hitched. The glass tilted slightly in her hand.

"You taste like trouble," I murmured, my voice gone rough.

Selene's gaze dropped to my mouth. "And you taste like good decisions I shouldn't make."

I took the glass from her hand and set it on the counter.

Then I dipped my head. "What if I want to taste it from somewhere else?"

Her pupils dilated, black swallowing hazel. I slid my hands around her hips, guided her back until she hit the edge of the table.

She didn't stop me.

I reached for the wineglass again and held it between us. "Tell me when to stop."

She didn't say anything, but she lifted her chin.

So I tipped it—just a little—and let a slow ribbon of wine trail from the hollow of her throat down to the swell of her chest, following the dip of her dress.

Selene shivered.

I followed the path with my mouth. Her breath caught when my tongue touched her skin. The wine was cool where it had landed, but her skin burned beneath it. I followed the trail slowly, deliberately, letting my lips brush the delicate line between reverence and hunger. Her fingers curled against the edge of the table, body taut and trembling under my mouth.

I paused just below the hollow of her throat and looked up. "You good?"

She nodded—small, sharp. "Yes."

Her voice wavered like she was on the edge of something she hadn't let herself want in a very long time.

I set the wineglass down and hooked my hands behind her knees, spreading her gently apart until she was open to me, breath shallow, dress gathered around her thighs. My palms slid over her skin, slow and steady, grounding her in every place I touched. I leaned forward, mouth dragging along the inside of her thigh, tasting the heat of her and the faint hint of red wine left in the air as I dragged her panties down her thighs.

I paused to stare at her, dress gathered at her hips, pussy bare and waiting. I yanked my shirt off before settling between her legs. Selene gasped when I licked her—just once, slow and sure—and then again when I buried my face between her legs like I'd been starving and this was the only thing that could bring me back to life.

She moaned my name—quiet and choked and wrecked.

I could have lived inside that sound.

The table creaked as her back arched, her fingers tangling in my hair like she didn't know whether she wanted to pull me closer or push me away. I didn't stop. Not until her legs were shaking, her breath ragged, her thighs clamped around my shoulders.

She came with a gasp that turned into a whimper, her whole body trembling under my hands.

I kissed the inside of her knee as I let her come down. I watched her, wild and undone, and knew I was a goner.

"You make me want more," I murmured, pressing my forehead to hers.

Selene blinked at me, dazed and flushed. "More?"

I stepped back just enough to grab the wineglass again, swirled what was left, and let the last of it dribble down the center of my chest. It followed the trail of my sternum, catching on the ridges of muscle before sliding lower.

Then I unbuckled my jeans, eased them down, and let the wine continue its descent.

Selene's eyes darkened.

The red wine curved over my abs, slid along the V of my hips, and dripped down the thick length of my cock, already hard and aching for her.

I wrapped my hand around the base and offered her a crooked smile. "Are you still thirsty, Selene?"

Her eyes met mine for half a second before she slid from the table and dropped to her knees.

Her hand came first—warm and sure, fingers wrapping around me like she already knew how I liked it. Her mouth followed, slow and devastating, tongue swirling against the wine-slick skin like she wanted to memorize the taste.

I groaned, one hand braced on the table, the other sinking into her hair.

Fuuuuuck.

She hummed around me, a smug little sound that nearly buckled my knees. Her mouth was hot and wet and perfect, sliding down inch by inch like she wasn't afraid of what I'd do to her. My breath hitched as I watched the glide of her lips over the thick length of my cock, the way her hand twisted at the base, working in tandem with her mouth like she wanted to ruin me.

"Jesus, Selene." My voice cracked, hand tightening in her hair. "You were made for this, weren't you?"

She moaned in response, the sound vibrating through me. My hips jerked.

Her tongue licked the underside of my cock, tracing the vein there before she hollowed her cheeks and took me deeper. My eyes rolled back. I could feel her throat working, feel the soft constriction around the head as she fought her reflex and swallowed me.

I looked down, and fuck—her lashes were wet.

She gagged once, pulling back with a gasp and spit slicking her lips and chin. Her hand never stopped moving. Her eyes lifted to mine, glassy and wild.

"Goddamn," I groaned, chest heaving. "You look so pretty like this. Eyes watering, mouth full of me. Do you know what that does to a man?"

I couldn't stop watching. Couldn't stop touching. I

thumbed her jaw gently, then dragged my fingers into her hair again, guiding her movements with a tenderness that proved how hard I was fighting not to come.

She whimpered, and it was like she wanted to prove something—because she went back down, deeper this time, taking me to the back of her throat with determined abandon. Her nails dug into my thigh as she swallowed again, and I nearly lost it right then.

"Fuck—just like that. Take it, baby. Take every fucking inch." My hips rocked forward, slow but insistent, and she let me. She moaned around me—wrecked and eager—and the sound, the feel, the utter trust of it, cracked something deep inside me.

"Such a good girl," I growled, tightening my grip just enough to steady her. "Letting me fuck your throat like it's mine."

She sucked like she had something to prove, or like she needed to claim me with her lips and tongue.

And she did.

Because I was hers now. There was absolutely no going back.

When I couldn't take it anymore—when the sharp edge of pleasure wound too tight to bear—I pulled her up, hauled her into my arms, and kissed her like it was the only language I had left.

Her legs wrapped around my waist. Her dress bunched at her hips. I grabbed her ass and slammed her back against the edge of the table, nudging the head of my cock at her entrance.

"I want this." My eyes never left hers.

She swallowed hard and nodded. "Me too."

I reached for my jeans, tugging out the condom I kept in my wallet. It wasn't cocky—it was careful. I was aware that

Selene would be alone this weekend, and some hopeful part of me hadn't been able to function without being ready.

I worked it down the length of my shaft, and in one slow, devastating thrust, I slid inside her.

We both gasped.

Selene clutched my shoulders, breath stuttering as I filled her. My hand slid up her back, holding her close, my forehead pressed to hers.

"I've got you," I said, voice low and rough.

Then I started to move. It wasn't soft. It wasn't slow. It was everything I hadn't let myself want. Everything I'd held back from her, now unleashed like a storm I couldn't outrun.

She moaned my name like a plea.

"Tell me," I growled, fucking into her so deep she cried out. "Tell me you need it."

"Yes," she gasped. "God, Austin, yes—I need it. Please don't stop."

Her words wrecked me. I drove harder. Rougher. One hand braced on the table, the other holding the back of her neck like I couldn't stand the thought of letting her go. She took everything I gave her, body clenching around me, mouth open in surrender.

"You feel so fucking good," I rasped against her throat. "Like you were made for this. For me."

She was unraveling beneath me, her body shaking, the table groaning under our weight, until she shattered. I felt her fall apart in the way she clung to me, in the way she cried out and buried her face in my neck, in the way her body gripped mine so tight I saw stars.

I followed her over the edge a breath later, cursing against her skin, hips stuttering as I emptied inside her.

It took a full minute to breathe again.

It was hard to remember where we were—who we were—but I never let her go.

Her forehead rested against mine. Her breath fanned over my lips.

"I think," I murmured, still buried inside her, "you've officially ruined me."

Selene's eyes fluttered open, dazed and soft and a little glassy.

And then she smiled.

EIGHTEEN

SELENE

I STAYED THERE FOR A MOMENT—PERCHED on the edge of the table, legs bare and trembling, Austin's chest still pressed to mine. My fingers were in his hair, slack now, no longer clinging like they had been a minute ago. The air between us shimmered with heat, but something colder had already started to crawl beneath my skin.

He was still holding me, and I couldn't remember the last time anyone had done that without needing to be asked.

The rise and fall of his breath moved against me, steady and solid. I'd forgotten what that felt like. That slow, grounding rhythm of another person simply being there without expectation or apology.

To simply be a woman in a man's arms.

My body was sated, aching in the best way, but my thoughts—those were less cooperative. They were already spinning, pulling me under like a riptide I hadn't prepared for.

What the hell had I just done? Again.

A smile played at my lips before I could stop it. Austin's head dipped, his mouth brushing against the edge of my jaw like it was second nature. It was so gentle, so instinctive, it almost broke me.

"Are you okay?" he asked, voice low and rough, the kind of voice you didn't forget even after the sound faded.

I nodded too quickly. "I think so."

A flicker of a grin pulled at his mouth. "I can't feel my legs."

I sucked in a breath, tried to laugh, but it came out thin and strange. I shifted slightly, the cool edge of the table pressing into my thighs—a reminder that I was still half naked and very much exposed. Not just physically, but in a way that went deeper than skin. I reached down, fingers fumbling slightly as I tugged the hem of my dress back into place, smoothing the fabric over my legs.

Austin didn't look away. He didn't leer or make a joke. He just watched me—quiet, present, and reverent in a way that made my throat go tight.

The intimacy of it all settled around us, heavy and a little bit strange. It was a connectedness that didn't come from sex, but from what came after. Just a man standing in my home after wrecking me in the most beautiful way, watching me like I was something sacred.

My underwear was somewhere on the floor, I was pretty sure, but modesty wasn't the point.

I needed the barrier. Something. *Anything.*

The truth was, the more I came back to myself, the more I realized I'd done something dangerous.

I had let him in.

Not just into my bed—or onto my table—but into the space I'd been keeping locked tight since the day Brian told me I was too much and not enough all at once.

I'd let Austin see the version of me that hadn't existed in years, and it had felt good.

Too good.

He was still watching me when I slid off the table, his eyes tracking the way my dress fluttered down to cover my hips. I tried to ignore the rush of heat that followed. My body was still very aware of him, even if my brain was throwing up every red flag it could muster.

Austin pushed off the counter with a quiet exhale. "Give me one sec," he murmured, brushing a hand lightly along my arm as he passed. He grabbed his jeans and disappeared down the hall toward the bathroom. I searched the floor for my discarded underwear. I found them in a rumpled pile, slipped them back on, and smoothed my skirt down with a shaky hand.

When he returned—bare-chested but freshly zipped and a little more composed—he leaned back against the counter, arms crossed over his chest, golden in the dim light.

"Well." I ran a hand through my hair and tried to laugh again. "That escalated quickly."

"No complaints here," he said with a smile. There it was. That smirk. That *spark*. The very one I should've ignored from the beginning. Instead, it made something flutter in my chest that I didn't have a name for.

I didn't respond, and instead I moved through the kitchen like I hadn't just had my legs around a man who knew exactly how to use his mouth *and* his dick.

His head tilted, not quite facing me. "Is this the part where you kick me out?" Austin's voice was light, but his tone was laced with a subtle hurt. The question was light, almost teasing, but it landed with more weight than I expected.

I blinked. "What?"

He turned then, eyes meeting mine with a look that was

too knowing. "It's okay. You're trying to figure out how to say it without hurting my feelings."

I opened my mouth, then closed it again, because . . . damn it, he wasn't wrong.

I had been thinking it. Not because I wanted him gone, but because the longer he stayed, the harder it became to pretend this was casual. The harder it was to pretend I wasn't already craving him again—for things that had nothing to do with sex.

Maybe that was what unsettled me the most—how naturally he fit here. In my space. In this moment. Like the edges of our lives had been stitched together when I wasn't paying attention.

I watched him from the corner of the kitchen, perched against the doorway like a woman debating whether to run or stay. So I did what I always did when emotions tangled too tight to name.

I dodged.

"Thank you for dinner," I said, my voice soft. "And . . . everything."

He didn't flinch. Austin nodded with a smile and turned toward the sink. He began rinsing plates, tanned skin exposed, forearms flexing as he moved like he belonged there.

I stood and stared, completely dumbfounded as to how I'd found myself in this exact scenario.

Then he set a wineglass down and stepped in close— close enough that I caught the scent of him again, woodsmoke and warm skin and something faintly citrus.

His fingers brushed a loose strand of hair from my cheek.

"Selene," he said, just my name. No question. No plea. Just . . . me.

It landed with more intimacy than anything we'd done on that table.

He kissed my temple, featherlight, and pulled back with a crooked smile. "For the record, I'm not in a rush."

I exhaled something between a laugh and a sigh. "I'm not kicking you out."

"Good." He turned back to the sink like that settled it, like he knew he could stay, at least for a little while.

Music still played low from the speaker on the counter —something moody and folksy, with a lilting guitar that wrapped around the room like candlelight. Austin hummed along under his breath, washing the last of the dishes like this was any normal night and not the one where I'd just let him see more of me than anyone had in years.

His hand brushed my lower back as he passed behind me to grab a dish towel and let it linger longer than it needed to.

I busied myself wiping the counter, even though it didn't need it. My mind felt louder than the music. Louder than the dishes or the hum of the fridge.

It wasn't just that he stayed.

It was the *way* he stayed.

Unrushed. Unbothered. It was as if I didn't need to be entertaining or funny or accommodating. It was almost like it was enough that I was just here, in my kitchen, breathing beside him.

I swallowed hard and leaned against the edge of the counter, watching him stack the glasses to dry.

Brian used to do the dishes, too, at first. He'd tell me to go sit down, to rest. That I did too much and I'd believed him.

Until it changed.

Until I was doing too little, asking too much, being too

needy, too tired, too soft. Until the very things he'd once found endearing became evidence of my failure.

A different ache bloomed behind my ribs. I shook it off and reached for the wine, pouring the last splash into my glass.

Austin turned to say something but paused, eyes searching mine.

"You're somewhere else," he said.

I forced a smile. "Just tired."

He didn't press, and I was grateful, because the truth was tangled and complicated.

The truth was, he made me feel too safe, too solid, and that was the danger. Not because I didn't want it, but because a part of me was starting to believe he might actually be different.

That maybe I wasn't the only one here hoping this could be more than what we were pretending it was.

I looked over at him again, lit by the glow of the kitchen light, jaw shadowed with stubble, towel slung over his shoulder like he was made to be in this exact moment.

And still humming.

Heaven help me, I was starting to hope.

I expected him to make a move, maybe kiss me again or reach for more. Instead, he rinsed the last dish, shut off the tap, and turned to me with a smile that didn't ask for anything. "I think you should take a bath."

The words caught me off guard. "I—what?"

"You've got the house all to yourself." He nodded toward the hallway. "Go take a long, hot bath. Put on music. Breathe."

My instinct was to deflect—to say I didn't need that. To stay standing in this kitchen like I had something to prove, but Austin was already drying his hands. He walked past me and upstairs toward my bathroom like it was a foregone conclusion. I followed him up, and by the time I stepped in behind him, steam was curling against the mirror as the tub filled.

He reached for a bottle and held it up, his eyes flicking to mine. "Is lavender honey okay? I found it in the linen closet."

I nodded. He had found the bubble bath tucked behind the soaps I used only when I wanted to pretend I was the kind of woman who had time for long soaks and luxury.

"I knew it." He poured slowly, letting it foam and build, a little smile tugging at the corner of his mouth.

"Knew what?" I stepped closer.

His cheeks pinched. "That you're a bubble bath girl."

"I'm a haven't-had-a-minute-to-myself-in-months girl," I said dryly.

He chuckled, then straightened. I realized, too late, that he wasn't leaving.

Austin stepped close, hands finding the hem of my dress. He didn't say anything—just waited, eyes steady on mine, giving me every chance to back out.

I didn't move.

Not when his fingers slid the zipper down my side. Not when the fabric slipped over my hips and fell to the floor with a whisper.

I stood there in my bra and underwear, suddenly hyper-aware of every scar and stretch mark, every place my body no longer felt like the one I'd lived in before becoming someone's mother.

I crossed my arms over my stomach, a flicker of apology already forming on my lips.

He stopped me with a look. "Selene."

Just my name, but it settled something restless inside me.

His eyes didn't drift. They didn't assess or compare or calculate. They devoured—hungry and awed and unashamed.

"You are incredibly beautiful," he said, like it was the most obvious truth in the world. "I wish you could see what I see."

Heat bloomed under my skin. Austin stepped in closer, fingers ghosting along the straps of my bra, easing them down with a reverence that made me want to cry.

He wasn't trying to get me naked.

He was giving me back to myself.

Once I was bare, he stepped back—not to admire, but to give me space to choose.

I climbed into the bath, easing down inch by inch, my whole body sighing as the hot water wrapped around me like a second skin. The bubbles hissed as I sank up to my collarbone, letting my head tip back against the porcelain.

It felt indulgent.

It felt earned.

Austin reached for my phone from the counter. "What do you want to listen to?"

He held the phone out to me so I could unlock it.

"Dean Martin," I murmured, closing my eyes again.

He paused, then laughed under his breath. "So you did hear."

A smirk formed on my lips. "I might have."

He scrolled through something, and a moment later the opening notes of "I Don't Know Why" drifted through the steam.

I let out a long breath, feeling the music bloom around me.

He lingered near the edge of the tub, fingers drumming against the side.

"Good night, Selene," he said.

When I opened my eyes and saw him turning to go, I reached for him without thinking. "Hey . . ." I blinked, gathering my courage. "Stay." The word was quiet. Uncertain. Hopeful.

He stilled.

When he turned back around, his expression was unreadable, but his hands went to the hem of his shirt and he started to undress.

This time, I watched.

The muscles in his shoulders flexed as he tugged his shirt over his head. The hard lines of his abdomen, the trail of dark hair that disappeared beneath the waistband of his jeans. His hands were confident, unhurried, as he unbuttoned his jeans and stepped out of them.

He wasn't posing and wasn't trying to impress me, but god help me, I was thoroughly impressed. He was thick and muscular, rough around the edges in all the ways that made my skin tingle. A man who used his body. Austin was a man who didn't just take up space—he filled it.

When he stepped into the tub, the water rising around him, I found myself leaning back against his chest without even thinking.

His arms came around me, solid, warm, and steady.

I closed my eyes, letting the music, the heat, and the hum of his breath against my neck wash over me.

This wasn't sex. It wasn't even seduction.

It was something deeper.

Something that had the power to unravel me completely.

NINETEEN

AUSTIN

Golden sunlight slid in through the kitchen window, touching the lip of the coffee mug in my hand. The scent of dark roast and toast drifted through the air, soft and anchoring. I went through the motions—cracking eggs, buttering toast, flipping bacon in the pan—not because anyone expected me to, but because it felt good. Real. Grounded in something that wasn't performance or duty.

Behind me, I heard the floorboards creak—slow and soft like bare feet on old wood. I turned just enough to catch a glimpse of her.

Selene stood in the doorway, her hair still damp and pulled into a loose braid that hung over one shoulder. One of her sleeves was slipping off, exposing a patch of skin just beneath her collarbone. She wore my worn-in T-shirt—washed a hundred times—and a pair of sleep shorts that made my mouth go dry. Her eyes met mine, still heavy with sleep but softer around the edges.

We'd kept each other awake half the night, but it had been more than worth it.

"Something smells amazing," she said, voice husky from the morning and lack of sleep.

I cleared my throat and gestured toward the table. "Coffee's fresh. Sit. I've got this."

She drifted in without a word, pulled out a chair, and curled one leg beneath her as she settled in. The light caught the edge of her cheekbone, casting a soft glow across her face. I plated her food, poured a second cup of coffee, and set it down in front of her before taking the seat across the table.

For a few minutes, neither of us spoke.

We just ate and breathed. It was a silence that wasn't begging to be filled—just existing, like we'd slipped into some secret margin between real life and something slower and sweeter.

"I forgot how nice the quiet could be," Selene said eventually, slathering the edge of her toast with jelly. "No cartoons, no glitter explosions. No one asking me to watch them do a cartwheel."

"You wanna watch me do a cartwheel?" I smiled, but I saw the flicker of guilt that crossed her face. It was like a tug-of-war between needing space and missing your child before they even walked out the door.

"She'll be back tomorrow," I said gently. "You're allowed to enjoy the in-between."

Selene looked down at her plate, then back at me. "How old are you again?"

I scoffed, knowing she already knew the answer to that question and hating that she questioned our eight-year age gap. "Forty-eight," I answered with a teasing grin. "Why? Are you grossed out that I'm so old?"

She shook her head with a smile. "You're dangerously good at knowing exactly what to say."

"It's a gift," I said with a shrug.

She reached for her coffee, wrapping both hands around the mug, and I let myself imagine mornings like this as a regular thing. Not a fluke. Not a borrowed moment between what was and what could be.

Just this.

Her. Me. The low hum of something beginning.

I didn't know what to call it yet, but it felt like the start of something that mattered.

"Can I ask you something?" she finally said, looking at me over the rim of her mug with her pretty eyes narrowed into slits. The inquisition was coming, so I braced for it.

I nodded. "Always."

She tucked her tongue against her cheek, like she wasn't exactly sure how to ask whatever it was she wanted to know. "Do you ever miss it?"

I frowned slightly. "Miss what?"

She glanced out the window, squinting at the stretch of blue beyond the trees. "The fast life. Being an untethered bachelor. Meeting whoever you want."

I stared at her as she barreled on. "It's just that I don't really see you go out—on dates or otherwise. You could be doing something big, something exciting, and instead you're . . . here. Making me bacon."

There was no bite in her words. Just quiet curiosity. Maybe even a little surprise that I'd chosen to spend my time with an incredible woman like her rather than waste my nights on someone whose name I wouldn't remember in the morning. It was almost as though she couldn't quite believe someone like me had landed here, in her kitchen, without trying to run.

"At first I thought I'd hate it in Star Harbor," I admitted. "But I wanted to get to know my brother, so I stuck it out." I chuckled and dragged a hand across the back of my neck. "There's just something about this place—the people, the ghost story, they get their hooks in you and don't let go."

I let that hang in the air, unsaid things tugging into a knot in my chest.

"But here"—I reached for her hand, brushing my thumb across her knuckles—"it feels like more than just Brody tying me to Star Harbor."

Selene stared at me, her expression unreadable. Then she slowly turned her hand, palm to palm, letting our fingers slot together. A breeze moved through the screen door, lifting the hem of the dish towel hanging from the oven handle.

The whole world felt quiet at that moment.

Not empty.

Just . . . waiting.

WE ENDED up on the floor.

Not in a tangled, half-naked kind of way—but the kind that came from too many pages spread across the table and nowhere else to set them. Selene had pulled out a box of old ledgers and archival files after breakfast, mentioning the need to spend time catching up on a few restoration projects while Winnie was away.

We sat cross-legged in a patch of sun on the worn rug in her living room, knees brushing, shoulders bumping as we flipped through delicate, century-old pages and penciled notes. A playlist played softly in the background—old-school crooners again, like a private joke we were still crafting. My back was against the couch. Her foot was tucked under my thigh.

She held what looked like a diary across both knees, one hand gliding carefully along the margin of a faded page. Her fingers paused over a line written in cursive so soft it almost disappeared into the yellowing paper.

"She wrote this," Selene murmured, voice reverent. "Listen: 'The sea was calm tonight. I pressed a flower in the pages for him. I wonder if he will ever know.'"

She looked up at me, eyes wide, luminous. "Can you imagine being so full of hope it spills onto the page like that? A pressed flower? A whole ocean between you and someone you might never see again?"

I didn't have an answer.

Not one I could say without telling her that I was beginning to understand that kind of hope. That I was starting to feel it bloom, quietly, when she looked at me like this. Like maybe I was good enough to not fuck this up.

She turned the page slowly, careful not to tear the edge.

"She wrote notes all through this. Tiny details—weather, visitors, little asides about which neighbor was stealing sugar from the pantry." Selene smiled faintly.

"You really love the work you do, don't you?" I asked, studying her face as she turned another page.

Her eyes met mine. "It was a time when women kept records of things no one else thought to write down. They weren't just wives or daughters. They were historians. They mattered."

I studied the pages most people would deem trash. Selene coveted each scrap of paper like it was her duty to not allow their words to be lost in time. I couldn't recall loving anything with such delicate reverence as Selene loved old words.

Her delicate voice broke my wandering train of thought.

"You're not what I expected," she said quietly, not looking at me.

That caught me off guard. "No?"

She shook her head, still reading. "I thought maybe you were just playing house. Like this was a sabbatical or a soft landing after something harder."

I tilted my head, unsure whether to be offended or flattered. "And now?" I asked.

Selene finally glanced at me. Her expression softened. "Now I think you might be dangerous."

I leaned in slightly, amused. "Dangerous?"

"Yes." Her lips quirked. "Dangerous in a way that sneaks up on you and makes you believe in things you swore you'd outgrown."

My heart kicked once. Then again. "Things like multiple orgasms?" I prowled toward her as I teased and was rewarded with the warmth of her laughter.

Selene leaned back until I was braced above her. Her hazel eyes shone up at me as her smile widened. A low growl formed in my throat, and my cock thickened. I eased her legs apart, then pressed into her, my mouth finding the delicate curve of her neck. Her back arched and she hummed, turning her head to allow me more access to her soft skin. My tongue smoothed over her silken flesh, my body begging for more.

With her head turned, something caught her eye. Instead of reaching for me, she stretched out her arm toward the stacks of old photographs and ledgers. Her fingers gently pinched the edge of the photograph, tugging it free from beneath a brittle stack of pages. The paper made a crackling sound as it gave way—like it hadn't been touched in decades.

I pushed up on one elbow, watching her expression shift

from amusement to something else entirely. The room held a stillness that suggested the air had changed around us, even though nothing moved.

The photo was warped slightly at the corners, the finish dulled with age. Sepia tones bled into one another, edges feathered by time. It had once been carefully framed, probably, or tucked into a book for safekeeping. Now it bore the signs of being forgotten—creased lines, water-stained edges, and a faint scent of mildew that clung to the paper like a memory.

The woman in the center of the frame stood stiffly, her spine straight, hands demurely clasped at her waist. She wore a high-necked blouse with puffy sleeves, the bodice cinched tight with a row of delicate buttons. Her skirt flared slightly, structured with layers of petticoat, the hem grazing the tips of her laced boots. The entire image had an eerie, formal softness to it—like she hadn't chosen to be captured and only tolerated it out of necessity.

Selene sat up straighter. "I know this dress."

I could instantly see her brain moving, frantic and searching. Selene delicately riffled through stacks of photographs that she had yet to organize. When she found what she was looking for, she stopped and held the portraits side by side. Each had the same woman, in the same dress, with the same background but with different positions.

It wasn't just the old-fashioned clothing or the haunted look in her posture that made me sit up straighter.

It was the face in the photo.

More accurately—what was left of it.

The woman's eyes had been scratched out. Not gently faded by light, not the victim of damage over time. Purposefully gouged. Like someone had pressed a nail or blade into the glossy surface and carved her sight away.

"Jesus," I murmured, inching closer beside her.

Selene didn't say anything at first. Her thumb ghosted over the marred space where the eyes should have been. "I found this photograph in a boarding ledger a few weeks ago. I think it has a name written on the back, but it's too faded to know for sure." She gestured to both images. "It's obviously the same woman, right?"

She showed me the back, where faint pencil markings in a cursive script were barely visible. Something flickered behind Selene's own gaze—an old instinct waking up and stretching.

I nodded, equal parts intrigued and creeped the fuck out.

"She's not alone in this one," she whispered after a beat, squinting as she looked more closely at the front of the unmarked picture.

She scooted closer to me, and I followed her line of sight.

In the far-right corner of the photograph, half in shadow, stood a man. He wasn't posed. He wasn't meant to be there, from the look of it. In shadow, the man was angled toward the woman—his gaze almost tender. The way his body leaned ever so slightly toward her made it clear he was watching her, not the camera.

He was dressed in a simple shirt and vest, trousers tucked into weather-worn boots. Not upper class. A laborer, maybe. Or someone trying to look like he belonged in her world when he didn't.

Selene squinted at it. "No freaking way," she whispered, holding it up to the light. Selene's finger poked at the man's image. "Who does this look like to you?"

Holy shit.

The man in the photo looked almost exactly like Hayes

Darling. Same bone structure. Same dark hair. Same tilted, half-grumpy smirk.

I let out a slow breath. "What the hell . . ."

Selene didn't answer. She turned the photograph over with reverent fingers. The back was stained and yellowed, but in the corner, barely visible beneath a smear of time, was a name. A single word, written in a slanted, looping hand.

"Alma," she read aloud. Her voice was almost too soft to hear. "Holy shit," she whispered, "it's *her*. The Lady."

Goose bumps prickled at my arms. I gave Selene space so she could crisscross her legs. She was examining the photograph, but I was looking at her.

Really looking.

I studied the way her eyes lit up when she uncovered something that mattered. The way she got lost in the margins of other people's stories but still made room to write her own. The way she gave herself so completely to the people she loved, even when it broke her a little.

It wasn't just Winnie's laughter or her smiles or her cinnamon muffins.

I wanted Selene.

All of her.

Not just in the flash-fire moments of stolen kisses or tangled sheets—but in the quiet ones. The ordinary seconds that strung together and became something worth holding on to.

Selene tucked the photo gently into the fold of her journal, slipping it between two blank pages like it had been waiting for a new story to live inside. I'd spent the majority of my adulthood enjoying the blank pages of my life, never worrying about what would come next and if it even mattered. Suddenly I found myself sitting on the floor of her living room wanting nothing more than for the woman next to me to see I was more than a stand-in until something real came along.

I was as real as those people in that long-forgotten photograph.

I wanted to crack a joke or think of *anything* to make the lump that expanded in my throat go away.

"You okay?" she asked, catching me staring.

I nodded slowly, unsure how to answer without telling her everything. That this mattered. That she mattered more than she knew.

You make me want more.

I almost said it out loud, but I didn't.

Instead, I reached for her hand and let our fingers thread together again, warm and steady in the sun.

TWENTY

SELENE

The afternoon light slanted across the floor, soft as a sigh, turning the worn oak boards golden beneath our bare feet. Everything felt a little hushed, peaceful in a way that I used to misname as loneliness.

Austin hadn't seemed to mind when I got lost in the restoration work. He flowed in and out, doing his own thing without making me feel as though I had to entertain or appease him. When he'd returned with a gentle knock, I couldn't help but smile.

He moved easily through my space—tidying throw blankets, stacking books, helping me draw the curtains against the bright midday glare. He didn't ask what needed doing. Somehow, he just knew. It seemed as though he slipped seamlessly into the quiet rhythm of my day like he'd always been part of it.

I watched him from across the living room as he reached for the last window. His muscular arm lifted, fingers pinching the edge of the linen panel, and in the angled glow of the early-afternoon sun, I caught something in his expression.

A flicker. Brief but unguarded. For a moment he looked almost confused.

It was the kind of look that passed through someone when they realized they'd been let in without quite knowing how it happened.

He pulled the curtain closed, his broad shoulders silhouetted for just a breath before the room settled into a warmer shade of shadow. I stood still, one hand resting against the worn wood of the doorway, something catching low in my chest.

This was the part that sneaked up on you—not the kisses or the incredible sex. It was the way someone turns off your kitchen light like it was theirs too.

"You keep this up and I'm going to have to start paying you," I said, reaching for levity as I stepped closer. "You've got live-in-nanny potential. Ten out of ten."

Austin looked over his shoulder, one eyebrow raised, lips twitching into a smirk. "As long as it comes with room, board, and occasional sex, I'm in."

I rolled my eyes, but my smile gave me away. "You have no shame."

"Not when it comes to you," he said without missing a beat, and damn it—my knees didn't stand a chance.

He crossed to me, fingers brushing mine as he took the empty glass from my hand and set it on the coffee table. His body was warm and familiar somehow, the scent of his cologne and cedar soap woven into the fabric of the afternoon. Being near him felt like something I didn't want to name for fear it might vanish.

Austin's fingers drummed a lazy rhythm. "Are you hungry?"

I blinked. "I mean, I could eat. Why?"

A sly half smile lifted one side of his mouth. "Because

I'm starving, and if I stay here much longer, I'm going to eat whatever weird cheese you've got aging in that fridge."

I snorted. "It's not weird. It's imported."

His face twisted in disgust. "It's moldy and suspicious."

I rolled my eyes. "Fine. Let's go get something, but I'm not changing."

His gaze swept over me slowly, taking in my faded jeans and soft, loose sweater like I was wrapped in silk. "You're perfect."

Heat licked up my neck. "Where did you have in mind?"

"There's that little place on the corner. The one with the red vinyl booths and the pancakes as big as your head?"

"Trudy's?" I asked.

He snapped his fingers. "That's the one. But I need to stop by my place first—wallet, hoodie, maybe shoes . . ." He looked down at his socked feet, one brow raised. "Unless we're going for full domestic bliss and you want to hold hands while wearing house slippers."

The words *domestic bliss* clanged against something inside me, but I shoved it aside. "Grab your stuff. I'll lock up."

We walked the short distance to his apartment side by side, the wind tugging strands of hair from my ponytail and making the hem of my sweater flap against my thighs. It wasn't cold yet, not really, but the air had that soft bite that hinted at what was coming.

He reached his door first and held it open with a little bow. "Welcome to my humble . . . rental."

The space was not exactly what I expected.

There wasn't clutter, but it felt temporary, like someone who hadn't fully unpacked. The couch was clean but threadbare, a mismatched blanket draped across the back like it had been stolen from an old camp trunk. His familiar pair of worn boots sat beside the door. The coffee table was stacked with a few books, a sports magazine, a half-finished water bottle, and a single photo in a basic black frame.

I paused.

In it, two boys grinned at the camera—one older, arms thrown around the shoulders of a younger kid with sun-bleached hair and a stubborn chin.

Brody and Austin.

I moved closer, studying the way the boys leaned into each other, full of that unspoken trust that lives between kids before the world gets too loud.

Austin returned from upstairs, now wearing a faded gray hoodie and jeans that hung low on his hips. He saw where my gaze had landed and paused, something flickering behind his eyes—quick, unreadable.

"That was the only summer we got to spend together," he said, his voice quieter. "Before the moms put an end to it."

I knew a little bit about Clint Sheperd's history. He was a well-respected officer who had cheated on his wife, Terri, and gotten the other woman pregnant—with Austin, presumably. It made my heart hurt to think of their cute little kid faces and how they were allowed only a single summer together. It was a time before adolescence and adult drama sank its claws in.

I offered a soft smile. "You kept it."

His shrug was casual, but the muscles in his jaw tightened just enough for me to notice. "It's the only picture I had of us. Figured it deserved a frame."

I didn't ask why it was the only one. I didn't have to. Some wounds don't bleed—they calcify.

I stepped forward and brushed my hand lightly across his as he passed.

Austin looked at the spot on his hand where I'd touched him, but changed the subject. "You ready? I found out the hard way that Trudy's closes early if they're short on staff."

"Let's go," I said, letting him nudge us past the moment, but I stored the flicker of pain away.

The walk into town was quiet at first, but not uncomfortable. Our strides synced without even trying. His shoulder bumped mine once, and neither of us moved away.

It felt like something new—like playing house, but outside the house.

We passed the bookstore, the fire station, and a chalkboard sign outside the coffee shop that read PUMPKIN EVERYTHING. People waved and I waved back. A few glanced curiously between us.

By the time Trudy's came into view, I felt that low-level flutter kick up in my stomach—the one that came not from being with him, but from being *seen* with him. Typically I had Winnie's presence to answer any questioning looks, but now I had to field them alone.

Austin pushed the door open and let me step in first. Warm air and the smell of hamburger patties greeted us like an old friend. The bell above the door jingled.

"Selene, hey!" Trudy's daughter, Marnie, chirped from behind the counter, her apron slightly askew, lipstick smudged like she'd just taken a bite of something buttery. "Is Winnie with you?"

"No, she's with her dad this weekend," I said, sliding into a booth along the window.

Marnie's eyes flicked to Austin as he followed me, settling in across from me with that easy grin of his. "Is Brody joining you?" She set down a third plastic menu.

"No, he . . . um . . ." My eyes pleaded with Austin, unsure of what to say.

"Oh . . . I thought maybe—never mind," Marnie said with a laugh and swat of her hand.

Austin chuckled. "It's just us today."

"I mean—great." She flushed. "That's fun."

"Thank you," he said, smoothly enough to leave it ambiguous. His gaze flicked to mine, unreadable.

Marnie seemed to recalibrate. "Well. Anyway, what can I get you two?"

We ordered—a patty melt for him, a double cheeseburger for me, Diet Coke all around—and once she was gone, I leaned back, feeling something unfamiliar twist behind my ribs.

"Are you okay?" he asked, watching me carefully.

"She thought you were here with Brody," I said with a crinkle in my nose.

"I got that." Austin leaned back in the booth like he was comfortable simply existing in his own skin.

"I didn't know how to explain—" My hand flicked across the table between us. "This."

He picked up his fork and traced a lazy circle on the table. "Would an explanation have made a difference?"

I opened my mouth, then immediately closed it. I didn't have an answer that didn't feel heavier than I wanted it to be.

Marnie returned with our drinks, and Austin thanked her, flashing that smile that could disarm just about anyone. She flushed again, and her appreciative eyes lingered a moment too long before she walked away.

Something pricked across my scalp.

The reality was that Marnie herself was closer in age to Austin than I was. It felt almost absurd to think anyone would assume he and I were anything other than a frazzled single mom and her devastatingly handsome nanny. It would be far more believable if it were Marnie sitting across the booth from him . . .

Jealousy. Real, bone-deep, breath-catching jealousy bloomed under my skin.

What the hell is that about?

He didn't notice. Or maybe he did and chose not to call it out. Either way, I didn't like how exposed I suddenly felt. I clasped my hands in my lap to get myself under control.

"Do you ever think about staying here longer than just a rental?" I asked, a little sharper than I meant to.

"Star Harbor wasn't exactly part of the five-year plan." Austin's head tilted as he shrugged. "But, like I said, it's growing on me."

"What is?" I asked. "The plan?"

He looked down at his drink. "I think I'm still figuring that out."

I hummed as Marnie silently dropped off the food. "And Brody?"

His smile faded just a bit. "That's a little different. He's my brother, but . . ."

"But?" I prodded.

"But . . . it's kind of complicated." He met my eyes then, and the flirty veneer slipped. "I'm not exactly what his mom would've chosen for a sibling. I think he's still trying to figure out what that means and where I fit in his life."

I didn't press, though I desperately wanted to pry. Instead, I swiped a fry through ketchup and popped it into my mouth.

"You've got good instincts," I said quietly. "You'll figure it out."

He smiled, but it didn't quite reach his eyes. Then he

licked his lower lip, letting his gaze drag up my front. "I've got good taste."

My heart did a slow, treacherous roll.

We finished the meal with lighter talk—music, food, the fact that I devoured my double cheeseburger with impressive speed. He paid without asking, tipping generously, and when we stepped out into the cool afternoon air, his hand found mine.

Not all the way. Just his pinkie brushing mine. I let my fingers drift toward his until they linked.

We didn't speak on the walk back. Not about what we were. Not about what it meant that we hadn't corrected anyone when they smiled in our direction and nodded greetings as they noticed our clasped hands. That we hadn't defined anything at all.

But I felt it.

The shift.

Whatever had been brewing between us was no longer contained by four walls and a cup of morning coffee.

This was the part where pretend started to fray . . . and I wasn't sure I ever wanted to stitch it back together.

TWENTY-ONE

SELENE

By the time we got back, the sun had dipped low enough that the living room glowed with that soft late-afternoon light—the kind that made everything feel a little slower, a little more golden around the edges. I dropped my keys in the bowl by the door and slipped off my shoes, trying to ignore how comfortable it all felt.

Austin followed behind me, pausing just inside the entryway. I could feel his gaze on my back before I turned. His hoodie was pushed up to his elbows, the worn fabric soft around his forearms, and his hair had gone tousled from the wind. He looked like he belonged here, and that was the part that kept knocking me off balance.

It wasn't just that he was hot, or funny, or that we'd slept together again. It was that I liked him here. I liked the way he moved through the house like it was familiar now. Like the space bent around him instead of the other way around.

I busied myself putting the kettle on, more for something to do than out of need. He stepped into the kitchen behind me and leaned a hip against the counter, watching me with that crooked smile that always made my stomach dip.

"I thought you had things to do today," I said, softer this time, more question than tease. "An actual life to get back to."

Austin shrugged. "I ran a couple errands this morning while you worked. But afterward?" His voice dropped an octave. "I guess I just didn't feel like being anywhere else."

He said it so simply. No grand gesture. No practiced charm. Just truth, plain and unvarnished.

"You spent the majority of a Saturday with me," I murmured, more to myself than to him. "That's commitment."

"You fed me. Let me touch your boobs. Let me help sort through haunted artifacts." His grin was wide. "It was basically a dream date."

I barked a laugh and swatted him, but the warmth he stirred didn't fade. If anything, it made my chest go gooey.

He was younger than me—eight years, to be exact—and in most ways, I felt it. He moved with a kind of unbothered energy that hadn't belonged to me in a long time. At least, not since Winnie was born. Not since the person I used to be slipped into the background beneath sticky fingers and grocery lists and late-night fevers.

But Austin made me feel something I hadn't expected.

Alive.

It was there in the way he teased me. In the way he noticed when I was tired and handed me tea without a word. In the way he looked at me like I wasn't just surviving womanhood and motherhood and personhood—I was still desirable, still *fun*. His eyes settled on me like I was still capable of being more than someone's caretaker.

Maybe that was what they meant by *spring awakening*.

Ironic I seemed to be feeling it as autumn wrapped its cool arms around us.

Austin turned toward me then, eyes catching mine in the dim glow from the stove light, his hand brushing my waist as he passed by—an absent touch that still felt deliberate.

His touch was possessive, like I belonged to him in ways neither of us had put into words yet. Desire danced across my skin.

He moved past me again, flipping off the last light in the living room. The house settled into a hush, and the quiet stretched between us—not empty, but full. Full of everything we weren't saying.

I stood still, heart beginning to thrum low and steady, as he came to stand behind me. His hand slid around my waist, warm and steady, pulling me back into his chest. I could feel the beat of his heart where it pressed against my spine.

"You ever think," he murmured, his mouth brushing the shell of my ear, "that maybe I like playing house with you?"

A shiver rolled down my spine.

His fingers drifted up, slow and reverent, grazing the underside of my breast through the soft cotton of my shirt. I let out a shaky breath.

"Because I do," he said, voice low. "I fucking love it." His mouth brushed against the thin skin of my neck.

I turned in his arms, my palms settling against his chest. That same cedar-and-skin scent I was starting to crave. "Austin . . ."

I didn't have a follow-up. Not really. Just his name, just the ache of it.

He leaned down, capturing my mouth in a kiss that started soft—tender enough to undo me. Then his hands slid beneath my shirt and everything shifted.

I didn't remember walking to the bedroom. I soaked up the feel of his mouth trailing heat down my throat, the way his body guided mine through the door, how my shirt disappeared without me noticing. I was vaguely aware of the way the last streak of light faded from the room behind us. It felt like everything we'd held back until now was crumbling between our bodies.

He laid me back against the sheets like he was offering up a prayer, his hands reverent against my skin.

I arched into him, thighs parting instinctively as he pressed his mouth to the space below my ribs.

"You are so fucking beautiful," he murmured, kissing the line of my stomach. "Every inch of you."

My body tensed, shame rising before I could stop it— automatic, conditioned. The soft places I usually covered. The faint stretch marks, the lines, the reality of motherhood etched across my skin.

He must've felt the shift, because he stilled and looked up at me.

"Don't do that," he said, gently caressing my skin with his mouth. "Don't hide from me."

"I'm not," I whispered, though it wasn't fully true.

Austin came up beside me, sliding his palm along my jaw until I was forced to look at him. His gaze held mine like a vow.

"Your body created a life. It's carried weight no one sees . . . and it turns me the fuck on, Selene. Every time I look at you, I want to drop to my knees."

Heat flooded me—too much and not enough. My thighs pressed together to ease the ache.

With one hand pressed to my throat, he kissed me again, slower this time, deeper. His hand skimmed down my side, finding the edge of my panties. When he peeled them away, I heard the sound of his breath hitch.

"You're soaked," he rasped, spreading me open with his fingers.

My legs opened wider on instinct.

He didn't rush. His fingertips stroked over me with maddening patience, circling, dipping, teasing—his mouth never far from mine, as if he didn't want to miss a single reaction. I moaned into his mouth as he slid two fingers inside, curling just right. My hips rocked against his palm, begging for more.

"You're fucking perfect," he said, kissing along my jaw, licking into the corner of my mouth like he owned it. "Let me take my time."

I nodded. Or maybe I whimpered. I wasn't sure. Everything was blurring at the edges.

His mouth moved across my breasts and rib cage. Lower again, this time across my hip bones until he settled between my thighs. He licked me like he meant it, like he was memorizing me from the inside out. My hands threaded through his hair and I swore, breath catching hard as he sucked my clit between his lips, then eased two fingers back inside me, working in slow tandem until my orgasm broke open like a storm.

When I came, he didn't stop. He groaned into my skin like my pleasure did something to him—like it wrecked him. He slid up my body, kissed me long and deep, and murmured, "I'm not done with you."

Austin reached for his jeans, but I gripped his forearm. Our eyes locked.

"I want to feel you . . . bare." A blush heated my cheeks.

Desire stormed in his green eyes. His jaw ticced as his body coiled. "I'm clean. I trust you. You can trust me."

I nodded, my body humming with anticipation. "Same."

We hurried to strip off our remaining clothes. Austin sat back on his heels, my legs spread open before him. He fingered me, spreading my desire and coating me in wetness. My eyes flashed to his when he sucked his own fingers, tasting me before positioning his cock at my entrance. My hips jerked upward, silently begging him to fill me.

When he finally sank into me, it was so slow it felt like my whole body was being remapped. Bracing himself above me Austin rocked into me with purpose—teasing, relentless, just the right pressure as his hand slid down to where we were joined.

"Austin," I gasped, already spiraling again.

"I know, baby." His voice was thick with want. "I got you."

He kissed the side of my throat as he fucked me through the edge of another climax, and this time when I came, it hit harder. My legs shook. My body clenched around him, and he growled—one hand bracing against the headboard as he thrust deeper, faster. The other rolled my nipple through his fingers, intensifying my pleasure.

Then his fingers brushed lower. Just a brush of his fingertip across my ass, tentative, asking.

My eyes flew open.

He stilled. "Too much?"

I shook my head, the word already on my lips. "No. Don't stop. I want more."

The pressure returned, slow and sinful. Austin guided his cock while his fingers teased me—circling, pressing, retreating—until my whole body trembled with need. My breath hitched at the unfamiliar sensation. It was a new, forbidden feeling. Intimate in a way I hadn't expected.

"I won't hurt you," he whispered, voice gritty. "I only want you to feel good."

And I did. *Fuck*, I did. Every cell in my body felt lit from within. My head dropped back as my body coiled, begging for more, wrung out of me by his name.

As his fingers caressed my delicate skin, my body relaxed, opening to him. "I've . . ." My voice was hoarse. "I've never done this."

He was steady and sure. "We'll only go as far as you're comfortable. I promise."

My bones were liquid. "More," I begged.

Then Austin slowed, his mouth brushing against my shoulder. "Do you have . . . ?" he asked, the unspoken part trailing between us like smoke. His voice was low. Careful. Not shy, just respectful.

Heat bloomed in my cheeks, but I didn't look away. I nodded toward the nightstand beside the bed. "Top drawer."

His eyes held mine as he reached for it, the quiet click of wood and metal sounding louder than it should have in the hush between us. He opened the drawer and found the small bottle of lube without comment, flipping the cap with one hand. I watched as he coated his fingers—slow, unhurried—the slick sound impossibly erotic.

His gaze never left mine.

"You still good?" he asked, voice low, thick with restraint.

I nodded, my lips parted, breath shallow. "Yes. Just . . . go slow."

"Always," he said like a vow.

He shifted as I spread my legs in front of him, one hand on my hip, the other trailing lower again. This time, the touch was slick, warm. He massaged gently, coaxing, not forcing—circling until my breath hitched and my spine arched of its own accord.

My nerves fluttered, but the ache between my legs was worse. He hadn't even filled me yet, and already I was clenching around nothing.

"That's it, sweetheart," he murmured, kissing the back of my shoulder. "You're doing so well for me."

I let out a shaky breath. "Austin . . ."

"I've got you." He was confident and steady—exactly what I needed when I felt like I was floating away.

One slick finger breached me slowly, the stretch unfamiliar but not painful. I gasped, surprised by how much I liked it—how intimate it felt, how raw.

He kept his movements shallow, gentle, his other hand stroking up my thigh in soothing patterns. Then he added more lube, more pressure. A second finger.

My breath caught and he stilled. "You okay?"

I swallowed, then nodded. "Yes. It's different, but . . . good."

His voice was like velvet against my skin. "You're so fucking sexy like this. Open. Trusting. Letting me touch you like this."

The words sent a pulse straight through me. My body ached for more—for him. My fingers reached for my clit, needing something. An idea popped into my head and I reached back, fumbling around the bedside table until I found my toy. I pulled it out, clutching it against my chest as I looked up at him.

His eyes were dark with need, but he waited for me to show him what I wanted. I turned it on, the small vibrator buzzing low, and pressed it against my clit as he continued to massage my ass.

"Austin . . . I want you." My entire body was on fire.

"Are you sure?" He paused, breath hard against my neck. "I'm happy to fill your tight little cunt if this is too much for you."

A groan of pleasure escaped me at his filthy words. "Yes," I whispered, not even recognizing the sound of my own voice. "I'm sure. I want all of you."

He moved slowly, carefully. I felt the blunt head of his cock nudge against me, his hands spreading me wider, holding my hips steady. I gripped the sheets, nerves tangled with need.

He pressed forward, stopping the moment my breath hitched, letting me adjust to his size.

The stretch burned—then melted into something deeper. My body trembled, half in shock, half in wonder.

"Talk to me," he said, voice hoarse, barely holding it together. "Tell me what you need."

"I'm okay," I whispered, heart pounding. "Keep going."

He eased in another inch, groaning through clenched teeth. "Fuck, Selene . . . you feel incredible. I want to fill you with my cum."

"Yes." My moan was barely coherent.

Once he was fully seated, he stayed still—stroking my sides, kissing any part of me he could reach, murmuring praises against my skin until the tension in my limbs gave way to pleasure.

He began to move, shallow at first, building in slow, deliberate thrusts. His grip tightened on my hips, angling me just right, until the sensation sharpened—rushed—everything low and tight and dizzying.

I cried out, half shocked by the pleasure ripping through me. He reached between my legs, taking the vibrator and making sure it stayed against me, buzzing my clit and stroking in time with his thrusts.

It didn't take long.

I shattered with his name on my lips, the climax blinding, drawn out by every inch of him still rocking into me with care and control.

"Fuck," he growled, his rhythm stuttering. "You're gonna kill me."

When he came, it was with a rough sound in my ear, holding me like he never wanted to let go.

We didn't speak at first. Just breathed, still tangled, slick and shivering in the aftershock. My body felt wrung out, boneless and raw in the best way. Austin stayed inside me, one hand gripping the flesh at my hip and the other splayed wide over my ribs like he needed to hold me together.

Eventually, he pulled out and inched back on the mattress. I winced at the sensitivity, but then he was soothing me with his mouth, pressing slow kisses along my rib cage as if he could seal every exposed nerve with warmth.

I turned my attention to him, and he was already watching me—eyes heavy lidded, hair wild, that same reverent look softening every hard edge of his face.

He smirked slightly, licking his lips. "Next time you let me take your ass," he murmured, lazy and low. "We'll fill that tight little cunt with your vibrator and see how you like it."

My breath caught. Heat flashed through me so fast I had to close my eyes. "Jesus, Austin."

He chuckled, slow and smug, his hand sliding down to squeeze my hip. "That's not a no."

It wasn't. Not even close.

What scared me wasn't how good he made me feel—it was how he completely rewrote the limits I thought I had. Somehow, with Austin, everything became a question I wanted to say yes to. He didn't push. He didn't demand. He offered and trusted me to answer.

And the trust—that was the part that undid me.

Later, after we showered, I curled into his chest, legs tangled beneath the sheets. He kissed my temple, murmured something low and unintelligible into my hair.

I drifted in and out of sleep, fingers trailing the lines of his arm, and somewhere in the back of my mind, I knew I was in trouble.

Because this wasn't just sex.

He was more than a man in my bed. It was trust. It was joy. It was someone knowing every inch of you and still reaching for more. He was the warmth sneaking into all the places I swore I'd hardened.

TWENTY-TWO

AUSTIN

THE SUNDAY-MORNING LIGHT poured through Selene's kitchen window, catching the edge of her smile as she handed me a mug of coffee. Her hair was a clump of wild waves, her bare feet silent on the old wood floors, and the hem of my T-shirt flirted with the tops of her thighs like it had secrets it was too shy to share.

I was warm. In my bones. In my chest. In the quiet, satisfied ache still lingering after what we'd done in her bed. She had been draped across me only a few hours ago, moaning my name like a secret she didn't mean to spill. It had been the kind of sex that stripped you bare—not just skin, but soul. Her body had taken everything I gave her, and then reached for more, like she didn't know how to stop.

Fuck, I couldn't stop either.

It hadn't just been good—it had been *real*. Messy and consuming and honest in a way I hadn't felt in . . . well, *ever*. I'd been high on her ever since. Maybe that was why the air felt sweeter, the coffee tasted better, and the light slanting across the floor looked like something out of a dream.

I leaned against the counter, sipping slowly, watching

her move around like she wasn't already taking up permanent residence under my skin. Everything felt soft. Easy.

I would have been happy to stay tucked into this lazy kind of rhythm all morning, the kind where time blurred and nothing needed to be decided right away. I was still barefoot, shirtless, wearing the same worn sweatpants I'd pulled on after our second round in her bed.

It was perfect.

I was about to ask her if she wanted lunch—or if she'd prefer a repeat performance upstairs—when a knock cracked through the quiet.

We both froze.

Her brows pinched. "That's odd . . ."

I shrugged. "Maybe one of your sisters?"

Her smile flickered. "They don't patiently wait outside."

My shoulders straightened instinctively. "You want me to get it?"

She hesitated, then nodded as her gaze landed on the front door. "Yeah. Okay."

I padded to the door and pulled it open—only to come face-to-face with Brian.

He looked like he'd just rolled out of bed and hadn't enjoyed it. His hair was a mess, his shirt wrinkled and untucked, and he was holding Winnie, who was clinging to his shoulder, flushed and sniffling with her face pressed against his neck.

Brian's gaze flicked over my bare chest with a flash of surprise.

"Hope I'm not interrupting anything," he said, his tone laced with embarrassment. "Winnie's not feeling great. Said she wanted her mom."

Brian looked wrecked. His jaw was tight, his gaze impatient as it flicked past me.

I had barely processed the words before Selene was beside me, reaching for her daughter with the kind of calm urgency I'd only ever seen in mothers. Her voice dropped an octave—low, soothing, steady—as she ran a hand over Winnie's hair and felt her forehead.

Selene nuzzled Winnie without hesitation. "Oh, sweet girl," she murmured, rocking her side to side. Winnie folded into her like a sigh, still sniffly, still fussy—but quieter now. "You're burning up."

Winnie's arms wound tighter around Selene's neck, her little fingers clutching like she was trying to anchor herself. The sight punched the breath out of me.

Selene's whole body had shifted. It was like watching someone switch dimensions. She was still the woman I'd had my hands all over this morning, but now? She was a mother, full and entire. Protective. Soft. Unshakable.

Something in my chest cracked open.

Brian's gaze shifted to me, and heat flashed in his eyes. Not a smile—more like a knowing smirk. His eyes dragged over me—bare chest, sweatpants, clearly not a neighbor stopping by for sugar.

The cat is definitely out of the bag.

"You're always so good with her. I knew no one would make her feel as good as Mom," he said with genuine affection woven into his words.

Selene offered him a tight smile and nod as she swayed with Winnie in her arms.

"Should I stay? We can take care of her together." Brian's hand landed on Selene's shoulder.

I watched him touch her, blood tightening in my temples. White-hot jealousy ripped through me.

Asshole.

Selene swallowed hard, but she said nothing in response. She simply adjusted Winnie on her hip and whispered something into her hair before easing away from Brian's touch. "No, thanks. She probably just needs a little Tylenol and some rest. I've got it."

I stood there, useless. My coffee cooling in the kitchen. My head spinning.

Brian lingered on the porch, clearly not wanting to leave, but he eventually relented. I tracked him as he moved down the porch steps and disappeared behind the wheel of his car.

Selene carried Winnie inside but didn't look at me right away. She was too busy shushing Winnie, too busy smoothing back her hair and guiding her to the couch. But when she did glance over, something in her expression had changed.

Our bubble had burst.

I wasn't her maybe-lover standing barefoot in her kitchen anymore. I was a bystander in the middle of her real life. Selene was already on the couch, cradling Winnie close, murmuring nonsense into her hair. She looked up at me once, eyes a little apologetic.

"Do you want me to stay?" I asked quietly, rubbing the back of my neck.

Selene looked up, eyes soft but distracted. "No, it's okay. I've got it."

She smiled—polite and grateful, but distant. It was not the smile I'd kissed this morning. Not the one that had broken me open an hour ago while she'd moaned my name into the pillows.

Was she embarrassed that Brian had caught us together?

He had known a part of Selene I would never be privy

to. Having a child together created an unbreakable bond, and I couldn't help but feel like the scum of the earth for wishing it weren't him that had that piece of her.

"I'll call you later," she added, her voice light but unreadable.

I nodded, even though I wanted to ask for more. Even though I hated leaving when she might need some help.

"Yeah," I said, forcing a smile. "Okay."

She nodded again. Her focus was already on the girl curled in her arms, her whole world shrunk to a sick child and the instinct to comfort.

I grabbed my sweatshirt and headed for the door. As I stepped out into the late-morning sun, I tried to shake the weight in my chest. I let myself out, the door clicking behind me, and crossed back to my side of the duplex with the oddest sensation in my chest.

Like I'd just stepped out of something warm and gone barefoot into snow.

THE MUFFLED sound reached me before the sun did. A soft thump. Then a hiccuping cough. Something wet. The strange noises filtered through the thin walls and were followed by Selene's voice—low and cracked and not quite right.

I sat up slowly, my hand braced against the bed, listening harder. Another sound. Not quite crying, but not *nothing* either.

I rubbed a hand over my face. It was the middle of the night—maybe three?—but this was usually the day I crossed the porch to help with breakfast or get Winnie dressed. Seeing Brian and Selene on the doorstep yesterday had sent me into an oddly jealous tailspin. I hadn't stopped thinking about either of them.

Not for a second.

I pulled on a shirt and headed downstairs. I crossed the porch steps and knocked, but there was no answer. After a beat, I used my key and pushed the door open gently.

"Selene?" I called, soft and low.

No answer.

Then—

"Oh, honey—no, no, no—wait—" I could hear Selene's voice from upstairs, sharper now. Panicked.

Something splattered, and when a barely audible whimper floated down the stairs, that was enough for me.

I took the stairs toward Selene's bedroom two at a time. I found my girls in a tangle on the floor of the primary bathroom—Selene crouched on the tile, cradling Winnie, who looked utterly miserable. Her dark waves were sweaty and stuck to her forehead, her face flushed, and her little hands clung to her mom's shirt like she was trying not to fall apart.

There was vomit. Not crime scene worthy, but enough to ruin a morning.

Selene was still in the same cotton shirt from yesterday —my shirt, technically. Her hair was messy, pulled half up in a clip that was losing the fight. She looked pale. Exhausted. Her knees were buckled like she might collapse.

"Hey," I said, moving toward them. "Let me help."

Selene looked up at me, startled. "I—I've got her. I just need a—"

"Selene." I crouched beside her and gently slid Winnie into my arms before she could argue. "You look like you're about to pass out."

"I'm fine," she lied unconvincingly, blinking too slowly.

Winnie pressed her overheated cheek against my chest.

She didn't even protest the transfer, which told me exactly how bad she felt.

"This is nothing," I said, giving her a small smile as I stood with Winnie. "I've seen worse. Locker rooms. College road trips. One time at the gym, a guy puked on my shoes mid–dead lift."

Selene made a weak noise that might've been a laugh—or a sob. I couldn't quite tell.

"Sit down," I told her. "You're running on fumes."

"I'll clean it—"

"I said sit." My voice was still soft, but firmer now. "You did the night shift. I've got this."

She swayed a little on her feet, then finally nodded, sinking back to her knees in front of the toilet.

I carried Winnie across the bathroom, cradling her against me as I ran cool water into the sink and grabbed a clean washcloth. She didn't say much, just clung tighter when I set her down on the countertop to rinse her off.

"You're okay, bug," I murmured, swiping the damp towel across her sticky cheeks. "You've got two grown adults who are absolute messes and still somehow trying to keep you alive. That's gotta count for something."

Winnie sniffled. "My tummy hurts."

"Yeah. I know." I patted her shoulder, feeling helpless. "Mine would too after chicken nuggets and four bites of a crayon yesterday."

She gave a faint giggle. At least the kid still had her sense of humor.

Once she was clean and wrapped in a fresh towel burrito, I walked her into Selene's bedroom and placed her on one side, tucking her into the plush comforter with a small trash can beside her, just in case.

Then I headed back into the bathroom to find Selene,

arm draped on the toilet seat, the other arm draped across her stomach. She was breathing slowly. Too slowly.

"Hey," I said gently, brushing the backs of my fingers against her neck. She was burning up. "Selene."

"Hey." Her eyes opened, heavy lidded and glazed. "I think I'm gonna—"

She didn't finish the sentence before bolting straight up.

Winnie whimpered and called for her mom, but I reassured her. "Mom's okay," I said, even as I heard the unmistakable sound of Selene losing her last meal. "Just a stomach bug, Win. It's nothing but a silly bug."

I worked quickly at the bathroom sink, running a clean washcloth under cool water. Selene was slumped beside the toilet, her knees tucked beneath her, one hand braced against the wall.

She looked absolutely miserable, and when she was wrung out, Selene rested her forehead on her arm.

"Hey there," I said, kneeling down beside her, flushing the toilet. "I told you. You need to lie down too."

"I'm not—" Her voice broke as she reached for the cold towel I handed her. "Ugh. I'm not usually like this."

"I know." I rubbed her back in slow, easy circles. "You're usually bossy as hell and a little scary before coffee."

She gave me a weak smile.

"Come on." I helped her to her feet, careful and slow. "Let me take care of you for a change."

She didn't argue that time. I lifted Selene in my arms and enjoyed the brief moment she sagged against my chest.

I tucked her in beside Winnie, both pale and drowsy, curled under the same soft blanket. I sat for a minute on the edge of the bed, just watching them breathe, unsure of what I should do next.

I'd never had to worry about taking care of anyone but myself, but I'd seen enough movies to know the basics.

I found a thermometer and checked both of their temps, confirming that whatever bug Winnie had come home with had been successfully passed to Selene. I grabbed the ginger ale from the pantry and dug around until I found some goldfish crackers and saltines. When they both drifted off again, I padded into the bathroom, rolled up my sleeves, and started cleaning.

I wiped down the counters and floor, then switched over the laundry. I rinsed out the towels and took the trash out before bleaching the toilet for good measure.

I called the school to let them know Winnie would be out for at least a day, then phoned in sick to work around nine. I didn't even hesitate—they needed me more, and the crew would be fine without me for a day or two.

And the weirdest thing? I liked it.

I'd never been the guy someone trusted with this kind of thing. I was the "fun one," the "casual one," the guy who always showed up with snacks and tequila but not the one who stayed to clean up the mess.

Playing house was never part of the plan. It wasn't sexy. It certainly wasn't smooth. It sure as hell wasn't easy, but it still felt like the best damn thing I'd ever done.

TWENTY-THREE

SELENE

The air smelled like cut grass and concession stand popcorn, sweet and faintly greasy, carried on a breeze that tugged at the loose strands of my hair. It had been three days since the stomach bug had swept through our side of the duplex like a wrecking ball—three long days of ginger ale, saltines, and an attempt to regain some semblance of normalcy. Winnie was back at school, chipper and loud as ever, while I was just starting to feel human again.

I tugged my cardigan tighter around my shoulders, not because it was too cold—Star Harbor's October sun was still warm enough—but because it felt like something to hold on to.

Winnie's laughter pealed across the playground toward the softball field, high and bright, as she and two classmates took turns chasing each other. She was flushed, her unruly waves bouncing as she darted away from the little boy trying to tag her, her shoes kicking up small clouds of dust.

I couldn't help smiling.

Beside me, Elodie and Kit occupied the other two folding chairs, their drinks balanced precariously on the metal armrests. Elodie had a notebook open on her lap, a pencil twirling between her fingers as she sketched something abstract and looping. Kit sat cross-legged, scrolling on her phone, the sunlight catching in her auburn hair.

"I'm so freaking excited." Her toes bounced. "This whole Lady of the Dunes theory is starting to unravel," Elodie said finally, not looking up from her page. "I mean, if that diary entry is real, then I was right. She wasn't waiting for someone—she was *running*."

Kit snorted. "Or maybe she was just bored out of her mind and decided to take a walk."

Elodie shot her a look full of sisterly exasperation. "You're a romantic cynic. The worst kind."

"I'm a realist," Kit said. "Which you'd know if you weren't trying to make this about tragic love and ghostly petticoats."

I sipped my lemonade, letting their bickering wash over me like comforting background noise.

"Speaking of tragic," Elodie said, tilting her head toward me. "I still can't believe Austin stayed and played nurse for two days straight. Cal told me he even called in sick to work."

"He didn't have to," I said quickly, my fingers knotting in my cardigan. "But he . . . he just did."

It had rattled me more than I wanted to admit.

For years I'd been the one holding everything together—late-night fevers, last-minute emergencies, the thousand tiny inconveniences that came with single motherhood. No one had ever stepped in, unasked, the way Austin had. No one had thought to. I didn't know what to do with that kind of care, with the quiet competence of a man who folded towels and rocked my daughter like it was the most natural thing in the world.

"Was Austin there when Brian dropped her off?" Kit asked with a bounce of her eyebrows.

I groaned, hoping to forget. I was still reeling from the fact that Brian had dropped Winnie off mere *moments* after Austin and I had just had sex. I was fully convinced the flush in my cheeks and rat's nest hair was a neon billboard that flashed *Just Been Fucked.*

"Yes," I grumbled. "There was a moment where the two just stared at each other like a pair of gorillas. I thought one of them was going to start beating his chest and grunting."

Elodie snorted. "Let him be jealous. He's the idiot who lost you anyway."

My sister had never liked Brian. While I was often reminded of the many, *many* reasons why we had divorced, he wasn't a horrible human being. We had been friends in college who'd fallen into a companionable rhythm. That rhythm had eventually turned into a relationship, and when he'd asked me to be his wife, I'd happily settled for a slow, comfortable life.

It had taken me a long time to realize how easy it was to mistake comfort for complacency. I would spend hours restoring and romanticizing old love stories while daydreaming of my own. I was three months postpartum when Brian calmly came to me one evening and told me he wasn't sure he'd ever been *in love* with me, and the only thing I could do was nod.

Because what else was there? I knew the truth—I was more heartbroken over the impact our divorce would have on Winnie than over anything else. I had been in love with the *idea* of a husband and never with the husband himself.

Pathetic.

My eyes strayed—again—to the outfield where Austin stood with his glove tucked lazily under one arm. He was laughing at something Hayes said, his smile easy and unguarded in a way that still did strange things to my stomach.

The early-evening sun cut across his broad shoulders, catching on the fine layer of sweat on his neck, and I *hated* how my pulse tripped.

"You're quiet over there." Elodie's voice drew me back. "Hey, I'm sorry if I was ragging on Brian."

I blinked and turned, schooling my expression. "It's fine. I'm just lost in my own thoughts."

Her brow arched, and I knew that look. Elodie had been reading me like a book since we were old enough to keep secrets. "No. You're doing that thing."

My brows pinched down. "What thing?"

Kit grinned. "The thing where you're pretending to care about the conversation while your eyes are undressing someone."

My mouth fell open as my cheeks flamed. "I am not—"

"You so are." Kit leaned forward, conspiratorial. "And honestly, same. I mean, have you seen Austin in a jersey? It's like the fabric doesn't know whether to cling or beg for mercy."

"Elodie," I said, desperate for backup.

But Elodie just shook her head and gave me a knowing smile. "You do watch him like someone who's trying very hard not to be caught watching."

Heat flared in my cheeks. I took another sip of lemonade to buy time, though it didn't cool me nearly enough.

"It's nothing," I said finally, waving a hand. "We're just . . . spending a little time together. Having fun."

Kit raised a brow. "Is that what we're calling mind-blowing sex these days? I could use some fun."

"Elodie," I hissed, praying no one around us heard.

"Don't look at me." She smirked. "I didn't say it. Kit did."

"I only implied it." Kit grinned. "But you just confirmed it."

My hands flew up. "God, you two are insufferable."

Kit nudged my knee with hers. "So when exactly did 'just spending time' become 'naked Olympic-level cardio'?"

My jaw dropped. "Kit!"

"What?" She sipped her drink like she wasn't openly broadcasting my business to anyone within earshot. "You're glowing. It's a dead giveaway."

"I am not glowing," I muttered, sinking lower into my chair.

"Sel," Elodie said. "You kind of are."

I stuck my tongue out at her. The worst of it was . . . I could feel it too. Lately it was as if some part of me I thought had been locked away for good was stirring. Waking up. Austin had a way of peeling back layers I didn't even realize I'd built, and that should have scared me more than it did.

"Don't read into it," I said finally. "It's not serious. It's just a little fun."

Elodie's lips curved. "Are you sure about that?"

"Yes." I drained the last of my lemonade. "Absolutely."

But my eyes betrayed me, darting back to the field where Austin was crouched to scoop up a stray ball. His shirt rode up just enough to flash a line of skin above his waistband, and I actively ignored the way my stomach swooped.

Kit followed my gaze and smirked. "Okay, sure. Totally casual."

I let out a groan and buried my face in my hands,

wishing I could melt straight into the folding chair. "You two really are the worst."

Kit's cackling laugh was quiet but smug as she clapped her hands together.

Elodie reached over and patted my knee. "We're just saying, it's a good thing. You deserve someone taking care of you for a change. Even if it's only for a little while."

I didn't have a response to that—at least not one I trusted myself to say out loud.

Across the field, the game wrapped up with shouts and easy laughter. Austin jogged toward the dugout, glove tucked under his shoulder. His grin was wide and unguarded as he high-fived one of his teammates, and for a second I hated how easily he fit here. Like this town—like my life—had always made room for him.

Elodie followed my gaze and let out a knowing sigh. "Well, Cal and I are skipping the Lantern tonight. I promised him a quiet night after wrangling farm chores all week. But if you want a little time-out, I could take Winnie for ice cream. Maybe let her run wild at the farm for a bit."

"She'd love that," I admitted, grateful for the offer even as hesitation pricked the back of my neck. "You'd really be okay?"

Elodie waved me off. "Please. She's an angel and loves hanging out with Levi."

"It's a school night," I said automatically. "Sorry."

Elodie's face crinkled. "You think I can't wrangle her? Compared to a teenager, Winnie's a breeze." Elodie's grin was pure mischief. "Come on . . . go have fun. Lord knows you've earned it."

"Actually," Kit chimed in, locking her phone screen with a smug little click, "I'll be at the Lantern later too. You

can text me when you get there—we'll grab a drink before
you and Austin inevitably start eye-fucking in public."

"Jesus, *Kit*," I hissed, heat rising in my cheeks.

"What?" she said innocently, sipping from her straw.
"I'm just being realistic here." She leaned in, conspiratorial.
"You can have a drink, dance a little . . ." Her eyes glinted.
"Maybe even let your hot not-boyfriend show you off
properly."

My cheeks warmed. "He's not—"

"Uh-huh." Kit cut me off with a wink and sauntered
toward the parking lot. "You should do it," she singsonged.

Elodie squeezed my arm as she gathered her sketchbook
and thermos. "You deserve a little fun, Sel. It's okay to let
yourself have it."

I watched her and Winnie head off together, a strange
ache blooming in my chest.

When had fun become such a foreign concept?

Indecision gnawed at me.

I looked back at Austin just in time to catch him glance
over his shoulder, his eyes finding mine like a magnet. He
smiled—easy, crooked, devastating—and raised a hand in a
lazy wave.

I called out to my sister and pinned her with a pointed
look when she turned around. "She has to be in bed by
nine."

Elodie let out a triumphant squeal before giving me a
playful salute. "Yes, Mother."

When I sneaked another glance at Austin, that flutter in
my stomach turned into a full-blown tumble.

THE DOOR to the Lantern swung shut behind me, muffling the night chill and wrapping me in the cozy haze of spiced whiskey and warm vanilla. Laughter rippled from the bar, the low hum of conversation blending with the strum of a guitar drifting from the corner stage. Light flickered off warm wood accents and glass bottles behind the bar, casting the whole place in a honeyed glow. My shoes clicked against the worn wood floors as I scanned the crowd, nerves prickling like static beneath my skin.

I paused just inside the door, tugging at the hem of my fitted sweater as my eyes swept the room. It wasn't packed, but the midweek crowd had staked their claims—regulars hunched over pool tables, couples tucked into booths, groups laughing a little too loudly over pitchers of beer.

My attention immediately snagged on Austin.

He was leaning casually against the bar, one ankle crossed over the other, a glass of something dark in his hand. His head tilted as soon as he saw me, and the grin that curved his mouth hit me square in the chest.

"Well, well," he said as I made my way over, his voice low enough to slide like warm honey along my spine. "Fancy meeting you here, gorgeous. You out trolling for tall, devastatingly handsome contractor-slash-nannies?"

I raised a brow, playing along as my nerves fluttered beneath my skin. "Just hoping one will buy me dinner. Or at least get me drunk enough to forget my responsibilities."

Austin chuckled, the sound deep and wicked. "I don't know about dinner in this place, but I've got your drinks covered." He slid a glass toward me—rich red wine, just the way I liked it.

I took it, our fingers brushing in the exchange. "What if I'm picky about my company?"

His grin sharpened as his eyes skimmed over me, slow

and unhurried. "You're not. At least not when it comes to me."

Heat pooled in my stomach.

The warmth of Austin's palm pressed into the small of my back, steady and grounding, as we shifted to make room for another couple squeezing past. His touch wasn't possessive in a loud, obnoxious way—it was quiet. Steady. Like he didn't even think about doing it, like his hand had been made to rest there. What once was a tiny voice nagging me that I was too old to be with him strangely morphed into a proud, confident woman.

Austin was hot as hell and his hands were on *me*.

The Lantern's lighting seemed to cling to him, highlighting the rough line of his jaw, the faint scar on his chin I'd never asked about, the way his shirt stretched across his shoulders like it resented the effort.

"You're staring," he murmured, leaning in close enough that his breath stirred the fine hairs at my temple.

"Am not," I said too quickly as I smothered my smile with a sip of wine.

"Sure, Selene. Keep lying to yourself." His palm pressed a little firmer against my back. "But if you keep looking at me like that, I'm gonna start thinking you want me to drag you out of here."

My breath hitched, and I felt brave. "I don't know if you've noticed, but you're hot. Maybe I just like looking."

"You know what I like?" He leaned in closer so only I could hear. "I like knowing every man in this room is wondering what it feels like to have you writhing under him." His voice was sinful now, meant only for me. "And only I fucking know."

My knees went weak, and it was unreal how easily he

could do that—how effortlessly he unraveled me with words alone.

Before I could respond, the strum of a slower song bled through the speakers, soft and bluesy. Austin's hand slid from my back to my waist, his fingers curling around my hip as he turned me toward the small dance floor.

"Dance with me," he said, not really asking.

I let him lead me onto the floor, my hand slipping into his as the music wrapped around us. He pulled me close—closer than was strictly appropriate for the public—and swayed us into an easy rhythm.

"See?" he murmured near my ear. "We're already the center of attention."

I risked a glance around, and sure enough, a few heads had turned. Small-town curiosity at its finest. But it wasn't the judgment I felt—it was hunger. The kind in Austin's touch, the way his thumbs brushed small, claiming circles over my hips. The way his eyes never left mine.

"You like showing me off," I said, my voice quieter than I meant.

His grin was pure sin. "Maybe I just like showing you what's already mine."

A light scoff pushed past my lips. "That's presumptuous."

"Mm. Maybe." His nose brushed my temple. "But tell me I'm wrong."

I couldn't.

As he shifted, I caught movement near the door—Kit slipping inside with a friend, her laugh bright as she waved at someone across the bar. My gaze flicked to Brody, who was mid-conversation with Hayes at a corner table.

His attention froze.

It was brief, but I caught it—the flicker of something

unreadable in Brody's eyes before he glanced toward Hayes. My brother, of course, didn't notice; he was too busy gesturing grumpily about whatever they were discussing.

I tucked the observation away for later.

Austin caught my wandering gaze and smirked. "What are you scheming, Selene?"

I shook my head, letting my thoughts slip from my siblings back to the man in front of me. "Just appreciating small-town secrets."

His brow arched as he spun me slightly, his hands tightening at my waist. "Careful. You almost sound like you're enjoying yourself."

"I might be," I admitted, surprising even myself.

Austin's grin softened into something warmer, quieter, though the heat in his eyes never dimmed. "Good. Because I plan to ruin you for all other men tonight."

I choked on a laugh, burying my face in his chest as my pulse thudded wildly.

I closed my eyes, a silent admission already humming through my veins: *You already have.*

"You're terrible," I mumbled.

"Yeah," he said, his lips ghosting over my hairline. "But you like me anyway."

I melted, my body betraying every ounce of restraint.

TWENTY-FOUR

AUSTIN

THE MORNING LIGHT spilled across Selene's bedroom in honey-colored streaks, catching on the loose waves of her hair where it fanned across the pillow. Her breathing was slow and steady. One bare arm curled beneath her flushed cheek; the other stretched across the sheets like she was reaching for something in her sleep.

Me.

I stayed still, flat on my back, one hand resting on my chest like it might hold in the ache lodged there.

This wasn't just good. It wasn't just the best night I'd had in years. It felt like something dangerous, something I wasn't supposed to want this badly.

She shifted in her sleep with a sigh, and the neckline of my T-shirt—stolen and stretched slightly on her—slipped just enough to expose the curve of her shoulder. The fabric shouldn't have looked erotic. But on her? It was lethal.

The thought came unbidden, hitting hard enough to leave a hollow echo behind my sternum.

What the hell was happening to me?

I'd never been the guy to catch feelings like this—messy,

reckless, clawing their way up my spine until they threatened to choke me. I liked keeping things light. Simple. I was good at being the easy one. The fun one. The one who didn't matter enough to hurt or get hurt.

Now I was staring at her ceiling and wondering whether I'd ever feel okay sleeping in my own bed again.

The sound of faint giggling tugged my attention toward the hall. Winnie had been asleep when we got back from the Lantern, but she was fully awake now, already conspiring, no doubt. Cal and Elodie had tuckered her out on the farm and put her to rest in her own bed before we'd gotten back to the duplex. Neither said anything about the way I followed Selene inside with a sheepish grin.

I stretched in bed, not ready to break the moment yet. I wasn't ready to leave the warmth of Selene's sheets or the way her body had curled toward mine during the night, like she couldn't help it even in sleep.

She stirred again, lashes fluttering as her eyes blinked open. For a second she looked disoriented—then her gaze landed on me, and a slow smile spread across her face.

"Morning," she murmured, her voice still thick with sleep.

Jesus Christ. I could feel it all over again—how she'd looked last night pressed against the Lantern's wall, how she'd tasted when I kissed her like I couldn't stop myself.

"Hey." My voice came out lower than I meant, rough around the edges.

She propped herself on an elbow, the sheets pooling at her waist. "You're staring."

"Can you blame me?" I said honestly, not bothering to hide the heat in my eyes as I brushed a rogue strand of hair from her face.

Color rose in her cheeks as she reached for the cup of

water waiting on her nightstand. She must've gotten up while I was still dead to the world.

Winnie's laugh carried again, louder this time.

Selene's smile softened as she glanced toward the door. "We probably don't need to . . . explain anything to her. At least not yet."

I hesitated. "Are you sure? She's a smart kid."

"She is," Selene agreed, tucking her legs beneath her as she sat up. "But she's also five. All she needs to know right now is that we're here." Her blush deepened as she glanced away. "And happy."

I nodded, but something tightened in my chest.

Here. Happy.

It was strange how *here* only ever meant her side of the duplex. Her walls. Her bed. Her life.

I tried to shove the thought down before it took root.

"You're right," I said, forcing a smile. "No need to over-complicate things."

"Exactly." She smiled, but it didn't quite reach her eyes.

I pushed myself upright and swung my legs over the edge of the bed, dragging a hand through my hair. "Come on. Let's get some fresh coffee before your little tyrant finds us." I stood and tugged on yesterday's jeans. "You know she's probably been plotting our downfall since sunrise."

Selene gave a soft laugh. "She'd make a terrifying general."

I laughed and agreed, offering a hand to help her out of bed.

Downstairs, the house felt still in that early-morning way—light filtering through gauzy curtains, the faint creak of old floorboards under our feet. Selene leaned against the kitchen counter, arms folded loosely across her chest as I found the coffee tin and started measuring out the grounds.

Nothing was in a rush.

The rhythm of it felt . . . good. Familiar in a way that had nothing to do with routine and everything to do with her standing there in my shirt, smiling like I was right where I belonged.

I sure could get used to this.

The thought came fast and sharp, leaving a hollow ache in its wake. I had never truly belonged anywhere. Being the by-product of an affair meant that I was relegated to the fringes. I had lived less than ten miles from my father and half brother but wasn't allowed to know them. Instead of drowning in those feelings, charm and humor became the armor to make sure no one could get close enough to poke at those old wounds.

Maybe deep down I had always wanted to matter. Not just to exist, but to *belong*. The realization made it hard to breathe.

I hit the brew button and leaned against the counter beside her as I steadied myself. My hand brushing hers just because I could.

"You're quiet," she said.

I shook my head, smiling down at her. "I'm just thinking."

She tilted her head, her gaze searching. "Good thinking?"

"Of course." I offered a smile that felt steadier than I actually was.

Before Selene could press, the sound of small feet pattering overhead pulled both of our gazes toward the stairs. A second later, Winnie appeared, clutching a plastic container filled with barrettes and her hairbrush.

Her grin was wide and conspiratorial. "Austin! You didn't leave yet!"

"You were right." Selene's lips twitched. "She *has* been plotting."

"I'm terrified." I chuckled as Winnie marched straight into the kitchen like a tiny commander with her finger pointed in my direction.

"I need your head," she declared solemnly, holding her hand out to me.

Selene choked on a laugh, covering her mouth with her hand.

"My head?" I repeated, brows raised.

"For practice." Winnie held up her brush. "I'm learning High Fae hair design. My friends say I'm getting good."

Selene leaned her hip against the counter, mug in hand now that the coffee had finished brewing, her expression soft and warm.

"Looks like you're booked for the morning," Selene teased, sipping her coffee.

"Booked?" I mock grumbled, holding Winnie's hand and allowing her to guide me to a chair. She climbed onto the table behind me.

I looked over my shoulder. "I better get a five-star review for this."

Winnie giggled as she set to work, tugging gently on my hair. "Hold still! You're too squirmy."

I shot Selene a look. "Your kid's a tyrant."

"She gets it from her mom," Selene said, smiling into her mug. "Besides, you love it."

Winnie clipped barrettes into my hair as she babbled about the new drama unfolding in her make-believe fairy kingdom. Selene's eyes lingered on me longer than I expected, something unreadable flickering there.

And hell, I *did* love it.

I loved the way this felt—easy and domestic, like I'd

always been part of their mornings. Like I wasn't just a guy Selene had let into her bed, but a man trusted with small, tender pieces of her life.

This feels so damn good. Easy. Right.

But even as Winnie anchored a clip into place with her tiny fingers and Selene's quiet laughter washed over me, I felt the flicker of unease in my gut.

The memory came unbidden, sharp as glass.

I couldn't have been much older than Winnie—maybe six or seven—when it happened. Mom had taken me to the park for the afternoon, her smile tight as she trailed me from bench to bench, pretending she didn't notice the way I kept craning my neck toward the walking path.

And then I saw him.

My dad.

He wasn't alone. A woman held his arm, laughing at something he'd said. A boy trailed beside them, years older than me and looking like the coolest kid I ever remembered seeing—Brody. My half brother.

My chest had tightened, but I raised my hand anyway, a reflex more than anything.

"Dad!" I called out, loud enough for it to carry.

His head jerked up. For the briefest moment our eyes locked. Recognition flickered—quick and almost reluctant.

Then his expression shuttered. He turned away like I wasn't even there, tugging the woman and Brody along with a hurried, "Let's walk this way."

"Dad!" I tried again, smaller this time.

But they didn't stop.

A weight settled on my shoulder—Mom's hand, warm but heavy. "Austin," she murmured, her voice low and tight. "Don't make a scene."

I didn't. I just stood there, watching their backs as they disappeared around the curve of the path.

That was the day I learned I wasn't just forgotten.

I was never supposed to exist.

I shoved the memory back down where it belonged, deep and tight.

Don't overthink. Just enjoy it.

I shut my eyes and let myself melt into the moment as Winnie hummed a tune, plotting her next braid like a true artist. Unaware of my internal meltdown, Selene laughed, hot coffee cradled in both hands as she watched Winnie secure the last pink barrette in my hair like she was putting the finishing touch on a masterpiece.

"You look perfect, Austin," Winnie declared, hands on her hips as she admired her handiwork.

I mock grumbled, catching my reflection in the toaster's chrome surface. A crooked row of clips sparkled like battle medals along my hairline. "I don't know, bug. Think this is OSHA approved for the jobsite?"

Selene's laugh curled around my chest, warm and easy. "You'll start a trend, I'm sure. Rugged construction men everywhere, begging for sparkly barrettes."

I turned my head just enough to catch her eye and muttered low, "Worth it to get that smile out of you."

Her lips curved, her fingers tightening slightly on the mug.

"All right, Princess of Hair," I said, standing. "We need to get you to school before you start charging clients for these salon appointments."

She giggled, admiring my hair. "I only take payment in cookies."

"Fair. But your mom said no cookies before nine a.m." I

winked at Selene as I gently lifted Winnie off the table and set her on the floor. "I tried negotiating for you."

Selene hummed, shaking her head as she set her mug in the sink. "Such a good influence." She settled her hands on her hips. "Let's get you ready for school. I've got a work meeting in less than an hour." Her arms opened wide, and Winnie tromped toward the stairs.

Before she left the kitchen, Selene's fingers brushed my forearm lightly—just enough to linger. "You're dangerous, you know. Making this all seem so effortless."

I didn't trust my voice, so I just grinned and tugged gently at the corner of her shirt. "You keep wearing my clothes like that, and I'll keep doing dangerous things." I shifted in one fluid movement, pressing her against the counter and gliding my hands over her hips. Her brows arched as her cheeks went pink. "I should go . . . before I start thinking about skipping work entirely."

I kissed her slow and deep, letting her taste course through my veins. When we were both breathless, I grinned at her. "We can't have that now, can we?" I stepped back, giving us both space to breathe. "Go on up. I can get Win off to school and you won't be late for your meeting."

Selene licked her lip like she was truly debating climbing me instead of the stairs to get herself ready for the day. The woman was irresistible.

Thankfully she was also the responsible one, because given an inkling of permission, I would have found a way to taste her again.

A few minutes later I wrestled Winnie's shoes on, helped her zip her jacket, and grabbed the lunch Selene had prepped. Winnie looked up at me, her eyes flicking to the sparkly barrettes still tucked into my hair.

"You're not going to embarrass me at drop-off, are you?" she asked solemnly.

"Me? Embarrass you? Never." I ruffled her curls. "Though I can bust out my air guitar at the school gates if you want."

She gasped in horror and shoved at my knee. "Noooo!"

Selene's happy laugh carried faintly through the open window as I led Winnie outside.

Dropping Winnie off was routine by now. She waved, disappearing into a knot of friends, and I lingered at the curb longer than I should've, my hand still half raised like an idiot.

The bubble wasn't gone, not entirely, but I could feel the edges thinning as I crossed the porch to my side of the duplex.

My place felt cold in comparison to Selene's.

Silent.

No giggles, no coffee smell, no soft sounds of Selene moving around in the kitchen.

I toed off my boots and set my keys on the counter. The single-serve coffee maker gurgled impatiently as I flipped it on, but even the smell wasn't the same. Selene's house smelled like vanilla and toast and her goddamn shampoo.

Mine smelled like . . . nothing.

I padded down the hall, stripping off my shirt and tossing it across the bed. The sunlight didn't hit these walls the same way. It didn't hit me the same way.

As the shower heated up, I caught my reflection in the fogged mirror. Sparkly barrettes still clipped across my hairline.

"Jesus," I muttered, pulling them free and setting them in a neat little pile on the counter. My thumb brushed over one of the plastic flowers, and I recalled how proud and sweet Winnie looked when she finished my hair. I could still hear Selene laughing—low and warm and soft enough to break something in me.

Don't get comfortable. This is where it all goes sideways.

I braced my hands on the sink and let out a breath.

I knew I was lying to myself, but it would have been so much easier if what was between Selene and me was just a fling. But flings didn't feel like this. They didn't seep into your mornings. Your evenings. Your goddamn bones.

I showered quickly, yanking on a fresh shirt and jeans. My hand hovered over my phone before I shoved it into my pocket. I didn't text her.

Not yet.

As I locked the door behind me, I told myself—again— not to overthink it.

Just enjoy it while it lasts.

But deep down I knew.

I was no one's first choice.

TWENTY-FIVE

SELENE

THE CARRIAGE HOUSE smelled faintly of old paper and cedar polish, a scent that clung to the edges of history. I sat at my desk, elbows propped on either side of the two faded photographs. Alma's photos stared back like the images might suddenly give up their secrets if I glared hard enough. My coffee had gone cold beside me, ignored. There was too much noise in my head—Austin's laughter from this morning, Winnie's conspiratorial giggle, the sound of a man's boots scuffing across my kitchen floor like he belonged there.

Alma didn't look like the ghostly figure the town whispered about on foggy nights. She wasn't ethereal or otherworldly. She looked solid. Real. A woman caught in the middle of a life she hadn't chosen, her spine stiff with duty and her eyes—well, whatever they once were, they were gone now. Scratched out so violently I could almost feel the sharp point of a blade digging into the photo's glossy surface.

I traced my thumb along the crease in the paper, my gaze drifting to the shadowy figure in the corner. He wasn't meant to be in the frame. You could tell by his posture, his watchfulness, the way his body tilted toward Alma like gravity insisted on it. And god help me, I couldn't stop seeing Hayes in him. The same angled jaw. The same stubborn set to his mouth. The faintest echo of my brother's smirk.

The Keepers would likely call it coincidence. A trick of heritage and shadow, but I wasn't so sure.

Hayes had always been sensitive about his so-called curse—the bad luck, the near misses, the way he'd never been able to hold on to anything good. What if it wasn't a joke at all? What if it started here, with Alma and the man in the corner who was never meant to stay?

I dragged my hands down my face and pushed away from the desk. Dwelling on old photos and ghost stories wasn't helping me. It wasn't answering the bigger question clawing at my ribs.

How the hell had I let Austin slip so easily into my life?

The memory of this morning came in sharp flashes. Austin sitting barefoot at my kitchen table, letting Winnie anchor pink barrettes in his hair with the same concentration she reserved for building her block towers. His wide, calloused hands brushing my hips as I reached past him for the coffeepot, the weight of his gaze sliding over me like a caress.

He'd been gone for less than an hour, and already the house felt . . . hollow.

This wasn't what I'd planned. This wasn't safe.

I didn't remember the last time I felt this wanted—this *seen*—and it terrified me. Wanting someone meant hoping, and hoping meant there was something to lose.

I rubbed at the ache in my chest, willing my pulse to settle.

Don't overcomplicate it. He's a good guy. It's just mind-blowing orgasms and a little harmless fun.

Except that lie was getting harder to hold on to with every quiet smile, every casual touch, and every night he stayed too long in my bed.

By the time I closed up the carriage house and slipped on my boots, the sun had burned off the last traces of morning fog. The afternoon was sunny and breezy, but fall was settling in. I found Austin waiting at the bottom of the front porch steps, Winnie perched high on his shoulders like she was queen of all she surveyed. Her pink sneakers bounced against his chest as she waved at a passing neighbor, and Austin—hands tucked loosely around her calves—grinned like he'd done this a thousand times.

The sight hit me square in the sternum.

He fits here so well.

"There she is," Austin teased as I descended the steps. "Thought you might need to pull an all-nighter."

"I was considering it," I said, my lips curving despite the twist in my stomach.

Winnie reached for me, fingers wiggling in the air. "Mama! We're going to the Crooked Spine! Austin says I can have a cookie the size of my face!"

"Only if it's okay with you." Austin shot me a mock-innocent look. "But I do like to be a man of my word."

"You're also a man who's not dealing with the sugar crash later," I countered with a stern look. He held my stare until I rolled my eyes with a laugh. "Let's go," I relented, falling into step beside them as we headed down Main Street.

Star Harbor was its usual Thursday-evening self—half asleep, half buzzing. The hardware store had propped its door open to let the scent of lumber and oil paint drift out, and somewhere nearby a radio played faint nineties country. Mrs. Donnelly waved from her florist's shop, the air sweet with late-season dahlias.

"Good evening, Selene! Hello, Miss Winnie! And . . ." Her eyes lingered on Austin, curious. "Austin, isn't it? I don't think we've been properly introduced. You're Officer Brody's brother, right?"

Austin's grin was easy. "Guilty as charged."

She eyed Winnie's hand tucked into his. "Well, I'd say you're settling in."

Austin sucked in a lungful of coastal air. "I'd say Star Harbor feels a lot like home," he said with a wink that made her blush and wave him off with a laugh.

We moved on, but I felt the weight of eyes tracking us down the street. Not hostile—just very, very curious. Small towns didn't need social media. They had sidewalks and sharp peripheral vision.

"Does it ever bother you?" I asked under my breath, increasing the space between his shoulder and mine, just a bit.

"What?" Austin adjusted Winnie's legs slightly.

I shrugged. "The staring. People wondering what's going on."

"Not really," he said simply. His shoulder bumped into mine, mischief sparking in his eyes. "Let 'em wonder."

My smile bloomed. I wanted that kind of ease, but my pulse still skittered. I had spent years keeping my private life tight to my chest, carefully curated to avoid giving anyone fodder for gossip.

"Faster!" Winnie giggled and tugged at Austin's ear. "Faster, horsey!"

Austin neighed dramatically and broke into a light jog down the sidewalk, her squeal of delight bouncing off brick storefronts.

I laughed and watched them play as the knot in my chest loosened.

Watching them together felt . . . dangerous yet exhilarating, like standing too close to the edge of something that promised both wonder and ruin.

The bakery inside the Crooked Spine smelled like sugar and butter and yeast, warm enough to feel like a hug as we stepped inside. Winnie pressed her face to the glass case, leaving a perfect smudge as she deliberated between a sprinkle doughnut and a chocolate chip cookie as big as her head.

Austin crouched to her level, his grin lazy. "Tough choice. But I hear cookies are better for maximum chocolaty face mess."

Winnie giggled and pointed decisively. "Cookie."

"Excellent choice, Your Majesty." He saluted and turned to the counter.

I slipped my phone from my pocket to check the time— and saw the text.

> BRIAN
>
> I need to swap next weekend. A new commitment came up. That works for you, right?

Polite. To the point. No greeting or asking how I was. Just dismissive brevity, as if our entire custody schedule was a puzzle piece he needed to work into his important schedule. In hindsight it was obvious to see that our relationship had always been like that—polite and little more. It was further proof that emotion mattered little to the man who'd once stood in front of our families and pledged his love and devotion.

I scoffed under my breath as my stomach twisted. Turns out, I got neither of those things during the course of our brief marriage.

Austin was still at the counter, paying for the cookie and a coffee I hadn't asked for but knew he'd hand me anyway. He shot me a cheeky grin over his shoulder, and I forced my lips into a faint smile that didn't quite land.

Fear crawled across my skin.

It wasn't Austin's charm, his ease in my life, or even the way he had seamlessly folded himself into our small-town rhythms. It was how fast he could make me forget that I had to keep my guard up.

Brian's text was a sharp, unexpected reminder that whatever this was with Austin—it wasn't built to last. I'd made the mistake of trusting someone else with my heart, and it had nearly cost me everything.

I thumbed out a terse reply.

ME

I'll see if I can adjust.

The screen felt heavy in my palm.

"Selene?" Austin's voice was a gentle nudge that pulled me back to the present. He was standing in front of me now, holding out a cup piled high with whipped cream. "It's a mocha-chip fratboy something," he said playfully. "Thought you could use the caffeine."

"Mmm, *frappe*. Yum." I took it automatically, my fingers brushing his, but the warmth from his hand didn't reach me. "Thanks," I murmured with a half smile.

His eyes narrowed, reading me like he always seemed to do. "You okay?"

I swallowed hard. "Yeah. Just life stuff. It's nothing."

The white lie sat bitter on my tongue.

Austin didn't push, but his thumb swept lightly over my knuckles as he handed Winnie her massive cookie. "Well, if life stuff needs punching, you know where to find me."

My laugh came out quicker than I intended. In hand-to-hand combat Brian wouldn't stand a chance against Austin. It was the one thing that made me feel the most shame: I had given myself completely to a man who never fought for anything, least of all me.

I glanced at Winnie and my shoulders relaxed. If I focused on her, everything else would fall into place.

Deep down I knew that Austin deserved more than this —more than my half smiles and subtle deflections, but he didn't know what it was like to carry the weight of a child's stability. It was exhausting to field every curveball life hurled at you alone. Too many times I had been left holding all the pieces when someone else decided they were done trying.

I took a deep breath and painted on a sunny smile for him and Winnie.

This is my mess, not his.

And I wasn't about to let him drown in it.

THE HOUSE HAD SETTLED into its evening hush, that weighty quiet that came only after Winnie was tucked in and the dishwasher hummed low in the background. I sat on the edge of my bed, scrolling mindlessly through my phone without actually seeing anything.

Austin hadn't stayed after dropping us off. He had walked us to the door, squeezed my hand—I think he knew I wasn't ready to kiss in front of Winnie—and said he had to check on something at his place.

It wasn't unusual. He still had his own life, his own space just a few feet across the porch, but for the first time I felt the absence of him like a cold draft slipping through a cracked window.

Maybe that was the problem. I wasn't supposed to notice.

Pushing the thought aside, I set my phone down, walked downstairs, and padded barefoot to the front door, drawn by the faint sound of crickets outside. I tugged it open just far enough to peek through the screen.

Like a dream, there he was.

Austin sat on the top step of his side of the porch, elbows resting on his knees, a half-empty beer bottle dangling loosely from his fingers. He wasn't scrolling on his phone or watching the street. He just . . . sat there.

Still and silent under the glow of a porch light.

The light haloed his profile in soft gold, catching on the sharp line of his jaw, the messy waves of his hair. He looked so different like this—quiet, almost contemplative.

I didn't want to interrupt, but my hand was already on the knob.

Before I could overthink it, I slipped outside, the screen door sighing shut behind me. My bare feet were silent on the worn wood planks as I crossed to him.

"You're brooding," I said.

Austin glanced up, surprise flashing in his eyes before it softened into something warmer. "I didn't hear you come out."

"I'm a part-time ninja," I said, easing down onto the step

beside him. The wood was cool beneath my thighs as I tucked my legs under me.

"You couldn't sneak up on me if you tried," he teased as he tipped his bottle toward me. "Beer?"

I shook my head. "Not tonight."

We sat in companionable silence, my head on his shoulder while the sound of insects and distant waves from the lake filled the air.

"You okay?" I asked finally.

He was quiet for a beat too long. Then he exhaled through his nose, giving a lopsided shrug. "Yeah. Just . . . well, brooding, I guess."

I chuckled as my heart lurched. "About?"

His thumb traced the label on the bottle. He was still before his shoulders jerked. "Nothing important."

I didn't push. God knew I wasn't eager to bare my own messy thoughts.

Then his voice dipped, quiet and rough around the edges. "My mom used to sit like this. She'd stare out at the road like she was waiting for him to come back and choose her. Maybe she thought if she stayed still enough, long enough, he'd walk right up the steps and everything would be fine."

I turned my head to watch him, my chest tightening.

"But he never did," Austin added, his smile brittle. "And she never moved on. Just . . . stayed stuck there waiting for a man who never loved her."

Waiting for a man who never loved her.

I wanted to say something—anything—but the words caught behind the lump in my throat. I knew the pain and embarrassment of realizing the person you had pinned your hopes on wasn't capable of loving you back. I couldn't imagine what it was like for his mother to have spent her life waiting for a man who never came. What was worse, it was clear she wasn't the only one who had spent countless hours waiting. *Hoping.*

My chest ached for that little boy.

Austin let out a soft laugh, shaking his head. "Sorry. I didn't mean to dump that on you."

"You didn't," I said quietly. "It's . . . I get it."

His gaze flicked to mine, searching. "Do you?"

I nodded, though I wasn't sure I did. But I understood enough about waiting—about the ache of hoping for something you couldn't name.

The porch light buzzed faintly overhead.

Austin set his bottle aside, his hands resting on his thighs as he leaned in, his voice low and steady. "Whatever's spinning in your head right now . . . you can trust me with it, you know."

I wanted to. Oh how I wanted to, but all that rose to the surface was fear. Fear that if I let myself lean on him—even for a moment—I'd never want to stand alone again. I couldn't afford that kind of weakness, not with a daughter who needed me steady. But a small, treacherous part of me ached for it anyway—for someone strong enough to stay, even when things got hard. I wasn't sure I believed such a person existed.

It wasn't attracting the attention of a younger, hotter man that scared me. It was the way he made me want things I'd buried years ago—safety, partnership, someone to come home to—and I didn't know if I'd survive losing them again.

So I kissed him. Harder than I meant to, like I could chase away his ghosts and quiet my own. Maybe I wasn't ready to give him all the words tangled up in my heart, but I could give him this—my hands in his hair, my mouth on his, the unspoken promise that, for tonight, he was seen.

Chosen.

Austin made a surprised sound against my mouth before his hands cupped my jaw, pulling me closer, anchoring me in the way only he could.

I broke the kiss first, tugging his hand. "Come inside."

His brows lifted slightly, a question in his eyes.

"Please," I said, my voice unsteady.

TWENTY-SIX

AUSTIN

She pulled back just enough to whisper it—soft, shaky, wrecking me in one syllable.

"Please."

Her fingers were still wrapped around mine, tight like she wasn't sure I'd follow. Like she didn't know I already would've followed her anywhere.

"Come inside," she repeated with a whisper, her voice unsteady, like she was afraid I might say no.

Like I ever could.

The porch step creaked under her bare feet, her eyes fixed on mine like I was something she wasn't sure she should want—but was about to take anyway.

Then her lips were on me again. Not soft and tentative, but hungry.

Selene kissed like she was trying to anchor herself in a storm, her fingers curling in my shirt as if to tether me closer. I didn't hesitate—I couldn't. My hands found her jaw, my thumbs brushing the delicate curve beneath her ears as I deepened the kiss.

She tasted like salted caramel and fear and something so

fucking addictive I already knew I'd crave it long after she let me go.

She was pulling me in. Pushing me away. Both at once. Honestly, I didn't care which—so long as she didn't stop.

The porch light flickered faintly overhead, moths circling, their wings whispering in the dark. It was the only sound besides our breathing, our lips, the needy noises catching in her throat.

Selene pressed closer, her hips brushing mine, and my restraint—always shaky around her—frayed to threads.

"Selene," I murmured against her mouth, unsure whether it was a warning or a prayer.

Her hands fisted in my hair, tugging just enough to make me groan, to make my pulse thunder against my ribs. I kissed her harder—desperate, frantic in a way that cracked something wide open inside me.

This wasn't casual.

This wasn't just fun.

For a flash, I was fifteen years old again, standing outside a house I wasn't allowed to call home. Cold hands. Cold nose. Watching through the glass as Brody set the table inside, laughter spilling past walls I could never breach.

I'd told myself I didn't need them, that I didn't need anyone.

But here? Selene's hands on me, her mouth claiming mine like I belonged to her? It undid me.

A sound broke from deep in my chest—rough, needy—as I pressed her back gently against the porch rail, my fore-head resting against hers as we both fought for air.

Her eyes searched mine, wide and dark and shining.

My throat was too full with the taste of her, my head

still spinning from the way she'd kissed me—like I was her last solid thing in a world slipping sideways.

Selene tugged gently, her palm warm against mine. I let her lead me through the door, the porch light buzzing faintly behind us as the night air clung to my skin.

And Christ—this woman. She didn't even know what she was doing to me.

Her hand fit so naturally in mine, her thumb brushing absent circles over my knuckles as we stepped inside. The door clicked behind us, shutting out the world like it wasn't even real anymore.

The house smelled faintly of her shampoo and vanilla candles. The hush was thick, intimate, broken only by the faint tick of the kitchen clock.

Selene stopped in the entryway. She turned toward me, her eyes shining in the glow from a lamp left on in the living room. Her lips were parted, still flushed from the kiss on the porch, and I couldn't help myself.

I cupped her jaw, my thumb grazing the delicate curve of her cheekbone. Her skin was warm, and there was a flicker in her eyes—hunger, yes, but also something rawer. Something that made my heart twist.

"Selene," I murmured. It wasn't a question, not exactly, but it felt like one anyway.

Her hands slid up my chest, fisting lightly in the fabric of my shirt. "Shh . . . don't overthink it," she whispered. "Just kiss me again."

I couldn't say no to her if I tried.

I kissed her like a starving man, my fingers tangling in her hair as she pressed against me, soft and insistent. She made a sound—quiet, desperate—that went straight to my gut.

I deepened the kiss, tasting passion and fear and

wanting all at once. Her mouth was hot and pliant beneath mine, her hands tugging at my shirt like she needed me closer than skin.

My back hit the wall with a muted thud as she pushed me there, her body slotting against mine. I gripped her hips, holding her steady as her tongue slid against mine, sweet and urgent.

There was a fragility in her urgency that nearly undid me. She wasn't kissing me for fun. She was kissing me like she was drowning and I was the only air left in her world.

And, fuck, if that understanding didn't make my skin feel too tight.

I kissed her harder, one hand sliding down to her lower back, anchoring her against me.

"Selene," I breathed between kisses, my forehead resting lightly against hers. "We don't have to rush."

But she shook her head, her fingers curling around my collar as she whispered, "Please don't stop."

That single, shaky plea burned through me.

"Okay," I murmured against her mouth. "Okay, baby."

Her hand caught mine again, tugging me toward the stairs. The movement wasn't hurried—it was deliberate. Like she'd made up her mind and there was no going back.

And god help me, I was already gone.

Selene tugged me toward the stairs, her steps light on the creaking wood floor. I followed without hesitation, my pulse thrumming low and heavy in my throat.

The house felt too quiet, like the stillness was a living, breathing thing. The hum of the refrigerator. The faint tick of a wall clock. The whisper of fabric as her sweater brushed against my arm.

Halfway up the stairs, I saw the faint sliver of light

spilling from under a door at the end of the hall. Winnie's room.

Selene glanced back at me, her hazel eyes glassy in the dim light. Her lips parted, but no sound came. She didn't need to say anything.

I understood.

We moved slower now. Careful. The air felt thick enough to drown in, charged with that precarious combination of want and restraint.

In the hallway, she stopped in front of her bedroom door. Her hand hesitated on the knob like she was weighing something—then she pushed it open and stepped inside, pulling me with her.

The door clicked shut behind us, muffling the world again.

Her room was dim, lit only by the faint glow of a lamp on the dresser. The curtains stirred gently with the breeze through the cracked window, carrying the faint scent of autumn air and her vanilla lotion. The bed was still slightly rumpled from the morning, an invitation that punched me right in the chest.

Selene turned to face me, her chest rising and falling fast. Her hands slid up my chest, fingers curling in the fabric of my shirt as if she couldn't decide whether to push me away or pull me closer.

She pulled.

I caught her face in my hands, my thumbs brushing her flushed cheeks as I kissed her—slower this time, but no less hungry. Her body melted into mine, the heat of her seeping through my clothes like a brand.

She felt unbearably good.

Her hands slipped under my shirt, palms skating over

my ribs and my stomach. I shuddered at the contrast of her soft fingers against my heated skin.

"Selene . . ." My voice was rough, too loud in the quiet room. I kissed her again to swallow it down, moving us backward until her knees hit the edge of the bed.

She sank onto it with an exhale, her legs parting slightly as her hands fisted in my shirt, tugging me down to her.

"Wait," I murmured, breaking the kiss just enough to search her eyes. "We don't have to—"

"I said don't stop," she whispered again. The plea in her voice was soft, but it cracked something open in me.

I kissed her harder, my hands sliding into her hair as she gasped against my mouth. Her thighs tightened around my hips, anchoring me there like she didn't plan on letting go.

Outside the door, the house creaked faintly, and my gut tensed with the awareness of a child sleeping down the hall.

We both froze for a heartbeat.

Then Selene's lips curved faintly against mine, her fingers tugging me down until our foreheads touched.

"We'll be quiet," she whispered.

The words lit a fire low in my stomach.

My voice went low and thick as my hands trailed down to her hips, pinning her to the mattress. "Then you better not let me hear a sound then," I murmured back.

Her answering smile was wicked. Her fingers curled in my shirt, tugging me down until our mouths found each other again. The kiss was slower this time but no less urgent—like we were both trying to memorize the shape of this want.

The quiet of the house pressed in on us, amplifying every sound. The rustle of the sheets as she shifted beneath me. The faint catch of her breath against my lips. The creak of the headboard when my knee brushed the mattress.

We both stilled at that, a silent agreement passing between us.

Be quiet.

Selene's lips curved faintly, her hands sliding up to frame my face. "You're heavy," she teased in the faintest whisper, though her eyes said the opposite—*stay*.

I shifted slightly to ease my weight off her, my forearms braced on either side of her head. My thumbs brushed her jaw, tracing the delicate line of her throat as I bent to kiss her again, softer this time.

"I'll always be careful with you," I murmured against her mouth.

Her hands skimmed down my chest, fingers slipping beneath the hem of my shirt. Her touch burned as she pushed it higher, higher, until I sat back on my heels just long enough to peel it over my head and toss it aside.

Her eyes swept over me in the low light, something raw flickering there. Not lust—not only lust.

Want.

Need.

Maybe even fear.

"You're staring," I whispered with a crooked smile, trying to keep the moment light even as my pulse roared in my ears.

"Can you blame me?" Her voice was barely audible, her thumb brushing over a faint scar near my lip.

I caught her hand, pressing a kiss to her knuckles before guiding it to my chest. "Touch me all you want." My voice was low, rough edged. "But you better let me return the favor."

Her lips parted, but no sound came, so I kissed her again, slow and deep.

When her hands tugged at the hem of her own shirt, my fingers wrapped gently around her wrists.

"Let me," I said, my voice steadier than I felt.

Selene hesitated, her lashes fluttering as she searched my face. For a moment I thought she'd argue. Then, with a small exhale, she let her arms fall back to the bed.

Trust.

The word echoed in my head like a bell.

I leaned down, brushing my lips across her temple, her cheek, the corner of her mouth, before trailing lower—down her throat, across her collarbone. Her fingers flexed against my bare shoulders, nails biting just enough to make my breath catch.

"You're killing me," she whispered, her voice breaking the hush of the room.

"Not yet," I murmured, nipping lightly at her skin. "But I plan to."

Her quiet laugh morphed into a gasp when my hands slipped under her shirt, palms splaying against the warm skin of her waist. I took my time, inching the fabric higher as my thumbs traced slow, lazy circles over her side.

"God, you're beautiful," I said reverently.

The words seemed to unravel something in her. She arched slightly, her hands threading into my hair as if to anchor herself.

"Say it again," she breathed.

"You're beautiful." I kissed the underside of her jaw, letting the words sink in. "Perfect. You feel like—" My voice faltered as I met her gaze, my chest tightening. "You feel like home, Selene."

Her lips trembled like she wanted to reply, but instead she tugged me down for another kiss, her hands desperate now, pulling at my shoulders like she couldn't get me close enough.

I didn't mind. I didn't ever want her to stop.

The quiet of the house pressed heavier around us as my hands traced the length of her thighs, slipping beneath the fabric of her shorts, mapping out every inch of her like I had all the time in the world.

I'd never had anything like this. And I already knew—if it all ended tomorrow, I'd still spend the rest of my life remembering how it felt to be here.

With her.

Selene's fingers tightened in my hair as I kissed down the curve of her throat, tasting the faint salt of her skin. Her breathing hitched, soft and shallow in the stillness of the room.

"Austin . . ." Her voice trembled like she wasn't sure whether it was a plea or a warning.

I drew back just enough to see her face, brushing a thumb over her flushed cheek. "What is it?"

Her lips parted, but she hesitated, lashes lowering like she was trying to hide.

"Selene," I murmured, pressing a kiss to her temple. "Look at me."

It took a beat, but her eyes finally lifted to mine. There was vulnerability there—naked and staggering—but she didn't look away.

And, Christ, she was devastating.

"I've got you," I whispered. "Every second. Every inch. I've got you."

Her fingers loosened in my hair, sliding down to my shoulders as if surrendering was the only choice left.

I tugged her shirt up slowly, giving her time to stop me,

but she didn't. When the fabric cleared her head and fell to the floor, my breath caught.

She was . . . everything.

"Fuck, Selene." My voice broke around her name.

Her hands came up to cover herself on instinct, but I caught her wrists gently, pulling them aside. "Don't," I said, my voice low. "Let me see you."

A shiver ran through her, but she nodded, her chest rising and falling like she'd just run a mile.

My palms moved down her sides, thumbs tracing the delicate line of her waist. "You're so damn beautiful."

The words seemed to sink into her skin, softening the tension in her shoulders. Her hands cupped my jaw, pulling me down for a kiss that was hungry and sweet all at once.

Her shorts followed her shirt, my fingers curling in the waistband as I worked them down slowly. She arched her hips to help, and the faint sigh that slipped from her lips nearly undid me.

When she lay bare beneath me, I had to pause—just for a second—because the sight of her like this wasn't something I could rush.

"Selene . . ." Her name was a reverent murmur on my lips as I pressed kisses along her collarbone, down her sternum, across the soft skin of her stomach.

Her hands threaded into my hair again, her hips shifting restlessly as a quiet sound escaped her throat.

"Please," she whispered.

I looked up at her, my chest tight. "Please what?"

"Don't make me say it," she breathed.

A slow smile curved my mouth. "I want to hear you say it."

Her fingers tightened in my hair. "Please touch me."

I was there to worship her.

I shifted higher, my hands mapping every curve as I kissed her again, slow and deep. Her thighs parted under my touch, her breath stuttering when my fingers teased her gently—just enough to make her gasp against my lips.

"You're already so wet for me," I murmured, my thumb stroking lazily through her pussy.

Her nails bit into my shoulders as she arched into my hand, her voice breaking on a quiet moan.

"Shhh," I soothed against her ear. "We have to be quiet, baby."

Her teeth sank into her bottom lip to stifle another whimpering sound. The restraint in her made my heart pound. She held so much in, but I could feel her unspooling.

"That's it," I whispered, my fingers working her higher, my mouth tracing her jaw. "Let go for me, Selene."

Her body trembled as she broke apart beneath my hand, her cries muffled against my shoulder.

I held her through it, murmuring quiet praises until her breathing slowed, her muscles loosening as she melted into the sheets. When her eyes fluttered open, there was something raw and unguarded in them.

"Come here," she whispered.

I didn't hesitate. I kissed her as I shed the last of my clothes, her hands roaming my chest like she couldn't decide where to touch first.

When I gripped my cock and settled between her thighs, her breath caught.

"I ache for you," I said, my forehead resting against hers.

"Yes." Her voice was sure now. "Please."

Sliding into her felt like coming home. Her warmth surrounded me, pulled me under, and I had to grit my teeth to keep from losing it right then.

We moved together slowly at first—deliberate, savoring. My hand cradled her jaw, my lips brushing hers with every thrust.

"Look at me," I whispered.

She did and it wrecked me.

"Selene," I groaned, my voice breaking as I pressed deeper into her heat. "You feel like everything I didn't know I was missing."

Her nails dragged down my back as her hips lifted to meet mine.

"Faster," she whispered, her voice desperate.

"Anything you want," I promised, my pace quickening as her moans grew harder to contain.

We were careful—so careful to stay quiet—but the headboard gave a faint creak with every roll of my hips, her breath stuttering into the curve of my neck.

"Please don't stop," she begged, her voice breaking.

"I won't," I vowed, kissing her temple as I thrust harder. "Not until you fall apart for me again."

She came undone beneath me a second time, her body clenching around me as I followed her over the edge, her name a groan on my lips.

When I collapsed beside her, my chest still heaving, I pulled her close—tucking her against me like I could shield her from everything outside these four walls.

Her fingers traced lazy patterns over my chest as our breathing slowed in tandem.

The room smelled faintly of vanilla and clean linen, the air still heavy with the warmth of skin and whispered pleas. Selene's breathing had settled into a slow, even rhythm, her head nestled in the hollow of my shoulder like she'd been made to fit there.

Her hair spilled across my chest in a soft wave, strands

catching on my stubble as I tilted my head, brushing my lips against her temple. She smelled like her shampoo and a little like me, and something about that gave me a full body rush.

The sheets had cooled, but her body was still warm against me—one leg tangled lazily with mine, her arm draped across my stomach like she owned the right to be there.

I shifted slightly, careful not to jostle her, and drew the blanket higher over her bare shoulders. My fingers brushed her skin as I tucked it in around her, and I felt her sigh—a quiet, contented sound that made my throat ache.

I could get used to this.

The thought came fast and uninvited, sharp enough to leave a hollow echo in its wake.

I could get used to her sleepy weight on my chest, to the faint crease between her brows smoothing as she drifted off. To the sound of Winnie's giggles in the morning, barrettes clutched in her small hands as she demanded another round of "practice" on my hair.

I could get used to being part of something.

A real part. Not just the fun guy or the temporary fix or the one who made it easy to forget.

Selene shifted slightly, her hand dragging across my stomach, fingers curling in the edge of the sheet as she murmured, "Don't leave."

I swallowed hard, my throat suddenly tight. "I'm not going anywhere," I whispered back, kissing the crown of her head.

Not tonight.

Not if it killed me.

Her breath hitched as she hummed, but she didn't stir, her body relaxing deeper into mine. I traced my thumb down her spine in a slow, absent pattern, memorizing the feel of her—every curve, every inch of soft skin that still carried my touch.

This felt so damn good.

My hand drifted to her hair, tucking a loose strand behind her ear so I could see her face. She was beautiful like this—unguarded, lips parted slightly, lashes resting against flushed cheeks.

The room's dim glow pooled over her shoulder, catching on the faint freckles I hadn't noticed before. My fingers itched to trace them, to map her like I had all the time in the world.

Because that was what I really wanted.

Time.

More mornings with them. More nights tangled in her sheets, her laughter in my ears, her daughter's tiny hand tugging mine toward some imaginary kingdom.

My nerves tightened into knots.

I'd spent my whole life trying to be the guy everyone wanted around—the one who kept things light, easy, fun. But sitting here, I couldn't shake the weight pressing in. The ache of wanting too much, of holding too tightly to something that wasn't mine to keep.

It felt too good—too close to perfect—and deep down I hated how easily I could believe I'd earned it. Like I deserved her, deserved Winnie, deserved this quiet life. It was a gnawing fear I'd never measure up—that no matter how much I wanted to be their constant, their safe place, wanting wouldn't be enough.

Selene shifted again, her breath warm against my skin.

I held her closer. I wasn't ready to let go, but deep down, beneath the buttery quiet and her soft sighs, I felt it— the truth pressing in and taking hold.

This wouldn't last, because nothing this good ever did.

I shut my eyes. I tried to ignore it and to hold the moment tighter, but the words lingered anyway.

She hummed and murmured in her sleep, "I like when you stay." Her words, almost too soft to catch, were a punch to the gut.

I smoothed her hair back, my thumb brushing the delicate curve of her cheek. I swallowed hard against the lump expanding in my throat.

"I'll stay as long as you'll let me," I whispered, though I wasn't sure if I meant it as a promise or a plea.

Because deep down, I knew I'd already fallen too far to pull myself back.

TWENTY-SEVEN

SELENE

I WOKE SLOWLY, my senses pulling me into the soft edges of morning before my thoughts caught up. The first thing I felt was warmth—steady and encompassing, curling around me like a cozy blanket knit just for me.

Then the weight of his arm draped across my waist. His hand spread over my ribs, fingers splayed as if even in sleep he couldn't stop holding me.

My cheek rested against his chest, and I could hear the slow, even rhythm of his heartbeat under my ear. It was unhurried. Certain.

For a moment I let myself stay perfectly still.

The air smelled faintly like soap and sawdust—Austin's scent—and his smooth skin was soft beneath my cheek. I breathed in, even though I knew I shouldn't.

He'd crash-landed into my life, and something about it felt like it wasn't ours to keep, but I would hold on anyway.

I tilted my head just enough to study him in the pale light spilling through the curtains. His face was softer in sleep—none of the playful grins or cocky smirks he wielded so easily when he was awake. He was just a man. His lashes cast faint shadows on his cheeks, his lips slightly parted as his breath puffed against my hair.

I let my gaze linger on the sharp line of his jaw, the faint stubble darkening his chin and upper lip. My eyes caught on the small scar near his mouth, the one I'd traced absent-mindedly with my thumb the night before. I wondered whether it was from some childhood playground accident or a reckless bar fight. There was still so much about him I didn't know.

Something tight coiled low in my chest, and I forced myself to look away.

These feelings didn't mean permanence. It didn't mean we were building anything.

It was just a moment. One perfect, fleeting moment.

The floorboards creaked faintly as I made my way down the hall, tugging the sleeves of Austin's sweatshirt over my hands. The kitchen was quiet when I slipped in, and I immediately started a fresh pot of coffee. When it was finished brewing, I wrapped my hands around the coffee mug, letting the warmth seep into my fingers as I stared out the window into the backyard.

The grass was bathed in gray light, an early-morning haze that made everything look gentler than it really was.

I should have felt triumphant, maybe even content. Last night had been . . . more than I ever let myself imagine.

But when I closed my eyes, I kept hearing the pain in his voice—low and hesitant in the dark as he talked about growing up in houses that never felt like home. How he'd grown up slipping through the cracks of other people's lives, never quite a son, never quite enough.

I hated that for him. I hated that he carried around this quiet ache like it was just a fact of life, the same way some people carried keys or loose change.

My heart rolled.

It was too easy to fall into this—too easy to want more. To want to *give* more.

I took a sip, letting the creamy coffee settle heavy on my tongue. I wasn't built for fragile things. I wasn't built for waking up in a man's arms and pretending it didn't cost me something every time I let my guard down.

Behind me, I heard the faint creak of floorboards upstairs. A door opened, followed by the unmistakable thump of Winnie's little feet hitting the carpeted floor.

Her laughter drifted down first—light and unburdened.

"Shhh," Austin's voice followed, low and rough with sleep. "Let's not be loud for Mom."

"She's awake already," Winnie whispered conspiratorially, though I could hear the grin in her voice.

"I know," he said. "But she seemed pretty tired last night."

"Did you keep her up past her bedtime?" Winnie's innocent question had me choking on my coffee.

I couldn't hear Austin's whispered response, but I pressed my lips together to keep from smiling. I knew the truth was he'd most definitely kept me up *well* past bedtime.

Moments later their footsteps padded into the kitchen. Winnie barreled straight for me, hair wild and her pajamas askew.

"Morning, Mommy!" she chirped, flinging her arms around my waist.

"Morning, my lovebug," I said, smoothing a hand over her wild curls.

Austin trailed in behind her, running a hand through his own messy hair. His T-shirt clung to him in places that made it hard to keep my eyes from catching.

"Good morning," he said, a faint smile on his lips before he leaned over and brushed a kiss to the top of my head.

"Morning." I tried to keep my tone neutral, my hands busy pouring a cup of coffee for him.

I sucked in a deep breath. "You're both up early," I added after a beat.

"Couldn't sleep," he said, a half smile tugging at his mouth. "Winnie's planning world domination from the sound of it."

"I am not," Winnie declared, climbing up on a chair. "I'm hungry. Can I have pancakes?"

"You're in luck," Austin said, brushing past me to grab a skillet from the cabinet. "Chef Austin is on duty."

"Chef Austin," Winnie repeated with a giggle. "You sound like a TV person."

Austin shot me a look, amused. For a second, something unspoken flickered between us—warmth, familiarity, a question I wasn't ready to answer.

I looked away first.

Winnie dangled her legs off the chair as Austin poured the first round of batter into the skillet. The warm, sweet scent of pancakes lingered in the air, mixing with the faint smell of syrup and coffee. The radio hummed low from the corner of the counter, a country tune filling the quiet spaces between their voices.

The room felt cozy and settled. It was like a snapshot of a life I wasn't sure I would ever find.

"Can we paint your nails after breakfast?" Winnie asked suddenly, swinging her legs like a metronome.

Austin blinked, flipping a pancake without missing a beat. "My nails?"

"Yeah." She held up her small hands, still sticky with

syrup. "I wanna practice before school. Mom said I can bring nail polish for my friends during recess."

I opened my mouth to intervene—save him, maybe. "Win, I'm sure Austin doesn't—"

He grinned. "Sure I do."

The words were so easy, so unhesitant, they caught me off guard.

"You do?" Winnie squealed.

Austin shot me a grin over his shoulder, his green eyes glinting with mischief. "Hey, a deal's a deal. She's been asking since last week."

"I have sparkly purple!" Winnie announced proudly. "You'll look fabulous."

Austin placed the spatula down and piled the pancakes high. "After you eat, you can do your worst, kiddo."

My heart gave a traitorous little tug.

After breakfast, he didn't flinch when Winnie started her work, her tiny brows furrowed in concentration as she painted each nail with meticulous care. He even blew on his fingers dramatically between coats, making her dissolve into laughter.

Even as thoughts tumbled through me and sharpened in my chest, a softer one unfurled beneath it.

Why does this feel so right?

By the time she was done, Winnie had painted all ten of Austin's nails, and most of the skin around them, a bright glittering purple. Satisfied with her work, Winnie bounded away from the table, and I caught her in a hug. "Not so fast. You know the rules. Clean up your mess, please. Then it's time to get dressed for school."

Winnie barely grumbled; she was used to my reminders. As she trudged away, her discarded backpack caught her attention, and she started rifling through it.

With a grin, Winnie waved a crumpled paper in my direction, her sticky fingers smudging the edges. "My music program! I'm gonna sing a solo!"

My brows rose as I reached for it, smoothing the creases. "You are? That's wonderful, baby."

"I'm gonna be so loud," she said with a grin, her front tooth still missing and her voice bubbling with excitement.

Then she turned those big hopeful eyes on Austin. "Will you come too?"

Austin placed a hand to his chest like she'd struck him straight through. "Front row. Loudest clapper in Star Harbor. Deal?"

"Deal!" Winnie giggled, flinging her arms around his neck.

Something in me ached as I watched them.

He wasn't her father. He wasn't mine to keep either—not really.

But in this small, sunlit kitchen, with the smell of pancakes in the air and Winnie's laughter bouncing off the walls, I let myself imagine what it would feel like if he was.

Just for a second.

The rest of the morning wrapped in a flurry of syrupy fingers, giggles, and Austin pretending he couldn't use his newly painted hands to clear plates. Winnie chattered nonstop about school as Austin pulled her jacket over her shoulders.

"I can't wait to show my friends your nail polish," she said to Austin, already halfway to the door.

"I love you," I called. "Have an amazing day!"

"I will!" Her head poked back through the door for only a moment. "Love you!"

Austin caught my gaze. There was something quiet in his expression, something that felt heavier than words.

"Have a good day," I said, my voice softer than I intended.

"You too," he replied before stepping forward and pressing a gentle kiss into my hair.

Then they were gone, the door clicking shut behind them, and the house felt too quiet all at once. I stood there, hands wrapped around my mug, staring at the space where they'd been. The sound of Winnie's laughter lingered like an echo, bright and fleeting.

It was dangerous how easy it felt. How natural.

By late morning, I'd settled into the quiet hum of the carriage house. The air inside carried the faint scent of old paper and whispered secrets, a smell that clung to your clothes and hair after a few hours.

Stacks of brittle ship manifests and faded photographs covered the long wooden table in front of me, their ink smudged and edges curled with time. My laptop screen glowed with scanned documents—obituaries, registries, and handwritten letters I'd been hired to digitize for the Star Harbor Maritime Museum.

I loved this work more than I'd ever admit out loud.

There was something haunting about the human traces left behind. A half-torn love letter, ink blurred from a tear that had fallen across the page decades ago. A ledger's faded dedication: *For my dearest, wherever the sea carries you.* Margins scribbled with notes in handwriting so careful it almost looked like art.

These tiny fragments of lives long past reminded me how easily people disappeared.

The photos of her had been haunting me all week.

Alma Barker, the Lady of the Dunes.

Two versions of her sat side by side on my screen. One pristine, her face serene and perfect, eyes staring straight into the camera. The other scarred—her eyes scratched out violently with something sharp, leaving behind hollow smudges where her gaze used to be.

And in the shadows behind her, a figure. Tall. Broad shouldered. Just visible enough to make my stomach knot.

I rubbed my temples and leaned back in my chair, staring at the cracked plaster ceiling.

I hadn't told my brother yet. Not about the second photo, not about the figure who looked alarmingly like him. Hayes wouldn't believe it anyway. He was already so weird about his supposed curse that mentioning something like this would probably put him over the edge.

Still, I couldn't shake the unease crawling up my spine.

The Lady's story was supposed to be romantic—tragic, yes, but soft at the edges. A woman waiting on the dunes for a lover lost at sea.

But this? The violence in that second photo? The man lurking in the background?

It didn't feel romantic. It felt like a warning.

My phone rang, startling me.

"Hey, Selene." It was Hannah from the museum board. "We're meeting about the new exhibit next week. Would it be possible for you to bring any artifacts you've flagged?"

"Of course," I said, forcing a smile. "I'll have them ready."

We said a quick goodbye, and I turned back to my screen, my eyes tracing the faint outline of the shadowy man again. Maybe my sisters would know what to do or how to tell Hayes that it was possible his silly curse wasn't so silly and unlikely after all.

I should have been thinking about the presentation. Or the pile of documents waiting for my attention, but my mind kept wandering back to Austin in my kitchen.

The way he'd let Winnie paint his nails without hesitation. The sound of her laughter as he blew on his fingers like he was waiting for them to dry. The kiss he'd pressed to the top of my head before he left.

It scared me how much space he took up in my thoughts. How easily he'd slipped into cracks I thought were sealed tight.

This was never supposed to be forever. It couldn't be, right?

For just a second I let myself imagine what it would feel like if it was. If the mornings started like this every day—Austin in our kitchen, coffee brewing, Winnie giggling as she looped her arms around his waist while he stirred pancake batter.

I pictured summer evenings on the porch, his hand resting low on my back as I leaned into him, belly round with our baby.

His laughter echoing through the house. His voice reading bedtime stories. His arms around me in the quiet hush after the world had gone still.

A life full of ordinary, beautiful things.

Warmth fluttered across my chest, and my eyes flew open. I swallowed hard as the stark realization washed over me.

I was head over heels in love with Austin Calloway.

I NEEDED AIR. I needed space. I needed to walk off the sharp, tangled knot of emotions sitting square in my rib cage. The air inside the carriage house had grown heavy, thick with the scent of other people's memories. I sat there for longer than I meant to, staring at the photo on my screen

—at Alma's hollowed-out eyes and the shadowed figure looming behind her—until the edges of the image blurred and my chest felt too tight to take a full breath.

I pushed away from the desk, the chair legs scraping against the worn wooden floor. My body hummed with a restless energy I couldn't seem to shake.

Grabbing my coat from the hook by the door, I stepped outside into the crisp autumn air.

The town was quiet at this time of day. A few cars passed lazily along Main Street, their tires whispering over damp pavement. Porch pumpkins were freshly carved, their grinning faces smiling back in the cool October air. The scent of woodsmoke drifted from somewhere nearby, curling with the sweet, earthy tang of fallen leaves. I tugged my coat tighter, the wool brushing my chin as I tucked it in, and let my boots carry me toward the heart of town.

Each step felt unsteady—not because of the cracked sidewalks, but because of the truth I'd finally let myself name.

I was in love with Austin Calloway.

The words settled in my chest like a stone tossed into still water, rippling outward until I felt them everywhere—in the curl of my fingers, the hitch of my breath, the quickened beat of my heart.

It felt too big, too heavy, too dangerous. Like it couldn't possibly belong to me.

But then—

Maybe it could.

For the first time in a very long time, the thought didn't send me into a tailspin. It wasn't panic that clutched at me—it was something else. Something lighter.

In town, I passed Mrs. Donnelly sweeping her stoop, the clatter of her broom bristles sharp against the wooden steps. She paused when she saw me, her gaze warming in that small-town way people had—like they knew something you didn't.

"Morning, Selene," she said, leaning on the broom handle. "Saw Austin walking Winnie to school earlier. Looked like he was made for it, the way she was chattering away to him."

A swell of emotion caught me off guard. I smiled softly. "She tends to do that."

Her eyes crinkled. "Well, it's nice to see her with someone so patient. And the way he carries her backpack?" She pressed a hand to her chest, practically swooning. "You'd think he'd been doing it all her life."

I nodded, my throat thick. "Yeah."

Mrs. Donnelly tilted her head, watching me a little too closely. "You look happy, Selene. Happier than I've seen you in a long time. Good for you, honey."

I murmured a thank-you and continued walking, my boots crunching over a scatter of brittle leaves.

By the time I reached Bay Street, my thoughts had looped back again. Austin with sparkly purple nails, holding his hands up to Winnie as if she'd just given him the finest manicure in the state. Her laughter was so full and unre-strained it had filled the whole kitchen. The gentle kiss he'd pressed to the top of my head before leaving, like it was the most natural thing in the world.

I wasn't supposed to want this.

But there it was—lodged like a splinter in my chest, tender and impossible to ignore.

Movement across the street caught my eye. A house. Mid-renovation.

The old place had been sitting empty for years, its porch sagging, shutters hanging crooked like tired eyelids.

But now it was alive again. Fresh siding stacked in neat piles. A crew moving in and out with purposeful energy.

My eyes snagged on the sign planted in the yard: WES VAUGHN CONSTRUCTION.

A familiar ache tugged at me. Wes. It had been months since the accident. Months since he'd been the easygoing guy everyone called when something needed fixing. I hadn't seen him out in public once.

Cal and Austin had both mentioned he wasn't doing well. I hadn't asked for details—I didn't have to.

Then my gaze drifted to the porch. It wasn't much yet—just bare boards and skeletal framing—but something about it pulled at me.

Sunday-morning coffee. Bare feet against cool wood. Winnie curled up in a blanket, humming to herself as Austin pressed a steaming mug into my hands.

The image came so easily I could almost feel the warmth of a coffee mug in my hands and hear Winnie's soft hum as she curled against Austin's side on that porch.

I drew in a sharp breath and tore my gaze away, boots clicking a little too quickly on the cracked sidewalk.

It wasn't real. He was too young, too untested, too full of possibilities I had no right to tether down . . . but even as I told myself all the reasons this couldn't last, hope bloomed in my chest anyway—quiet, stubborn, and utterly impossible to ignore.

TWENTY-EIGHT

AUSTIN

My SUV RUMBLED over the gravel lot, tires crunching in a steady rhythm that matched the thrum of contentment low in my chest. Outside the windshield, the world looked dipped in gold—maple trees flaming with orange and crimson, sunlight slipping through their branches in hazy sheets.

From the back seat, Winnie's voice rose, bright and uncontainable.

"Do you think they have the giant pumpkins yet? The ones so big they need a wheelbarrow?"

"I don't know, bug," I said, throwing a grin over my shoulder as I eased the car into a parking spot. "You think you're strong enough to carry one of those?"

"I'm very strong," she declared, flexing her small arms with all the seriousness of a bodybuilder. "Look at these arms. I'm basically a superhero."

I clicked my tongue. "I don't know . . ." I teased.

"Besides," she said with a shrug, "I have you."

"Fair point." My grin widened as aching warmth spread from the center of my chest to my limbs.

As I cut the engine, the faint scent of hay and

woodsmoke drifted through the cracked window. Star Harbor Family Farm sprawled out ahead of us like something pulled from a postcard—kids racing toward a towering tire mountain, hayrides lining up with red-cheeked families bundled in scarves and jackets, a farm stand surrounded by pumpkins in every shade of orange. The smell of cinnamon sugar doughnuts hung thick in the air, undercut by the earthy sweetness of straw bales stacked high along the barn.

The bright-blue barn itself loomed half finished beyond the pumpkin patch, its frame sturdy but already hinting at what it would become. I felt a flicker of pride tug at my chest.

"Wow." Selene's voice was thick with wonder as she looked out the window at the barn. "I haven't been here in a while. You guys are making a lot of progress."

"It's really coming together," I said as I cut the engine, nodding toward the construction site.

Selene's gaze drifted to the barn, her expression softening. "I know how much this place means to them. It's incredible to see Elodie's dreams coming true like this."

"It feels special, right?" I agreed, but then I hesitated, a smile tugging at my mouth. "Cal's added a few quiet touches no one really talks about yet."

Her brow arched slightly in curiosity.

"He had the crew carve Levi's initials into one of the main support beams. Said he wanted him to feel like he'd left his mark on the place too. And there's a little alcove in the dining room where they're hanging a framed photo of the barn raising—the whole community out there lifting beams together. Even the Amish neighbors."

Selene's lips curved, and she instinctively found Winnie's hand, which was clutching at her coat hem.

"That's really beautiful. So much history packed into four walls."

"Yeah." My voice came out softer than I meant it to. "It feels good—working on something that means this much to people."

Winnie's voice piped up before either of us could say more. "Will there be dessert?" she asked, craning her neck for a better look at the barn.

"You know your uncle Cal . . . best desserts in Star Harbor," I said solemnly. "That's a requirement."

Selene laughed, the sound warm and unguarded, and I felt it settle low in my chest like it belonged there.

Together we wandered away from the parking lot, but we didn't make it far before Elodie appeared. Her canvas work pants were streaked with dirt and tucked into a pair of green rubber boots, a grin splitting her face.

"Well, well. Looks like Winnie's dragging you into fall festivities, huh?" she teased, hands planted on her hips.

"She's convincing," I said, smiling as I hooked my thumbs into the pockets of my jacket. My nails—still painted sparkly purple—caught in the sunlight, and Elodie's gaze flicked there before her grin deepened.

"Convincing and stylish," she said with a wink.

"Hey, I don't do anything halfway," I replied.

Winnie giggled, already bouncing on her toes. "Aunt Elodie! Where are the best pumpkins? Tell me the secret!"

Elodie crouched slightly, lowering her voice like she was imparting classified information.

"Go all the way to the back, near the corn maze. Everyone picks over the ones in front. That's where you'll find the hidden gems—the big round ones and the knobby warty ones too."

Winnie's eyes went wide. "The warty ones are the *best*. They look like witches."

"Exactly," Elodie agreed.

Selene gave her sister a hug before we had to scramble behind Winnie. As we headed into the patch, the sound of laughter and crunching leaves followed us. Winnie darted ahead, already scouting her options like a tiny general surveying her troops. Selene trailed after her, phone in hand, snapping pictures as Winnie scrambled over vines and tugged on stems.

I kept pace behind them, taking in the way the sun caught the edges of Selene's hair, the faint flush on her cheeks from the crisp air. She glanced back once, her eyes warm and almost wistful as they met mine.

My stomach dropped.

She doesn't even realize she's already my whole damn world.

We didn't make it far before Winnie darted toward a squat, lopsided pumpkin that looked like it had been left behind for a reason. Its skin was a mottled orange and green, covered in warts like a witch's nose.

"This one!" she announced, throwing her arms out dramatically. "It's perfect."

I crouched beside her, studying it with an exaggerated seriousness that made her giggle. "Perfect, huh? Are you sure about that? It looks like it's been through a lot."

"It's special," she said, placing both hands on its misshapen sides. "No one else wanted it, so I'm gonna love it extra hard."

Something twisted in my chest as I looked at her—this fierce, tender little kid who seemed to love the overlooked things instinctively.

"Then I guess this is the one," I said, and Winnie's grin

widened as if I'd just told her she'd won the lottery. I looked up at Selene. "What do you think, Mom?"

She was snapping pictures on her phone from a few steps back, her laughter warm in the cool autumn air. "I think it's perfect."

"Would you like me to get a picture of all three of you?"

We turned to see an older woman standing nearby, her hands tucked into her puffer vest and a knowing smile curving her lips. She gestured toward the pumpkin Winnie was hugging. "That looks like a memory worth keeping."

Selene hesitated, but before she could respond, Winnie piped up. "Yes! A family picture!"

My chest went tight at the word, but I smiled anyway, trying to play it cool. "Sure. Why not?"

Selene passed her phone over, and we knelt beside Winnie, the pumpkin nestled between us like a fourth member of the group. Winnie leaned her head against my shoulder without a second thought, and Selene's arm brushed mine as she shifted closer for the shot.

The woman took a few photos, then handed the phone back with a wink. "Looks like a keeper to me."

I glanced at the screen as Selene thanked her. Winnie's gap-toothed smile beamed up at us, her tiny fingers gripping the pumpkin. Selene's hair was windblown, her smile unguarded. And there I was, in the middle of it, looking every bit like I belonged.

The sight nearly knocked the air from my lungs. Even as I warned myself this was almost too perfect to be true, I couldn't stop staring at that photo. "Send that to me, would you?"

Selene smiled and nodded.

I bent and scooped up the pumpkin like it weighed

nothing, cradling it in the crook of my arm as we headed back toward the farm stand.

Winnie skipped beside me, her boots crunching over fallen leaves. "You carry it like it doesn't weigh anything at all," she said, tilting her head up at me with a grin.

"Guess I've been working out just for this moment," I teased, flexing my biceps dramatically and shooting Selene a playful wink, just to watch the color rise in her cheeks. "You think this one's going to need its own bedroom?"

Winnie giggled, the sound like wind chimes in the crisp air.

The woman who'd taken our photo was still standing nearby, still deciding on her own choice of pumpkin with what appeared to be her grandkids running circles around her.

As Selene fell into step beside me, the woman gave Selene a gentle nudge and a knowing smile. "Looks like you also found yourself a keeper."

Heat crept up Selene's neck, painting her cheeks the faintest shade of rose. She opened her mouth to respond, but before she could get a word out, Winnie piped up from her spot, skipping a few paces ahead.

"He's my nanny!" she declared proudly, as if I'd just been knighted.

The woman's brows shot up in surprise, but her smile only deepened. "Well, lucky you, sweet girl."

Selene's lips twitched like she was trying not to laugh— or cringe—and her eyes darted to mine for a half second before she looked away.

I bit back a grin and adjusted the pumpkin in my arms.

"Best damn nanny in Star Harbor," I said lightly, and Winnie let out a little giggle.

The air smelled faintly of cinnamon and fried dough as

we followed Winnie's determined little march toward the tire mountain—a towering pile of massive black tractor tires stacked in a pyramid built into a hill. It was well over twice her size. I gently placed the pumpkin at our feet.

Winnie dropped her jacket at the base like a knight shedding armor. "Austin! Watch this!" she called as she scrambled onto the first tire, her tiny hands gripping the edges. "I'm the queen of the mountain!"

I chuckled and moved closer, ready to catch her if she slipped. "Queen, huh? Should I kneel or bow?"

"Both." Her legs pumped as she climbed higher.

Selene hung back a few steps, her phone angled as she snapped pictures, laughter slipping past her lips in soft bursts. I caught her gaze once—her eyes warm, almost wistful—and electricity crackled beneath my skin.

I steadied Winnie with a hand at her back as she reached for the top tire, her boots slipping slightly.

"Careful, bug," I said, my voice low but sure. "You got it."

She clambered over the edge with a triumphant squeal, planting her hands on her hips as she stood tall against the autumn sky. "I did it! I'm the fairy queen!"

"You sure are," I said, my grin stretching wide.

It was ridiculous how easy it felt. Like I was meant to be there—meant to catch her when she fell, meant to laugh with Selene, meant to carry the ugliest pumpkin in the patch like it was the most important thing in the world.

Winnie made it halfway back down the tire mountain before deciding she'd conquered enough territory for one day.

"My hands are cold," she announced as she hopped down the last tire and landed with a triumphant little bounce. "I think we need doughnuts now."

Selene laughed, tucking her phone back into her jacket pocket. "Doughnuts sound like the perfect plan."

At the farm stand, Winnie hovered close to her prized pumpkin as I set it carefully on the counter, its warty sides gleaming in the weak autumn sunlight.

"One lopsided beauty for the queen of the mountain." Elodie grinned as a cashier rang it up. "This one's pretty ugly. Maybe we should give it to you for half price since no one else wanted it."

Winnie stood taller at the title, her chin lifting with a grin. "It's worth full price to me. I love it."

Selene reached into her bag for her wallet, but I was already sliding my card across the counter. "Austin—"

"I've got it," I said easily. "Don't argue. It'll hurt my feelings."

Selene rolled her eyes, but there was a flicker of warmth in them that I didn't miss.

After dropping the pumpkin off at the car, I lingered, watching Selene and Winnie through the windshield as they chatted near a display of multicolored corn and gourds. The way they leaned toward each other, their voices lost in the breeze—it was a sight I could've watched all day.

But my hands were cold too.

I turned back toward the farm stand, drawn by the faint smell of warm cider drifting on the breeze.

Elodie was behind the counter helping again, her sleeves pushed up to her elbows as she filled a customer's order. The ease in her movements struck me—like she was born for this, the hum of a busy farm, the laughter of kids climbing hay bales, the sound of coins clinking in a cash box.

"Hey, Austin," she said as I stepped up, already reaching for three paper cups. "Cider?"

I nodded. "Yeah. Three, please."

As she filled them from a steaming kettle, I let my gaze wander back to the barn.

"You know," I said casually, "Wes and the crew have done amazing work on the inside so far. The attention to detail—hell, even the beams feel like art. Wes's vision really made the place feel alive."

Elodie's easy smile faltered slightly. Her hands stilled on the cups.

"It does," she said. Then her brow furrowed as she sighed. "It breaks my heart, but he's . . . really not doing great lately. Cal said he stopped coming out to jobs altogether. Won't answer calls. Says he won't even leave his house anymore. We're all worried about him."

The words settled heavily between us, the steam from the kettle curling lazily in the cool air.

"He was always the first one to show up for everyone else," she added, almost to herself.

I nodded slowly, the weight of her concern pressing into my chest. Wes had been the guy who threw himself in front of a moving car to save Hayes—the guy who never hesitated to help.

Now he's the one who needs showing up for.

"Sorry. I didn't mean to bring down the happy mood." Elodie handed over the cups with a small, distracted smile. "Thanks for saying something, Austin. Not many people have."

"Of course," I said quietly.

I walked toward Selene and Winnie with the warm paper cups balancing in hand, the sweet-spiced smell of cider curling around me like a hug.

Selene looked up as I approached, her lips curving into

a smile that melted my insides. Winnie's eyes lit up at the sight of the paper cups.

"Cider! Yes!" she cheered, reaching for one.

"Careful. It's hot," I warned, crouching to help her hold it steady.

Selene's fingers brushed mine as she took hers, and our eyes caught.

The air between us felt warm in a way that had nothing to do with the cider.

We started walking the rest of the farm, Winnie skipping ahead with her cider cup clutched in both hands, the steam swirling around her flushed cheeks.

The path wound past rows of late-blooming mums, their colors like spilled paint—deep burgundy, burnt orange, buttercream yellow. I kept my pace slow, matching Selene's without even thinking about it, every few steps scanning ahead to make sure Winnie didn't trip over a root or wander too close to the small pen of goats without one of us close by.

The air smelled like hay and something sweet—baked apples, maybe—and it sank deep into my bones. I felt steady, like that was where I was supposed to be—with them.

"Think you can handle this place without me for a few minutes?" I asked, glancing over as we reached a split in the path.

Selene tilted her head, her wavy hair glinting in the afternoon light. "Depends. Where are you off to?"

"I see my brother over there," I said, nodding toward Brody, who stood near the tractor shed, his uniform catching the light as he spoke to one of the farmhands.

Selene's gaze followed mine. "Go on. We'll check out the corn maze. If we're not back in fifteen minutes . . ."

She let the warning hang with a faint smirk.

I grinned. "I'll come in after you, but only if I get to carry you out like a heroic farm rescue."

Her laugh curled around me, warm and unguarded. "You're ridiculous."

"Ridiculously heroic, you mean." My eyebrows bounced.

"More like ridiculously full of yourself," she called over her shoulder, Winnie tugging her toward the maze entrance.

My laugh cracked into the autumn air and I turned toward Brody.

The sound of boots crunching on gravel preceded me as I crossed the open space.

Brody glanced up, his mouth twitching into a wry half smile. "Well, look who wandered in from the pumpkin patch."

"Don't knock it till you try it," I said, clapping him lightly on the shoulder. "Pumpkin picking is serious business."

His smile widened a fraction. "So I've heard."

I gave him a jab of my elbow. "You mean to tell me the local cops have nothing better to do than protect the local family farm?"

Brody took my ribbing in stride as he ran a hand across his vest. "Last week I went on a call because Phyllis Clayborne was convinced the Lady had possessed her cat. I'll *happily* take a drama-free afternoon at the farm."

Our mutual chuckle was easy enough, but under the surface there was still that faint hum of something unspoken. Years of being brothers without ever quite feeling like it.

"How's the build going?" Brody asked, nodding toward the barn.

My gaze followed his. "It's good. Busy and makes for a long day sometimes, but it feels . . . important, you know?"

He nodded. "They're lucky to have you on it. You're good with your hands—always have been."

Something in my chest tightened at the words. A compliment, casual and light, but from Brody it felt heavier.

"Thanks," I said, rubbing a hand over the back of my neck.

Brody's gaze drifted toward the fields before he spoke again.

"Listen, I've been going through some of Dad's old stuff. There's a lot. More than I can handle alone. You'd really be helping me out if you came by."

I blinked, caught off guard by the ask but surprised by how quickly I wanted to say yes.

I cleared my throat. "Yeah. Absolutely. Whatever you need."

His mouth tugged into that faint smile again, and I felt the tiniest crack of something shift—some small barrier loosening between us.

"Appreciate it," he said simply.

"Of course." I shrugged, trying to play it cool even as a quiet warmth spread through my chest.

For once this didn't feel like chasing something unattainable. It all felt possible.

I leaned against the fence post, the wood cool and rough beneath my palm, and watched Selene and Winnie disappear into the maze.

Selene's brown hair caught in the wind as she followed Winnie through the archway of bundled cornstalks, her shoulders shaking with laughter at something Winnie had said. A second later, they were swallowed up by the rows, the rustle of dry husks the only sign they'd been there at all.

I just stood there, the late-afternoon light stretching long and golden over the fields.

It felt good. Surreal, even. Like I'd stumbled into a life I wasn't supposed to have but wanted more than I could admit.

Selene. Winnie. This town. All of it.

I couldn't remember the last time I'd felt this steady, like I had roots sinking in deep and fast before I even realized it.

A grin tugged at my mouth as a new thought took hold —mischievous and stupid in the best way.

Maybe I'd give them their fifteen minutes.

Then I'd sneak in behind them—find Selene in some narrow row and sweep her right off her feet.

Literally.

If she thought I was ridiculous now, she hadn't seen anything yet.

TWENTY-NINE

SELENE

THE BEDROOM WAS STEEPED in golden light, the kind that only came late in the afternoon, warm and slow like honey poured over the edge of a spoon. It bled through the gauzy curtains, painting the walls in a soft glow, catching on the floorboards and the abandoned trail of clothes we hadn't bothered to pick up.

Winnie was with her dad and I was draped across Austin's chest, my cheek resting against the steady rise and fall of his breathing, with one leg tangled with his beneath the sheets. The air smelled faintly of him—salt and cedar and whatever soap he kept in my shower now. His fingertips traced lazy circles along the small of my back, occasionally stretching wider, dragging like he didn't want to forget I was here.

I didn't want him to.

For a long time, neither of us said a word. The quiet wasn't awkward or loaded. It was comfortable. Sacred. I could still feel the echo of his mouth on mine, the press of his body, the way he looked at me like I was something he wanted to keep.

Outside, I could hear a dog bark down the street. A machine buzzed in the distance. Life was still happening beyond this room, but inside, time had slowed to something languid and lovely.

"If we take a nap, are you going to steal all the covers," he said eventually, voice still thick with sleep and sex, "or just most of them?"

I smiled, barely lifting my head to glance up at him. "Depends. Are you planning to hog all the pillows again?"

He scoffed. "I'm a man of comfort. I require at least three."

"Diva." I snorted. "You use one. The other two are just for decoration."

He grinned, and I couldn't help myself—I leaned up and kissed him, slow and soft, right at the corner of his mouth. The kind of kiss that didn't ask for more. It simply promised that I was still here.

I settled back against his chest, my hand tracing the faint lines of the tattoos that trailed down his forearm, disappearing beneath the edge of the sheet. Everything about him felt solid and safe.

His body. His presence. His heart.

I wasn't scared. Not right now and not with him.

Not anymore.

For once, the future didn't feel like something I needed to outmaneuver. It felt like something I could actually want and look forward to.

I pressed a kiss to his shoulder and closed my eyes.

After a stretch of silence, he shifted beneath me. "You know this thing with us?"

I lifted my chin, met his gaze. "Yeah?"

His eyes held mine. "It's not just a thing."

The air left my lungs in a quiet breath. I didn't smile. I

didn't tease. I just nodded, letting my hand rest over his heart.

"I know," I whispered.

Austin shifted beneath me, brushing my hair off my shoulder as he leaned in, lips close to my ear. "So what'll it be?" he murmured, his voice a low, teasing rumble. "A nap? Round two? Or . . . hear me out—both?"

I snorted, eyes still closed, too comfortable to move. "Are those my only options?"

He pretended to think. "I mean, there's also late lunch. Or a motorcycle ride. We could probably manage both of those things if you're up for it."

I turned my head, just enough to meet his eyes. "A motorcycle ride?"

His grin deepened. "Yeah. I want to take you out. A proper date. You, me, a stretch of road. Maybe a place with pie."

I blinked up at him, heart thudding, caught off guard by how much the idea made me feel . . . giddy. Like a teenager being asked out for the first time. "A date?"

His thumb stroked the curve of my hip. "Yes, a date. You've been letting me hang around your house and paint my nails with your daughter, so I figure I should try to romance you a little."

I smiled slowly. "Well, when you put it like that."

His lips quirked. "Is that a yes?"

I nodded, holding his gaze. "It might be."

He rolled on top of me as my smile grew, his mouth brushing mine, fingers sliding down my waist like he already knew I'd said yes.

"We've got time before I wow you with my pie-selection skills," he whispered, voice gravel and heat, "so I'm going to vote for option two."

I arched beneath him as he nudged my thighs apart with his knee, the sheet slipping away. He reached down, guiding himself between my legs with a tenderness that only made it hotter.

He stretched me slow and reverent, like every time was its own kind of worship.

And when his cock finally filled me—deep and warm, his forehead pressed to mine—I knew I'd say yes to him a thousand times over.

I DIDN'T REMEMBER FALLING asleep, but at some point we were both thoroughly fucked and his breath slowed against my neck. Mine quickly followed.

We must've drifted off tangled together, skin warm against skin, because the next time I opened my eyes, golden light had deepened to soft amber. The shadows stretched longer across the floor. Outside the window, the breeze swayed the oak tree, shaking off dry leaves into the yard.

Austin stirred beneath me, groaning as he stretched.

"That was . . . productive," he muttered, voice still rough from sleep.

I smiled against his shoulder. "Is that what we're calling it now?"

He chuckled, then pressed a kiss to the top of my head. "Productive. Enlightening. Nap adjacent."

I rolled to my side and propped myself on an elbow, the sheet clinging to my chest. "Is a motorcycle date still on the table?"

He tilted his head toward the window. "Looks like perfect riding weather."

My heart fluttered again—an involuntary little thrill I didn't bother to tamp down this time.

Ten minutes later I was sliding into jeans and a soft Henley, watching him zip his jeans up over bare skin.

He caught me looking, and that crooked smile of his kicked up in one corner. "What?"

"Nothing," I said, biting the inside of my cheek. "Just appreciating the view."

His eyes swept over me in return, warm and intoxicating in a way that made me feel claimed without ever saying a word. "I'll grab the helmets."

We roared out of town with the sun low behind us, wind in our hair and laughter in our throats. The bike was old and loud, but steady beneath us. The rumble of it pressed between my thighs, and Austin's body was warm against mine. I clung to him, arms wrapped snug around his middle, and let myself lean in. Trusting the turn. Trusting him.

The road twisted along the edge of the lake, flanked by trees turning orange and red, leaves tumbling across the shoulder in lazy spirals. Every time he took a curve, I felt the shift of his muscles, the subtle lean that told me he'd done this a thousand times.

And yet, when we pulled into the little diner he'd mentioned—hand-painted sign out front boasting "Homemade Pie, Hot Coffee, No Nonsense"—he turned off the engine and sat there for a second, hands still gripping the bars.

The bell above the door jingled as we stepped into the diner, the kind of place that smelled like burned coffee, fryer oil, and cinnamon. The booths were vinyl, the tabletops scuffed from years of elbows and gossip and lazy Sunday mornings. An older woman behind the counter gave us a once-over and a knowing smile, like she already knew what kind of date this was.

We slid into a corner booth, his knee bumping mine under the table.

A waitress with a high ponytail and three pens tucked into her apron pocket came by and handed us two laminated menus. "You folks here for dinner or just the important stuff?"

Austin glanced up at her. "We came for pie."

She grinned. "Smart man. What kind?"

Austin looked at me.

I chewed the inside of my cheek, overwhelmed by choices that somehow all sounded like the right one. "What do you recommend?"

"Apple crumb, if you like classic," she said. "But we've also got maple pecan and a seasonal one—pear with honey and rosemary. That one's new."

My brows lifted. "Pear and rosemary?"

She winked. "Don't knock it till you try it."

Austin reached across the table, placing his hand over mine. "Let's get three slices. Try them all."

"Three?" I laughed. "We are not getting three slices of pie."

"Sure we are." He leaned back in the booth, impossibly pleased with himself. "Live a little, Selene."

The waitress chuckled as she scribbled on her pad. "I like him."

"Me too," I said, squeezing his hand.

By the time she brought the plates—each slice warmed just enough to let the filling ooze slightly onto the ceramic— I was already buzzed on endorphins and the way Austin kept looking at me like he couldn't believe I was real.

He pushed the apple slice toward me. "Start with a classic."

I took a bite, the tart-sweet crunch melting on my tongue, the crumble crisp and buttery.

"Oh my god," I said around a mouthful. "That's stupid good."

He grinned and picked up a fork. "Now, try the pear."

He fed me a bite over the table, his elbow on the edge as he watched my reaction like it was the only thing he cared about.

My eyes widened. "Okay, that's unfair. That might be the best pie I've ever had."

His lips curved. "Told you."

I leaned forward, stealing a bite of the maple pecan from his plate. He made a noise of protest as I licked my fork, slow and smug.

"Rude," he muttered, but he was smiling.

"You invited me on this date," I teased. "You should've known pie thievery was inevitable."

He tilted his head, the corners of his eyes crinkling. "Honestly, I'm just glad you said yes."

I froze, just for a second, then softened. "Me too."

We took the last of the pie in to-go containers and walked across the street to the beach, shoes in hand, the light beginning to shift into something duskier, moodier. Lake Michigan was calm, glassy and gold, stretching out toward the horizon in a manner that made everything else fall away.

We found a quiet spot just off the path, tucked near a drift of tall dune grass. He shrugged off his hoodie and spread it across the sand for us to sit on.

I curled up beside him, the pie forgotten in my lap, my

body leaned into his. A few gulls called overhead. Waves lapped lazily at the shore.

For a long moment, neither of us spoke.

Then he exhaled. "There was this one time . . . I was maybe eleven. My dad decided he was ready for a relationship. He picked me up, took me for a ride on the road out here, like maybe he needed to blow off steam. I rode on the back of the bike, arms around his waist, pretending I wasn't scared shitless."

I looked up at him, my chest pulling tight. "You never talk about him."

He exhaled, gaze fixed on the water. "We didn't really have a relationship, not a real one. He wasn't around much. My mom was the other woman—he didn't exactly sign up for fatherhood."

I stayed quiet, my chest tightening.

"He showed up a few times when I was a kid. Once with a cheap toy police car, once with a milkshake I wasn't allowed to tell anyone about. And then . . . nothing. Not until I was older and already angry enough to pretend I didn't care."

He glanced down at our hands, his thumb brushing across mine absently. "After he died, I got a call. He left me this bike and a letter I never read."

"You never read it?" I whispered. The wind shifted, lifting the edge of my hair. I tucked a strand behind my ear and reached for his hand.

He shook his head. "I didn't want his words. I wanted him to want me, and he never did. Not enough to matter, at least."

Silence settled between us again, broken only by the distant rush of waves and the cry of a gull overhead.

"But this bike," he said finally, nodding toward where it

sat parked along the sand, "it's the only thing I have from him. I don't ride it much. But tonight . . . I don't know. I guess I wanted to rewrite something. Make a new good memory."

I leaned into him, pressing my cheek to his shoulder, the ache in his voice curling around something deep in my chest.

"You are not him," I said gently. "You're so much better."

He didn't answer. Just turned his head and kissed the top of mine like he didn't quite know what to say.

"You know . . . I understand what it feels like to wish a relationship was something it isn't." I couldn't look at Austin, so I just kept talking. "Brian and I were always friends, but . . ." I exhaled, fumbling for the words to explain it all. "I think, in my head, things would get better, more passionate, or just feel . . . right, somehow? I don't know. Things like shared interests, caring enough to be on time, my needs as a woman . . . it was like they never even crossed his mind."

I blew a sad stream of air through my lips. "I learned too late that the *idea* of him was different from the man I married. He was perfectly content with a comfortable companion, but I needed *more*. When I realized I was slowly becoming the shell of who I was, I had to leave. For myself, sure, but also for Winnie. She deserved a home where there was never a question that she was fiercely loved. I knew I could give that to her, but not if I lost myself completely."

Austin turned to me. "You do deserve that, Selene. You deserve everything."

Tears flooded my eyes as I tried to blink them away. Grit

lodged in my throat so tightly I could only nod and nestle closer into him.

A beat passed. Then another.

That was when I saw her.

Just beyond the curve of the dunes, where the golden sand met the shadows of the woods, stood a woman in white.

Still. Barefoot. A pale white dress fluttering slightly in the breeze.

Goose bumps lifted on my arms as I stiffened and sat upright.

"What is it?" Austin asked, following my gaze, but she was gone.

I blinked, heart pounding harder than it should have. "Nothing," I whispered, pressing my face to his shoulder like that could keep the moment from slipping through my fingers.

It was the wind, I told myself. Just a play of the light.

But part of me wasn't so sure.

I shivered in the cold, and Austin's arm tightened around me. "You're frozen. Let's get you home."

I nodded and stood, my gaze still drifting to the spot where I saw her.

Was she like me? Yearning for something more but terrified it wasn't meant for her?

I tried to shake her from my thoughts as we packed up, but I knew what I had seen.

The ride back was quieter. Nothing had changed, really, but something had settled between us. There was a kind of hush that came when you've said something real and the other person held it gently in their hands without crushing it.

The sun was low now, casting long streaks of amber

across the two-lane road as we wound back toward Star Harbor. The breeze was cooler, tinged with the first signs of evening, but I didn't mind. I was tucked against Austin's back, arms wrapped around him, chin resting on his shoulder. One of his hands stayed curled around my calf—a small, unspoken check that I was still with him.

And I was. Still there. Still his.

The rhythmic hum of the engine beneath us, the steady way he leaned into each curve—it all lulled me into something warm and wool soft. It was a quiet that made space for my thoughts to stretch out. For the first time in a long while, I let them wander where they wanted to go.

Not into fear. Not into worst-case scenarios or escape plans of ghost sightings.

But forward.

I let myself imagine what it might look like to wake up to mornings with him in our lives—slow and golden, tangled in his arms, sunlight painting the sheets. I pictured Winnie curled up on the couch with a bowl of popcorn while Austin read to her in that gravelly, steady voice of his. I imagined holidays and grocery lists and the little things— socks folded in the wrong drawers, toothpaste left in the sink, fights and forgiveness and the ache of ordinary love.

I imagined laughing with him in a kitchen that didn't quite feel like mine yet. Watching him dance Winnie around the living room while I stood at the sink, dish towel in hand, pretending I wasn't completely, utterly wrecked by the sight of it.

I imagined a life.

Not just a moment, but a life.

When we pulled into my driveway, the sky had slipped fully into violet. The porch light spilled gold over the walk, and the duplex stood there waiting—familiar and quiet and suddenly not quite big enough for all the dreams crowding my chest.

Austin cut the engine and reached down to steady the bike. I didn't move right away, didn't let go. My arms stayed around him a second longer than necessary.

He looked back at me over his shoulder, helmet hiding most of his face, but I saw it in his eyes.

"You good?" he asked, his voice soft through the visor.

I nodded, heart swelling with something I couldn't name just yet. "Yes," I said with a deep sigh. "I'm perfect."

He smiled, slow and crooked. "Yeah you are."

Even after the helmets were off and we were walking toward the door, our fingers laced together, I kept that vision close to my heart.

Just in case it wasn't a fantasy.

Just in case it was a beginning.

THIRTY

SELENE

I HAD TAKEN a rare day off and the house smelled like lavender and warm cotton. It was one of those quiet, in-between afternoons where the sun lingered at the edge of the sky, painting the windows in gold and peach while the rest of the world slipped toward evening. I stood in front of the couch, folding a blue towel into thirds, then again into a neat square. The dryer rumbled faintly down the hall, rhythmic and low, like the sound of a distant train.

A mug of peppermint tea rested on the arm of the couch, half cold. Something acoustic played from the Blue-tooth speaker on the kitchen counter—easy, open chords and a woman's voice low and raspy, like she knew exactly what it meant to miss someone she couldn't name out loud.

Behind me, Winnie sang over the music. Off-key and unapologetic.

Her voice bobbed in and out of the chorus, occasionally breaking off mid-word to talk to herself or narrate her outfit choices for tonight's concert.

"Do you think the boots are too much?" she asked, appearing at the edge of the hallway with one sparkly boot in hand and her hair half brushed. "Like, what if I look like I'm trying too hard?"

"You are trying," I said gently, smoothing my palm over the crease of a pillowcase before folding it. "That's the whole point of performing. But no, they're not too much. I think they're very you."

She made a satisfied noise and spun on her heel, disappearing again. Above me, I heard the closet door creak, then the scuffle of a hanger dragged too fast along the rod.

I smiled to myself, folding another towel, but the feeling snagged—soft and sweet and a little too close to hope.

Things hadn't changed, not really.

Austin still dropped Winnie off at school, hair windswept, his hoodie rumpled like he'd been in a rush—because he always was. Construction all day, then school pickup, then maybe dinner here if the timing worked out. Sometimes he'd lean against the kitchen counter and eat leftovers with a fork straight from the Tupperware. Sometimes he'd stay long enough to steal the remote and flip through channels until my feet found his lap.

There was a familiarity in the way time slipped between us now, stretched thin by work and responsibility and the pieces of his life I wasn't part of. Not yet.

And still, every day, I found myself listening for the sound of his boots at the back door. I wondered whether his texts—brief and busy and laced with humor—meant what I wanted them to mean.

I didn't need constant reassurance. I didn't. I just liked knowing he was still out there, thinking of us too.

He texted often. Brief and sweet, but busy.

Hope today's not a shit show.

Save me a bite of that soup.

Miss your face.

They often weren't long messages, but they were warm. Warm enough that I reread them more than I probably should have. Warm enough that I felt pathetic for missing him while he was still orbiting my life like he always had.

What we had wasn't a relationship. Not really. But on quiet nights, and smiles over dinner, and in the space between kisses, it certainly felt like *more*.

The washer clunked to a stop. I reached for another shirt from the basket, the cotton still smelling like dryer sheets. Outside the window, the tree in the front yard danced in the breeze, its last few leaves clinging for life before they drifted to the ground.

Winnie padded back into the room, one boot on, one off, holding a sequined cardigan against her chest. "Does this go with the dress?"

"It doesn't *not* go," I said, tilting my head. "Let's see."

She slipped it on and turned in a circle.

"I think it's a win," I said. "You look like a star."

Her smile bloomed, bright and immediate. "Do you think Austin will like it? I hope he sits in the front row, like he said."

My fingers froze in the middle of a hem. Just long enough to feel the sharp little tug behind my ribs. She wasn't asking about whether her dad would show up or like her outfit; she was asking about Austin.

I forced my face into something gentle. "Yeah, baby. He said he'd be there. He wasn't around today because I was, remember?"

She nodded like that was enough. I hoped it was.

When it came to Austin, I wasn't asking for everything.

I just wanted a little piece of the future to feel steady. I picked up the next towel and folded it slowly, methodically. The domestic rhythm of it calmed my hands even if it didn't quiet my thoughts.

Behind me, Winnie went back to humming, trailing into the kitchen. The floor creaked under her little feet. The afternoon pressed in softer around the edges, dusky light slipping through the windows like a secret.

I sipped the cold tea and didn't bother reheating it.

THE SCHOOL GYM buzzed with too many bodies and too much sound—squeaking sneakers, folding chairs scraping against polished wood, the shriek of a mic being tested at the front. It smelled like popcorn and some kind of janitor's cleaner, with an underlying tang of cafeteria food still clinging to the air.

Winnie tugged at my hand, her excitement vibrating through her small frame like she might float right off the ground. I gave her fingers a gentle squeeze before letting go, and she darted off through the crowd toward the long hallway that led backstage.

I lingered a moment, watching the wave of sequins on her dress catch the overhead lights as she disappeared into a sea of tiny performers, all lined up and jittering like wind-up toys. Their show was going to be brief, each grade level singing a song or two to celebrate autumn and their music program. Excited giggles filled the hallway, and my cheeks pinched when Winnie's head popped out and she gave me a delighted little wave.

I waved back before finding a spot in the gymnasium. Rows of chairs spread across the gym floor in chaotic half rows. I spotted my parents near the third row—Dad in his good flannel, Mom with her purse clutched in her lap. Elodie and Cal sat beside them, their hands knotted quietly between them. Levi slouched one seat over, earbuds tucked in until showtime. Kit waved me over from the end of the row, already halfway through a handful of candy corns and beaming like she'd been appointed Head Cheerleader of the Night.

I dropped into the open chair next to her, then immediately thought better of it and stood again, draping my coat across the one beside me.

Austin's seat.

"Where's your hot nanny?" Kit asked, not bothering to keep her teasing voice low.

"He had work," I said simply, smoothing my hands down my dress before sitting again. "But he said he'd be here."

Kit gave me a look I couldn't quite interpret, then nodded and handed me a crumpled program. The top corner had a faint smudge.

I took it gratefully and let my eyes skim the list of class names and songs, pretending to care about the order of the medley.

"Selene?" a voice said beside me.

I turned to find one of the moms from Winnie's class sliding into the seat behind me. She was tall and smiley and always seemed to have her life together in a way that made me feel vaguely sticky and underdressed. Tonight was no exception—her curls were shiny, her lipstick flawless, and she smelled like expensive perfume and eucalyptus baby wipes.

"Hey," I said, managing a smile.

"Can you believe how packed it is?" she asked, fanning

herself with the program. "I swear, every time it's like this. My husband's late, of course. Probably still circling the parking lot."

I nodded like I knew exactly what that was like. As though I hadn't checked my phone twice already since sitting down.

She leaned in conspiratorially. "Or maybe he stopped for beer. He always does this thing where he gets here just as the lights go down and then acts like he didn't miss anything."

I gave a polite laugh, my thumb brushing over my phone screen again. Still blank.

It's just traffic. Or overtime. Or a last-minute hiccup at the jobsite.

That was all. I knew there had to be a reason Austin was running later than expected.

I tucked the phone into my bag, folded my hands in my lap, and tried not to think about the coat beside me. I tried not to hope he'd walk through the doors any second, cheeks flushed from the cold, apologizing with his eyes before he even reached me.

The gym lights flickered once, then again. A hush rippled through the crowd as the overhead fluorescents dimmed to half bright.

The show was starting, and the seat beside me was still empty.

THIRTY-ONE

AUSTIN

THE SMELL of spackle and drywall dust clung to my hoodie. I'd been smoothing and sanding all morning, and by the time I climbed into my SUV, my hands were raw and my shoulders were stiff. I cracked the window, letting in a wash of cold air that smelled like woodsmoke and October.

My phone buzzed against the dash. I glanced at the screen, thumb already mid-reach to decline whatever spam was trying to get my vote or my soul or my subscription—but it wasn't spam.

It was Brody.

That alone made me pause. He didn't call. We texted. Short things. Things with no weight. Memes about him being an old man or sarcastic remarks about small-town life, the kind of conversations that didn't ask for anything and didn't offer much either.

I swiped to answer.

"Hey," I said, adjusting the volume with my knuckle.

There was a brief delay, just long enough to make me think he might've pocket-dialed me.

Then his voice came through—low, like he was already regretting whatever he was about to say. "Hey. I know you've been stretched thin. You good?"

I blinked. "Uh . . . yeah."

It came out slower than I meant it to. Not because it wasn't true—just because he'd asked.

Brody didn't always ask about things. Not in that tone, anyway.

He cleared his throat. I heard the faint creak of a chair, a metallic shuffle. Somewhere behind him, a muffled voice over a radio squawked in and out.

"Are you around?" he asked. "I found something I wanted to show you." There was a beat. And then he said, "It's not a trap, if that's what you're thinking."

I let out a short breath, halfway between a scoff and a laugh. "Didn't cross my mind."

"Liar," he joked.

I smiled despite myself.

He gave me the address to the back entrance of the police station near Main Street, and I told him I'd swing by. Just for a bit.

The kindergarten concert wasn't for a few hours, and Selene had the day off.

I had plenty of time.

THE PRECINCT SMELLED like old paper and cheap floor cleaner, the kind that lingered in your throat long after you left. The linoleum curled at the corners and the hallway buzzed with lights that looked like they hadn't been replaced since the place was built.

Brody met me at the back door and nodded like we'd just run into each other at the grocery store instead of planning it.

"I appreciate you coming," he said.

"Wasn't doing anything important," I lied, following him through the maze of hallways.

We passed two officers I didn't recognize and a bulletin board littered with faded flyers. One still advertised the holiday potluck from last year.

Brody led me to a room I didn't know existed. It had no windows, just four gray walls and a table covered in file boxes. He flicked on the light and crossed to the corner where a single frame leaned against a stack of evidence folders.

"I found this last night," he said, rubbing a hand over the back of his neck. "We were clearing out a storage closet. This box probably hasn't been touched since the nineties."

He picked up the frame and turned it toward me.

It was an old photo, slightly yellowed at the edges. Five men stood in front of a police cruiser, arms crossed, smiles crooked with youth and pride.

I knew which one was ours instantly.

Same build. Same eyes, but softer and smiling.

"He couldn't have been older than twenty-two," I murmured.

"Twenty-one," Brody said. "Fresh out of the academy. My mom wrote the year on the back."

I took the frame. It was lighter than I expected, but the weight of it still pulled at my hands.

"I thought about tossing it," he said after a second. "I didn't want it. I guess I don't need it, but I figured . . . maybe you would."

I didn't say anything. Just stared at the photo of our

father like it would answer questions I wasn't brave enough to ask.

Brody sat down with a groan, as if his body remembered years that weren't his to carry. "You know, I used to wonder what it'd be like if we'd grown up together."

I looked up.

"I didn't even know the truth about you until I was fifteen," he said. "Then when I found out, I was pissed. Not at you—just at him. For keeping it quiet. For acting like it wasn't real."

He shrugged. "But I think what pisses me off more now is that I didn't do anything with it once I did know. You were out there and I didn't reach out."

There was no emotion in his voice. No edge. Just the kind of quiet honesty that made the room feel too small.

"You were a kid," I said. "And it wasn't exactly advertised."

He shook his head. "Still. I could've done better."

I set the photo down and sat across from him, my boots scraping against the tile. "Yeah," I said. "Me too."

The room didn't have a clock. Or maybe it did, but I wasn't paying enough attention to see it. Time stretched differently in spaces like that—stale air, low ceilings, walls that hadn't been painted in a decade. The hum of fluorescent lights softened everything around the edges, like the day was underwater.

Brody slid a folder toward me. Not with ceremony, just an offhand flick of his wrist like it wasn't something that had been sitting in a box collecting dust since before I was born.

"He kept everything," he said. "Weird, right?"

I opened the flap.

Inside were old notes, clipped articles. A few faded printouts from training sessions. A ticket stub from a Tigers game from decades ago. My chest pulled tight around a breath I didn't realize I was holding.

"Seemed like he had a good life," I said quietly, thumbing a photo of three uniforms standing arm in arm in front of the old station. "People respected him."

Brody nodded. "Yeah. That was the thing. Out there, in the public eye, he was different."

I glanced at him.

Brody leaned back in the chair, ankle hooked over his knee, elbow resting on the edge of the table like we were just shooting the shit after a shift, but his jaw had gone tight.

"I mean," he went on, voice measured, "he could be a hard-ass. He was rigid. Ran his precinct like it was the damn Marines. But the guys here? They looked up to him. They called him honorable."

I swallowed. "That's not the word I'd use."

He huffed a sound that might've been agreement. Or regret. Maybe both.

"I keep trying to reconcile it," he said. "This version of him and the one you got."

I nodded, slow. "Me too."

Silence settled. Not awkward—just impossibly heavy.

I looked down at the folder again. Nestled between two sheets was a picture I hadn't noticed before. It was folded in half, like someone had carried it in a wallet too long.

I opened it carefully.

A boy. Maybe six or seven. In a Halloween costume— some kind of superhero getup with a crooked mask. He was standing in a front yard I didn't recognize, holding up a plastic pumpkin like he'd just pulled off the heist of the century.

"Is that you?" Brody asked.

I nodded, my mouth tipping in a wry smile. "First grade.

My mom sewed that cape herself. She said if I wanted to save the world, I needed to look the part."

I held the photo a second longer, then set it gently back in the folder, still confused as to why my dad had held on to it at all.

Somewhere in the distance, a phone rang. A door opened and closed. A printer choked out a few pages and fell silent again.

I rubbed the back of my neck and stood, stretching out a cramp in my shoulder.

"I should probably get going," I said, not quite checking the time.

Brody nodded but didn't move.

"I know it doesn't change anything," he said quietly, "but for what it's worth . . . I'm glad I know you now."

That one caught me right between the ribs.

"I'm glad too," I said, meaning it more than I expected.

He stood and clapped a hand on my shoulder, firm and brief—like any more than that would tip the moment into something we wouldn't know how to carry.

I walked back out into the chill of late afternoon with the folder tucked under my arm and a strange ache behind my sternum.

The sky was softening, low and gray at the edges. My phone buzzed in my pocket, a calendar alert flashing across the screen.

Winnie's performance—6:30 p.m.

I cursed under my breath and glanced at the time.

6:01.

Shit.

I sent a quick text to Selene.

ME

Almost there.

Then I threw the car into gear and peeled out of the lot like I still had a chance.

The first stoplight took too long.

Some minivan stalled in the intersection, the driver waving cars around like she was directing traffic instead of causing it. I tapped my fingers on the steering wheel, every tick of the turn signal syncing with the pulse in my neck.

6:07.

It was fine. The elementary school was close. Close enough that if everything else went smoothly, I'd slide in with a minute to spare. Maybe two. Just enough time to sneak into the gym, find the seat Selene had probably saved for me, and catch Winnie's crooked ponytail and wide, determined eyes right before the music started.

The light changed. I took the turn too fast, tires squealing a little as I veered around a van and gunned it.

Almost there. Come on.

But then there was the construction.

Orange cones lined the two-lane road like a fucking obstacle course. Flashing arrows pushed traffic into one narrow lane, crawling past a backhoe and a guy in a neon vest who didn't look like he gave a shit that the clock was chasing me down.

"Come on," I muttered, inching forward behind a dump truck hauling gravel and regret.

I tried not to picture it. I tried not to imagine the gym packed shoulder to shoulder, folding chairs squealing across the tile, parents fanning themselves with paper programs and checking their watches.

I tried not to see Selene scanning the crowd or her holding a spot beside her that stayed empty.

I tried not to picture Winnie stepping onto the risers, eyes flicking toward the back of the room with that quiet, hopeful expectation.

I gripped the steering wheel tighter, trying to stay focused. The car finally crawled past the last cone and I gunned it, tearing through a yellow light, letting the curse catch in my throat.

I turned onto school grounds at 6:40, the tires crunching across the gravel shoulder as I pulled into the overflow lot.

I didn't even park straight. I threw it into park, slammed the door, and sprinted.

My boots hit pavement hard, lungs burning as I jogged up the sidewalk. The front entrance buzzed with late arrivals, but the gym doors were already closed.

A woman stood outside with a clipboard. She smiled politely as I approached, chest heaving.

"The first group just finished," she said gently, stepping aside to let someone out. "You can head in, though. Grade one is performing next."

I was frozen.

I stood there, one hand on the frame of the open door, as the sound of applause swelled inside—loud and proud and final.

My heart dropped like a stone in my chest.

I stepped through the door.

The gym was exactly how I pictured it—humid with body heat, the scent of popcorn and old wax clinging to the air. Metal chairs clattered as parents shifted and clapped. A row of kids in their Sunday best filed off the risers, faces glowing, some waving frantically at the crowd.

Winnie was in the middle.

Her wild hair poking in all directions, cheeks flushed pink, eyes scanning the audience.

She was smiling. Proud. Brave.

But there was that little flicker—so quick most people wouldn't have caught it. That quick drop of her smile as she looked to the spot next to her mother.

Where I should've been.

I couldn't move, couldn't breathe.

Then she spotted me, just as she stepped off the riser. Her face didn't crumple. Winnie was tougher than that, but her smile didn't reach her eyes this time. Not quite.

When she looked away, it wasn't sulking or pouting. It was worse. It was quiet disappointment. The kind that sat still and waited, hoping no one noticed the ache blooming in her chest.

Across the room, just past a cluster of parents, I saw Selene.

Her back was ramrod straight, her fingers laced in her lap. Her coat was draped over the back of the folding chair beside her—the one she'd saved.

The one I never made it to.

Her expression shifted when she saw me. Something in her shoulders flinched, then softened, like she didn't know which reaction would hurt less.

She didn't frown or scowl, but she didn't smile, either, and for the first time in weeks, I didn't know what came next.

I missed it.

I missed the song. Her solo. The way Winnie's excited eyes searched the crowd for her people. The chance to prove—for once—that the people who loved her would show up when it mattered.

I didn't have an excuse. At least not one that was enough.

Sure, I had finally got what I wanted—a connection with my brother, a piece of my dad's past, something that felt like belonging.

But it still wasn't enough.

Not when the thing that mattered most was walking off the stage, wondering why I hadn't been there to see her shine.

THIRTY-TWO

SELENE

HE'D MISSED IT. He'd really, truly missed it.

An ache gripped my heart as realization washed over me. The past few minutes played over in my mind like a blur.

A hush had pulled through the gym like a drawn breath as the concert waited to begin. The chaotic rustle of candy wrappers and folding chairs fell still. Parents leaned forward. Programs crackled quietly in their laps. Someone's perfume hung sweet and powdery in the air, mixing with the sharper tang of disinfectant and warm metal bleachers. The faint squeak of sneakers echoed from behind the curtain.

Beside me, the seat had stayed empty.

I sat up straighter, smoothing the hem of my dress over my knees even though I hadn't moved. My palms were folded together, tight and deliberate, the way you press your fingers in prayer—not to ask for anything, just to anchor yourself in place.

The stage lights flared a soft amber. A teacher's voice

came over the mic, cheerful and a little too loud, announcing the start of the kindergarten medley.

I hadn't realized I was holding my breath until the curtain finally opened.

My smile bloomed when I saw her. Front row, second from the end. Sparkly boots. Sequined cardigan. Ponytail bouncing with the beat of the opening chords.

My whole world.

Winnie had smiled so wide I could see it from thirty feet away, even through the haze of gym lights and the shimmer of movement all around her. Her voice joined the others, sweet and slightly off-key, and my heart squeezed so hard I had to press my thumb into the meat of my palm to keep from crying.

She looked radiant.

She looked proud.

And every few seconds she looked into the crowd.

Searching.

Waiting.

Hoping.

My eyes had stayed on her. I didn't let them wander. Not to the doors. Not to the back wall. Not to the seat beside me that sat empty.

Instead, I had given Winnie everything I had. I smiled like I could make up the difference. Like my love could stretch wide enough to cover the empty space beside me. Like I wasn't fraying at the edges.

The kids began the second song, something about falling leaves and sharing and neighborly cheer. They swayed side to side in unison, arms rising and falling like clumsy leaves. A few got distracted and waved at parents. One picked her nose. A boy in the back row lifted his shirt and proudly scratched his belly. The audience laughed politely.

Winnie didn't wave. She didn't lose focus, but her eyes still moved.

She had been searching. Still hoping.

When her solo came, she had stepped forward with practiced poise, her shoulders pulled back, her hands at her sides. She was small and steady and so heartbreakingly brave.

Her voice had wobbled at the start, just slightly, then found its footing and rose into the space like it belonged there.

I knew every word. Every note. We'd practiced in the living room for days, her voice bouncing off the walls, off-key and perfect. She'd sung it into her hairbrush, into the shampoo bottle, into the quiet corners of bedtime when she thought I wasn't listening.

Tonight she sang it to me. Just me.

Because that was all there was. It was no surprise her dad didn't show up, but Austin had promised. Shame rippled through me as I realized I'd let it happen *again*. Only this time, it wasn't just me who was affected.

Halfway through the verse, her gaze had flicked again toward the crowd—one final, hopeful sweep—and when it landed back on me, something in it faltered. The corner of her smile dimmed, not quite a frown, just . . . the faintest dip. Like a curtain lowering an inch too early. Like she was folding up something she hadn't even gotten to fully share.

She finished the song with a quiet bow. Another student stepped forward to enjoy his time in the spotlight. When the song ended, the applause came like a wave, loud and proud, echoing off the high ceilings. Parents clapped and cheered and rose to their feet. Cameras flashed. Kit let out a whoop.

I clapped, too, but I couldn't feel my hands.

The space beside me was still empty. Cold air clung to it like a ghost. My coat lay draped over the seat, untouched.

I glanced around and noted polite smiles and interested stares. There were whispers behind their curious glances, as if to say, "We all see it. You're still doing this alone."

As the grade levels transitioned, movement at the door caught my attention. Austin's frantic gaze snagged on me, but I swallowed back tears.

He missed the whole thing.

I stared ahead as the rest of the grade levels completed their performances. I willed myself to keep it together. Finally, the lights came up and the kids started filing offstage, giggling and bumping into each other, cheeks flushed and glittering under the lights.

I caught sight of Winnie at the edge of the curtain, her cardigan slipping from one shoulder, her hair a little lopsided now. She looked toward the seats again, just once.

This time, she didn't even bother to hide the heavy sigh.

I stood quietly. Smoothed my dress again. Gathered our coats and the little purse she'd insisted on bringing.

When I turned to make my way toward the backstage door, I didn't glance at the entrance once.

The backstage hallway smelled like pencil shavings and tempera paint, a familiar cocktail of elementary school chaos. Kids poured out of the side door in a burst of noise and color—jackets half on, glitter shedding like confetti, sneakers scuffing linoleum.

I scanned the crowd until I saw her.

Winnie's cheeks were flushed, her cardigan hanging to her elbow and her boots a little crooked. She looked up, eyes sweeping once more toward the gym behind me, before they landed on my face.

There was a second—just a heartbeat—when her expression brightened, and I knew she thought maybe, just maybe, he was with me.

But then she looked past me and her smile dropped.

Not all the way. Just enough that the air between us lost its shimmer.

"You were amazing," I said, crouching in front of her. I tugged the cardigan back up over her shoulder and buttoned the top clasp with slow, careful fingers. "You sang so beautifully, sweetheart. I'm so proud of you."

She gave a little shrug and looked down at her boots. "It wasn't that good."

"It was," I said firmly, tipping her chin up with my fingers. "It was perfect."

She didn't argue, but she didn't smile either. Just nodded, polite and small.

"I thought . . ." she began.

I waited.

She swallowed. "I thought Austin said he was going to be there."

I kept my face soft. I didn't flinch. At least not where she could see.

"I know, baby," I said, putting on the bravest face I could muster. "Me too."

I stood and helped her into her coat, tucking the sleeves over her sparkly cuffs, brushing glitter from her shoulders. All the while my mind replayed the last moments like a highlight reel I hadn't asked for.

Winnie practicing in front of the mirror. Winnie asking about her boots. Winnie lighting up at the idea of Austin seeing her perform.

I wasn't mad, not exactly. I was tired.

So tired of the way hope kept sneaking in, even when I knew better.

"I'm hungry," Winnie said, rubbing her eyes. "Can we go home?"

"You don't want to stick around and visit with your friends?" I asked.

Winnie shook her head, her eyes staying glued to my shoes.

"Of course, baby," I said, looping her hand into mine. "You want to stop for ice cream on the way?"

She glanced up at me. "Only if you're not mad."

That was the part that broke me. Not the missing seat. Not the phone that stayed quiet. Not even the sight of her standing alone in a sea of kindergartners, her hope slowly unraveling like thread.

It was her thinking that she needed to tiptoe around my feelings.

I stopped walking. Knelt again so I was level with her.

"I'm not mad. Not at you, okay? Not even a little bit. I'm just proud. So, so proud. You were the best part of my whole day, and I want you to have whatever kind of night makes you happy."

She nodded, her lip wobbling just a little before she smiled again.

I stood and led her toward the exit, the hallway growing quieter behind us.

We were almost to the front doors when I heard it—the quick, echoing thud of boots across the polished floor.

My body went still before I turned.

Austin stood just inside the hallway entrance, breathless, eyes sweeping the crowd until they landed on us. His face was flushed, jaw tight, shoulders stiff beneath his coat like he hadn't even stopped moving long enough to let the air settle in his lungs.

Winnie's hand went tight in mine.

"Hi, Austin," she said, her voice small but hopeful. She'd already forgiven him.

He stepped forward fast. "I'm so sorry. Traffic was—I thought I could—" His eyes flicked from her to me. "I swear, I tried. I wanted to be here."

Winnie looked up at him. "You missed it."

She didn't say it with anger. There was no accusation in her voice.

Just quiet disappointment, and somehow I knew that hurt more.

Austin opened his mouth, then closed it again, like he didn't know what to say that would make it better.

"Your boots look awesome," he offered.

Winnie didn't respond.

I looked at him then—really looked at him. The wrinkle between his brows. The regret clinging to his features like soot. The part of him that still thought being sorry could fix things.

"It's okay," I said, cutting through the quiet. "We're heading out."

"Selene—"

"No," I said gently, but with finality. "Let's not do this here. Not now."

I didn't raise my voice. I didn't cry. I didn't ask for more than he could give.

I just turned back toward the door, fingers tightening around Winnie's hand.

"We're okay," I said again, but this time it was for her.

Winnie's hand felt smaller than usual as it gently squeezed mine, her pink coat half buttoned over her dress.

She didn't bounce or skip or ask a million questions about ice cream. Her spark had dimmed into something quieter, more inward, like all her extra glitter had settled beneath her skin and weighed her down.

The gym doors thudded shut behind us, the air outside cool and damp with the first hint of late autumn. Night had fallen fast—slate sky, breath in clouds. The parking lot was a mess of brake lights and uneven idling, parents calling to each other over too-tight parking spaces.

I guided Winnie between puddles, her boots squelching against the pavement. She didn't speak, just climbed into the back seat when I opened the door. I helped her shrug off the coat, fastened the seat belt snug across her lap, and leaned in to press a kiss to her forehead.

"You were the best one up there," I whispered.

She gave me a quiet smile that didn't quite reach her eyes.

I stood with my hand still resting on the door for a breath longer than necessary. Then I closed it gently and circled to the driver's side, blinking against the sting gathering behind my lashes.

My hands found the steering wheel but didn't turn the key. I sat there, staring straight ahead as headlights swept across the lot, illuminating corners I didn't want to look at too closely.

Across the row of cars, under the yellow glare of the gymnasium's exterior light, Austin stood just outside the doors, his hoodie sleeves pulled down over his hands, shoulders hunched like he wasn't sure whether to come closer or turn around and disappear.

His eyes were on the car.

On *us*.

My heart twisted, low and mean, an ache that knew exactly where to press.

I could've rolled down the window. I could have waved or gotten out or told him it was okay—that I understood. That maybe it didn't matter as much as it did.

Instead, I reached into the back seat for Winnie's hand, gave it a squeeze, and turned the key in the ignition.

I didn't know what I'd say if I let myself say anything at all.

Because this—this wasn't a breakup.

It wasn't even a relationship.

It was hope, thin and tender, folded into corners I should've left untouched, and now it hurt in ways I hadn't let anything hurt in a long, long time.

I pulled out of the lot without looking back.

Maybe that was the worst part—he wasn't even mine, and it still felt like an ending.

THIRTY-THREE

AUSTIN

THE PORCH LIGHT on Selene's side of the duplex was still on.

It glowed soft and amber against the navy night, casting long shadows across the railing and turning the potted mums by the steps into something almost golden. A fat moth knocked clumsily against the glass bulb, over and over, like it hadn't figured out it would never get through.

My boots crunched against the gravel path as I crossed the small strip of yard that used to feel invisible—like nothing more than an extension of home.

Tonight, it felt like enemy territory.

I shifted the take-out container in my hand—chicken nuggets and honey mustard from that diner Winnie loved, still warm in the brown paper bag I'd gripped too tight. My intention was to get myself dinner while giving Selene some space, but I was too nauseated to eat. The cardboard had softened along the edges where my fingers had sweated through it, and a smear of grease marked the side where my thumb wouldn't stop pressing.

My palms were damp again. I wiped one against my

jeans, but the moisture clung, cold and clammy. My throat was dry. Swallowing felt like dragging glass through cotton.

I hadn't changed out of my work hoodie. There were still paint flecks along the hem and a dried smear of spackle on my forearm. I looked like someone who didn't care enough. Like someone who hadn't planned this right.

Fuck.

I'd barely made it home before dragging myself next door, my thoughts tangled with all the things I should've said hours ago but hadn't. The silence between us had stretched so long it felt alive now—tight and watching, coiled like a wire waiting to snap.

I stopped at the bottom step.

The house was still. A stillness that felt dangerous.

I should've told Brody I didn't have time to stop by. I should've showered and cleaned up for them. I should've been in that gymnasium. Front row. Clapping loud. Lifting Winnie into a spin like she was made of magic. I should've been steady and present, proudly pressing my hand to the small of Selene's back when the lights came up.

Instead, I stood in the dark, holding a sagging bag of lukewarm food, and wondering how many times a man could ruin something good before it was gone forever.

I looked up at her door.

My feet wouldn't move.

For half a second—maybe longer—I thought about turning around. I considered leaving the food on the step like a sad little peace offering and slinking back through my own door without knocking. At least that way I wouldn't have to watch Selene look at me like she was bracing for disappointment.

The porch bulb flickered once, then held steady.

I climbed the steps slowly, every movement deliberate.

My knees felt stiff, my chest tight enough that I couldn't take a full breath. The wood creaked beneath me—familiar in a way that nearly undid me. I remembered walking up those steps with shopping bags and groceries. I remembered Selene opening the door barefoot and smiling after she'd just pulled an apple pie from the oven. I remembered Winnie in her pajamas, holding up a picture she'd drawn of the three of us.

I remembered it all.

I couldn't shake the feeling that it might already be too late to fix my fuckup.

I raised my hand and knocked—three slow taps that sounded too loud in the quiet night—and waited with my breath caught behind my teeth.

The porch light buzzed above me. The moth bumped again against the glass.

Somewhere down the road, a car passed without slowing. The moment stretched long and taut, my pulse thudding behind my eyes.

The door opened and the world tilted.

Selene stood there in pajama pants and a long-sleeved tee, her bare face lit in amber. No mascara. No gloss. Just clean skin and tired eyes that looked right through me.

Her hair was tied up in one of those loose, half-fallen knots, strands curling around her cheek like they were trying to shield her. From me.

She didn't say anything.

I tried to smile, but my lips wouldn't move right. I held out the bag of food like it might fix something, even though I knew it wouldn't.

"I brought dinner," I said, voice rough and too small. "For Winnie."

Selene's gaze dropped to the bag. "She's already asleep."

Her voice was soft. Gentle, even. But there wasn't a trace of warmth beneath it. Only quiet finality, like a door halfway closed.

I swallowed, the motion sharp in my throat. "I—I thought I could make it," I said. "I really did. Brody called and said he needed to show me something last minute. He said it was important, and I didn't think it'd take as long as it did. I wasn't watching the clock. I thought I had time, but it got away from me."

She nodded once, barely. Her hand stayed curled around the edge of the door. No invitation to step inside. No sign I was welcome.

"I'm not making excuses," I added quickly, my words hitching over themselves. "I'm just . . . I messed up. I know that. I should've been there."

A pause stretched between us, thick with everything I wanted to say and everything she didn't want to hear.

"I was trying to be there for everyone," I said again, slower now as I tried to catch my breath. "For the guys at work. For Brody. I was trying to be the type of person who could handle it all. But I should've been here. With you. With her. Nothing else matters more than that."

The words came too fast—tumbling out like they'd been waiting all night to escape. "I thought I could do both. I thought I could make it work. And then when I saw the time—fuck, Selene. I drove straight from the station. I ran. I didn't even think, just—I had to get here. But I was too late. I know that."

She exhaled slowly, but nothing eased between us. Her eyes didn't narrow. They didn't soften. They just stayed steady on mine. Watching. Measuring.

"I missed it," I said, barely above a whisper. "I missed her. I missed the opportunity to be there for you."

A silence fell. One that swallowed every sound of the night.

Selene's hand finally released the doorframe. She folded her arms gently across her chest, like she was holding herself up from the inside. Her expression didn't crack, but something in her gaze flickered—like a candle struggling to stay lit.

"Thank you for explaining what happened," she said at last. "But I think I need a little space, Austin." Her voice was so even, so heartbreakingly composed, it took me a second to understand the words. "I've done this before—believed someone when they said I could count on them, and I can't afford to be wrong again."

My heart lodged behind my ribs as my panic rose. "Selene . . ."

She shook her head—not in anger, but with quiet certainty. "You were trying. I know that. But I need more than good intentions."

I took a step forward without thinking. "Let me fix it."

"You can't," she said gently, like it hurt her to say it.

Panic bubbled up inside me. "I fucked up *once*, Selene. Can't I—"

"I know, Austin." Her eyes shimmered with unshed tears, and it gutted me. "I just . . . I'm not even sure what I'm doing here. All I know is I have a five-year-old little girl who cried herself to sleep and looks to *me* to understand how I could let that happen."

The thought of Winnie crying because of me was too much. The porch boards groaned beneath my feet. I clutched the bag of food tighter, as if there was anything left in it worth offering.

"Please," I begged. "Just . . . let me apologize to Winnie."

Her mouth parted like she wanted to say no—but then she sighed, glancing toward the hallway behind her.

"She's asleep," she said. "You can come by tomorrow."

I nodded, though everything in me was screaming to stay. To fight. To grab her hand and tell her she was the only thing I was sure about in my whole damn life.

Selene turned to retreat back into her house when I panicked and shouted the first thing that came to mind. "I love you!"

Fuck.

Selene's mouth dropped open as I stepped forward. "Selene, I'm sorry, I—I didn't mean to just yell it at you like that, I'm . . . shit."

My eyes bounced between hers as I dragged a hand through my hair. I had shocked her silent with the world's most unhinged declaration of love, and while I meant it, she deserved more than a hasty *I love you* on the heels of my fuckup, like those words would fix what I did.

"I can't do this right now," she finally whispered. "Good night, Austin." I stood there as she stepped back inside and closed the door with an almost unbearable softness.

The click of the latch might as well have been the sound of something breaking clean in two.

I stood on the porch until the moth disappeared, until the porch light flickered again and went out, until I couldn't feel my fingers around the now-cold paper bag.

Just one wall between us, and it might as well have been a canyon.

Inside, I sat on the edge of my bed, hands clenched so tight in my lap they'd gone white at the knuckles.

The room didn't feel like mine anymore.

Same boots by the door. Same hoodie tossed over the chair. Same dent in the mattress where I always crashed after long days, but something had shifted. Or maybe everything had.

The silence felt wrong. It was loud and cavernous all at once.

I glanced at the wall beside me—the one that separated my room from Selene's. It used to be nothing more than drywall and studs. Something we laughed about when I had first moved in. How we'd have to keep it down. How thin the walls were. How close we were.

Now it might as well have been a fucking mountain.

I leaned forward, elbows on my knees, and stared at that stretch of painted plaster like it might answer for me. Like maybe, if I looked hard enough, it would give me a way through.

A thump echoed faintly—a drawer closing. Then footsteps, soft but unmistakable. The creak of floorboards under Selene's feet.

She was still awake.

Still moving. Still holding everything together on the other side, because she always did. Even when she was breaking.

I closed my eyes and tried to picture her tucking Winnie in. Folding her little pajamas, brushing crumbs from the kitchen counter, flipping off the porch light and going to bed alone.

Fuck.

My chest tightened, breath catching hard behind my ribs as I walked toward the wall. I pressed a hand to the surface. Flat palm, fingers splayed like maybe if I held still enough, she'd feel it.

"I'm sorry," I whispered into the darkness.

I didn't expect an answer, but I hoped maybe she'd feel

something in the way I said it. If she heard, I only hoped she knew I meant it with every part of my soul.

I was sorry for missing the performance. For being too late. For not immediately choosing them over anything else.

Regret pulsed so thick I thought I might drown in it.

I didn't know how to fix what I'd broken. I only knew that wall had never felt so impossibly solid.

I let my head fall forward, resting my forehead against the cool sheet of plaster, and stayed there in the quiet. Listening for her and reaching out for nothing.

Just one wall away. She was only feet from me and I had never felt farther from home.

THIRTY-FOUR

SELENE

THE HOUSE WAS DARK.

Not the kind of quiet dark stillness that soothed, but the kind that pressed in from all sides. As if the walls themselves knew something had shifted and were holding their breath along with me.

Winnie's breathing had finally deepened, soft and rhythmic from the other room. I'd kissed her forehead three times before tucking the blanket higher on her shoulder. She didn't stir. Winnie had whispered something incoherent in her sleep and curled tighter onto her side, completely untouched by the crack that had split the night wide open.

I was glad for her capacity to forget so quickly, to rebound like a rubber band while I felt like shattered glass wrapped in tissue.

I stepped quietly down the hallway, fingers brushing the wall as I went. On the other side, I could still feel him. Not in any literal way—but like an echo caught in the drywall, pulsing low and persistent. *Austin.* Just a few feet away, separated from me by nothing more than plaster and paint and everything I didn't say.

I paused outside my bedroom and closed my eyes.

A wave of something thick and hot curled through my chest. It was grief, but not clean. It was stitched through with shame, with anger, with that sick twist of embarrassment I hated more than anything.

Because I'd *hoped*.

I'd let myself believe—really believe—that I could have something different this time. That he was different. That maybe we were building something steady. Something real. Something that could last longer than the breathless beginning.

He loves me.

I turned the knob and pushed the door to my bedroom open.

The room felt unfamiliar in the dark. Maybe it was me who didn't belong anymore. I moved by muscle memory, stepping around a laundry basket, reaching for the edge of the bed before my hand dropped to the basket instead. I crouched and pulled out the shirt that I had tossed in earlier that week—something Austin had worn when he had stayed over last.

I pressed it to my face.

It still smelled like him. Like cedar and sunlight and salt. Like sweat and soap and something I hadn't let myself name until now.

Home.

I sank to the floor.

Just folded down onto the hardwood like my body couldn't bear its own weight. The shirt was crushed against my chest, my arms locked around it like a shield. My spine curled, my forehead met my knees, and I stopped pretending.

The sob that broke free was ugly. It cracked open my throat and left me raw.

I tried to muffle it into the cotton—tears swallowed down so Winnie wouldn't hear—but another followed, and another. There was no fixing it, no gathering the pieces into something presentable.

I cried the way a woman cries when she's been too strong for too long. When her body forgets how to carry it all without collapsing under the load.

When she realizes, too late, that she let someone in past the gates.

I should've known better. I *did* know better. Every instinct had warned me, and still I'd done it—I'd let my guard down. I'd let him in. I'd let myself fall in love and believe in a future I hadn't dared imagine before.

And for what?

It wasn't even about the missed performance. It was about letting *myself* down. It had become achingly clear that the pattern was *me*. The one where I gave and hoped and controlled everything around me so I couldn't be let down again. I was making the same mistakes all over again, and I didn't know how to stop it.

I'd gotten comfortable with Austin's help. For so long I'd waited for someone to meet me halfway that I forgot how painful it was to realize that no one was rescuing me but myself. I had desperately wanted things to be different.

Being a mother meant that I needed to be stronger than that.

I gasped through a sob, breath hitching hard in my chest. The shirt slipped from my hands, crumpling in my lap.

I wasn't mad at Austin because he didn't show up. I was mad because I'd counted on him to, and I was madder still that some part of me still wanted to count on him.

The wall beside me stayed quiet. No footsteps. Just silence.

But I swore I could still feel him there, just on the other side.

Like maybe he was sitting with his back to the wall, too, wishing the distance between us was easier to cross. I stayed curled on the floor until the tears slowed, then stopped. My face was hot, sticky, and raw.

I didn't move. I didn't want to go to bed. I didn't want to be strong again tomorrow.

But I knew I would. Because Winnie would need breakfast. Because the world would keep spinning.

Still, tonight . . . I let myself sit there, alone in the dark, holding the shape of something I almost had but was too scared to hold.

THE MORNING CAME SLOWLY, like the world knew I couldn't take the sharp edges of the day.

Sunlight filtered through the kitchen curtains in lazy beams, striping the floor in pale gold. The scent of coffee filled the air, rich and grounding. I stood at the counter in an old sweatshirt and pajama pants, hands wrapped around a chipped ceramic mug, letting the warmth soak into my palms.

Winnie sat at the kitchen table in a pink hoodie, legs swinging beneath the bench as she nibbled at a piece of toast slathered in strawberry jam. She hummed to herself between bites, completely unfazed by last night. Her hair stuck out in a dozen directions, eyes soft from sleep.

"You feeling okay, bug?" I asked, voice still raw at the edges.

"Yep." She shrugged and licked jam off her thumb. "I'm good."

She didn't even mention the performance. There was no lingering sadness. No weight in her chest. Just toast and a morning hum and the blissful magic of childhood resilience.

I blinked and looked down at my coffee. The floor felt too solid under my feet.

A knock came at the front door, and before I could move, it creaked open.

Elodie's voice filled the space, low and cheerful. "You decent?"

"Unfortunately," I muttered, though the knot in my chest loosened.

She stepped inside with Levi behind her, already unzipping his coat. "We're stealing your kid for a bit," she announced. "The goats are restless, and Levi made blueberry muffins."

Levi held up a Tupperware with a proud grin. "We even remembered to let them cool this time."

"Levi!" Winnie scrambled off the bench. "Can I go, Mama? *Please.*"

I hesitated for half a breath—then nodded. "Of course, baby. Just put on your boots."

Levi helped her get ready in the mudroom, leaving Elodie to watch me from across the room.

Her gaze lingered too long.

"You look like you've been hit by a train," she said, eyeing me gently and stepping toward the counter.

"Thanks," I murmured, sipping my coffee. "I was going for *functional wreck*."

She reached for the second mug I'd left beside the coffeepot and poured herself a cup. "Did you talk to him?"

I didn't answer right away, staring out the window where frost clung to the glass in thin threads.

"He came by late last night," I said finally.

"And?" Elodie's brows were in her hairline.

"He told me he loves me." I swallowed. "I told him I needed a little space."

Elodie blinked. At first she didn't speak, didn't push. She sipped her coffee and waited.

"I thought I was smarter than this," I whispered. "I thought I was past hoping for something I couldn't rely on. He's twenty-eight, for fuck's sake."

"You know his age has nothing to do with this." Elodie's face softened as her head shook. "You didn't mess up by loving him back, Selene."

The words landed like a warm hand to my back—steadying. Not healing, but grounding.

I blinked fast. My eyes still gritty from last night's tears.

"Do you love him?" she finally asked.

"Yes." I swallowed hard. "But I'm afraid. I just keep thinking about Brian," I said. "About the time he didn't show up for that doctor's appointment when I was pregnant. The nurse asked if my husband would be joining us, and I laughed like it was a joke, and then I sat there alone, listening to her heartbeat."

Elodie's jaw tensed.

"I didn't even cry," I said quietly. "I just sat there and smiled because I didn't want the nurse to feel awkward. I've spent so long making things easier for everyone else that I forgot I was allowed to need something. It was the first of many, *many* times that Brian was too caught up in some-thing to show up for me."

"That's because he's a dick," Elodie shot back.

I gritted my teeth and gave her a plain look.

She raised her hands in surrender. "*Fine*. I'll take a break from Brian bashing for *one* day." Her hand settled on her hip. "But needing someone isn't weak," she said. "It's human. Plus, Austin is not Brian. It's unfair to compare them."

"I know that." I nodded, throat tight. "Honestly, I don't think this is about Austin missing one thing," I said. "I think it's about how fast I felt real panic. Like it proved all my worst fears. That I was alone again. That I'd always be the only one showing up."

"Maybe you set an impossible standard," Elodie said in a way that only a sister could. "You don't need him to be perfect. Just . . . present."

I stared at her, my hackles going up in immediate defense of Austin. "He has been. Every time. Except this one." I blew out a breath, knowing she was absolutely right. "Shit. Maybe I overreacted."

Elodie reached across the counter and squeezed my hand. "I'm proud that you're standing up for yourself. I am. You've had to do a lot by yourself, and that's bound to change a woman. But . . . you do tend to be a little rigid."

My chin wobbled and I nodded.

"You said you love him," she continued. "So find the courage to tell him that. Talk to him, Selene. Don't let fear of being wrong steal something good."

My phone buzzed on the counter.

I didn't have to look to know who the text was from.

Still, I picked it up.

AUSTIN

I need to say it again. I'm so sorry. Not for
missing the performance—but for not
seeing how much it meant. I'd like to say it
in person when you're both ready.

My thumb hovered over the screen.

I didn't respond, not yet, but I didn't delete it either. Instead, I stared until the screen faded to black and sat there in the quiet, feeling the faintest hum of something I hadn't felt since before last night—not pain, but *hopeful possibility*.

THIRTY-FIVE

AUSTIN

The car idled for a full minute before I finally killed the engine.

Downtown Star Harbor hadn't changed in the thirty minutes I'd been circling it. Same green awnings over the Crooked Spine, same bike rack still missing a bolt, same tilted campaign sign for the mayor's reelection propped outside the hardware store. I'd meant to stop in—I needed sandpaper or caulk or something equally unimportant—but instead I parked two spaces past the bakery and just sat there.

The streets were quiet in that lazy Saturday way. Slow and unhurried. A couple of kids zipped past on scooters. Someone had chalked a hopscotch board on the sidewalk near the mailbox, the colors soft and dusty from wear. The air smelled like dead leaves and exhaust, sun-warmed pavement, and the icy drag of winter creeping closer.

I hadn't eaten. I couldn't eat. There was still a half-crushed protein bar in the console, but the thought of chewing made my stomach flip.

Across the street, the bell above the bakery door jingled

and a family stepped out—a woman, a man, and a little girl with dark hair and freckles along her nose. She looked about Winnie's age, maybe younger, with a messy braid and cookie crumbs clinging to her shirt.

She held up a half-eaten sugar cookie in one hand, the other tucked securely in her dad's. Her voice carried across the street in bursts—telling a story with wild hand gestures and animated eyebrows, completely unaware of the world around her.

The mom smiled, brushing crumbs from the girl's cheek with her thumb. The dad leaned down to say something only they could hear, and the girl tipped her head back in a full-bellied giggle.

They walked off, just like that. Three people, one unit. Easy. Unbroken.

A burn started behind my eyes, sharp and immediate. I blinked it back.

That should've been me.

Not the bakery, not the cookie. Just the together part. Winnie bouncing between us, arms flung around Selene's waist. Me holding a backpack, Selene carrying a bag of cookies she'd insist was a "business expense."

I used to picture that without even meaning to. I would go to sleep thinking about it and wake up hoping I hadn't dreamed it.

And now?

I didn't even know if Selene would look at me again. If Winnie would forgive me.

I turned toward the passenger seat, suddenly desperate for something—anything—to hold on to. That was when I saw the photo, still tucked partway under the visor where I'd shoved it.

I pulled it down carefully, like it might shatter. A

printed snapshot, sun-faded around the edges. My dad in uniform, grinning at someone off camera, looking proud and half cocky the way guys do before the world wears them down.

He looked young. Younger than I am now.

I stared at the photo for a long time, like it might answer the question I couldn't even say out loud.

How do you come back from fucking up the best thing in your life?

He didn't answer, of course. Dad just smiled that same frozen smile, stuck in time.

I leaned my head back against the headrest, closed my eyes, and let the silence settle.

A couple passed on the sidewalk—a guy with a stroller, his partner walking beside him with a to-go coffee—and they didn't even glance at me.

Why would they? I was just a guy sitting alone in a parked car, creepily watching other people live the life I wanted.

I'd had it. I'd had everything worth looking at, and I let it walk away.

I didn't remember driving home. All I recalled was the ache in my jaw from clenching my teeth and the imprint of that photo still burned into my palm.

By the time I pulled into the driveway, the sun was sagging behind the trees. Shadows stretched long across the gravel, and the breeze had picked up, rustling the edges of Selene's wind chimes like they couldn't decide on a melody. The porch light on my side flicked on automatically, too early, casting a sharp triangle of gold across the siding.

I didn't go inside right away.

I didn't want to be back in that empty house with too much quiet and the hum of guilt ricocheting off the walls. I sank down onto the top step, elbows on my knees, and let the weight of the day press down on me like a second skin.

The screen door creaked open behind me.

Brody didn't say anything as he stepped out, just handed me a coffee—black, still hot, still somehow perfect.

I took it without a word.

He lowered himself onto the step beside me, letting out a sigh that sounded like it came from somewhere deeper than his lungs.

"Isn't going into someone's home without permission breaking and entering?" I asked.

He scoffed and looked at me. "Fuck off. I have a key." His legs stretched in front of him as we stared into the lawn. "Besides, I saw you parked downtown," he said finally, voice low and even.

I shrugged. "I didn't feel like being here."

He nodded like he understood but still had questions. "You were in front of the bakery for almost forty minutes."

I grunted. "I wasn't counting."

He sipped. "You looked like shit."

I scoffed. "That's because I feel like shit."

His brow twitched in what might've been sympathy. Or amusement. Maybe both. "Heard there might be a little riff between you and Selene."

I shook my head as sarcasm dripped from my tongue. "Good news travels fast, apparently."

Brody shrugged. "It's a small town. What did you expect?" His legs stretched out in front of him, and he sighed. "So your plan is to sit here feeling sorry for yourself all night?"

My eyes twitched toward Selene's half of the duplex. "I don't know what else to do."

Brody didn't answer right away. He stared out at the

street, eyes narrowed like he was watching something far off. Then he took another drink, set the mug down beside him, and leaned forward, forearms resting on his thighs.

"Did you cheat on her?" he asked.

My head whipped to the side. "What? Fuck, no. I'm not a total idiot."

Brody nodded as though he liked that answer. "So what then?"

"I promised Selene and Winnie I'd see her kindergarten performance, but I blew it. I was late and missed the whole thing." I exhaled hard, guilt tightening like a belt around my ribs. "You called and I stayed at the station longer than I should've," I admitted, voice rough. "I thought —I don't know—I thought I could do both. Be the guy who shows up for everyone. Be the kind of brother you want around."

Brody looked surprised, but he nodded slowly, his jaw flexing.

Fuck it, might as well lay it all out there.

"I like being near you," I added, quieter now. "After everything with Dad . . . and growing up the way I did . . . I didn't want to mess it up. Not with you finally letting me in."

Brody turned his head, met my eyes. "You can't mess that up, Austin."

I let out a breathless laugh. "Can't I?"

"You could've said something." His voice was firm but not cruel. "You should've told me. Hell, I would've understood. You didn't have to choose."

I rubbed my hands over my face. "I didn't want to let you down. We were talking and laughing and then . . . I lost track of time and it all went sideways."

"You wouldn't have let me down," he said, shrugging.

"But you did let her down. That's the part you have to own."

Silence settled between us, sharp and clean.

Then Brody softened, barely. "You're always going to be my brother. That doesn't change. Even when you fuck up. Hell, especially then."

Love for my brother filled my chest. I shook my head and scoffed under my breath. "You think Selene wants anything to do with me right now?"

"You're not the first guy to screw up a good thing with her," he said quietly. "But you might be the first one who gives a damn enough to fix it." He shrugged. "She might not forgive you today. Maybe not even tomorrow, but that doesn't mean you stop trying."

"I said I love her," I murmured, voice breaking on the edge of it. "I practically yelled it in her face. It was so desperate." I laughed at myself for how epically poorly timed it had been. "But I meant it. Somehow I still blew it."

Brody glanced sideways. "You think saying it is what counts the most?"

I blinked. "Isn't it?"

He shook his head, slow and sure. "Love's not just the saying-it part. It's what you do after the screwup. When it's hard. When it's inconvenient. When it costs you something. That's where it lives." He took a sip of his coffee. "At least . . . that's my best guess, anyway."

I stared down at the coffee cup, the heat long gone from the ceramic. "I don't know how to fix this."

"You don't," he said simply. "Not all at once."

I eyeballed him. "So then what?"

Brody stood, his boots scuffing the wood. He looked at me like he saw right through the mess I was, straight into whatever pieces were still salvageable underneath. "You start by doing what Dad didn't. You start showing up, and then you keep showing up. Prove that you meant it when you told her you loved her . . . even if you did yell it in her face."

He turned and walked back inside, letting the screen door ease shut behind him.

I sat there for a long time, the quiet heavier than before —but different. Less suffocating. Like silence that waits for something new to begin.

I looked down at my phone, at the empty screen, at the string of unanswered texts I hadn't sent yet.

Then I stood up.

Time to prove I was a man of my word.

THIRTY-SIX

SELENE

THE HOUSE WAS STILL AGAIN.

Not quiet—still, more like it was waiting to see what I would do.

I stood at the edge of the kitchen, my fingers curled around the handle of my coffee mug, half full and long since gone cold. I hadn't sipped it in twenty minutes. The ceramic was lukewarm now, and my other hand kept drifting to the knot forming at the back of my neck.

I'd been up since six. I made Winnie breakfast and brushed her hair into pigtails that went crooked the second she put on her jacket. I packed her backpack, double-checked her folder, zipped up her coat, and tied her shoes.

All the things Austin usually helped with.

All the things I could do on my own. Things I *had* done on my own, for years.

I told myself I needed the time off work. That staying home these last few mornings and afternoons was good for Winnie. That I liked being the one to pick her up from school and make dinner without glancing at the clock. That it had nothing to do with needing space to clear my own head.

The truth clung to my lungs like smoke.

I hated how respectful he was being. How he'd backed off completely. I hated that I hadn't heard his key in the lock. That there hadn't been a quiet knock or a note left on the counter or one of his sweatshirts slung over the arm of the couch like it still belonged there.

It would've been easier if he'd pushed. If he'd knocked and begged and made me feel justified in keeping him at arm's length before collapsing in his arms and begging for a chance to love him again.

Instead, Austin was giving me space, and somehow that hurt more.

My phone buzzed against the counter, and I smiled when I saw the photo.

Winnie, sitting at her desk, cheeks dusted with powdered sugar, grinning so wide I could count all her baby teeth. Her hands were covered in orange frosting, and a half-eaten Halloween doughnut sat on a paper napkin in front of her.

Below the photo, the message from her teacher read:

Big thank you to Mr. Calloway for the surprise treats! He brought enough for the whole class. We loved the spooky spider doughnuts! He also gave Winnie the sweetest note. Thought you might want to see.

A second image loaded. A folded piece of notebook paper in Winnie's tiny fingers. Scrawled in Austin's all-caps handwriting:

HEY BUG,

I HOPE THE SPIDER DOUGHNUTS WERE SPOOKY ENOUGH. SO PROUD OF YOU. ALWAYS.

Love, Austin

I pressed my lips together and stared at the screen until my vision blurred. Then I blinked and looked away, willing the tears back down where they belonged.

I set the phone on the counter. My thumb hovered above the reply, then moved to lock the screen instead.

I could hear the deep timbre of his voice in my head.

So proud of you.

Of course he knew exactly what to say. He always had. Austin Calloway was the kind of man who listened, even when you didn't think he was paying attention. He was the kind of man who knew that Winnie hated plain glazed and loved anything with crunchy sugar eyes. Who remembered which day she had library and when her spelling tests were. Who called her *his girl* like it was the best honor he'd ever been given.

A man who said he loved me. A man I knew I loved with every fiber of my being.

I exhaled a shaky breath. I should have let him explain better. Maybe Elodie was right and I was letting the weight of my past shape the way I viewed the present.

Maybe I was still scared.

I stood still and listened to the thrum of my own heartbeat.

The house stayed eerily quiet.

I picked up my cold coffee and poured it down the sink. Then I pulled my hair into a bun, changed into clean jeans, and got ready for work.

By the time we made it home, Winnie's mouth was stained blue from the cotton candy twist cone she'd insisted on. I had chosen a small espresso chip I'd barely touched— my excuse for extending the walk as long as I could.

That was what it was, after all. An excuse.

Our walk was a way to loop the long way through town, past the library and over the footbridge, to delay the inevitable moment we'd round the corner and see the duplex.

I wasn't ready for an accidental run-in, because I hadn't figured out how I was going to explain the jumbled-up emotions knotted in my heart and that maybe they didn't really matter, because at the end of the day I was in love with him.

My chest tightened the second the house came into view. The pale golden light of late afternoon stretched across the sidewalk, catching in the hair at Winnie's temple and making her glow like something out of a memory.

She skipped ahead, trailing melted drips down her wrist, and I shifted my gaze to the yard.

It was clean. *Too clean.*

The brittle, rust-colored leaves that had been curling along the edge of the walk all week were gone. Raked into neat piles and bagged, the grass showing in soft patches beneath.

My feet slowed. I hadn't touched the rake. To be honest, I hadn't even thought about the yard.

I glanced up the steps and stopped.

A simple, woven basket sat in the middle of the porch.

I swallowed and moved toward it, my fingers curling around Winnie's sticky hand as she danced up the steps.

"Go wash up, okay, baby?" I said, and Winnie darted inside.

The screen door clattered shut behind her, leaving me in a pool of quiet. I crouched in front of the basket.

Inside were peas—still damp, their skins taut and cold—and a handful of sugar snap vines, tangled together like they'd just been tugged free. A few sprigs of basil, wilting slightly but still fragrant. And then, nestled in a dish towel in the corner, a tiny bunch of rainbow carrots.

Not the uniform kind you find at the store. These were knobby and strange, like they'd been shaped by the stubbornness of the earth itself. Crooked stems. Mud-caked ends. One of them was such a deep purple, it looked almost bruised.

I reached for it without thinking.

The root trailed like a thin ribbon, curling at the end. It was still cool from the dirt. I let my thumb trace the ridges in the skin, the places where it had grown wild and a little misshapen. I remembered the day we planted them—Austin kneeling in the dirt beside Winnie, brushing soil from her knuckles and promising her that yes, carrots really could come in funky colors.

He'd smiled at me over her head like it wasn't the first time he'd imagined a future in our garden.

I didn't cry, but I wanted to.

Instead, I sat with the quiet ache that pressed against the inside of my ribs and held that crooked little carrot like it had something important to say.

I scanned the basket again.

No note.

Nothing tucked beneath the towel or wedged between the peas and basil. Nothing that said my name. Nothing that was just for me, and somehow that absence made the ache worse.

I realized then that I wanted one. I wanted a message. A word. Some small offering that said he saw me too.

Not just Winnie.

Not just the little life we were building around her, but *me*.

I curled my fingers tighter around the carrot and stood.

With sure steps, I walked to his door and knocked —*hard*.

"Austin? Are you there? I'm sorry, I'd like to talk. Please open up." My heartbeat drummed in time with my tapping toes. I knocked again. "Austin?"

Silence greeted me as I slunk away. The porch creaked beneath my weight as I stepped inside and let the screen door close behind me. The scent of basil followed, earthy and green, clinging to the air as I set the basket on the counter.

The carrot stayed in my hand, and I stared at it for a long moment, heart tight in my chest, and smiled.

He was still showing up, and I knew exactly what I'd say the second I saw him again.

Winnie's thunderous footsteps pulled me from my spiraling thoughts.

"Mama! I figured it out!" Winnie declared, breathless as she made her way to the kitchen. "Our Halloween costumes. We should be the Lady of the Dunes!"

I turned from the sink, raising an eyebrow. "Oh yeah?"

"Yes!" She nodded hard. "You'll be the Lady. Like, with a long floaty dress and a crown made of seaweed or shells or something cool. Austin can be her long-lost love—the sailor who got lost at sea—and I'll be the grizzliest, grossest sea captain ever."

She paused, grinning. "I'll have a fake beard and a peg leg and one eyeball hanging out."

"Oh wow," I said, trying not to laugh. "You've really thought this through."

"I think it's perfect," she said proudly. "We'll be spooky and tragic and hilarious. The best kind of Halloween."

Her smile was blinding, so wide and hopeful it almost hurt to look at. She bounced on her toes, then spun in a little circle like the sheer joy of planning was too big for her body.

"We can all go together," she said, nodding fiercely. "Me and you and Dad—"

She stopped.

I blinked.

Her eyes widened. "I mean Austin." She covered her slip with a laugh. "You know what I meant."

My heart gave the faintest lurch, and I reached for the counter behind me like I could anchor myself to it. The edge bit into my palm.

I sat down on the nearest stool, slowly, like anything more abrupt might crack me open.

"Sweetie . . ." My voice was thinner than I wanted it to be. I swallowed. "Austin, he . . ."

I didn't know how to finish.

I didn't want to correct her, not when I understood *exactly* what she meant. Not when I'd spent the last few days trying not to think about what he meant to me too.

I didn't want to make it a lesson in biology or legality or complicated relationships that I thought were just supposed to be sex but turned my whole world upside down. I also didn't want to dim the light in her face by drawing boundaries she didn't understand.

So instead I offered the only truth I could manage. "He might not be able to come trick-or-treating with us, but we can ask."

Winnie didn't flinch. She just shrugged, casual and certain. "He will."

The faith in her voice—so pure, so unshaken—was a sucker punch to the chest.

Winnie set her shoulders. "I know you're sad about him for being late to my concert," she said, climbing onto the stool beside mine. "But you don't need to be. I already forgave him."

My breath caught.

"You two just need to talk," she added, swinging her feet. "It'll be fine."

I didn't say anything. I couldn't.

In her small, unbothered voice, she'd spoken the one thing I was too afraid to believe in—that maybe it really was that simple. That maybe forgiveness didn't have to be tangled and conditional and hard-earned.

Maybe it could just be offered. Freely. Lovingly. Like a handful of crooked carrots pulled from the earth.

She leaned against me, her little head warm against my shoulder.

I looked down at her, this wise little person in a tiny body, and felt the crack deepen.

Because I wanted to believe her. I wanted to believe in a world where all it took was a conversation and a costume.

So I smiled, small and tired, but real.

"Okay," I said. "We'll see."

THIRTY-SEVEN

AUSTIN

I OFFICIALLY HATED my half of the duplex.

It was quiet in that way that made my ears ring a little—like the silence was trying too hard. I was busy pretending not to miss the sound of bare feet thumping across hardwood or a little girl humming the theme from her cartoons for the thousandth time.

I sat at the small kitchen table, surrounded by the wreckage of a late dinner I barely remembered eating. There was a half-finished container of lo mein, sweet-and-sour sauce smeared across a napkin, and a sweating beer I had taken three sips of and then forgotten.

Across from me, my laptop glowed with an open tab for air-filtration systems. Beside it sat a manila folder filled with bank statements and loan applications for a house I didn't own yet.

I leaned back in the chair, dragged a hand over my face, and let the silence stretch.

It wasn't that I regretted giving Selene space.

I had promised I wouldn't crowd her. I had an insatiable

need to show her I could listen—that I could learn. And I meant it.

But *fuck*, I missed them.

I missed the way Winnie would barrel into me with a fierce hug, all wild ponytails and snack requests. I missed seeing Selene's face when she'd laugh at something on TV that was genuinely stupid. I missed the feel of them in my life—messy, noisy, beautiful.

Now?

The air felt thin, like something vital had been sucked out of it.

I stared at the condensation dripping down the bottle in my hand. Water pooled at the base, the cardboard take-out bag damp and curling beneath it.

My side of the duplex didn't feel like home anymore, and maybe it never really had.

At the time, it had felt like enough. Enough space. Enough privacy. Enough for me to pretend I wasn't still carrying things I hadn't named yet.

I could never have guessed a chance meeting with Selene in a lonely jazz bar would have turned into me *craving* everything about domestic life with her.

I let out a breath and pushed the beer away, grabbing the blueprints instead.

Selene didn't need promises or pressure. Instead, I wanted to give her something real that would show them both how I felt.

I wasn't trying to win her back. I was trying to prove I'd never left.

~

WES'S PLACE sat at the edge of town, just past the split in the road where the woods thickened and the lake breeze grew sharper. The house was mostly hidden by towering evergreens, the gravel driveway barely visible from the road. I pulled in slowly, tires crunching under scattered pine needles, and rolled to a stop in front of a house that didn't look anything like a man trying to disappear.

It was gorgeous.

Clean lines, weathered cedar, long glass windows that caught the trees like paintings. It was a place you built when you had nothing to prove but wanted everything to feel intentional. Of course it was—Wes Vaughn had always been a genius with his hands.

I shut the car door and climbed the steps. No doorbell. Just a knotted iron knocker shaped like a ship's anchor. I knocked once. Waited. Nothing.

Knocked again—harder this time. "Wes? It's me, Austin. Brody's brother. Come on, man. Open up."

More seconds passed, until I heard the sound of footsteps, shuffling behind the door, slow and uneven.

The door opened, and Wes looked like someone who'd stepped out of a storm and hadn't decided whether he wanted to come back inside.

He had an unkempt beard, and the shadows under his eyes made the blue look almost metallic. He leaned slightly to one side, a shift you might not notice unless you were looking for it.

"Austin," he said flatly. "Didn't know we had a meeting."

"We don't," I said. "Can I come in?"

Wes hesitated. "Your brother send you?"

I shook my head. "No. I, uh, had a construction question for you."

His eyes narrowed, but he stepped aside with a grunt.

Inside, the house was exactly what you'd expect from one of Wes Vaughn's designs—clean lines, rich wood tones, everything crafted with purpose. The bones of the house were perfect.

But the rest? It looked like the man had stopped caring.

Take-out containers were stacked on the kitchen island, most of them half closed, a few buzzing faintly with fruit flies. An abandoned broom leaned against a cabinet, the dustpan still half full. The sink was piled with dishes, some of them clearly from last week.

The entire space felt like it had been built for a life that never arrived. Beautiful and functional on the outside, but hollow in all the places that mattered.

I let the door fall shut behind me and glanced over at Wes, who didn't seem to notice—or didn't care that I did.

He wasn't embarrassed. Just . . . resigned, like this was the best it was going to get.

The house smelled like old food and coffee gone cold. Every inch of the place looked lived in and left behind all at once.

"You doing okay, man?" I asked, rubbing a hand across the back of my neck.

Wes stared at me until I shifted my gaze. "Did you need something?"

I cleared my throat and reached for the folder in my coat pocket. "It's about the house on Cherrytree."

Wes didn't move.

"I want to buy it," I said. "The whole thing. What would it take to get you to sell it to me?"

He dropped onto a stool at the kitchen counter and reached for a half-eaten protein bar. "It's not finished," he said, voice low and flat. "The house hasn't been touched in months. Why would I give a shit if you take it off my hands?"

I studied him for a beat. The apathy wasn't a performance. It hung on him like old clothes, comfortable but too heavy.

"I remember when you started it," I said, trying to salvage our conversation. "You called it your next masterpiece."

"Yeah, well." He gave a dry laugh. "Turns out masterpieces don't matter when you wake up every day wondering if you still give a damn."

The words landed between us like dust.

I didn't pity him—I wouldn't do that to a man like Wes —but I felt the grief in that sentence like a bruise. Deep and dull and still healing.

I let the quiet stretch until it felt like enough.

"I've seen it," I said. "The porch isn't done, but the bones are there. I know what it could be."

Wes didn't look at me, but his jaw twitched. "Then finish it. Maybe you can make it something."

I stretched out my hand to him. "Thank you."

He gripped it fiercely and shook before letting it drop. He turned, depression hovering over his shoulders like a heavy blanket.

"Hey," I offered. "I think some of the guys from the team are going to go up to the Lantern for a few beers. You should join us."

His blue eyes pierced through me. His jaw ticced before he shook his head. "No, thanks, man."

I swallowed hard. He didn't need pity, but it was clear Wes needed people to show up for him, because he was too deep in it to show up for himself. I made a mental note to call Brody and figure *something* out.

"Well, then, I'll see you around," I called to his back.

Wes didn't bother turning around or walking me to the door. He simply raised one hand in a dismissive goodbye. I exited his house with a strange mix of emotions swirling inside me.

The drive back was quiet, the sky overcast and low like it hadn't decided whether to rain or hold off. I rolled the window down halfway, letting the sharp cold bite at my skin while I let the hope settle in.

It scared the hell out of me.

The idea that it might not be enough. That Selene might never let me all the way back in. But that didn't change a thing.

I was going to build it anyway.

Even if it took the rest of my life.

THIRTY-EIGHT

AUSTIN

By the time Halloween night came around, I was crawling out of my skin. Excitement and unease warred in my chest, pulsing just beneath the surface like a second heartbeat.

I'd spent the past hour pacing the living room, pretending to eat and watch television, all while listening to Selene and Winnie through the wall. The lights were dimmed low, my boots were by the door, and the last piece of my costume hung over the kitchen chair like it was waiting for courage.

Through the wall, Selene's voice floated in—soft and teasing.

Then came Winnie's giggle, unmistakable and wild with energy. "I'm gonna be the grossest sea captain ever!" she announced like a battle cry.

I smiled despite the tension stringing through my chest.

There was a rustle of movement, the thud of something being dropped—maybe a bag or one of those big plastic pumpkins she insisted on dragging everywhere.

Then Winnie got louder. "Mom! Please hurry up! My beard isn't sticking!"

I leaned back against the wall, head tipped just enough to catch every sound I shouldn't have been listening to. Selene's voice was too quiet to catch all the words, but it was warm. Light. It curled under my skin like heat from a long-forgotten fire.

Winnie giggled. "Austin's gonna freak out when he sees you. You look so ghosty."

I held my breath in the beat of silence. Something muffled. Selene must've said something back, but the words didn't carry.

I heard the front door open—hinges groaning gently—and the slam of it closing. Their footsteps padded across the porch.

It was finally time.

I reached for the last piece of my costume. My hands shook a little—not from nerves, I told myself. From hope.

From trying.

From still loving them more than anything else in the world and finally doing something about it.

The porch creaked under my boots as I eased the door open. The night air was cool and sharp, the scent of crushed leaves rising up from the walkway. Porch lights blinked across the neighborhood in warm, flickering bursts. Jack-o'-lanterns flickered like quiet sentinels.

Selene stood at the edge of the porch, her hand resting gently on Winnie's shoulder. For a second I forgot how to breathe.

She wore layers of gauzy white that shimmered under the porch light, the edges frayed like seafoam and storm-snatched lace. Her hair had been twisted loosely, wisps catching the breeze like kelp beneath the surface. A dusting of silver shimmer traced her collarbone. She didn't look like a woman in costume. She looked like a legend pulled from the tide—like the Lady of the Dunes stepping out of a whispered dream.

I had tried to match that magic. Her eyes widened as she turned and looked at me.

A sun-faded button-up clung to my chest, sleeves rolled to my forearms, with flashes of my tattoos peeking beneath them. Worn suspenders crossed my back. I'd thrifted an old sailor's scarf from the antique shop in town—sea-glass green and fraying at the ends. My hair was messier than usual, salt tossed, and as unruly as I could get it. I'd added a streak of fake dirt along my jawline, a few rips in my pants.

A shipwrecked soul from another time, lost and finally returned.

Her long-lost love.

I didn't know if she'd recognize it right away, but when her eyes finally found mine, something in her went very still.

Winnie spun around, her fake beard askew and an enormous pirate hat tilting on her head. Seaweed dangled from her curls, tangled with a rubber crab. One of her sleeves was stuffed with cotton batting to mimic a missing arm, and a plastic hook jutted out like she'd won it in a bar fight. The best part—a fake eyeball on a string—bobbed against her cheek as she grinned at me.

"Ahoy!" she cried, jabbing the hook in my direction. "It's the ghost of Shippy McShipface's crew!"

I barked a laugh and crouched low, holding my hands up in surrender. "You're terrifying, Captain. Can I take a look at you?"

Winnie beamed, bouncing on the balls of her feet. "Only if you walk the plank with us."

I looked at Selene again. She hadn't moved, not really. Just stood there, her lips parted slightly like she'd been caught off guard. Like she wasn't sure whether to smile or cry.

I didn't speak. Not yet.

I just stood up slowly, brushing off my knees, and held out my hand.

Winnie's grin stretched beneath the beard. "Told you, Mama."

Her hook hand waved triumphantly as she raced down the path, seaweed streaming behind her.

Selene turned to me fully.

Her dress caught the breeze and fluttered around her ankles, the gauzy fabric whispering against the sidewalk like sea-foam lapping the hull of a boat. Her hair glowed in the soft light, haloed in strands of gold and pearl. Even like this —dressed as a ghost, her makeup hollowing her cheeks and smudging around her eyes—she was the most alive thing I'd ever seen.

"How did you know about the costumes?" she asked, voice fragile but steady.

I swallowed. My scarf felt too tight.

"Thin walls," I said, softer this time. "I heard her talking to you. I heard you laugh."

Her eyes flickered and her breath hitched. Selene wrapped her arms around her waist like she needed to hold herself together.

"I didn't know if I'd see you tonight," she whispered.

I took a small step forward. Careful. Reverent.

"I missed you," she said suddenly, voice breaking like brittle glass.

I reached for her before I could think better of it. My hand cupped her jaw, thumb brushing the edge of her cheekbone. "I've been walking around missing you so hard I forget how to breathe."

Her eyes filled. "I was upset."

"I know." My chest squeezed.

Her head shook. "I was upset because you missed the performance, but I was too harsh. I let—" She released a shaky breath, but she didn't pull away. Her hands found my chest, curled lightly in the front of my shirt. "I let one mistake take away everything you've done for me. For us. I didn't even hear you out. I was wrong."

I shook my head. We both had played a part in how everything went to shit. "I fucked up. I never should have put *anything* before you and Winnie. It won't happen again."

"I don't want to do this halfway, but I'm so scared," she whispered.

"I'm not halfway *anything* with you. I'm all in. I have been since the first time we met in that shitty jazz bar." My fingers tipped up her chin so she'd look at me. "Once I realized the incredible woman I thought had gotten away was right here? I was done for."

A small chuckle rumbled in my chest. "You know, I missed waking up to your hair on my pillow," I said, voice low and tight. "I missed the sound of you laughing. I missed the way you hum when you're washing up, and the way the corners of your mouth lift when you're pretending not to smile."

Selene blinked, the tears trembling there. "I missed you asking if I needed gas. I missed the way you always handed me the little fork because you know I like it best, and the way you check the door twice even though I already locked it. I missed . . . the way it felt when I wasn't holding it all together alone."

I touched my forehead to hers, our breath mingling. "I never wanted you to feel alone. Not again. Not with me."

Her lips brushed mine—barely. A tremble. A ghost of a kiss. Selene leaned in, and I met her the rest of the way.

The kiss was slow. Lingering. Not a reunion, not really. It was a remembering. A returning. A rebuilding.

Her lips opened under mine with a quiet, vulnerable sigh that hit me harder than any shouted confession. It wrecked me, the way she leaned into me like she wanted to memorize the shape of this. Of us.

I kissed her slowly, reverently. Letting it build.

One hand on her jaw, the other sliding around her waist, anchoring her to me. Her body curved into mine, and my restraint thinned.

She made a broken noise against my mouth, and I felt it in the hollow of my throat and the bend of my knees. Her kiss filled the ache that had lived in my chest in her absence.

I pulled her closer, and then I kissed her deeper, hungrier.

That kiss was full of every goddamn thing I'd wanted to say and hadn't. Every time I'd reached for her in a dream and woken up alone. Every time I'd caught her scent in the hallway and had to stop myself from knocking on her door.

Her fingers threaded into my hair, tugging just enough to make me groan.

I kissed her again, and again, and again, until the heat bloomed between us—low and heady.

The world disappeared, and all that was left was the woman in my arms and the taste of her.

"AHEM."

We froze.

Selene blinked up at me, wide-eyed. Her lips were swollen, cheeks flushed. I wasn't doing much better.

We turned our heads slowly—like a pair of teenagers caught behind the bleachers—and found Winnie standing three steps away with her arms crossed, her fake eyeball swinging on its string, and a suspicious amount of smugness in her eyes.

"Am I gonna have to steer this whole ship by myself or . . . ?" she asked, her little hand slapping the outside of her thigh.

Selene choked on a laugh. I bit back a groan.

"I mean, I'm just saying . . ." Winnie continued, adjusting her crooked pirate hat. "We've got a whole neighborhood of candy to plunder, and the lovebirds are smooching on the porch."

Selene covered her mouth, her shoulders shaking with laughter.

I dragged a hand down my face and muttered, "She's only five, right?"

"Five and highly observant," Selene said.

Turning on her heel, Winnie said brightly, "C'mon, the captain doesn't wait for romance."

She stomped off down the sidewalk, hook hand raised in triumph.

I glanced at Selene, still breathless beside me.

"We should . . ." I nodded toward the retreating pirate. "You know."

"Right," she said, smoothing her dress and grinning up at me. "Before she mutinies."

I offered her my arm and Selene took it.

Together, we followed our fearless, one-eyed, seaweed-haired captain into the night.

THIRTY-NINE

SELENE

I STOOD BAREFOOT in the kitchen, one of Austin's shirts hanging off my shoulders, sleeves rolled up past my elbows as I spooned batter into the waffle iron. The house smelled like cinnamon and browned butter, and the faint hum of something upbeat came from the living room—Austin, humming off-key through a mouthful of coffee.

Winnie was off with her dad for the weekend, with plans for rebuilding the fallen Fae kingdom in the woods behind the school playground. She'd packed two granola bars, a half-empty roll of duct tape, and a hand-drawn map that she insisted Brian take very seriously.

Brian had taken Winnie for his overnight, and I'd watched in awe as Brian and Austin shook hands. It still struck me how easy it could be if I just let things *be*.

Now it was just the two of us in the morning. Quiet. Easy. Full.

The waffle iron hissed, steam curling into the air as I leaned back against the counter and watched him. He was lounging at the table now, his hair was still a little mussed from sleep, and he hadn't bothered with shoes—just flannel pants and that worn gray T-shirt I liked a little too much.

He smiled at me like I was the sunrise.

It wasn't flashy, this life we were building. It didn't come with guarantees or perfect days, but I'd never felt safer.

Austin had been humming more lately. Sometimes I'd catch him running his hand along the doorway or fixing something he'd already fixed. Winnie had started asking for double tuck-ins—one from me and one from him. Then she'd whisper something about how he made the best monster voices and demand he do one more story before lights out.

Somehow, without planning it, we'd slid into something that felt suspiciously like forever.

The waffle iron clicked. I opened it, then glanced up when Austin's voice drifted across the space between us.

"Hey," he said.

I turned, catching the light in his eyes, the way his mouth tilted like he was holding back a secret. "Yeah?"

His brows furrowed. "Can I show you something?"

I smirked, bouncing my eyebrows at him. "Is it a sexy something?"

He laughed, low and rough, standing from his chair. "It could be afterward."

I raised a brow as he crossed the room, took the spatula from my hand, and set it aside. He unplugged the waffle iron, then reached for my coat—the tan one I loved—and held it out.

"No pressure," he said. "Just something I've been working on that I want you to see."

"Should it wait until after breakfast?" I asked.

He glanced up at me. "I'm too excited."

The way he said it—soft and sure—sent a flicker of heat low in my stomach. I didn't know where we were going, but I knew better than to say no to that look on his face.

So I stepped into my coat and followed him out the door.

I walked beside him down our street, hands tucked into the pockets of my coat. The sky was soft with clouds, pale light stretching long shadows across the sidewalk. We passed porches still scattered with half-deflated Halloween decorations—grinning ghosts with slumped shoulders, a skeleton reclining in a tipped-over wheelbarrow, and a spiderweb sagging under the weight of actual leaves.

Austin didn't say where we were going.

He just walked beside me with that quiet smile he wore when something was brewing—half nerves, half hope.

I bumped his shoulder. "So, is this a romantic stroll or the long, winding lead-up to a murder in the woods?"

His mouth curved. "Would I lure you into the woods in broad daylight?"

I chuckled. "Yes. And you'd probably pack me snacks to keep me calm."

"I'm thoughtful that way," he said, nudging me with his elbow.

"You'd carry my body out gently and call the coroner yourself. Gentleman serial killer vibes."

"Now I know where Winnie gets it." Austin glanced at me sideways, laughing. "You're so weird."

"I'm just saying. If I go missing, everyone will say you were charming but suspiciously handy with power tools." I poked his side.

He shook his head, smile twitching, and pulled me under his arm. We turned onto a smaller side street that edged toward the back of the neighborhood. The houses thinned out, newer construction sprouting between wooded patches. Gravel crunched under our boots as we veered off the sidewalk toward a lot nestled in a quiet cul-de-sac.

The structure in front of us looked familiar, though I couldn't place why at first. Two stories, dark-blue siding with creamy trim. Still half finished—some landscaping undone, the porch railings unpainted. The windows were in, but there was no mailbox yet. A blank canvas.

I tilted my head. "I've seen this house before on one of my walks. It was one of Wes's projects."

Austin didn't respond immediately. He reached into his jacket pocket and pulled out a key, running his fingers along the metal.

"Yeah, well . . ." he said. "It's my project now."

I blinked. "Wait—what?"

He didn't look at me right away. Just stared at the house with a strange mix of reverence and nerves. "I talked to Wes and he agreed to sell it to me. I'll be working on a few things inside whenever I get the chance."

I stopped walking. "You're buying it?"

He nodded.

I frowned. "So you're moving out of the duplex?"

He scratched the back of his neck. "Well . . . I was kind of hoping the two of you would want to move out too."

I turned to look at him fully. Austin's eyes were steady, but his voice had gone tentative. Careful. Like the words were heavier than he expected.

My heart stumbled. "You—wait. *What?*"

He didn't try to explain it away, didn't make a big show of it. He just pulled my hand and stepped up to the porch. The wood creaked faintly beneath our feet as he turned the lock and pushed the door open.

Warm light spilled across the floor from the tall front

windows. The inside still smelled faintly of sawdust and lemon cleaner and something else I couldn't name—something that smelled like possibility.

Like new dreams.

Austin turned to me and, with the gentlest smile, held the door wide. "Come inside."

I stepped through the doorway, the hinges groaning gently as the door closed behind me.

The house wasn't finished—not yet—but it already felt like it had a soul. Hardwood floors stretched across the open living space, still dusty in the corners. The walls were primed but not yet painted, pale like the start of a canvas. Exposed light bulbs dangled from the ceiling, and in the far corner the makings of a kitchen took shape—cabinets without hardware, counters still waiting to be installed. But there was light streaming through the windows, and warmth beneath the quiet.

Austin tucked his hands in his jacket pockets like he didn't know what to do with them.

"I know it's not done," he said. "But when I walked through it the first time, I couldn't stop thinking about the three of us here. Movie nights in that corner." He pointed. "Winnie's art project explosions all over the kitchen. You stealing my side of the bed upstairs. The whole third floor can be converted into a restoration space for you. Winnie will still go to her same school. It just . . . felt right."

I turned slowly, taking it all in. The unfinished walls. The wide-open promise of it. "Austin . . ."

He stepped forward, eyes locked on mine. "I can't promise I'll never screw up," he said, voice thick with emotion. "But I can promise I'll never stop showing up. You and Winnie—you're it for me. You're my home."

My breath caught.

He reached into his jacket again—this time pulling out a small box. His hands didn't shake, but mine did as I raised them to my mouth.

"Selene," he said, sinking to one knee on the bare wood floor, "for most of my life, I didn't know what it meant to feel safe with someone. To feel chosen. To choose back. But you . . . you cracked me open. You gave me a reason to try. I want to build something with you that doesn't fall apart the second it gets hard."

He flipped the box open—inside was a ring that looked like it belonged under moonlight and stars. The ring had a delicate, vintage setting—an antique-style gold band etched with tiny, imperfect scrollwork, like something pulled from the pages of a forgotten fairy tale. At its center sat an old European-cut diamond, soft and warm in the light, not flashy but full of quiet fire. The kind of ring that had history. The kind of ring that had been loved before—and was ready to be loved again.

"I want it all," he said. "The hard parts, the boring parts, the magic. I want coffee in the mornings and brushing our teeth side by side and putting together furniture and falling asleep with your cold feet against my leg. I want to build a life with you."

My vision blurred.

"I love you," he said simply. "And I'd really, really like to marry you."

Something cracked in me then. The last of the walls I'd been holding up. The ones built out of fear and years of telling myself not to need too much.

I dropped to my knees in front of him, laughing through tears as I cupped his face in my hands.

"I love you too," I whispered. I had been too scared to

say it out loud, but once I did, I had never been more certain of anything else.

Austin exhaled like he'd been holding his breath for years. His arms wrapped around me, pulling me in as I kissed him—desperate, real, full of everything I hadn't known how to say until this moment.

Our kiss was messy, tear-damp, and perfect.

He pressed his forehead to mine, smiling so widely I could feel it against my skin. "So . . . is that a yes?"

I nodded, still breathless. "That's a *hell* yes."

His laugh rumbled through his chest as he wrapped me up, holding me close on the floor of our not-yet-finished home.

We stayed there for a while—just us and the dust and the light—and I didn't care that the house wasn't done yet.

It already had everything we needed.

EPILOGUE

Selene

SUNLIGHT SPILLED through the wide kitchen windows, warming the countertops and painting golden streaks across the floor. The porch swing outside creaked, keeping time with the breeze that drifted through the screens.

A vase of wildflowers—half wilted but still lovely—sat in the center of the table, their petals curling just slightly at the edges. Austin had picked them a week ago on our walk to the farmers' market. He had called them *whimsical as hell* and insisted we needed to take them home.

A faint jazz record spun in the background—something slow and brassy with a whisper of old romance in its bones. We still kind of disliked it, but jazz never failed to remind me of that fateful night Austin and I stumbled on each other and changed everything.

Over all of it, I heard Austin's low, steady voice. "Pinch the edge, not too hard. Just enough to seal it."

Winnie giggled. "I am pinching it. This pie is going to be iconic."

He chuckled. "Can't argue with that, bug."

I padded in quietly, barefoot and still warm from my shower, wearing one of Austin's old T-shirts that hit halfway down my thighs. I clutched a chipped mug of hazelnut coffee in both hands, the rim still warm against my lips.

They didn't notice me at first.

Winnie stood on a stool at the island, her hair in two messy braids—the complicated Dutch ones that Austin had perfected—and flour dusting her cheeks. Austin hovered beside her, guiding her dough-covered fingers with the same calm gentleness he used to fix a cabinet hinge or straighten a picture frame. His inked forearm flexed as he reached across the counter, the edge of his shirt damp from dishwater, and his hair still tousled from sleep.

I leaned against the doorframe and watched them, my heart so full it felt like it might swell out of my chest and float away entirely.

This was it—the extraordinary ordinary.

Quiet mornings with soft music and too many dishes in the sink. Pie crust under fingernails and giggles over too much cinnamon. Winnie narrated everything like she was hosting her own baking show.

I never thought normal could feel like this. Like freedom. Like coming home.

Austin still kissed me like it was the first time. My favorite moments were when he looked at me across the dinner table like I was made of some impossible dream. I'd spent so long convincing myself I wasn't the kind of person who got a forever. But he was different. With every slow breath and gentle word. With every night he stayed and every morning he reached for me first.

"Mom." Winnie spotted me over her shoulder. "Is this

not the greatest thing you've ever seen?" She threw her arms out, nearly knocking over a mixing bowl.

"Whoa." Austin laughed, catching it just in time. "Chaos gremlin, reel it in."

I crossed the kitchen and kissed Winnie's floury cheek before winding my arms around Austin's waist from behind. He leaned into me, smiling as I pressed my lips to the back of his shoulder.

"Morning," I murmured.

He turned just enough to kiss me. It was soft, quick, and familiar—like punctuation on a thought we'd been finishing together for months.

"Hey," he said, voice still scratchy from sleep. "We're making blueberry pie. Win thinks we're going to win the whole contest this year."

"I'm rigging it," Winnie stage-whispered. "We're baking in the magic."

I smirked. "Obviously."

Austin's hand slid to rest against my lower back, warm and steady. "You good?"

I nodded, sipping my coffee and soaking in the light, the laughter, the easy way it all fit together now. "Great."

I was more than good. I was home.

By late morning, the pie was cooling on the counter, the kitchen was only slightly less of a disaster, and Winnie had shifted gears completely.

She raced through the hallway in her socks, trying to decide which sparkly headband went best with her outfit for the party. I could hear her in her room narrating to her stuffed animals like she was the star of a red-carpet event.

"She's got main character energy today," Austin said, stepping beside me as I finished wiping down the counter. His hand settled on my lower back. "Also, I think I'm still finding glitter in my hair from her unicorn costume last week."

"Good luck." I laughed. "That stuff never goes away."

"I hope this stage lasts forever," he said quietly, but with a smile that told me it wasn't the kind that wore you out—it was the kind that rooted you. "It's the best."

My chest pinched. Winnie was starting first grade next week.

She was equal parts excited and anxious, but mostly just thrilled that she got to stay in the neighborhood she knew after we moved. Her friends were close, the school was just a few blocks away, and she liked that we'd kept her routine as steady as possible.

What she didn't say out loud—but I could see it in the way she held Austin's hand a little tighter lately—was that it made all the difference having him there.

He meant it when he said he'd take care of the before-and-after-school stuff. He was the one who packed her lunch just the way she liked it, with the extra pickles in a little cup. He made her brush her teeth when she was stalling. He braided her hair—after many, *many* online tutorials—and she beamed the whole time.

He was steady. Present. Everything I once thought I couldn't count on.

Austin worked full-time for Wes now—officially on the books. He came home most days with sawdust in his hair and stories about the latest drama happening between guys on the crew. He loved it. Not just the work, but the purpose behind it.

Last month, with leftover materials from a custom sunroom project, he'd built Winnie a tiny playhouse in the backyard. Painted it lavender with a yellow door and little flower boxes under the windows.

She called it the Sparkle Fort and declared it a fairy-friendly zone.

Sometimes when I was working late on a restoration piece, I'd glance out the window and catch Austin sitting on the back porch steps, listening patiently while she explained her fairy kingdom's bylaws or read him a chapter from one of her dog-eared books.

It was such a small life. So ordinary in the very best way.

But the way he loved us—fully, fiercely, without ever once flinching—made it feel big.

I set down the dish towel and leaned back into him. "She's going to crush first grade."

"Ha!" he cackled. "She's going to run that school by Halloween."

I winked in his direction. "She gets that from me."

He laughed. "Obviously."

I reached for the mixing bowl Austin had abandoned in favor of playing sous-chef to Winnie and started stirring what was left of the whipped cream.

"You know," I said, eyeing the slightly lopsided crust on our pie, "I don't want to insult your skills or anything, but this crust looks like it was rolled out by a pirate with a hook hand."

Winnie gasped from her stool. "The captain would never! He's very precise with his hook!"

Austin tried to look wounded. "I'll have you know I followed the recipe exactly."

"Uh-huh." I tapped the spoon against the bowl and smirked.

"I was distracted," he said. "Someone came in here in my favorite shirt and ruined my concentration."

I shot him a slow, exaggerated look. "Is that so?"

Before he could reply, Winnie let out a dramatic groan and covered her eyes. "You guys are being mushy again."

Austin grinned and flicked a bit of flour at her. "Just wait till you're older. Being mushy is the best part."

Winnie wrinkled her nose but didn't argue. She was too busy sneaking a fingerful of filling from the pie tin.

Outside, a breeze swept through the open windows, fluttering the corner of the flyer and rustling the wildflowers in the vase.

The porch swing creaked gently.

It had been the first thing Austin built for me when we moved in—a surprise I found one evening after a long day of work, complete with two mismatched throw pillows and a handwritten note on the back: *For slow mornings, long talks, and everything in between.*

I smiled as I looked at it now, swaying just enough to remind me how much we'd grown here already. How much further we would go.

Austin's arm slipped around my waist. "What are you smiling at?"

I leaned into him. "Just . . . everything."

THE SCREEN DOOR creaked open behind me just as I slid the finished pie onto the cooling rack.

"I think I see Brody's truck," Austin called from the porch. "Winnie! Go make sure your kingdom is ready!"

"Already did!" she shouted back, scampering past in a blur of bare feet and braids flying. "The fairy throne is sparkly and OFF LIMITS."

I grinned and turned back toward the sink, rinsing the last of the crumbs from my hands. Outside, the warm summer air drifted in through the open windows, carrying with it the sound of distant laughter, birdsong, and the buzz of cicadas tucked in the tall grass.

Music played low on the record player—something old and easy, a song that made you want to swing your feet and drink something cold. The kitchen smelled like sugar and lemon zest. The porch swing groaned contentedly as it rocked back and forth, a lazy rhythm to the hum of our little corner of the world.

A knock came at the front door, followed by a familiar voice.

"Don't make me use my key," Brody said with a laugh.

"You don't have a key," Austin replied, opening the door.

Brody gave him a playful shove. "Not yet."

I wiped my hands and stepped out to greet them.

Kit was behind Brody, holding a casserole dish and wearing cherry-red lipstick that matched her earrings. Wes followed, his gait still slightly uneven, but more confident now. My sister Clara walked beside him, laughing at something he whispered to her—his expression softer than I'd ever seen it.

Elodie came next, holding a giant bowl of fruit and waving her elbow in the air as she passed me. "Don't ask. Levi made me carry the healthy stuff. I'm hoping it's a phase."

Levi trailed behind, even taller than I remembered, with Cal at his side, both of them already eyeing the ice-cold lemonade at the table.

As Elodie stepped inside, I leaned in and murmured, "I still can't believe Clara is here."

She bumped her shoulder against mine and smiled. "Me neither. But it's kind of nice, isn't it?"

I glanced back at the porch where Clara now stood, nudging Wes's arm and laughing as he pretended to glare at her.

"Yeah," I said. "It really is."

The house buzzed with movement—doors opening and closing, bare feet on the wood floors, chairs scooting across the deck. There were easy hugs and second helpings and the clink of glasses raised in toast.

The windows were wide open, letting in the warmth of the summer dusk, and the breeze caught the edge of the linen curtain, lifting it just enough to feel like the whole house was breathing.

We had made it.

Not perfectly. Not easily. But fully.

And with everyone here, the house didn't feel new anymore.

It felt lived in. It felt like home.

The last of the dishes clinked into the sink. Outside, the fireflies had taken over, blinking in a lazy rhythm beyond the porch rail. The chatter of friends had faded, the music long stopped. Now it was just the two of us, moving quietly through the kitchen like it was a ritual we'd practiced for years.

Austin's hand brushed across the small of my back as I reached for a dish towel.

"You did good," I murmured.

"So did you," he said, pressing a kiss to my shoulder.

His touch lingered, his hand slipping beneath the hem of my shirt. His thumb dragged against my bare hip bone like he couldn't help himself.

That warmth—that easy, electric thrum that always came alive between us—it bloomed again. Familiar. Safe. Irresistible.

This.

Not the walls. Not the porch swing or the smell of the grill outside.

This was home.

I turned and caught the look in his eyes. That slow-burn, storm-on-the-horizon kind of gaze he always gave me when the world quieted and we were just us.

Something passed between us—hot and steady.

Our mouths met in a kiss that was slow and certain, built from memory and longing and promise.

I could taste the day on his lips—laughter and lemonade and cinnamon sugar.

His hands settled on my hips. Mine curled around the back of his neck.

Later wasn't soon enough.

The house was dark and still.

Winnie had fallen asleep on the couch halfway through a movie. Austin carried her upstairs with a gentleness that made my heart ache, and I watched them disappear down the hallway, the soft hush of her bedroom door clicking closed behind him.

By the time he returned, I was already under the covers, curled on my side, wearing one of his old tees and nothing else.

He leaned in the doorway, arms crossed, watching me like I was the only thing he'd ever wanted.

"You just going to stand there all night?" I teased, voice low.

He hummed and moved closer. "I'm just thinking about all the ways I want to ruin you."

Heat flushed beneath my skin. I sat up slowly, the sheet sliding off my legs. "Then show me."

That was all it took. He crossed the room like a man starved.

His mouth crashed into mine, hot and hungry, hands already beneath my shirt. The kiss deepened, his tongue stroking against mine, pulling a whimper from my throat as he guided me back onto the pillows.

"You have no idea what you do to me," he growled against my neck. "Every damn day, Selene. I wake up hard just thinking about your legs around me."

My breath hitched.

He peeled off my shirt like it was sacred, like unwrapping a gift he'd waited years to open. His hands roamed—palms and fingertips and knuckles grazing skin that had only ever felt this alive beneath his touch.

"You're so fucking beautiful," he murmured. "This body? Mine. This mouth?" He kissed me, deeper now. "Mine too."

His words weren't filthy. They were worship.

When he slid down between my thighs, I moaned. He didn't rush—he savored, devoured, like he was learning me all over again, even though he already knew every inch of me by heart.

His name broke from my lips again and again—plea and praise and promise.

When he finally sank into me, I gasped. He groaned, low and deep, like he was home.

Our bodies moved together, slow and desperate, chasing something ancient and tender and hungry. He kissed every part of me, whispering filth against my skin until I came undone beneath him, trembling and gasping his name.

After, we lay tangled in the sheets, limbs knotted, his hand tracing lazy circles over my hip.

He looked at me like there was no other life before this

one. In his arms, with our whole messy, beautiful life unfolding around us, I realized—sometimes the best kind of magic isn't the kind you chase.

It's the kind that's waiting to catch us when we fall.

WANT MORE of Selene and Austin? Read a very special bonus scene here: http://www.lenahendrix.com/get-selene-and-austins-bonus-scene

UP NEXT: BENEATH THE FROST

Weston Vaughn has always been the most charming man in any room. That is, until he saved my brother's life and the accident took his leg. Now, he's a gruff recluse and my new roommate.

When my life goes up in flames on my wedding day, I become my small town's favorite scandal. I want to lie low while the gossip dies down, but living with my parents feels impossible. Moving in with my brother's best friend is my best option.

He won't ask for help and I won't be dismissed. Trouble is, I like this gruff side of Wes and despite his rules, I enjoy showing up for him. He's adjusting to his new life and when he finally admits his confidence is shot, well . . . I know exactly what he needs.

I'm a *hands-on* kind of caretaker.

Tensions rise as our tentative arrangement melts into sexy, forbidden lessons aimed to rebuild the confidence he's lost. He thinks he's broken, but all I see is an irresistible man with a firm grip and a filthy mouth.

He's walled off his heart, but all it takes is a woman who's willing to see what lies beneath the frost.

Pre-order BOOK 3 in the Star Harbor Series, ***Beneath the Frost*** here: https://geni.us/beneaththefrost 1

ACKNOWLEDGMENTS

To my readers, you're the best in the world. I wake up every day so incredibly grateful that I get to write stories for a living. Meeting (and exceeding) your expectations is always a highlight. Thanks for coming on this journey with me.

Page, thank you for jumping in and taking Team Lena to the next level. Your creative ideas and thoughtful execution are unmatched. I am positively giddy over how far we can go together!

A huge thank you to my cover designer Cat for seeing my vision and creating the most gorgeous, cohesive covers. I couldn't decide whether I love the models or discreet more—they're both that good!

To my beta readers Trinity and Ashley, thank you for always taking the time to help my stories shine. I love seeing that we share the same favorite scenes and your comments always make me laugh!

Stephanie, this book would not exist without you putting the reverse-age gap trope into my head! I hope they lived up to every one of your dreams.

I cannot thank Dawn and James enough for outstanding editing and help with creating swoony hero serving of such an incredible woman like Selene. Your insights and guidance means more than I could ever say!

To Kandi, Corinne, Elsie, Catherine, and the rest of my incredible writer friends—without our sprint session, plotting chats, and your general encouragement, writing would be a sad and lonely job. I love our unhinged text threads, random voice memos, and the gentle reminders that the characters that live in our heads are, unfortunately, fictional. You're the best friends a gal could have.

Want to connect? Come hang out with the Hendrix Heartthrobs on Facebook to laugh & chat with Lena! Special sneak peeks, announcements, exclusive content, & general shenanigans all happen there.

Come join us!

ABOUT THE AUTHOR

Lena Hendrix is a *USA Today* and Amazon Top 5 Bestselling contemporary romance author living in the Midwest. Her love for romance stared with sneaking racy Harlequin paperbacks and now she writes her own hot-as-sin small town romance novels. Lena has a soft spot for strong alphas with marshmallow insides, heroines who clap back, and sizzling tension. Her novels pack in small town heart with a whole lotta heat.

When she's not writing or devouring new novels, you can find her hiking, camping, fishing, and sipping a spicy margarita!

Want to hang out? Find Lena on Tiktok or IG!

ALSO BY LENA HENDRIX

Star Harbor

Chasing the Sun

When We Fall

Beneath the Frost

The Sullivans

One Look

One Touch

One Chance

One Night

One Taste (prequel novella)

The Kings

Just This Once

Just My Luck

Just Between Us

Just Like That

Just Say Yes

Redemption Ranch

The Badge

The Alias

The Rebel

The Target

Chikalu Falls

Finding You

Keeping You

Protecting You

Choosing You (origin novella)